LUNA

The Adventures of

RHONE & STONE

book 2

by:

<u>**Luna**</u>

book 2 of,

The Adventures of Rhone & Stone

1st edition, 2023

Copyright © 2023 by Strider S.R. Klusman

Published by Duramen Publishing

Contact at: DuramenPublishing@gmail.com

Duramen
Publishing

ISBN: 979-8-9851196-6-4 (paperback)

ISBN: 979-8-9851196-5-7 (ebook)

Cover Art by: James T Egan, BookFly Designs

Contents

Prologue

"Hurry up now. Get this stuff stashed below, and make sure it's secure! I don't want them coming loose if we hit heavy water."

A sailor's curt nod and ducked head acknowledged the harsh words, scurrying off with the first bundle from a stack of cargo sitting dockside of a heavily armed ship. The slick wood of the dock wasn't helping with loading, but the crew was well used to working in these conditions. The darkness and clouds were custom-made for their evening's adventure. No one would be out wandering the docks at this hour, especially in the rain. The ship would be loaded and gone well before daylight, though even dawn wouldn't make the storm-covered sky much lighter.

Unexpected steps from the town side of the dock brought the captain around in a spin, reaching for his ever-present cutlass.

"A bit jumpy, aren't you?" came the voice, far too cheery for a dark night in the rain.

The well-muscled and well-dressed captain let out a strangled snarl as the sword slammed back into its scabbard, polished steel striking the brass furring of the sheath with a solid clack. In undisguised distaste he asked,

1

"Why are you out here? I thought you wanted this done unnoticed, mister Mayor. You know you can't go anywhere without people talking. Being noticed is part of your job."

"Oh quit worrying," the mayor said easily. "I've had the dock watch called to the other end of town, so we have a few minutes. Now, have you got it all?"

"Whatever's here we've got, the captain replied unimpressed. "But if you've jeopardized the shipment, and we get seen on our way out, I'm blaming it on you, not me and my ship."

The words were clipped, without the normal deference the mayor normally received, but he shook off the insult with a snide sneer down his long, eloquent nose. "I told you, it's covered. Now, be sure to tell your bosses that as far as I'm concerned, our business is complete. They will have to look elsewhere for goods. We're stripped bare. You have approximately thirty minutes before the watch returns, so be done, and be gone. And... good luck. Looks like it's a rough night out there."

With that said, the mayor drew his long coat tight around his tall frame and headed back up the heavily worn wharf. He would preserve his town, even if it meant a few deals with the riffraff.

Within half a minute, his shadowy silhouette had disappeared into the blowing raindrops.

CHAPTER 1

One Step Forward

Aundrea barely recognize the corrugated surfaces of the dry labyrinthian pathways they inched through. The heat haze in the rocky passages made distant viewing unsure, but certainly no worse than the fog her mind struggled with, or the feelings she never knew she had missed. With the little Jewel secured in her hands, the trek was an unfamiliar blur.

Rhone led Pasha between the tortuous basalt walls, their echoing hoof beats reverberating like a heartbeat in the desert air, a hot breeze drifting behind them as surely as a kitten following milk. It was an odd feeling, as though their vibrations rolled along with them, sometimes following, sometimes ahead.

To Aundrea, the sounds of the hoof beats went as un-noticed as the uniquely pillared walls, but Rhone had been here before and knew the tricks of the badlands. Stone lay securely in his setting on Rhone's collar, tracking their progress, his awareness keeping them from getting lost in the jigsaw-like passages of the badland's maze.

Jewel was a perfect name for Aundrea's little crystalline entity. She'd had been part of the much larger crystalline construct called the We, known to each other by their mental signature rather than a name, but since Rhone had given Stone one, it only seemed proper for Jewel to have a name too.

Since their partnering, Aundrea and Jewel spent every waking moment learning about each other, trying to understand each other's thoughts. It was a long process, matching dissimilar concepts of motion and action, picture and personality, a unique experience which created Aundrea's mental haze. It hadn't quite come together yet, but they were learning. And there was so much to learn.

Simple things like speech were progressing nicely. On the other hand, motion, while not a new concept, was definitely a difference. Jewel had drifted through space as part of the crystalline community, but being able to move about randomly with a human was totally new.

When the cataclysmic breakup of the crystalline community left Jewel alone, without her companions thinking their thoughts of calculation and definition, she was orphaned, and had weathered the intervening years in solitude. Eventually, she had been collected as a bauble, ending up in Commissioner Dodge's vault of treasures. That horror had nearly broken the little creature, but a timely rescue by Rhone, searching for his own crystalline friend, saved her. Now she had Aundrea, while Stone once again had Rhone.

As Aundrea cuddled the golden-pink crystal in her palms, cooing sweet nothings to the little jewel, quiet echoes of color began to tickle her mind. Wisps like gossamer veils drifted across her mental vision, transforming the hard rock of the walls into a patterned mosaic much like tiles in a sunken bath. The mystery of it overwhelmed her senses, until the colors converted to a word standing directly before her mind.

Pretty?

"Oh yes," she whispered. "It's beautiful! I understand!"

Aundrea's speech intruded into Rhone's mind-numbing plod and he glanced up.

"Ma'am? Were you talking to me?"

Aundrea roused herself as though waking from a dream. "Oh... Rhone, I'm sorry, no. Jewel just spoke to me again. Only a word, but the colors are absolutely amazing! I would never have considered them arranged in such a way."

"Arranged?" Rhone asked carefully, unsure what she meant. "I don't think Stone and I went through anything like that."

No, we did not, Stone answered matter-of-factly, speaking directly into Rhone's mind. *I had already developed an understanding of your visual receptors. It was simply a matter of properly transferring the data in both directions. These two are still in the discovery segment of their partnering, but it should correct itself in time.*

Rhone squinted up at the blinding sun, before silently commenting, *Okay, I think I've got it,* then repeated everything for Aundrea's benefit.

Surprised, she asked, "So, you don't see colors swirling along the walls? I'm almost sorry for you. It's absolutely dazzling."

Rhone wasn't sure if his, 'not seeing', was all that bad. His connection with Stone was just fine the way it was.

Stone sent his own comment on the subject. *Thank you, Rhone. I enjoy our connection too. Theirs will be similar, but not exactly the same. Now, will you tell Aundrea that Jewel will probably need rest soon. She is still recovering from her ordeal in the vault. Too much stimulation, too soon, may cause a setback.*

Once again, Rhone recited Stone's words to Aundrea. He would be glad when the two 'We' would be able to communicate directly with each other. Technically they could now, but any distance between them made it difficult.

"Of course she needs a nap," Aundrea said, chastising herself for not having considered her little friend. "I should have thought of it." With a shift of her concentration, Aundrea began her thought talk to Jewel. *Hello my beauty. Stone just told me you need your rest. I am very sorry. I shouldn't have kept you working so hard. You rest now and I'll take care of you. Have a good nap my love.*

Aundrea's eyes lost the faraway look she had when she talked with Jewel, and she smiled to Rhone. "How much further to the flatlands? I left my buggy out there somewhere, and if we come out near it, I'll switch Pasha to the harness and take the buggy back to the OPR stables. It will be a long drive, but it will take me at least that long to figure what to say in my report."

"Your office? Where's that?" Rhone asked with a curious note. The badlands were the furthest he had ever been from home, and he had only been to Skragmoore the once. Mom hadn't liked town much, and only went when she had to, leaving him at home.

"Far to the south," Aundrea said, knowing he wouldn't understand, even if she said more. "It's actually located in The Capital Stronghold."

But again, Rhone's look said he had no idea, other than it must be some place special.

Aundrea sighed, recognizing his total lack of worldly knowledge. But it was a fair trade. She would teach him about the world outside his little town, and he could teach her more about Jewel. Even thinking Jewel's name was enough to draw her mind back, just to check.

"Everything okay?" Rhone asked, understanding her sudden shift.

"She's warm and cozy," Aundrea said, slightly embarrassed by Rhone noticing her lapse. "This must be what it's like having a baby. I've watched new mamas continuously checking on their little one, making sure they're covered and safe."

Rhone knew the feeling. He and Stone had gone through that process, though not exactly the same. Their connection had come about gradually, melding before they had actually met. It took time to figure out how to connect and understand.

They trudged for another hour through the hot basalt corridors before the pillars began to thin, changing from long walls, to groupings, then finally into single spires jutting from the desert floor.

"There it is," Aundrea cried, spying the little buggy parked alongside a massive rocky outcropping. The stone spire was the last bastion of the badlands, disappearing as though being absorbed into the flat terrain of the brush land. The rolling countryside beyond was sparsely scattered with sage and antelope brush, intermingled with an assortment of dry grasses. Between the scattered clumps lay a shallow layer of gravelly soil overlaying coarse rock. It wasn't much to look at, and at this time of year had very little color, unless you considered grey and dust-brown colorful. But it reminded Rhone of home.

His poor and heavily weathered house was miles from here, standing vacant in a dry rocky valley a short way from the little town of Skragmoore.

It was a perfect name for the worn-out place. But while Skragmoore was small, the area was at least large enough to have a commissioner. It was The Council that oversaw the political workings of the government and placed commissioners to oversee the outlying areas. Rhone only knew that much because Mom wanted him to know something of the government of their country, but that was about all he remembered, mostly because she had mentioned The Council in her disgusted comments about Commissioner Dodge. Apparently, their commissioner was supposed to oversee the polit-ical and economic affairs of the region around Skragmoore, but his sticky fingers had found every excuse to slide any small gain into his own pockets, leaving the people destitute.

Somehow his profits had included the beautiful little gem he had stashed away in his vault. She hadn't been Jewel at that point, or even a she. 'We' didn't have gender identities.

But Jewel was free now, and the commissioner had disappeared, much to the relief of Skragmoore.

"That's a nice rig, ma'am," Rhone said appreciatively. "You drove that little thing across the flatland without a road? It must have been quite a ride."

He actually wondered how the tall slim wheels had managed to make it over the rough and rocky ground, but the old tracks were still visible across the sandy areas showed they had. Awed by the buggy, Rhone walked around it, running a hand over the smooth wood of the thin spokes and the fine leather seat padded and as soft as anything he had ever seen.

"It wasn't much fun," Aundrea agreed, "but I made it. Don't forget, I didn't just close my eyes and head north. I was following a map. But it was a long trip, and will be the same going back."

The buggy looked far too delicate for the journey, but it had made it once, so would probably make it again. Still, Rhone had never ridden in a buggy, and wondered if maybe he should walk.

His concern must have shown, as Aundrea took control. "Come on. I'll teach you how to hitch up the horse, and how to drive. It will be a pretty rough ride cutting cross country, but once we hit the road, it will be easy enough." Her mind was already busy, working on the future.

The offer had Rhone's eyes wide in surprise. "You would teach me? Really?"

"Of course. Every man should know how to hitch up a team, and how to drive. It will be expected."

Rhone wasn't so sure. He had gotten along without knowing, and his two legs did just fine. But, there was a big world out there, and who knew where he would end up. Her suggestion eventually won out. "Yeah, I'd like that. We never had a horse. Couldn't afford one I guess."

"Perfect," Aundrea said with a smile, "besides, I could use a driver. I can't very well drive myself with Jewel in my palms." She lifted her cupped hands as if to prove her statement. "Now, I know you had plans, but I was also wondering..." She paused, sizing him up before continuing. "I could use a good assistant, and I'm not sure how well things are going for you around here. You would have to work hard, of course, but I would teach you all you need to know."

"You want me to go with you?" Rhone asked, startled by the question. But he had heard enough already. With a grin, he blurted, "Stone and I were already planning to leave, so I can't see any reason not to." Then he thought to ask Stone. *Sorry, Stone, what do you think?*

I go where you go, Stone answered stiffly, *but it does sound exciting. I've never been to the big city before.*

Me either, Rhone thought back, suddenly not so sure.

Aundrea waited for Rhone's attention to return, before carefully asking, "Well, what did he say?" She was excited at the prospect, and could use the two of them. Their skills would be priceless in her line of work. But, she did need to make one thing clear. "You'll find the city quite different from what you know, and possibly confusing. So if you feel a bit on the outside of things for a while, don't worry. We'll get past it."

Rhone gave a shrug before he had time for his worries to grow, "I think we can handle it," he said, "and Stone says yes."

I most certainly did not, Stone commented in his mind. *I said, I go where you go, but I suppose that is inherently the same thing. If, you were planning on going.*

Rhone chuckled to himself, but didn't answer, knowing Stone certainly wasn't going without him.

"Just wait until you see the big city," Aundrea said with a dimpled smile. "It is a pretty amazing place, even if you weren't coming from somewhere like Skragmoore. I'll tell you more as we travel. It will help time go by faster."

Pasha stood patiently between the traces while Rhone worked at setting the collar comfortably over his muscular shoulders. Horses were amazing creatures. He wished again they had been able to afford one, but as mom had said, "If wishes were horses, then beggars would ride," whatever that meant. Mom was always saying strange things, and honestly, he hadn't understood most of them.

Holding up a strap, Rhone looked blankly at the harness draping over Pasha. "So does this strap buckle up here?"

"You got it," Aundrea said happily. "By the way, Pasha likes you. He doesn't often stand still for other people. He usually gets squirmy when they get too close, but he's standing like a tree today."

Pasha must have heard, because he gave a sharp snort, blowing out a snotty mist.

Rhone wasn't sure if it was in agreement, but the horse hadn't tried to bite him, so he felt welcomed. "You're a good boy Pasha. Thank you for letting me learn on you. I really appreciate it."

Aundrea gave Rhone an approving smile, but to him, talking to a horse wasn't much different than talking to a rock.

I heard that, came Stone's snide remark. He hadn't been saying much lately, with Aundrea and Jewel taking up his time.

I didn't say you were like a horse, Rhone thought to Stone. *I was just saying, if I didn't have a problem talking to you, I shouldn't have a problem talking to a horse.*

Oh, I heard you quite well, Stone muttered. *What you were thinking was, a horse is no different than a rock, being we are both hard headed.*

What? Of course I wasn't thinking that, Rhone retorted, quickly blocking the rest of his thoughts. *I've never known a horse before.*

His thoughts had been slipping past far too often, but this conversation was no different than a hundred others he and Stone had been through. It wasn't always easy understanding an entirely different view of every single piece of information. Stone saw things through his rock-like vision, which wasn't vision at all, and Rhone saw and did things that a rock couldn't

11

possibly understand, having never experienced action. Considering that, things were going pretty well.

Rhone's unexpected laugh caused Aundrea to glance up with a look of question.

"You have no idea," Rhone told her, unable to corral his mirth. "Stone was concerned about me talking to a horse. But you have to understand, he once told me, anyone can talk to a cow, but not everyone expects the cow to understand and answer." He was enjoying the fact he could use Stone as the object of his humor. It wasn't often he got to win one over his friend.

Aundrea raised her eyebrows in a knowing look. "It sounds to me like he was correct. Not every creature is as intelligent as We are," she said, giving him a wink.

Rhone caught her word play, and was about to respond, but Stone beat him to it.

I like this young lady. You may keep her, Stone said graciously.

Rhone almost choked, but managed to pass off the actual message by saying, "Stone just said he likes you," not mentioning the rest of the line. The very thought sent his heart into double time.

Ahh, Just as I thought, Stone murmured. *You do fancy her.*

Of course I like her, Rhone said evasively, instantly beginning to blush. *"But it's not like that. She's way too old."* Then speaking aloud, said, "Whew, it's sure getting hot," fanning his face as he bent to finish hitching the harness, and effectively cover his sudden flush.

The teenage blush hadn't escaped Aundrea, but she let it pass without comment. It was nice to be appreciated. He was a nice young man, but still just a kid. "When you've finished with the traces we'll be ready to go."

CHAPTER 2

The Big City

The drive took days, with every mile bringing things Rhone had never seen before. Stone too for that matter. This was a long way from the river where Rhone had found him.

The further they traveled from Skragmoore the better the land, leaving the dry wastelands to more fertile ground and rocky slopes clad in trees.

After some days they began to see people and homes, but by that time, Rhone was becoming pretty handy with the buggy. Pasha had accepted his hand on the reins, making the journey a gentle drive. The road gave him time to realize just how backward his life had been. Where he had walked before, he now he rode in a buggy, and that was just a start. Aundrea talked of the wonders of the big city, but said he would have to see for himself just how magnificent things were. He shuddered knowing he was a babe in the woods, and would have to start all over again.

Even with new things around every corner, Rhone was startled when Stone broke into his thoughts.

What is that? Stone pulsed, the energy his question enough to make the collar vibrate.

Suddenly worried of an attack, Rhone asked, "Is there a problem?" Then he heard an odd hissing noise as a strange buggy pulled onto the road.

He would have asked more, but Pasha took that moment to reject the odd vehicle, showing his belief that distance would make things better. Ears back, Pasha bolted forward, straining against the harness and racking every joint on the buggy as he lunged against the traces. Rhone worked frantically at the reins, trying to get the buggy back under control, and direct Pasha's explosive effort to remain on the roadway. A wheel slipping into the ditch wouldn't bode well for the light vehicle, let alone its occupants.

"Whoa boy! Easy now," Rhone called, his voice anything but calm. But it must have worked, as Pasha suddenly high-stepped to the edge of the road, coming to a snorting stop, hide shivering violently as agitated hooves beat the hard ground like a metronome.

"Rhone, that was exceptionally well done!" Aundrea exclaimed, righting herself from a near dumping from the buggy seat. "I doubt I could have done as well."

Stone however, didn't show the same excitement, as he asked, *What was that contraption? It seemed to be mechanical in nature. Quite basic, yet marvelous. I could feel the resonance of the drive, although I have never encountered such manipulation of mechanical forces.*

Little shivers zipped up and down Rhone's body as he settled himself. He would hate to admit it, but he had been ready to jump and hope for the best. blowing out a breath in relief, he turned to Aundrea. "I didn't do anything special," he announced with a shrug. "He just stopped."

Ahhh..., I may have had something to do with that, Stone mumbled apologetically. *Our Pasha seemed a bit agitated, and I thought a calming influence might be appreciated.*

"You did that?" Rhone asked in surprise.

"I didn't do anything," Aundrea responded, confused at Rhone's suggestion. "I was too busy falling off the seat."

"No, Stone did," Rhone explained, slumping in relief from his recent adrenaline surge. The driving had been bad enough, but talking between persons was as confusing as ever.

Do not be so dramatic, Stone declared dismissively. *You are just fine. But what was that mechanism? It was most unique.*

Rhone scowled before flicking the reins with a "giddy-up boy," guiding the buggy back onto the main roadway. It was a moment before he answered his friend. *How am I supposed to know? But it's obviously a buggy of some kind.* After another moment to catch up with his driving, he gave up any pretense of anger. *Never mind, I'll ask* Aundrea,' he commented. silently "Stone wants to know about that buggy thing."

"Of course, you wouldn't know," Aundrea said, a huff showing disappointment in herself. "That was one of our steam buggies. They are quite new even, in the big city, but there are more and more all the time. Someday, the roads will be full of them. Unfortunately, Pasha doesn't think much of the idea."

"Does he always do that?" Rhone asked, suddenly worried about his new driving skills.

"No. At least not always, but why don't I take over from here. We're almost to the outskirts of town, and it's only going to get worse. For a country boy, this is going to be a real eye opener."

A half hour later, Rhone stared with wonder as they passed another of the unique buggies, its high-pitched hiss spewing a slim sliver of steam into the air as it made its way along the dirt road with nothing to pull it.

Pasha tossed his head wildly, making Rhone more than happy he had already handed Aundrea the reins. Besides, his neck was already sore from turning first to one side, then the other, attempting to see everything in the clustered mass of humanity.

There was just no way to catch it all. The city was far larger than he had even dreamed. Buildings stood as tall as the badlands' strange cliffs, if not any cleaner, and the streets were clogged with so much traffic until they could hardly move. The number of people simply boggled his mind, with every single street holding more people than the entire town of Skrag-moore.

But it was the clothing that caught his attention most, some of the most outlandish things he could imagine anyone wearing. He gawked at the colors, layers, and odd attachments connected with leather straps and buckles, unable to figure what it was all for. His only comfort lay in the sight of the more conventional clothing the workers wore. Worn-out fabric looked the same no matter who wore it.

He actually thought he was doing pretty well, until he saw a man with an odd hat towering nearly a yard above his head. Gizmos and buttons plastered its surface, making Rhone want to laugh aloud, until the man turned to stare at him with wide eyes.

Suddenly, Rhone wondered if he looked just as odd to the city folk, and lowered his gaze, trying hard not to stare.

As the raucous noises and odd colors assailed his senses, it was the smells that had him wishing he had thought a bit longer before throwing himself into Aundrea's well-meaning hands. Rotting vegetables were a familiar smell, as well as the heavy odor of horses and their droppings, but the scent of bodies, and the filth in the ditches lining the cobbled streets, was beyond his nose's appreciation.

Aundrea took the moment to glance at Rhone, sagging on the bench seat, looking all-together like a lost puppy in a crowded market. "Hey, are you doing okay?" she asked in concern. "This must seem pretty strange."

His face held the answer, and while it wasn't necessarily fear, it certainly wasn't confidence. "Yeah, it's fine," he answered, giving a one shouldered, non-committal shrug.

Aundrea's eyes softened as she reached to pat his leg in sympathy. "It is. Things have changed a lot in the last few years, and I can only think it's going to get more interesting as time goes on. It's hard to stop innovation once it starts. The government is trying desperately to keep some controls on new technology, but it's developing regardless." She shrugged casually. "First everyone wants change, then they look back and wish things were like the good old days."

As Rhone nodded his understanding, his attention was caught by a lady on the street corner. Unconsciously, Rhone stiffening in his seat, swinging his face forward, eyes as big as silver dollars.

Aundrea turned to see what had caused his odd reaction, then flicked the reins, driving them forward with the traffic. "Just think of it as an education," she said calmly, trying to keep a straight face. But his strained expression made her wonder if she was doing the right thing. "It's not much further," she said with a light sigh. "You'll be fine."

Rhone managed a nod, but kept his eyes fixed on the road.

Venders of every kind hawked their wares, while crowds pushed their way down the wooden walkways fronting the tall stone and brick buildings. The streets were clogged almost to a standstill, as buggies pulled by prancing teams, people, and carts, vied for space with the odd mechanical contraptions that made high-pitched screeching noises, and puffed billows of foggy mist into the heavy air. The city was alive, and Rhone knew his life would never be the same again.

"There it is," Aundrea said with relief. "This is my place. You'll be staying here for a while, at least until we can find somewhere better for you to go. And don't worry, I live by myself."

Rhone looked up at the neat multistoried brick building, wondering how she could possibly use a place this big. And she lived all by herself? Just the cleaning must have taken an entire crew a solid week. She must be rich.

But walking past the front entrance stairs, Aundrea turned at the corner and unlocked a door in a small, partially hidden alcove. "Welcome home," she said proudly, before greedily sweeping into the hallway.

Rhone followed slowly, working his way past the heavy door that reminded him of a similar door into The Commissioner's hidden basement. But this hall headed up a flight of stairs, into a wide apartment with large windows overlooking the street.

"Isn't it wonderful?" Aundrea gushed, standing by the window and looking out at the city.

Rhone wasn't so sure he would have said the same. He had seen grand views of mountain vistas, and tortured rocky passageways, heart wrenchingly beautiful crystalline caverns and desert lakes, but the dirty, noisy and smelly streets of the city didn't live up to his definition of wonderful. Interesting maybe, but not wonderful.

Aundrea, however, was perfectly happy with her own description. "It took me ages to find this place. Let me tell you, they're hard to come by. It costs a fortune too, but when I got the job at the department, I just couldn't turn it down. It's perfect."

He had to admit, it was a nice room. Far better than any he had ever been in. "What do you do with the rest of the building?" he asked casually. "You must have a lot of stuff."

It was a very reasonable question, and Aundrea blinked before breaking into a bubbling laugh, laughing so hard she had to cover her mouth to keep from snorting. "Oh, Rhone," she huffed between chortles, "I don't know what to say. That is absolutely the best question I think I've ever heard. But I do apologize. I keep forgetting how new you are to city life."

Rhone accepted her comment, but it didn't answer his question. And why was it so funny?

His face must have given away his thoughts, because she began laughing again.

"Sorry. I'm not normally this poor a hostess. I'll just blame it on the trip, and say, I'm more tired than I thought."

That much he could believe. He was certainly tired of sitting on the hard bench seat of the buggy. It had springs and padding, which helped a lot going over the rough terrain of the flatlands, but it was still a long ride. That and the almost foreboding sense of the city made for a disquieting first impression. Quietly he wondered if he had made the wrong decision. He wasn't a city boy, and was glad of it. It was just too different.

Aundrea motioned toward the kitchen, diverting his thoughts. It was obviously the kitchen, although there was nothing dividing the big room, other than the furnishings. A table sat in one corner, and a counter was built onto the outer wall. Kitchen utensils stuck up from a crockery jug next to the chopping block, and at the other end sat a large metal tub, looking exactly like the one his mom had used in their kitchen. Suddenly, he felt very far from home.

I am here, Stone whispered, having felt Rhone's emotions shift. *Today it is new, but we will learn. Tomorrow will be easier.*

"I suppose so," Rhone replied in a low breath, "but what if we're doing the wrong thing? What if I can't learn this stuff? It's really strange, and... it's just different." He sighed in aching despair.

We will do it together, Stone whispered to his friend.

They had weathered a lot together. They could handle this too.

Aundrea saw Rhone's far-off look and knew what it meant. "How's Stone taking all this? Is it too much?"

She watched his lips purse as he tried to come up with an answer.

"If you would like, I could take you somewhere else," she said, feeling responsible for his disquiet. "We'll get things figured out once I get to the office."

Rhone nodded unenthusiastically.

None of this had been planned. She had only gone to the badlands because of a tip from Maynard, her old friend and Keeper of Histories. It was the tiny drop of blue ink in the center of the puzzle-perfect paths that had drawn her, and where she had unexpectedly found Rhone. Now she had Jewel, and Rhone had Stone. And she had come home without a plan. Some department head she had turned out to be. Even so, the Office of Public Recrimination would never be the same. Not only did she have the best network in the entire government, she now had We to assist her in helping the people. The very thought made her heart race. They could make a huge difference.

Hello, are you all right? came the tiny voice, echoing in alarm through Aundrea's mind, and sending her hand automatically to the little bag tied around her neck.

"Oh Jewel. I am so sorry my little one. Did I wake you?" She spoke aloud, forgetting to think the thoughts to the little rock.

I am fine, but your system began to accelerate, and I did not understand.

"Oh, You're talking!" Aundrea gasped. "This is wonderful!" Dropping somewhat un-ladylike into a fragile looking settee, she began to coo softly to the little We entity.

Rhone grinned as Stone confirmed his guess. *The little one has completed the patterning of Aundrea's mental receptors,* came the inaudible comment. *They will now proceed rapidly through the data connection portion, and on from here on.*

"I thought they were already doing a good job," Rhone said quietly, watching the almost embarrassing love emanating from the two.

But the sound like a harsh throat clearing caught his attention.

Are you about done here? Stone asked archly. *We have more to do than stand around observing others.*

Rhone slumped with sigh. "All right. So, what's going on in that cynical mind of yours? Planning a takeover? Or maybe a way back home? I'm not sure we're going to make it here."

But we did make it here, Stone commented in confusion. *How can you say that we might not make it, when you are standing here? Again, I do not understand your words.*

Rhone gazed imploringly at the ceiling, but knew Stone was right. "Okay, we are here, but I'm not sure we belong here. Is that better? The city's a weird place. You saw all those strange devices, and what about the people? That woman had more chest showing than ...."

Indeed impressive, Stone broke in. *I, of course, was speaking of the machinery.*

When Rhone's ears began to reddened, Stone kindly changed the subject.

Actually, the term machinery is a definition of the process by which the mechanism is created. It is simply a collection of machined elements, assembled into a unique structure, creating an output greater than the sum of the parts.

"Is that right," Rhone said sarcastically, quite used to Stone's instructional mannerism. Stone did, after all, know an amazing number of things, and was usually worth listening to.

I am simply saying, it is good to be educated, and this is a new place. We must be awake to new things. Tally ho, and all that.

"Tally Ho? Where did you get that?" Rhone asked. "Anyway, I get the picture. You like it here and you're saying, I need to get with the program."

Exactly, Stone agreed. *I believe this will be a very stimulating environment, and we should do our best to catch up.*

"Catch up?" Rhone sputtered. "But I don't even know where everyone's going. What if they're all going the wrong way?"

Take a breath, Rhone. You are beginning to panic. We cannot be of assistance if we are in such a state.

Rhone knew it was true and tried to relax. "Okay, but I still don't have any answers. What am I supposed to do in the city? Aundrea wanted an assistant, but I don't how I could even help, unless she wanted me to hunt rats. I'm sure there are plenty of those around. I know how to hunt, but other than that, what good am I? What could I possibly do that she would want me for? I'll just end up in the streets, and I already hate them."

Stone didn't answer for a moment, perhaps giving Rhone a chance to cool off, or maybe calculating the odds, but when he did respond, Rhone felt the impact of his words. *You will need to educate yourself to your new environment. Certainly it will be a change, but you are capable.*

And again, Stone was right. But what he hadn't mentioned was, he would simply be along for the ride. Rhone would be doing all the work.

Rhone had forgotten Aundrea and Jewel, until she called excitedly, "Rhone, we did it! Jewel can talk. It's so amazing."

I told you they were doing well, Stone commented, sounding almost as pleased with his prediction as he was with their accomplishment.

You did, Rhone agreed half-heartedly. *But I'm still glad to see it.* Then he spoke to Aundrea. "You two can really have fun now. You have no idea how much Jewel will be commenting on everything you do, and even what you think. Communication just becomes natural."

"We'll do great," Aundrea said with certainty. "My little Jewel is perfect!"

Rhone wanted to roll his eyes, but decided to look on the bright side. "You will," he stated emphatically. "and if there are any problems, Stone is here to help. Aren't you Stone?"

You do not need to shout, Stone commented. *I have already offered my assistance to the little one, and everything seems to be in order.*

"What? You spoke directly to Jewel?" Rhone asked excitedly, realizing he would no longer need to interpret everything.

She and I can now communicate, Yes, Stone agreed, *and with a much greater efficiency than you were accomplishing, although I am certain you were doing your best.*

Rhone made a wry face before passed the information to Aundrea. "Stone just told me, he can talk directly to Jewel now. at least for close distances. Now you won't have to listen to my halfway translations."

"I know. Jewel just told me!" Aundrea said happily. "This is so exciting. Isn't she a wonder?"

Rhone wondered how many times he was going to hear that before it got old, but then remembered his own first days with Stone. It really had been perfect.

CHAPTER 3

The Department

"Come on. It's not far," Aundrea called over her shoulder, indicating the direction with a tip of her head.

Everything seemed to be 'not far', yet totally out of reach as Rhone followed her lithe form, seeming to slide through the crowds like a warm knife through butter.

How does she do that? he thought, watching in amazement as she again disappeared into the throng. Rousing himself, Rhone hustled double-time to catch up. Her movement was obviously a skill in itself, and one he would have to learn. Luckily, within a few steps he caught up with her, and congratulated himself. Maybe he was getting the hang of it.

The bewildering mass of humanity seemed to buck his motion no matter which way he went. It was lucky he had Aundrea to follow, as she flitted through the crowd with ease. But it only took one second of people watching, and she was gone.

Rhone searched for her, standing on his tip-toes for a better view. In sudden panic, he realized there was no way he could find his way back without her. It had only been a few blocks, but already he was as lost as a lamb in the wilderness.

Spinning back and forth in search, Rhone caught his toe on an unseen cobble and stumbled, tripping awkwardly with arms flailing. He tried desperately to stop his fall, but instead of hitting the cobbled pavement, his fall was abruptly corrected as a firm grip caught his elbow, righting him and allowing him to regain his footing.

With a shocked breath, Rhone glanced up to thank his rescuer, seeing Aundrea's wry smile of concern. Her quick once-over was enough to change her concern to a look of amusement, verifying he was unharmed, but also noted his shock, like an animal ready to bolt and run for its life.

"Hold my hand so we don't get separated again," she said, giving his arm a comforting squeeze. Then tipping her head in the correct direction, held his gaze a moment longer to be certain he was listening. "It's not very far. It's the main reason I pay so much for my apartment."

Almost numb with embarrassment, Rhone gave a nod, knowing he wasn't ready for the city. It was just too much for a country kid.

He followed, holding tightly to her hand, while trying valiantly not to allow the rise of his heart rate to trigger a comment from Stone.

It was only a couple of blocks before they took a flight of steps up to a massive stony edifice. The doorway arch itself could easily have spanned his entire house back in Skragmoore. It was humbling to think about, and Rhone couldn't help slowing his steps as he gazed up at the enormous structure.

Aundrea too slowed as she saw his interest. She had forgotten her own first time entering. She had been in Maynard's secure grasp that trip, and understood the power of the moment. "Pretty impressive isn't it?" she asked, turning her gaze up at the huge building. "I should have given you a bit more introduction, but I guess this works. This is The Capital Stronghold. What do you think?"

Rhone stood on the wide flow of block steps, reminding him of the steep talus slopes below Skragmoore's craggy ramparts. Tipping his head back, he looked up at the massive stonework of the Capital Stronghold, its grey stone walls rising as grandly as any cliff face he had ever seen. Briefly he wondered how many years it had taken to build.

"It's huge," he mumbled in awe. "Do you really work here?"

Maybe she was more important than he thought.

"Yes sir, I do. Actually, I run the office. Well, the entire department I suppose," she said with a depreciating shrug. "It's The Office of Public Recrimination, or the OPR to us, and I guess you could say we're pretty important. Our job is to oversee the effects of policy, as seen by the people. When the people give comment or complaint, it's up to us to find out the what and why, and if anything can be done to mitigate the problem. Our favorite saying is, If the people are happy, the government is happy. It seems to work, most of the time. When it doesn't, we do double time to get it fixed."

Glancing up at the tall walls, Rhone cautiously asked, "Is that why you were in Skragmoore?"

"You're pretty sharp for a young man," she said, giving him a serious look. "We knew Commissioner Dodge was dealing underhanded, but we didn't know how, or about you. That came later."

"But I thought you were following a map, and looking for treasure," Rhone stated, somewhat confused by her comment.

Aundrea's eyes twinkled as she grinned. "It all fits together, and yes, I did follow a map, but I didn't know you were at the other end." With a very girlish grin, she said, "Sometimes things just work out. Like this time. Who could have guessed?"

That was something he could understand. Who could have guessed he would find a rock that turned out to be a crystalline entity? And who would have guessed he would leave home to search the world? Or break into a vault and end up in the big city? It sounded like a fairy tale, but everyone knew fairy tales end up good. With Stone's support and Aundrea's guidance, maybe he could make this work.

With that thought in mind, he followed Aundrea as she climbed the steps below the archway, entering the massive building to an equally massive foyer.

"It's called The Stronghold for a reason," Aundrea instructed like a tour guide, "but while it was built much like a castle it's not as old as you might think. It came sometime after the collapse, and has been growing ever since. New parts get added, and old parts are rebuilt for new reasons. Who knows, maybe it will continue forever. For now, it's where I work. I had to connive my way in, but it is a real convenience for us to be in close proximity to the offices of The Council. I need to be where we can talk, without the delays of transportation back and forth across the city. They saw my point and voila, here we are.

The stonework corridors stretched off the entrance foyer into the distance, with steep stairways rising upward level after level. The ceiling rose several stories high, a spider-work of detailed art crisscrossing the span in honeycombed panels and flying buttresses, their delicate ribs belying the strength of the massive building.

Stone was equally awed. *I did not realize mankind had such knowledge of stress and support. This is wonderfully structured. Do you see the interlace of bracing and bridging?*

Rhone wasn't certain what parts Stone was admiring, but he had never seen anything like this before. In open admiration he asked Aundrea, "How many people work here?"

"I have no idea," she answered, actually surprised she didn't know. "I've never asked." With a sweep of her arm toward a corridor, she grabbed his hand with her other and led the way up a staircase, not noticing his embarrassment.

"This is quite a climb the first few times, but you get used to it. Two more floors and we're there."

Climbing wasn't a problem. He had grown up with rocky cliffs rising on both side of their dry valley, and had climbed them often. Often enough that he had worn a trail into the dirt of the rocky hillsides.

No, the racing of his heart had nothing to do with the climb. It was the warm hand holding his. It had been a long time since Mom had passed, but his feeling for Aundrea was nothing like that, even if in some way similar. She was easily the most impressive woman he had ever met. The remembered glimpses of her swimming in the little lake sent a chill shiver through his body.

"How are you doing?" she asked in concern. "I don't want to wear you out before we even get there."

"Ahh, I'm fine. Just getting a little warm I guess."

He truly was getting warm, but not for any reason he could admit. Realizing she had released his hand, Rhone remembered the story of the fool, who had been in such an intent conversation with himself, he walked off the edge of the cliff. *I'm such a dumb head,* he chided himself.

Not my words, came Stone's reply.

Frustrated, Rhone returned the thought in the same tone. *Well, maybe the guy had a rock in his pocket too, and spent so much time arguing, he couldn't see straight,* then he almost stumbled on a tread as he hurried to catch up, feeling as stupid as the man in the story. Speaking with Stone and keeping an eye on Aundrea at the same time were almost too many distractions.

I believe you hit it very well, Stone offered. *You are being distracted, and not setting to our task.*

Our task? Rhone thought, surprise by the accusation. *How can I do that when I can't even walk down the street without help? It's not easy being on this side of the team, you know.*

I do realize the difficulty, Stone commented, *and I wish I could help more, but the conditions are such that I cannot focus effectively.*

"Ah ha! So it's not just me," Rhone replied jubilantly.

"It's not just you?" Aundrea asked, turning with a look of question.

"Sorry, I was talking to Stone," Rhone mumbled in embarrassment.

Aundrea laughed gently as they climbed the last flight of stairs, stopping before a heavy wooden door. The bold letters on the engraved brass plaque said, 'Office of Public Recrimination', and with an elegant flourish, Aundrea swung the door wide. "Welcome to the office."

The room was a bustling hive of activity. Papers shuffled, drawers clacked shut, and the voices of dozens filled the open space as work proceeded at the pace of a horse race.

"It gets a bit noisy," Aundrea said, smiling warmly at the scene, and obviously proud. "Come on, I'll show you my part of the office."

Aundrea received occasional hellos and a wave or two, as she led the way, but managed to outdistance potential questions. Rhone followed like a child at his mother's skirts, head swiveling back and forth, trying to catch every intriguing scene. He could hardly believe it when she stopped at a door with hazy glass in the upper half, painted with the words 'The Boss' in fancy gold lettering.

So, she truly was the boss of all these people. Rhone felt tiny compared to that. He had nothing to offer, having simply followed her from the badlands.

His eyes wandered the fine office as Aundrea plopped dramatically into her chair like it was a feather bed.

"I'm back," she sighed nostalgically, placing her booted feet up on the desk and leaning back to scan the ceiling thoughtfully. "I probably shouldn't have gone, but I knew something was there. I just didn't know what."

Rhone stared in shock at the almost dainty boots propped on the desk top, a definite first for him. He had never seen a woman's foot lifted higher than the next step, and seldom then. Once again, realization struck of just how little experience he had in the world, and yet another thing mom hadn't mentioned.

Quickly averting his eyes, he asked, "So, if all these people work for you, why did you come to the badlands yourself? Why didn't you send some of them?" He nodded vaguely to the outer office.

"Do you believe in fate?" Aundrea asked, tipping her head to look at him closely.

"I don't know. Maybe." Was it fate that his life had changed after meeting Stone? He certainly hadn't planned it, so maybe it was. "I think I make up my own mind, so I'm not sure if that discounts fate."

"Well said, Rhone, and I certainly hope not. We all plan for a best outcome, yet seem to get directed to where we hadn't intended. Is that fate, or just happenstance?"

It wasn't any more of an answer than what he had said, but it was comforting to hear her say it. Nodding his agreement, he again asked, "But why were you out there by yourself? Aren't you too important?"

"Let's call it a technical maybe," she dithered with a wave of her hand. "But I also sent a team, and they should be back soon. Right now, the only things we're certain about are that I have you, and Commissioner Dodge attempted your murder and the theft of Stone. There's a lot more that still needs answers. We had reports Commissioner Dodge was all up in arms about something, with men out searching, but we didn't know what he was looking for. I'm not sure he did either, until his men ran into you."

"That's true," Rhone said. "We met them, twice."

"Twice? And you came out on top? Even the little I know about Commissioner Dodge tells me that's pretty impressive."

For a few sun-starred moments, Rhone basked in the approval of her warm smile.

"I told you my job is exciting," Aundrea said, straightening in her chair. "We get to track down problems, and try to fix them. In your case, we were hoping to gain enough information to make The Council recall Dodge for breach of contract. Although, on that topic, I had two more agents in Skragmoore I need to check on. I'm like a mother hen, always on the watch for hawks."

"And coyotes," Rhone added. "They're sneakier."

Aundrea grinned at his metaphor. "I'll have to remember that one. It's far too true." Rising from her chair she shook out her skirt. "Come on. Time to meet the natives."

"Natives?" Rhone asked in surprise. Then it clicked. Her staff.

They were barely out her door, when Aundrea put two fingers to her mouth and gave a short, ear-cracking whistle. Rhone jerked reflexively at the unexpected sound, but no one else seemed disturbed, or even surprised, and within moments, all attention was focused in their direction.

Then with practiced authority, Aundrea's voice filled the space, not shouting, but definitely heard. "Everyone to the committee room for a short meeting. We'll start in five." Turning to Rhone she gave a wicked grin. "We may be somewhat short on protocol, but we get the job done."

He wasn't sure how to respond. Having never had a job before, maybe this was how it was done.

Rhone felt the curious glances as people began moving toward a set of double doors in the far wall. Concern washed over him realizing his collar was an obvious attention grabber. He had been set on more than once, because of it, ending up almost dead, twice. Just having people notice it made him nervous.

Aundrea moved easily through the milling group, making her way to the front of the room before motioning him up beside her. "Good morning all. Thanks for dropping whatever you were doing. I've just returned from an interesting trip, and want to check on what's been happening."

"Welcome back, Boss," called a woman from the rear of the crowded room. "Maybe these guys will get some work done now."

A skinny man across from her met the comment squarely. "Hey, I've been doing plenty, and half of that was Bran's. When is he getting back Boss? He can have his job."

Several derisive remarks flew, regarding the validity and parenthood of the speaker, until Aundrea raised a placating hand. "Settle down. We have a guest, and believe it or not, I've been bragging about you. I'd hate to have him see what you're really like." But she said it with a smile. These were after all, her people, and she was proud of them.

"Who you got there, Boss? Seems a bit young to be hooked up in this office."

Aundrea acknowledged the speaker with a nod. "I would like you all to meet Rhone. He and I met on this assignment, and I wanted to show him around."

Rhone gave an apologetic shrug as all eyes focused on him, feeing his imminent blush begin to rise. He wasn't much for crowds, and as someone once said, anything over two was a crowd in Skragmoore.

"Rhone and I will be working closely for a while, but it shouldn't intrude into whatever each of you are working on. As for Bran..."

The main doors to the outer office chose that moment to swing wide, slamming against the wall with a resounding crash as a male voice called, "Hello all. We're home."

"Bran, we're in the meeting room. Come on in," Aundrea returned, recognizing Bran's voice, brash, but with a new tone of authority. Things must have gone well.

A few moments later a young man, with a questioning look on his sunburnt face, popped into the room, closely followed by several others.

"Howdy all," he chortled mischievously. "Glad you all got together for our home coming. Makes us feel all warm and welcome."

Rhone kept to the wall, instinctively staying out of the way.

"Welcome home Bran," Aundrea said cheerfully. "Is the whole team with you?"

"Yes Ma'am. Every single one of them."

A worn and dirty team trickled past, jostling for space in the now overly crowded room. Hellos and hands shakes were handed off, until Aundrea settled them, waving Bran to the front.

"You can give me the full rundown later, but how about a quick summary of the trip? It seems like it went well."

"No problem," Bran said, making a show of readying himself before starting his recitation. Using both hands he mimed the actions of their journey. "So there we were, totally surrounded by Commissioner Dodge's men." A quick glance made sure his audience was following before he continued. "Yup, Looked like it was going to be a free for all, and no way out. But we were ready, or as close as you can get to it in the badlands. It's a bad place, and no doubt about it. Turned out, we hadn't run into just anyone. It was Commissioner Dodge's foreman, Manny, and his select few. Interestingly, they were there for the same reason we were. Looking for the kid. We had already found the tracks of their previous run-in, where he was lost, and funny thing was, we were able to prove it, right down to the number of horses. It's not often you actually prove the stories right. Anyway, we had just finished with that and were working our way back out of the maze... when we ran right into 'em. Darn place is so messed up, you can't tell if the sounds are coming at you, or from behind, and I'm serious. It's totally messed up."

Rhone began putting things together as he listened, realizing they were talking about his story. He had managed to live through it, but now it was coming back to haunt him. Shrinking further against the wall, he began to look for a way out, when Andrea's voice smoothly broke into the ongoing story.

"Bran, I would like to introduce you to someone. This is Rhone." Her subtle wink let him know it was going to be okay.

"Sure Aundrea, whatever you…" Bran stopped mid-sentence as he turned, finally taking in the youth looking very uncomfortable at being in the spotlight. Then his eyes focused on the collar around Rhone's neck, the pillow shaped golden-pink stone dazzling even at a distance. "So you are alive," he whispered almost soundlessly. "But how'd you get here? We searched for days, and the commissioner's men were searching even longer, but never found anything."

Uncomfortable with the scrutiny, Rhone glanced around nervously until Bran stopped him with a dismissive gesture. "Hey, don't worry about it. You're here." Reaching out, he gave Rhone's shoulder a friendly pat. "Glad to meet you Rhone. Welcome to the OPR."

The honest warmth of Bran's words made Rhone's nervousness relax, but he did have a question. "The Commissioner let you go?"

"Well, not exactly," Bran said, his face losing some of its cockiness. "Interesting you should mention it. Seems mister commissioner up and disappeared." He paused, bobbing his brows for effect. "Nobody in town's seen him. Not since he hightailed it out to the badlands, presumably to catch us. Mighty strange if you ask me, but it is the badlands." Then breaking into an easy laugh, he motioned a gorgeous redhead to come forward. "Rhone, this is MarryEllen. She was part of our team, and played backup. And of course, since it was the badlands, we needed it."

Rhone was getting lost in the players, and couldn't imagine what this lady had to do with backing up.

She was there as a final failsafe, Stone spoke quietly in his mind. *It is a common strategy for military maneuvers when the outcome is questioned.*

Thanking Stone with a thought, Rhone nodded with his new understanding and summarized for Bran, "So you knew there was going to be trouble."

Bran's snort more than described his feeling on the matter. "We were dealing with Commissioner Dodge, so I was pretty sure there would be trouble. Remember, he was the reason we were there in the first place, so it only made sense. If he was underhanded on a normal basis, we weren't going to walk in and play patty cake."

With the story getting more interesting, Aundrea took over. "It looks like we're going to need a bit more of the story than I had planned," she said, speaking to MaryEllen. "At least this will get it out in the open and won't need to go through the grape vine. So what brought you into their devious machinations?" She herself could come up with several possibilities, and knowing MaryEllen's file, this could prove interesting.

Luckily, MaryEllen wasn't shy, which, considering of her looks, was a good thing. She would draw attention wherever she went. Thankfully, she had the skills to back up her beauty.

"It really wasn't much," she said, as demurely as Aundrea had ever heard her. "The Commissioner was a man, so I simply spoke to him like he was a man." Which sounded quite acceptable, until she made a sour face. "Really though, he was just a creep, so I had to use force."

Even knowing MaryEllen's dossier, Aundrea was surprised. "You used force on Commissioner Dodge? But he's huge. 6 foot 4, and 300 pounds, or something like that." It was impressive enough to be almost unbelievable.

"Probably bigger," MarryEllen said matter-of-factly, "but I did cheat."

The sounds of applause were punctuated by cheers of approval. Even Rhone smiled, understanding she had outmaneuvered The Commissioner.

"So what happened?" Aundrea asked, still needing information. "Is he dead?"

While dead wouldn't necessarily be the best outcome, it probably wasn't the worst either, except for him.

"Oh no," MarryEllen replied, almost regretfully. "Although he might wish he was. He was pretty smelly by the time I dropped him off for The Council to deal with."

"*You* dropped him off? By yourself?" Aundrea asked, again surprised by this slim girl. She looked to Bran for some explanation, but only received a raised shoulder in posed innocence.

"I wasn't there," he said, enjoying the moment. "We just met coming up to The Stronghold."

Still confused, Aundrea regarded MaryEllen questioningly.

"It wasn't so difficult," MaryEllen stated almost shyly. "No harder than hoisting a steer for slaughter." But with the looks of disbelief in the room, she dipped her head, embarrassed at needing to explain. "I used a hoist and grapples."

Mumbled comments weren't quite so prolific this time around, but the wide-eyed appraising stares certainly were.

"You're quite a girl Emmy," Bran chortled with appreciation. "Glad you're on our side."

Aundrea could only agree. "Only a couple more questions for now," she said, redirecting everyone's attention, and saving MaryEllen from more scrutiny. "So, I presume Commissioner Dodge is being seen to by The Council's gaoler? I can't think of a better outcome. While I'm not sure how you accomplished it, I must say, I'm impressed." She turned to Bran who was beaming at his team. "A good job to you too, Bran. I sent you on a hopeless task, and you all come back smelling like roses. No, change that. I can smell you from here. The whole lot of you, go home and get bathed, then show up tomorrow. And thank you."

With a nod and a wave, Bran escorted his team out like gladiators, the men beating each other on the back, lifting clouds of road dust into the still air, while the ladies, a bit more circumspect, drifted out behind the noisy men.

CHAPTER 4

And Now what?

They were simply going to the market, but it felt more like a jungle trek Rhone had once read about. He marveled at the number of unidentifiable machines and gadgets passing by, but actually wading through the crowds like a swollen river, brought everything much too close. The mass of people was simply too constricting, and he yearned for the freedom of the wild countryside.

At least the big city's crush was giving him a better understanding of Stone's incarceration in the commissioner's safe. No wonder Stone had been grumpy when he was rescued. What must it have been like, being in total isolation, when Rhone felt isolated even in the midst of a crowd?

He was again following Aundrea through the crowded streets, when the spectacle of a woman's pleated patchwork skirt, worn thin and raggedly torn at the hem, caught his eye. The alluring glimpses of her many-hued leggings reaching from heavy leather ankle boots to her knees was so different he was instantly embarrassed. It seemed every day's walk left him in a daze.

Aundrea herself wore an interesting assortment of clothing as though trying to fit in with the rowdy crowd. Her burgundy leather bustier matched nicely with her rose-colored silken blouse, but Rhone was glad the buttons were done well up her neck. He had already seen more than enough of her to have daydreams, and that just wasn't right. This woman had brought him out of the badlands, and if he played it right, might even become his boss. She was already giving him free room and board while he learned his way around, trying to get his feet under him.

The odd 'auuuuga' sound of a horn caused Aundrea to quick-step out of the road, mere moments before a proverbial bucket-full of cold muddy water doused Rhone, wrenching a sputtering gasp from his throat and dragging him from his haze.

Glancing back, Aundrea only half succeeded in covering her laughter as Rhone stepped onto the boardwalk, dripping arms held out to the sides while muddy water drained down his pant legs, creating little puddles around his boots.

"Are you all right?" The question came from both Aundrea and Stone at the same time; one with concern, and one with covered humor. It was odd, hearing the words echo both inside and out simultaneously.

Rhone's clothes stuck to him like a second skin, soaking him to the bone. Almost immediately, he felt his body's heat being sapped away by the light breeze. He must have looked more than a little stupid standing on a street corner, dripping like a tree in a winter storm. But the rest of the world couldn't have cared less. The traffic, both pedestrian and vehicular, passed by without concern, not even noticing his awkward condition.

"Rhone, are you okay?" Aundrea asked again, quickly assessing his situation. "I'm so sorry. I wasn't watching close enough."

He wasn't about to blame her. It was his fault. He was simply in the wrong environment. At least he knew what to expect from coyotes and snakes.

"I'm fine," he said with shiver. "A bit of a drip, but I'm fine."

Aundrea grinned at him and chuckled, "You're okay fella." But seeing something of the wild and lost confusion in his eyes, she took his hand and guided him further from the roadway. "You are quite the young man Rhone. I dragged you out of the wilderness into the big city, and no matter what happens, you take it all in stride. I appreciate seeing that ability in a man."

Rhone managed an awkward smile, thinking he was anything but, yet it steadied his nerves. With a shrug he said, "I guess it isn't so bad. I've been wet before."

Aundrea's second once-over noted the mud from the drenching he had taken. "I still blame myself," she apologized. "If I was really good at my job, you wouldn't be standing there soaking wet. Let's head back and you can get cleaned up."

Rhone drooped, feeling he had disappointed her. He had been tired of sitting at the window watching the world roll past, and asked to come along.

"Come on," she said gently. "We have plenty of time. We'll try again this afternoon. First we have to get you dry."

It was amazing how her smile made his world fine again. Other than his being cold, the whole thing really was almost funny. "I guess I could use a clean shirt," he acknowledged. Then quickly added, "Maybe pants too."

Two hours after his soaking, Rhone was sitting propped in the window seat, blowing on his hot tea as he watched the traffic flow by in spurts and drizzles. High-stepping matched teams pulling tall wheeled buggies, mixed in uneasily with the odd mechanical vehicles belching clouds of vapor. Each vied for space with the pony carts and heavily laden wagons, while the pedestrians, often in their uniquely styled clothing of various colors and cuts, attempted to cross between the traffic, hopefully without becoming splattered with the ever-present mud. While the scene wasn't quite pandemonium, it was definitely high activity. Everyone seemed to have somewhere to go, and were obviously late in getting there.

But it was the gadgetry that had Rhone mesmerized. A multitude of different pieces, each with a different look and obviously different use. Some, he was pretty sure were weapons, more by the look of those carrying them than the items themselves. Other items he understood, such as the goggles used to protect eyes from the belching steam and the splattering mud. The long coats and dusters had been common even in Skragmoore, and made sense when traveling on dusty and muddy roads. But it was the other odd items he couldn't figure out, such as with the gentleman crossing the street. The tubes, gears and dials on his vestment had him baffled, but it was, after all, the big city, and almost everything he had seen was a bit odd.

A shrill shrieking whistle caught Rhone's attention as a heavy rig went racing past, pulled by an excited team of horses. The man beside the driver bellowed through a mouth horn to the clogged traffic, then pulled a dangling cord, producing the shrieking sound as a warning to those ahead. The rig was coming through, whether they were ready or not.

"Isn't it exciting?" Aundrea asked, coming to stand beside him and noticing the action below. "That's the new fire department rig. The big boiler in the wagon pumps water directly onto a fire. It's terribly effective from what I hear. I read, they even managed to put out an entire house fire last month."

Stone, of course, had his own comment on the proceedings. *It is merely a system of mechanics, creating hydraulic pressure to push the water. Not a difficult process at all.*

But it sounded difficult to Rhone. He thought about the brush pile he had burned last year, and how much work it had been to put out after it unexpectedly spread into the grass. He could see how the rig would be a definite improvement over buckets. It had taken many trips before he got it under control, carrying water from the pump in the yard to the fire. Luckily the grass had been sparse in the rocky soil, and the fire hadn't spread far.

Rhone watched as the fire wagon passed, then slumped back into boredom as Aundrea slid gracefully onto the settee, removing the little leather bag from around her neck. Pouring Jewel into her palm, she smiled warmly as she whispered, "Hello little one. I have a surprise for you."

A surprise? came the small voice speaking clearly in her mind. *Do I like surprises?*

"This is a very good surprise," Aundrea said encouragingly. "I spoke with a jeweler, and he's going to make a setting for you. Soon I will be able to wear you every day, and I won't need to leave you home by yourself. Won't that be wonderful?"

Although Rhone could only hear Aundrea talking, he was used to the interaction between the two, and could usually follow their conversations.

"Will it be a ring?" He asked, pleased with the idea.

Aundrea nodded happily. "Yes. I saw a pattern I just loved, and need to take Jewel in for them to measure. They said it wouldn't be any problem at all."

Rhone couldn't help but smile. He was happy for her, but a question had been bothering him.

Swinging his feet around to face her, he asked, "Aundrea, what am I doing here? I can't just sit around your house all day doing nothing. I need to do work of some kind." As the reality of his situation truly settled on him, his eyes took on a pained look of dejection. "I honestly don't know what I can do for you. All I really know is hunting and gardening, and I don't see much use for either of those around here."

Aundrea heard the need in his voice, and slipped Jewel back into the pouch. Leaning forward, she study him closely. "I can understand your worry, but our teams don't just fix the problems of the big city. They go all over the country. With you and Stone as a team, you could be a huge asset to us. How does that sound?"

"But I don't know anything about being an agent," Rhone voiced in concern.

"Don't worry. I won't send you to the field untrained. Our agents are required to study both method and manner. It will be a lot of hard work, but I know you can do it."

I could help, Stone said with interest. *As you know, I have very good recall.*

Rhone couldn't help but smile at his friend's enthusiasm. "Stone says he's all for it, but I think he's just bored."

"Thank you, Stone," Aundrea said aloud. "I was hoping you would be." Her enthusiasm grew as she explained more of her plan. "With you and Stone in the field, Jewel and I can work from the inside. Together, we can build a solid unit for fighting problems, and we won't have to worry about anyone leaking information."

It is a good plan, Jewel added, speaking directly to Stone.

Jewel has just agreed, Stone commented, and with more enthusiasm than Rhone had heard for a long time. *Which, I believe, makes it unanimous. So, when do we start?*

Resigned, Rhone let Aundrea know. "Stone just asked when we can start."

"Yesssss," Andrea said, with an almost predatory grin, "but you already have. Why do you think I brought you all this way? The city is quite a place, but not somewhere you would have come by yourself."

"But, what if I had said no?" Rhone asked, suddenly aware he could have goofed up her entire plan.

"You wouldn't," Aundrea said with certainty. "I watched you. I even studied up on you before I went to the badlands. There was no way you would let this pass."

"Wait, You knew you were going to meet me?" Rhone asked, his concern growing again.

"Not at all. That was totally by accident, but I knew 'of' you. You were an unknown quantity, and possibly, one with mysterious powers. Pretty exciting actually, but we had no idea who, or what, you really were."

Rhone nodded as he began to understand. "So that's why they asked if I was a wizard. But did they really think so?"

"We honestly didn't know," Aundrea said with a shrug and a smile, "but in this game you have to keep an open mind. What if you had been, and we hadn't considered the idea? While it may not have been on the top of our list of probabilities, we did consider it."

Perplexed, Rhone had to ask, "But what if I was? Would it have changed anything?"

"Oh, we had a plan. I wanted you on our side, so it was up to Bran's team to find out what you needed, or what would convince you that we were trying to fix things. If they made contact, they had been tasked to offer what we could. We wanted you to work *with* us. Not *against* us."

Rhone considered this. "So you're really saying, I would have been working with you, no matter which way it went."

"No, not quite," she said with a wistful look. "What if you had been a black mage, or simply desired to be left alone? Some people are that way. You would have had the power to work against us, and we would have had very little ability to do anything about it. It was a gamble, but I put Bran on it, and trusted him not to goof up." She smiled at those words. "I have to trust all my people. We're a team."

"And you want Stone and me to be part of the team," Rhone said, nodding with understanding.

"I do. And with Jewel, it will be an entirely different game."

The talk had Aundrea so animated she could no longer sit still. "Want some dinner?" she asked, shoulders shivering with her energy. "I know this great little diner down the street. Let's celebrate."

CHAPTER 5

Training is Hard Work

R hone sat in deep concentration, fingers steepled at his lips.

It is not all that difficult, Stone complained. *Can you not see the connection? When the catalyst is added, a reaction occurs, but the catalyst is not consumed.*

Rhone tried to visualize the meaning, squeezing his eyes closed to remove any distraction. "But, why isn't it used up? When I put wood on a fire, it burns by changing to a gas, and the gas burns. So it gets used up. Why not the catalyst?"

Ah, not a bad question, but the reaction is already occurring naturally. The presence of the catalyst simply speeds up the process, allowing it to occur more rapidly. Try this concept. Sliding on ice is much easier than on the rough ground, because the ice removes the friction, yet is not used up. It simply speeds your progress. It is not the same at all, but I thought you might enjoy the concept.

Rhone's mood brightened as he caught at least some of the idea. "That makes sense. Since the ice is slippery, it has less friction and I go faster. So the ice would be the catalyst."

As I said, it is not a perfect understanding, but it will work for now.

Rhone took a long breath, allowing his mind to clear. Studying was about as exciting as watching the sun dry the apples slices mom had prepared for winter storage.

But you enjoyed the apples in winter, did you not? Stone asked encouragingly. *Therefore, the preparatory time was well spent. Do not get discouraged my young friend. Training is good for you. Personally, it is somewhat satisfying to note, I am not the only one having difficulty teaching you.*

"Well thanks. Glad I'm good for something," Rhone commented dryly.

He wasn't really grumpy at his friend. Without Stone's help, he was basically worthless. He hadn't realized just how unschooled he was. In fact, his only redemption was that he and Stone had already worked on many of the concepts they were now using.

"I never considered an agent needing this kind of knowledge," Rhone admitted. "I figured it was all secret stuff, and fighting. Things like that."

Those are important elements too, I am certain, Stone commented, heading off onto another of his teaching moments, *but background information is vital to understanding future possibilities. When you understand what could happen, you will be better prepared for any upcoming action that does happen.*

Rhone crinkled his nose, trying to listen, but without really hearing, as his mind kept drifting off track. "I still like the sneaky stuff better. You've got to admit, I was pretty good at knife throwing," he commented proudly.

He didn't mention, he had been throwing knives ever since he was old enough not to cut himself regularly.

Agreed, you were, but what about the calculations for the launched weapon's drop rate?

Rhone's puff of annoyance said he knew he hadn't done so well on that one. He had managed it, eventually, but only with Stone's tutoring.

Diverting from the subject, Rhone asked, "I wonder when we get to the section on mechanics?"

He had seen so many unique pieces in the city he could hardly wait to learn what they were, and what they did. He was considering those, when a feminine voice broke into his thoughts.

"Thought you might like a break. You've been at it for hours." MaryEllen's gorgeous features would make any man's day seem brighter, and Rhone was quick to agree.

"Sure," Rhone said, both relieved and happily surprised. Taking the proffered cup, he patently ignoring Stone's snide comment about his heart rate's sudden increase. "What time is it anyway?" he asked, careful not to look directly at her. No sense fueling the fire.

"Poor boy, works so hard he doesn't even know when it's time to eat," she said with a playful pout. "I noticed you missed lunch, and that's pretty sad for someone your age."

He hadn't even realized he had missed lunch. It must have been during one of Stone's never-ending lectures.

"It's close to two already," MaryEllen continued in her sultry tone, "so I thought, if you're interested, we're all going to the cantina later."

Interested? He was being asked out by the most beautiful woman he had ever seen! But guiltily thought of Aundrea. They were both beautiful.

And, they were both older than he was. That was one problem when working with adults. Still, it was a problem for another time.

"Yeah, I'd love to!" he answered. "But I should probably ask Aundrea first."

"Good idea," MaryEllen agreed with a light smile. "Stay on the up and up with the boss, and you won't have to make excuses later. Let me know. Maybe we could head over together." Her eyes crinkled in that perfectly cute way she had, and with a wave, she swept back out of the room.

Rhone relaxed, staring vacantly at the coffered ceiling with a dumb grin on his face.

But Stone broke into his revery, always ready to chastise. *Excuse me,* but *your work is not yet completed. If you are planning to skip your homework later, you had better set your mind to your task now.*

Party pooper, Rhone thought wryly, but was anticipating the evening too much to be grumpy. "Okay, where were we?"

Party pooper? Stone asked in question.

Rhone smiled to himself, feeling the shaking of Stone's non-existent head.

At 4:00 sharp, Rhone set down the book and stood up for a long-needed stretch. He had put in a good day, and his brain was numb, but he still needed to make sure the evening's plan would work.

As expected, he found Aundrea sitting at her desk, pouring through the ever-present paperwork. His plopping into the chair across from her desk caused Aundrea to look up abruptly.

"Rough day?" she asked knowingly.

She had been through the entire process herself once, and knew it was a lot of work, but it was worth it. Now she ran the entire organization, and literally told everyone where they could go.

But Rhone's thoughts were headed in other directions. "I was wondering, would it be okay if I went out with the gang tonight? MaryEllen dropped by and mentioned they were heading to the cantina after work."

What he didn't mention, was that she had asked if he wanted to go with her. That was personal somehow.

"I don't know why not," Aundrea responded, but her lips pursed as she seemed to reconsider. "You are a bit young to be drinking." It took a moment before her face brightened in decision. "I'm sure we could make it work. Let's do it. I haven't been out for ages, and it will be good for us."

Rhone made sure not to show his minor disappointment. They were going, and that was the main thing. While he wouldn't be going out with MaryEllen, it really wouldn't be so bad. He knew better than to think it was an actual date, and Aundrea was almost as cool.

Smiling his thanks, he sagged back into the chair, watching as she returned to her papers. He managed a few long minutes, before rising from his slumped position. "I'll just let them know we'll be there, but maybe a bit late."

"Good idea," Aundrea said without looking up, "I shouldn't be more than a few minutes," and raised a hand to acknowledge his departure.

Rhone wandered off to find MaryEllen, figuring he wouldn't have to rush. 'Hurry up and wait' seemed to be the by-law of adults.

The cantina was packed, and so noisy that everyone seemed to be talking at the top of their voice just to be heard. No one could hear what anyone said, but no one seemed to mind.

Rhone had never been in a place like this before, but he seemed to be saying that a lot lately. Aundrea saw arms waving for their attention, and motioned to a table in the back. Rhone stumbled along behind, blindly following as she moved almost effortlessly through the crowd. They eventually reached their table and crammed in, Aundrea on one side, and Rhone, up against MaryEllen on the other. It was just fine as far as he was concerned.

"Thanks for inviting us," Aundrea shouted. Rhone shyly glanced at MaryEllen, managing a dumb smile, but in full agreement.

"Glad you could make it," MaryEllen shouted back cheerfully.

Bran was there too. "What can we order for you?" he called over the din. "I can guess yours, Aundrea, but what about the pup?"

With a thoughtful look, she answered, "I doubt he's ever had anything, but let's try the ginger ale. It's spicy, and a good place to start."

Bran raised a hand, flagging for the harried waiter's attention. "We'll have another round of the same, plus one, and a ginger ale for the kid."

The waiter looked surprised at having a teenager in the group, but nodded and quickly left. The place was hopping, and there was no time for unneeded questions.

MaryEllen leaned in close enough to be heard, and asked, "How did it go today?"

Rhone could hardly think with her perfume so close, and valiantly tried not to notice the amount of chest she was showing as she leaned toward him. "I ahh... I think I did pretty good. Up until the part about ballistic drop."

"I remember that part," she relied with an easy laugh. "Don't let it get to you. It's a poorly worded question, but the easy answer is, know your weapon, and don't miss."

Which made a ton more sense than learning tables and calculations, but he didn't say so. Feeling dumb, he tried not to stare at her, which was truly difficult when he was close enough to feel her body's heat.

He was saved when Bran called, breaking him from his revery. "Hey Rhone, you look kinda lost down there. Glad you made it," giving a thumbs up of approval.

Rhone didn't know what to say. Was 'thanks' appropriate, or maybe, 'what ever'? But his shrug and a smile, seemed to work. They all laughed, but they weren't laughing at him, simply laughing and having fun as friends. Rhone hadn't known much of that in his life, but he was warmed just to be part of it.

The drinks finally arrived, and were passed down the table with an almost ceremonial fanfare. Rhone took his, and not knowing what to expect, sniffed.

When the spicy bubbles sparkled up his nose, Rhone jerked back reflexively, startled but grinning like a jack o'lantern. "Woooow, that's different," he exclaimed with wide eyes.

He hadn't noticed, but the entire table had stilled, watching for his reaction to the drink. Laughs and cat calls broke out with mugs and glasses raised in a toast. In that odd moment, Rhone truly felt part of the team. It seemed, he had a place.

The group broke into several conversations as Rhone intently studied his mug, watching the bubbles rise and burst as he inhaled the scent of intoxicating spices. It was like nothing he had ever had before.

Sitting close, MaryEllen watched his reaction, grinning at his wide eyes. "You like?" she asked appreciatively. "It has a bit of a burn as it goes down, but it's not beer. Still, it does a pretty good job."

Rhone could only nod as he almost inhaled the amazing liquid in large gulps.

Two rounds later, they decided to call it a day. There was work to do tomorrow, and fat heads wouldn't help.

Rhone caught MaryEllen's hand as she slid from the table. "Hey, Thanks for inviting me," he said happily, actually feeling free enough to talk to her. "I've never been to a place like this before. It was super."

Her smile was approval enough. "I figured, anyone putting in as much work as you are ought to get some of the good side too. It takes a lot to be a team. Some of it's good, some not so much. We try to make sure we keep a balance." With a wave and a nod, she headed off through the tables.

It was a simple statement, but Rhone knew he would never forget it.

As the room cleared somewhat, Rhone scooched off the end of the bench and stood quietly beside Aundrea. "Thanks," he said reflectively.

She turned and eyed him carefully. She was good at her job, and saw the thoughtfulness in his face. "What is it? You've got something in there, and it wants to come out."

He shrugged, only mildly embarrassed by her scrutiny. "I just wanted to say, thank you. Not just for tonight, but everything. I know you went to the badlands to find something, but it wasn't really me. Except, it was. It is, I guess. Me and Stone, but I know you took a chance when you took us in. You didn't have to, and it's not just the clothes and things. They're super great, but it's the friends, and the work, and a future, and... maybe something important to work for." He stopped, reviewing his thoughts. "Stone and I were planning to travel the world, looking for other We, but I didn't know how. Then we got caught, and things fell apart. Stone was stolen, and I found the cave, then you came along." He paused again as his lips drew into a tight line, trying to find a way to bring it together. "I think you saved us, Stone and I. If you hadn't, we would still be tromping around in the badlands, going nowhere, probably forever. I just wanted to say, this is way better. Stone thinks so too. He just hasn't said it yet.

I do, Stone agreed quietly. *Well done my friend.*

"We did do good," Aundrea's said, eyes sparkling with sudden moisture. "But you are the special one here. The rest of us are just along for the ride."

I could not have said it better, Stone agreed in pride.

CHAPTER 6

One Plus One Makes One

Over the next few months, the partnership between Jewel and Aundrea melded into a solid unit, much as Rhone and Stone had. Stone had finished testing Jewel, and his early calculations seemed to indicate that for the We, size had something to do with mental capacity. It made sense, but Rhone refrained from mentioning the fact to Aundrea. Some things just weren't all that important. Jewel was a perfect lady, mirroring Aundrea in every way.

Even Rhone hadn't known the We had no sex equivalent until they partnered with a human. It seemed they took on the sexual attributes of their host, becoming as one. At least, that was how it worked for the only two subjects they knew. If other We were eventually found, they might know for sure.

Now that Jewel was set in a ring, she and Aundrea never parted. It also turned out to be a perfect placement for them, as Jewel picked up the energies of everything she saw, passing the information on to Aundrea. Now when she met with someone, Jewel's input gave Aundrea in-depth information as to skin temperature, pupil size and heart rate, even the energy output of their contact. All Aundrea had to do was keep track of the conversations. Jewel's data collection allowed her to know when to agree, disagree, or even when to run. Where Aundrea had been good before, she now became perspicacious in her dealings with her staff and the public. The OPR was actually beginning to make headway against the constant problems in the stronghold. But they were becoming so effective, they were gathering attention from The Council. Sometimes, in government circles, it wasn't necessarily a good thing to be noticed.

R hone used his sleeve to wipe the sweat from his forehead. With the day's training done, it was time for the field test. He cringed, knowing a senior team member would be judging his work. The outcome would determine whether he continued, or called it quits. While it would undoubtably be exciting, the thought of testing made his whole body tense.

"I just can't fail," Rhone groaned, mostly for Stone's benefit.

Stone already understood, of course, but he was learning almost as much as Rhone. Stone had also learned that sometimes Rhone just needed to talk it through, without someone giving him the answers. There were tricks to becoming an effective team of one, together.

"I honestly don't think I'll fail, but I don't want to disappoint Aundrea either," Rhone continued. "She's put a lot into us, including money." Then miming an actor in a play, he stood and took a regal stance, fist held to the sky as he began reciting epic words he had learned in a class. "We cannot change our past steps. We can only work to make our next steps more sure."

He made a silent promise to do just that, then a thought struck him. "Stone, you know I'll do my best. I really will, but I'd like to do it on my own." *Do you understand?* he asked silently, wanting to be sure Stone really understood. *I don't want to hurt your feelings. You're my best friend, my collar-mate, but I think I need to do this on my own. What do you think?* Somehow, asking mind to mind felt more personal.

Stone's thoughts drifted through his head as if they were his own. *I think you are growing up my friend. Your mother would have been proud of you. Possibly a bit lonely too, but she would still wish you to grow. Do not worry about me. I will be here, and I will watch. When you need my help, let me know. Until then, I will wait. Remember, I am like a rock, and very good at waiting.*

Emotion flooded Rhone as he wondered what had he done before Stone had come into his life. But he already knew. He had been alone.

It was funny how he could laugh and cry at the same time.

———

Bran watched in detached observance as Rhone slid silently up to the old cobbler, and past, leaving the building without having been seen or heard. In his hand he held the cobbler's tack hammer and a dozen nails. Exactly twelve.

Rhone's grin reached from ear to ear, until Bran raised an eyebrow.

"Now, put them back. The poor man can't afford to buy more, and those shoes need finishing."

"Put them back?" Rhone sputtered in disbelief. "But you said..."

"I said... put them back. It should be simple. Just don't get caught."

Rhone sucked on a tooth for a moment, then with a harsh breath, slid his way back into the little shed as quietly as a shadow. *I should just walk in and hand them to him,* he grumbled silently in his mind. Then realizing what he was doing, grimaced self-consciously. He had spent so much time talking with Stone it was just normal, except Stone hadn't answered back. *Thanks, Stone. At least one of us is doing good.*

There was no answer, but he did feel what might have been a chuckle vibrate from his collar.

Rhone watched warily as MaryEllen flew through an elaborate series of maneuvers, each making him almost dizzy. Then with a deft move, his hand shot out, grabbing for the handle of the little knife flying toward him. In one efficient motion, his defensive posture switched to an attack. The little blade pivoted up and under her arm, slipping forward just enough for the razor sharp tip to touch her. He was already grinning as he readied to call a hit, then suddenly realized the knife, and MaryEllen, were gone, with her spinning away in another eloquent maneuver.

He never saw the weapon as it sliced through the air, but he heard the dull *thunk* as it struck, quivering between his feet.

Open mouthed, and in total disbelief, Rhone felt the cold wash of absolute shock sweep through him.

"Rhone, that was great!" MaryEllen called cheerily, coming to a perfect ballerina-like pause, arms extended and one foot lifting slowly, sliding up her beautiful calf. When it stilled, as though molded to her leg, she bowed, tilting from the waist, and still on one foot.

The entire thing had Rhone awestruck, or perhaps dumbstruck. He had followed her fighting motions, seen the flight of the weapon, and timed his catch to perfection. But the rest? The rest was like a dream, or perhaps a nightmare. He simply couldn't keep up. Then came her finale! It was totally unimaginable that someone could be so, incredibly..., he huffed, not even able to come up with a word for it. She was beyond great... and he had just failed, his second test.

MaryEllen beamed as though he had just won a race, but Rhone hardly saw it. He had lost. His face held an awkward smile, but he couldn't keep the moisture from collecting in his eyes. He had wanted so much to succeed. For Aundrea's sake as much as his own. She had spent so much energy on him, and he had just let her down, twice, and he hadn't even taken the written test yet.

Miserable, and feeling sick, Rhone didn't know what to do. Perhaps he should gather his things and head back to his gardening at the worn-out home where he had grown up. Then an unexpected thought fluttered past. Maybe someone else lived there now. He had been away a long time.

Closing his eyes at his almost heart-breaking failure, Rhone took several long breaths before he could even think further.

When a flicker of warmth touched the skin of his neck, Rhone managed an equally silent, *I know. You're there*, but his breath caught, and he wanted to throw up. *I'm sorry, Stone. I tried, but it's a lot harder than I thought.*

Straightening, he plastered a smile on his stricken face and walked over to MaryEllen, shaking his head in disbelief. "I have no idea how you did what you did, but it was totally awesome. I hate to keep saying that, but I don't know what else to call it." Then dropping his shoulders in surrender, he had to ask, "So, how did you do it? I had you dead to rights... and then, well..." he almost choked as he said, "then you had me dead." He really would be dead had it been for real. And he had thought he was so good.

"I have no idea what you mean," MaryEllen said, shaking out her flaming red hair. "You did wonderfully, and you almost had me." Then a sly grin broke across her pretty face. "To be honest, I just hate to lose. Blame it on my past, but it makes me better. If you don't allow yourself to lose, anything goes in order to win." Her grin morphed into a pretty pout as she corrected her words. "Or maybe, I just put everything into winning. When it looked like *you* were going to win, my mind wouldn't allow it, and sped up until everything was almost in slow motion."

But Rhone had stopped listening at the words, 'you almost had me'. He knew it! He really had almost won! Where a moment before he had felt failure, his mind now spun into a series of silent whoops of joy.

At his neck, Stone warmed in his collar.

With his fieldcraft finished, only the written test remained. This would be his first written test without Stone's help. There would be no one to slip him hints when he came up empty handed, no one to give the moral support when he was floundering, and no one to double check his answers before he turned it in. But they had agreed, and Stone had kept his part of the bargain.

Rhone however, was losing his conviction as he sat at one end of the heavy wooden table, with Bran at the other. A thickly bound notebook lay open before Bran, which Rhone was sure was full of unanswerable questions. Why couldn't it all be knife throwing, or going unnoticed, or even using invisible ink? He had those down pat, but writing long complicated answers had him wishing he had spent more time at the books.

The dull clunk of Bran's heavy cup being set on the table broke Rhone from his self-induced misery.

"You look a bit jumpy," Bran commented sympathetically. "You doing okay? We could put it off awhile if you need."

Which only made it worse. Everyone here had been so nice, but Rhone knew they would hate him if he messed up. He would have wasted all their time for nothing.

"No, I'm okay," he answered evasively. "I'm just tired of waiting."

"Good," Bran said with a nod. "Give me a second here. I'm almost ready. I'm trying to find some really good questions. A few of these are a bit vague, and don't allow for a range of answers."

Rhone wasn't sure if that was good or not, but it certainly sounded like more writing. While his penmanship had gotten better, it was far from being the best part of his training. Aundrea had even mentioned it, saying, "It is simply expected, a gentleman will have good penmanship. So if you are going to pass as one, you will need to work on it. It is simply a skill, just like the rest."

Which was probably true, but the workouts with quarterstaff didn't give his hands half the cramps writing with a quill did. But he wasn't going to let her down, so he had practiced. The thought of practice brought sword work to mind. Funny how swords weren't as easy for him as knives. The list of things he needed to work on continued to grow.

"I'm ready if you are," Bran said, slapping the notebook shut with a mischievous smile.

Startled, Rhone jumped, then groaned, "Okay, how do we do this?"

"Don't you worry yourself. I've got a quill and paper right here. All you need to do is answer each question as I ask them. It's pretty straightforward."

Rhone relaxed just a bit, until Bran threw in a qualifier. "There is a time limit however."

"It's timed?" Rhone's voice cracked unexpectedly, instantly as worried as Bran had just told him not to be.

"Well of course it's timed. I don't want to be sitting here all night and miss dinner." But his conniving grin belied the comment. "Don't worry. You'll have plenty of time. The timer is just to give some of the slower trainees an easy way out. It's much easier to say you didn't finish in time, than to admit you flunked."

Now Rhone had something else to worry about, suddenly wondering which way he would end up.

With a sigh, he gave his go ahead. "I guess I'm ready then."

<hr>

Two and a half long hours later, Rhone set the pen in its holder and flopped back in the chair, totally exhausted.

Glancing up at the big clock ticking loudly in its cabinet, Bran grunted an acknowledgment. "Not bad. Almost as fast as I did," then slapped the table happily. "I didn't expect anything less. You've practiced hard to get here, and from now on, you can try it for real."

Uncomprehending, Rhone sat up in surprise. "Try for real? I don't get it." But with only Bran's grin for an answer, he worked it out. "I passed? But you haven't corrected the papers yet."

"Don't need to," Bran answered with a conspiratorial wink. "I already know you know the answers. I watched you writing. Nobody puts that much effort into something they're going to fail at. Just doesn't happen. Besides, I've been watching you for weeks. You've known the answer to every single question I, or anyone else, has asked. Welcome aboard employee."

Rhone blinked dumbly, hardly able to believe his ears. It was almost under-whelming, not at all what he had expected, but he did believe it. He could read the truth in Bran's face.

I am proud of you, Stone said in a thought, full of congratulations and deserving every bit of their connection. *I hope it is all right we talk again. You have completed your training, and I have maintained my 'tight lipped' status, as I believe you say.*

Rhone almost cried at hearing Stone's voice, but held it together. Bran was still in the room, and didn't know of their connection. Nobody but Aundrea and Jewel knew, and they too were a secret.

I missed you, Rhone said in their quiet link. *I'm so glad we can be together again. I proved... to myself I suppose, that I can do it alone, but honestly, I would rather do it with you.*

We do make a good team, Stone said proudly. *Now, you need to find Aundrea. She will want to know.*

Somewhat surprised by the statement, Rhone asked, *Can't you just send it to Jewel?*

He had been so separated from Stone, he wasn't up on their news.

I could, Stone admitted easily, *but this is something you need to do.*

A undrea's happy and well-muscled hug lasted so long he was becoming embarrassed, as well as running out of breath.

"I'm so proud of you," she said, with one last squeeze, eyes sparkling like they wanted to break into tears. But she was the boss now, and stepped back slightly, holding him at arms-length. "It wasn't so very long ago, I saw a kid walking along the edge of a desert lake, asking if I had been sent by The Commissioner. My, how things have changed." She gripped his shoulders with an appreciative squeeze, feeling the toned muscles under his classy jacket. "You belong here. I couldn't have planned it better if I had dreamed up the whole thing. When I sent the team out to the badlands, I considered the possibility of finding someone I could use for information against Commissioner Dodge, but I never imagined this. Now you're part of the team, and we may actually make a difference in the big picture.

With Jewel learning so quickly, I haven't even been in the office much, instead, training with her most of the day. But with so much needing done, I'm going to put you directly in the field. I would say by yourself, but you have Stone, so you aren't really alone. With Jewel and me here, and you two in the field, we'll make one great team."

Rhone was startled at the thought of an assignment so soon, and started to make a comment about not being ready, but she cut him off with a wave.

"I know, you are really new at this, but since the work never stops, we either keep up, or we get swamped."

Rhone responded with a snarky grin. "I guess that really does make it sink or swim, doesn't it?"

Aundrea smiled, appreciating his humor. "Don't worry. I'm giving you an easy first assignment. Try it out and see how it fits. I have full faith in you."

Rhone blew out a soft breath, realizing he really was part of the team. He hoped he was ready.

CHAPTER 7

To Shop or Not

"**B**rass buttons! Shiny brass buttons!"

Rhone flinched as the bullhorn-like cry rang out just inches from his ear.

"The perfect attachment for every wardrobe. You want 'em. We've got 'em!"

Trying to be polite, Rhone turned toward the man to say he wasn't interested, but Aundrea's firm grip quickly dragged him past the stall.

"Just ignore them," she said with an air of exasperation. "You can't stop at all of them or we'll never get where we're headed."

Flustered, Rhone had to ask, "Where are we headed?"

Aundrea grinned back in pleasure. "There's a great shop just up the line. You need a few things for your assignment, and while we're there, I might just grab an item or two. With so much going on at the office, I don't get much time to shop."

Rhone nodded noncommittally, knowing it was best to simply follow her lead while it was still there.

A few more minutes jostling through the crowds, and Aundrea stopped at an awning-covered storefront displaying top hats and ladies' underthings. It didn't seem an appropriate match to Rhone, but he was far too aware of 'not' staring at the lady things to really give it proper consideration.

"Here we are," Aundrea said, confidently guiding him into the establishment. An astonishing assortment of men's wear, women's wear, and various items he couldn't quite figure out, hung on racks, lay in stacks, and piled haphazardly on tables. It was a puzzling arrangement, dominated by a monstrous figurine, displaying a filmy parasol and goggles. The shop was more confusing than anything he had seen in the crowds outside.

Aundrea waved to someone in the rear of the establishment, calling out through the unrelenting din, "Tigan, Halloo. I have a customer for you." Turning to a stupefied Rhone, she gave his hand a squeeze. "Tigan will know exactly what it will take."

"What it will take?" Rhone mumbled. "But...," was all he managed, as Aundrea was grabbed by the shoulders and swung around into the arms of a good-looking black man.

The unexpected action sent a surge of worry through Rhone, quickly followed by a wave of jealousy. Did she needed help? But her quick laughter made that a pretty low bet. Still, when she returned the hug in obvious joy, he couldn't just stand there and gawk.

"Excuse me, Sir!" Rhone said firmly, reaching out to tap the man on the shoulder. He would take care of her, even if she didn't think she was in trouble.

The man turned at Rhone's touch, quizzically sweeping his gaze back to Aundrea. "Miss Aundrea, it seems you have a young protector. Good for you. I have told you many times, you take too many chances."

The words surprised Rhone, suddenly making him less sure.

"Tigan, this is Rhone," Aundrea said smoothly. "He's a new graduate, and needs to be outfitted. I couldn't think of a better person do the job. Are you up to it?"

"Hoohoo," Tigan chortled in seemingly honest mirth. "You think I cannot make a silk purse out of a sow's ear? Well, you are wrong my girl. I have sold more pig's-ear purses than you can count. Only one question." With a pensive look, he asked. "How much time do I have?"

"Take your time. I'll be shopping while you gentleman work."

Nodding as one accepting a challenge, Tigan pinched his chin between finger and thumb, scrutinizing Rhone with the seriousness of a diamond cutter. From foot to shaggy head, and front to back, he patted and smoothed, his clicks and mumbles making Rhone wonder for the umpteenth time what he had gotten into.

Satisfied he would be in good hands, Aundrea gave a smiling wave and turned to her own shopping.

Cupping a hand to the corner of his mouth, Tigan leaned toward Rhone and whispered, "You have to watch out for this one. She will have you in trouble before you even know you have arrived." He chuckled at his own joke, but Rhone was beginning to agree.

Deep into his project, Tigan delivered more than one, "tisk, tisk," as he considered the severity of his task.

Not sure what was expected of him, Rhone stood where he was, but kept a wary eye on Aundrea as she admiringly ran her fingers through the long laces of displayed leather vests. She seemed to be enjoying herself and making good use of her time. The least he could do was wait patiently, without causing problems.

Apparently satisfied with his survey, Tigan stepped back and addressed Rhone. "Now, young sir, what things do you need?"

The intriguing accent effectively caught Rhone's wandering attention, but he had no answer. He was wearing what he always wore, and had no idea what Aundrea expected. "I'm not from around here," he began, trying to explain.

"Ho!" came an explosive burst from Tigan. "That much I could guess. You stand out more than the newfangled gas lights they are placing around the market. Which of course, they make us pay for. But they say it will be good for business. We shall see."

Rhone had no idea what Tigan was talking about, or what lights had to do with his clothes, but Tigan was running the show, so he tried a different route. "I think I need just about everything, although I have this," he said, motioning to his outfit, "I have one other pair, but they're pretty worn, and honestly, I don't know what she expects. Do you?"

"You say, the other set is worn out?" Tigan asked, sounding as though he expected these to actually fall off Rhone's body. But with a wink and a knowing nod, he took over, doing what Aundrea had come for him to do. "Have no fear. You have come to the right place. I will take care of everything."

Suddenly the realization flitted through Rhone's mind that he was broke. In embarrassment, he blurted, "I don't know how much..." Pausing mid-sentence. The only thing he had of value was Stone. But he wouldn't part with his collar for everything in the shop.

"Do not worry about such things," Tigan soothed, instantly understanding the problem. "Aundrea has brought you, so we are now friends. That carries more weight with me than an equal amount of gold."

"Really?" Rhone mumbled, shocked at hearing a shop keeper talk that way. He had never even seen gold.

His awkward surprise sent Tigan into a laughing bray, slapping Rhone's shoulder solidly. "You are a good man, Master Rhone. I like you. No wonder Miss Aundrea keeps you close."

At least the words were comforting, until he noticed Tigan studying his collar. A sliver of fear shot through his body, realizing too late that Stone would catch anyone's attention. He should have put the collar in his pouch before going shopping. Now he was alone with this man, both bigger and undoubtedly stronger than he was. Tigan's broad shoulders and fit waist made that pretty clear.

Again catching the worried look, Tigan raised a hand in denial. "Not to worry Master Rhone. I am only looking. It is truly a beautiful piece, and I cannot think I have ever seeing anything like it."

"Thanks," Rhone said, pleased despite his unease. "I found the stone in a river, and made the collar myself." All that was true, but he felt guilty, hiding the truth of Stone.

I believe you are being wise my friend, Stone said silently. *You do not know this man. And even if Aundrea trusts him, it is best to keep some things to one's self.*

Rhone was glad to hear Stone's thought on it, and silently answered, *If you're okay with it. I don't want you to feel like I'm neglecting you.*

I am fine, but you need to pay attention, Stone commented. *This man is quite aware, and you are not listening.*

Rhone's senses snapped back to Tigan in time to catch a curious look. Perhaps a little late he realized, the city was more dangerous than even the badlands had been, in its own way.

"Master Rhone," Tigan began again, "I was asking if you were desiring a full kit, or just a few pieces?" He didn't mention Rhone's disconnect, although he must have noticed.

Once again, Rhone's face flushed, not knowing what a kit was, full or otherwise. He was expecting a pair of pants, or maybe a shirt, but what was a kit?

"I can see this is a bit beyond you," Tigan said, taking it in stride. "Obviously you have come from a very different environment than we offer here in the city. I tell you though, do not be concerned. I too came from elsewhere, and it too was nothing like this." He gave a comfortable smile as his brow creased in thought. "Miss Aundrea would not have brought you here if she did not want my best effort. So, if you will allow, I will pull a full kit, with several options as to look and effect. Does that sound agreeable?"

Rhone found it hard to believe it could be this much work. He had only purchased one pair of pants at a store, with Aundrea doing the actual shopping. On the other hand, it only took one glance around to see it was far beyond his expertise. "Okay. Might as well go for it," he said, giving up with a sigh. "I just hope she likes it."

"Ahh, that she will," Tigan said, his teeth-gleaming smile brightening the room. "I know just the right amount of embellishment for good effect, yet not ostentatious. No one wishes to be ostentatious, now do they?"

Rhone thought he knew the word, but if the outfits he had seen on the streets weren't ostentatious, he wasn't sure exactly what it could mean.

Luckily, Stone was there, coving for his lack of knowledge. *You are quite correct. Ostentatious would be, a conspicuous show, specifically to draw attention to one's self. Although I too am not certain on its use here.*

Being tired of the entire affair, Rhone merely said, "Just make it something that fits."

Tigan smiled softly, lowering his voice conspiratorially. "Do not worry Master Rhone. I only sell things that fit," and motioned to a plushly pillowed chair sitting to the side. "You sit there, and I will select a few pieces for you to try." Then he was gone, sweeping away through the narrow isles tucked between counters and racks.

With a relieved breath, Rhone slumped into the cushy chair, squiggling his rump appreciatively into the plush cushion. He was surprised to find it as comfortable as it looked. Back home, the chairs had all been hard wood with doweled backs. They had worked well enough, but weren't all that comfortable.

In less time than it would have taken Rhone to find his way out of the shop, Tigan was back, arms loaded with merchandise. With a sigh of the righteous, he carefully deposited the stack on a nearby table, obviously set there for that purpose. Then hands on hips, he faced Rhone. "Are you ready?" his smile more like a challenge. "With my vision, you will be transformed from a confused child of the country, to a young gentleman of status. You have only to follow my directions and make your choices."

It certainly sounded good, but now Rhone was even less sure of what he had signed up for.

"First will be the britches," Tigan said, pointing off-handedly toward Rhone. "Off with them."

"You want my pants off?" Rhone asked with a hint of panic.

"You will need to change, yes."

The quick response didn't ease Rhone's mind. He simply was not going to strip down in the middle of a public shop.

Recognizing the problem, Tigan pointed to a curtained alcove in the corner. "In there. When you have changed, come out, and we will see the new you. A veritable picture in motion." His expansive gesture was as extravagant as the giant stuffed dummy in the center of the shop. Seeming very pleased with his artistic vision, Tigan handed Rhone an armful of clothing, and drew back the drape to the alcove. "Now change," Tigan demanded pleasantly. "Miss Aundrea will be returning soon, and you will not be ready. Go, go!"

Rhone allowed himself to be guided into the little space before Tigan flipped the curtain closed and gave his final directions. "Quickly now. Time is wasting."

With no table, chair or bench, Rhone dumped the clothes onto the floor and looked over the pile. First things first. Pants he could figure out, or so he thought. Other than having two legs, the pants were different from anything he had ever worn. In confusion, he stood looking at the garment with far more buckles and straps than he could find any reason for. With a sigh, he patiently worked his way through the task of dressing.

Dark leather straps swept across deep grey material, fitting the material snuggly, but comfortably. Once started, it was almost fun figuring which buckles attached to which belts. The shirt wasn't much easier, as two rows of buttons attached a pleated placket to a hard backing, together making it virtually solid. Probably strong enough to keep a thrown dagger from plunging through. It was odd, and difficult to put on, but fit better than he expected.

The waistcoat was next. Its fine wool, large lapels, and standing collar looking like something he might expect on a king in a picture book, not a kid from the sticks, but it too was in the pile. Lastly came the boots. Their tall leather calves holding additional buckles, running from the instep to the thick cuff just below his knee. Finally, he was out of items.

Having managed to dress himself, Rhone gazed down, shaking his head in bewilderment. This couldn't be him, but he had to admit, it felt amazing. Rolling a shoulder to settle the outfit more comfortably, he squared himself, and took a deep breath.

His timing was none too soon, as Tigan's voice caused him to turn in alarm. "Master Rhone, is your ensemble completed? We are ready for the viewing."

We? In panic, Rhone realized that Aundrea must have returned. His chest tightened, wondering if she would laugh, or just as bad, balk at the expense. He had only expected a pair of pants, and knew this was far too much.

He had just decided to undress, when he heard Aundrea's eager voice calling.

"Rhone? Come on out, I can hardly wait."

Too late. He would have to accept whatever reception he got. Plan thwarted, Rhone squeezed his eyes closed, wishing he was back at home. With a worried smile, he slowly pulled the drape aside and warily stepped out.

Aundrea's smile morph into something... different. Her open-mouthed expression caused Rhone's heart to fall.

"Oh... my..." she whispered, reluctantly tearing her gaze away from Rhone, to Tigan.

Tigan stood with arms folded over his wide chest, grinning in an oh so-knowing way. "I have told you. I know what I do. It is good, no?"

Aundrea almost forgot to breathe as she nodded absently, trying to answer. "He looks... like an aristocrat, and one of the top tier. Even his collar fits in perfectly."

"Is it okay?" Rhone asked, stomach curdling under Aundrea's wide-eyed stare. Taking another cautious step from the alcove, he suddenly understood. It was the money, and began stammering an excuse. "I'm sorry," I... I don't know how much it costs, but I'll pay it back, somehow."

"Rhone, shut up," Aundrea sated flatly, then mumbled in disbelief, "This outfit was made for you."

Rhone wasn't sure how that could be, since Tigan had just pulled it from the shelves. "But it's far too much," he evaded. "All I need are some pants." But her single look stopped his apology, and he set his face to acceptance.

Aundrea shifted positions as she continued looking him over. Putting hands to hips, she took a breath and smiled. "Tigan, this is unbelievably perfect for the first set. I can't imagine anything better for uptown, but he will need something for daily wear."

"Oh, Miss Aundrea, just you wait. If you like this, you will love the next." Without a pause, Tigan turned to Rhone. "Master Rhone, time to put those things aside while I gather the next outfit. I will not be but a moment."

Rhone stepped back into the alcove as commanded, and began disengaging himself from the clothing. Disengaging was the correct term, since undressing hardly seemed to fit. He could hear Tigan shuffling back and forth as he gathered more items, and had just managed to get the pants off, stepping awkwardly out of the last leg, when the curtain flipped back and Tigan deposited another bundle of clothing.

Caught with his back to the door, and shiny hiney facing the opening, Rhone reflexively turned his head, catching Aundrea's less than subtle grin. His own face instantly blossomed into a vivid blush.

Tigan, on the other hand, didn't appear fazed in the least. "I think you will like this set," he said cheerfully. "It will allow for a good range of motion, and sports multiple attachment points for your various tools of the trade. I have made certain to choose sturdy materials for everyday use and long wear, so quickly now, the lady is waiting."

She may be waiting, but Rhone was frozen in place. Turning would only make things worse.

"Okay, I'll get right on it," came his strangled reply, as his ears heated to glowing coals.

Aundrea's quick wink only made it worse, burning itself into his memory the moment before the curtain drew together, blocking the view.

Rhone suddenly found it difficult to breathe, the confines of the small alcove beginning to draw in unbearably tight around him.

But the ringing in his ears also brought Stone's voice alive in his head. *Rhone, snap out of it. Your heart is racing as though The Commissioner himself was after you again. What is the problem? I simply do not understand your system's overcharge.*

Rhone braced himself against the wall as he finished stepping out of the pant leg, then sagged tiredly to the hard floor. "I'm pretty sure you couldn't understand," he sighed wearily, "but don't worry. I'll be all right in a sec." He felt like a fool, and so far out of his natural environment he could do nothing but chuckle dumbly into the dark.

"Master Rhone?" Tigan called from outside. "Is everything all right? I did not catch your last comment."

With a last defeated chuckle, Rhone pulled himself together. "I'm fine, he called through the drape. Just got my foot caught."

A rms full of bundles, Rhone struggled valiantly to keep up. The market experience was somewhat more than he had expected, but Aundrea had come to shop. When he'd raised his brows at the number of packages, she had merely responded with, "If you are going to dress like that, then I need to upgrade my own wardrobe, or I'll look totally out of place. We certainly can't have that." Her smile let him know she was enjoying herself, which was at least some consolation.

Unused to the weight of his new boots, and arms already feeling the burn of carrying the packages, Rhone's awareness of his debt grew. "Aundrea, I'm really sorry I got so much stuff," he tried to explain. "I guess I got carried away. But don't worry, I'll pay you back. I will. I'm just not sure when."

Aundrea stopped, and turned with a frown. "I already told you not to worry. I have funds. Besides, for this, I'm digging into the office account. You sir, are an investment, just as much as buying a horse might be. Honestly though, I think you look far better in those clothes than a horse would," and her face lit with a grin.

Although still uneasy at the expense, Rhone couldn't help but smile. For someone that had never owned a pair of store-bought pants, his purchases were beyond extravagant. The clothes were awesome, but he couldn't imagine when he might actually wear the fancy getup.

"Well, what do you think of your new outfit?" Aundrea asked, guessing his thoughts. "Pretty comfortable?"

"It's good," Rhone admitted, shrugging his shoulder to better feel the fit. "I like the material. It's a lot softer than the stuff mom made, but I'm not sure what all the buckles and pockets are for. I don't have anything to put in them."

"Maybe not right now," she agreed, half-suppressing a laugh at his discomfort, "but you'll find things. It's better to have too many than not enough."

Rhone accepted her answer, and considered his other new things. "These boots are super nice, but why do I have two pairs? I can only wear one at a time."

"Let's see," Aundrea said, tapping a finger against her lips playfully. "You own more than one pair of pants, but you can only wear one at a time." Then lifting a shoulder, she answered, "One is for everyday, and the other is a nicer pair, for more dressy occasions."

"But these look great? Why would I need anything nicer?"

Again she raised a shoulder in resignation. "You never know, but let's just say, it's always good to be prepared."

"I get it," Rhone said dryly. "Like, you can never have too many pockets?"

"Exactly."

He rolled his eyes as she grinned, but as long as he had her attention, he was going to use it. "Okay, one more thing. Why did Tigan keep calling me Master. I'm nobody's master, and don't want to be."

Aundrea gave a little laugh before explaining. "Like many words, master has more than one meaning. It can indeed mean a person with power over another, but as in this case, it can simply mean a young man. If he had been speaking to a young lady, he would have said mistress. Miss is simply a shortened version of mistress."

You have much to learn, Stone murmured wisely. At least his summary was short and sweet, a factor Rhone appreciated.

He did indeed have a lot to learn, but he quietly doubted Stone had known the answer either.

CHAPTER 8

Corgy

Now that he was a graduate, Rhone expected life to be hours of work, sitting at a desk like so many others at the office. Instead, he continued to sit through boring classes.

Do you believe you have gathered all the information available on every subject? Stone asked clinically.

"Well no. I just figured it would be enough, or they wouldn't have hired me... Us," he corrected quickly.

Indeed, Stone rumbled. *We did manage to acquire extensive information relating to the manipulation of elemental components. And you obtained passing marks in knife throwing,* a comment that gave Rhone a warm feeling of accomplishment. *What we did not do, was learn sufficient details regarding the structure of the working establishment outside of this compound. The 'real world'.* His tone, and the fact that Rhone began to squirm, scratching futilely at his armpit, brought a suspicious query.

"Stone, is that you?"

I was simply making sure you were paying attention, Stone acknowledged. Rhone could have sworn he felt a devious grin, but that was impossible, and Stone continued as though nothing had happened. *You have no experience whatsoever in the real world, and I, most certainly have not. Together, we are no better than the lowest street urchin fighting for survival.*

"Wow, you certainly know how to cheer up a guy," Rhone said derisively. "But I think we've got this. Remember, we're agents of the OPR. Nobody's going to challenge us."

Actually, he felt pretty good saying so. After all, who would consider working against the organization that protected the people? Everybody knew the good guys won.

Prepared or not, his days of boredom were quickly coming to an end.

"Rhone, Aundrea is looking for you. She asked if you would meet her in her office."

It wasn't the words that sent a chill through Rhone, it was Stone, as a flash of awareness seared his mind at Bran's comment.

"Aundrea?" Rhone asked, feeling a sudden pulse of panic. "Like, right now?"

Bran circumspective squint regarded their youngest agent. "Yeah. I'd say, if the boss called me to her office, I'd probably want to head that direction, like right now. Any problems with that?"

"Ahh, no. I was just wondering."

"Well, best get to it then," Bran commented off-handedly. "I know I wouldn't want to keep her waiting." His subtly devious snicker didn't lessen Rhone's growing anxiety.

"Sure, ahh, thanks Bran. I'll go now." But even before Bran left, Rhone was already questioning his best friend and collar-mate. *Hey Stone, what's going on?*

I do not know, Stone answered warily. *Bran's physical responses were far beyond his normal composure levels. Thus you need to be wary. I believe there is a game afoot.*

Rhone considered the unique comment. Stone had used it once before, but in that case, 'they' were the game. What could it mean here, in the OPR office? "It's just Aundrea, so I think we're safe," Rhone said, feeling better as he said it.

With only a single-knuckle knock to her glass-topped door, he heard her answer.

"Come in Rhone, and close the door."

Never before had he felt trepidation at being around Aundrea, but today he was almost sweating as he entered.

"Take a seat. I'll be with you in a moment."

Rhone took his normal chair across from her desk, and slumped into its cushions, wondering if he was going to be expelled from the organization. Maybe they had decided he was too young after all. Or maybe his grades weren't going the way they had hoped. Those may not be the real reason of course, but they were reasonable. He waited uneasily, sweating the minutes away.

With a flip of her wrist, Aundrea closed the file she had been working on and smiled, but her eyebrows rose in an unquestionable arc, sending goosebumps down Rhone's neck.

"I see you got my message," she said amiably, arching her back until even Rhone heard the crackle. "Best we take care of this behind closed doors."

Speaking of hearing things, Rhone's uneasy stomach groaned with acid, producing enough volume to easily be heard through her office. He blanched, embarrassed by the sound, and suddenly worried he was going to be sick.

"Hungry," Aundrea asked, "or not feeling well? We could put this off until later."

"No, sorry," Rhone groaned. "What did you want me for?" Hopefully he could simply get it over with, and move on. Even if the move meant back to Skragmoore.

Aundrea studied her protege' with concern, before giving a nod and scooting her chair back. "We have run out of time," she announced, glancing to a sheet on her desktop. "I am afraid we are going to send you..."

"Wait," Rhone cried, breaking into her sentence, and jumping up in panic. "I can do better. I promise."

"What are you talking about?" Aundrea asked in confusion.

Rhone was almost panting in anxiety, as he muttered, "Aren't you sending me away?"

"Yes, that was my plan. But not unless you agree," Aundrea answered, still not comprehending. "I won't send anyone on an assignment they refuse. That would be fruitless."

Rhone was caught somewhere between terror and questioning, but neither seemed to fit. "But you're sending me away?" he managed.

"Yes, and I'm sorry it is so soon," Aundrea said carefully, still feeling the disconnect. "A need came up with the new dispatches, and I couldn't think of a better place for your first assignment."

Rhone's heart suddenly began to pump again, flooding blood back into his brain. He was being sent on assignment, not back home. Almost faint with the change, Rhone could only manage a nod and a feeble, "That sounds great. Thank you Aundrea," before slumping exhaustedly back into the chair.

⚬ ⚬⚬ ⚬

Today he was a young gentleman. The women had decided it would be his best disguise, and had worked to develop his persona, spending hours going over his wardrobe, adjusting his clothes and gear, adding this, and removing that. In the end, they had done what they could and were satisfied. The rest would be up to him.

Aundrea had gone over Rhone's assignment in detail, including what was expected of him. She had also given him a few pointers on how to deal with people in new places, but it was MaryEllen who had given him true directions.

"You look the part of one of the well-to-do, so use it. Act as though the world owes you, and people will walk all over each other to agree. I've seen it a hundred times and it never goes wrong. It's only the pitiful and poor that get walked on, so don't lie in the ditch, unless that's your best way out."

"The ditch is the best way out?" Rhone questioned in confusion.

MaryEllen pursed her lips, eyebrows raised pointedly before answering. "You never know. The best way out may be doing what no one would ever want to, or be expected to do." Then with a quick smile, she leaned forward and gave him a gentle peck on the cheek. "Do what they don't expect, and you'll do fine."

He would try to put that lesson to use.

86

"Attitude," was all Aundrea said, her smile quivering as her eyes sparkled with sudden moisture. It was her parting comment, as Rhone turned his horse away from the stables.

Rhone felt like someone from a story book as he looked down at himself fitted out in his new outfit. But while he had a story, he was pretty sure no one wanted to hear it, and the new gear would take some getting used to.

It was to be an easy first assignment, or so Aundrea said. But after a few days of travel, and now close to his new post, he began to worry. Aundrea needed to test him out on his own, and though she would keep track of his reports, the work would be up to him. He and Stone.

So here he was, weary days of riding from The Capital Stronghold, and glad to be out of the big city. Luckily, part of his training had been horsemanship. Having never ridden a horse, the simple task of learning to mount correctly had taken some time, but as with all his training, he worked hard and learned quickly. He now sat comfortably even if his seat was sore, astride a horse simply named Blue. He was actually grey, so why he was called Blue, Rhone didn't know, but he was a loaner from the OPR stables, and well mannered. For the time being Blue was in his charge.

When the wind picked up, whipping Blue's main and tail into an excited dance, Rhone huddled deep into the warmth of his heavy billowing cloak. He was used to chill wind, so this was no any worse than the biting winter at home, although this air was filled with a damp chill instead of the moister-wicking dry of their rough valley.

The sharp wind pierced through his layers of clothing, and he gripped the cloak firmly with both hands, tucking his head down into the cloak's folds to hold in the warmth. Rhone let the reins drape over Blue's neck, accepting the set pace. Blue would stay to the road, as any smart horse would, knowing the going was easier here than over the rough country. Eventually, Blue brought him to where the land gave way, showing a great expanse of water stretching out to the horizon.

The small harbor town of Corgy lay in a crook of the rugged coastline, seeming to grow from the edges of a river cutting its way out to the ocean. Rhone could see a few boats tied to the quay, and workers laboring up and down the dock in both directions. It was a busy place for being so small, and Rhone understood a bit more of why his home town of Skragmoore had been so poor. It took trade to bring prosperity, and thanks to Commissioner Dodge's sticky fingers, there was no money left in the town to risk on business ventures.

There is much activity in the harbor, Stone agreed. *I can sense the water and the big floating things, which must be boats.*

"Good guess," Rhone complemented his friend. "I've never been on one, but it might be fun. Maybe we could get a ride and try it out."

If you wouldn't mind, Stone said, with a hopefulness Rhone could feel. *I would find it quite interesting, studying the difference in resistance and directional stability of a floating craft. Note the sails. Would that not be similar to the resistance you felt with the wind in your cloak? Very exciting, I must say.*

Rhone considered how helpless it must feel being on a boat, unable to go wherever, or do whatever he wanted, when he wanted. It was up to the wind. It must also be frustrating for Stone, waiting for him to do things. But riding on a boat did sound like fun.

"Let's get settled in first," he commented. "Then we can ask around. Maybe I could help out on one of the boats for a free ride."

Then why are we not moving? Stone asked quickly. For a rock-like thing, he wasn't nearly as patient as he pretended to be.

Their plan was to find the town's mayor, and introduce Rhone as an agent of the OPR. Their work was well known amongst political people, and Aundrea didn't think he would have any problem finding his way into the happenings of the small town.

Small towns he could do, there being so much less to keep track of than in the big city.

Stone had mentioned his own difficulty with the city's many overlapping connections and happenings. Even his crystalline matrix had a limit. He had learned to filter the data, but it had taken the entire time they had been there.

The small town was calming after the frantic bustle of the big city, although the wind must not have been aware of the contradiction, as it whipped even harder, catching at Rhone's cloak like it wanted to blow him from the saddle. Blue plodded patiently along the narrow road, following the harbor's edge as the land rose steeply around the town. The coastal hills had been cut sharply by the flow of the dark river, and below the road, a marsh lay like a slimy film, filling the nooks and crannies of the flats. The river itself made a darker blue-brown swath near the center of the marsh, snaking through the green-brown stalks and squishy mud. Sheep wandered aimlessly over the steep hills, cutting their own trails in the green slopes, their fleece proof against the chilling wind. The place was isolated, but seemed content, willing to accept its place.

Rhone progressed down the frontage road, following the flow of sparse traffic, past the bigger buildings and on to the docks. The town's waterfront ran both directions along the bay, with docks poking out to meet the waves sloshing quietly up onto the shallow strand of silted beach.

Dismounting stiffly, Rhone tied Blue to a handy rail, then clutched his cloak tighter in the blustery wind and sauntered out onto the dock. He kept a wary eye on the workers hauling goods from the boats to the warehouses lining the timbered quay. Their heavily laden carts and trollies made hollow clopping sounds as they passed over the thick boards that kept them out of the potholes of the roadway itself.

"Out of the way kid," came the annoyed call of the stevedore coming up quickly behind him. His empty dolly said he was headed back for another load, and Rhone wasn't walking fast enough.

"Sorry," Rhone answered automatically, stepping to the edge, but very aware that while the water wasn't deep, it wasn't desirable either.

The man quickly lumbered past, but did offer a helpful comment. "If you can't make up your mind, head to the port office. They can take care of you there."

Rhone gladly nodded as he returned the comment, "A good idea, thank you," but the worker had already forgotten him as he hurried to his next load.

At least Rhone now knew where to go, and the sign saying 'Port Office' made the direction an easy guess. With his cloak billowing around him, Rhone walked the boardwalk with the confident air of someone sure of themselves and not bound to a timeline. After an interested perusal of the ships and dock, he made his way back to the office.

He had just swung open the door when a heavy gust grabbed it, causing him to lunge forward, barely managing to keep it from slamming against the wall. Only slightly ruffled, he apologized with a tip of his head. "A bit blustery today."

Unfortunately, the man wasn't impressed, but Rhone couldn't tell if it was over him, or the fact that his entrance had allowed the wind to invade the small office. The poor man scurried about, attempting to gather errant papers that had been tossed about by the untimely blast.

Now out of the chilly wind, Rhone allowed the cloak to hang loose, inadvertently showing the collar fastened around his throat. Stone's flashing brilliance danced in the lamplight, the flickering reflection catching the clerk's eyes, where they slid to the bauble and didn't leave until Rhone cleared his throat.

"Excuse me," Rhone said with an easy smile. "A man on the dock told me to come by the office if I couldn't make up my mind. Would this be the place?"

The harried clerk smoothed out the newly stacked papers, looking patently nervous at Rhone's presence. Uncertain, he answered, "Ah, yes sir! It is if you wanted something shipped."

Obviously, there are not many of the gentry using this port, Stone murmured in silence, making Rhone hide his smile. Even he could read the signs of awe from the man.

"Exactly," Rhone answered, then sent a quick message to Stone. *This might be easier than I expected.* Stepping up to the counter, he gave a short nod. "I am new to town, having come directly from The Stronghold itself. I was hoping to find a boat willing to take a jaunt out into the bay. It would be a joy to see the town from the water side."

He couldn't help but swagger a bit. It was expected after all.

"Why, I don't know sir. Things are pretty busy right now with two ships just coming into port."

"Two, is that all? I'm afraid I was expecting a slightly larger place. Would the Mayor be around? I will need to speak with him."

"The mayor? You want to speak with Mayor Dugan? Well, I'm not sure about that either. I believe he's out of town for a few days." The clerk's eyebrows started to bob as his worry grew.

In apparent disappointment, Rhone released a sigh and walked to the window. "I understand, no ships available. I can't blame you on that accord, since I gave no warning of my coming, but perhaps a smaller vessel?"

The clerk's nose had begun to twitch at Rhone's questioning glance, then his eyes brightened. "I think I have just the boat. I'll have to check with the captain of course, but if you would stand by at The Common House, I'll see to it. Would that be acceptable sir?"

MaryEllen had been right. People would walk all over themselves to do his bidding.

"That would be perfect. Thank you," Rhone said with a slight tip of his head. "And where would this Common House be?"

Twenty minutes later, Rhone was sitting at a tiny round table lit with a magnificently colored lamp and shade, its hundreds of tiny pieces throwing flecks of brilliance around the room, the midnight blues and ruby reds balanced perfectly with the deep emerald greens that seemed to dance along the walls and ceiling. Its delicacy spoke of a culture far deeper than he had expected of this little sea town, and was only out-done by Stone's own flash of color, as though trying to show his superiority. When the maid, in a crisp white pinafore over a well-worn gingham dress, came by with his cup, Rhone asked her about the building. "This place is quite nice for a little town like Corgy, if not quite what I'm used to. What can you tell me about it?"

Rhone's smile, and his up-town apparel, made it a requirement she answer, but she hesitated, not sure how much to say. "Sir? This is the best place in town, but if it's not good enough..."

"Not at all." Rhone replied, cutting her off with a quick wave before she could go further. "It's quite acceptable, thank you." He didn't need to glance out to the quaint harbor. She understood his meaning.

"Yes sir," she mumbled. "Mr. Jorstad owns the place. He bought it when the original owner died sudden like. It was a couple of years ago now, but we haven't done so good since." She was beginning to stammer apologetically, as a rosy hue grew on her cheeks. "He owns a few of the ships too, but he spends more money on them than he does on this place." Realizing she was talking about her boss, and to a stranger, she covertly glanced about, suddenly concerned that someone might have overheard.

"It's all right," Rhone whispered conspiratorially. "I won't tell a soul. And thank you for the confidence. I plan on working here for a while, and it's good to understand the community before I, 'put a foot into it', as they say." He smiled at his choice of words, trying to ease her worry. He was falling into his new role like it was a pool of water.

Trying not to grin at his comment, she delivered the cup and bobbed a quick retreat. But before she got a step away, Rhone called to her.

"Oh, miss, I am expecting someone to meet me here. A captain I believe. If you will keep an eye out for him, I would appreciate it."

Another of his smiles, and he had her.

"Absolutely sir. I know most of them, so it will be no problem at all."

With a shy glance, she began talking a little easier. "You're here for work? Aren't you a bit young for that?" Instantly appalled at what she said, and to a gentleman at that, her cheeks went scarlet and she blurted an apology. "I'm sorry sir! I didn't mean it like that. Oh, my mouth gets me in trouble all the time. Please don't say anything, or I'll get fired for sure."

Rhone raised a hand in assurance. "Miss... I'm sorry, I don't know your name."

"Bella. I'm Isabella," she whispered in chagrin.

"Miss Bella, I understand entirely. I am indeed young, but I have been dealing with my father's business for years already. He's a firm believer in teaching me the business from the bottom up."

"That certainly makes sense," Bella said with a faint smile.

"Now, Miss Bella, if you wouldn't mind keeping a watch out, I would most certainly appreciate it."

Still embarrassed, Bella dipped a nod and a curtsey, and slipped away, glancing back from the corner to verify he wasn't going to make trouble for her.

This was far too easy, and Rhone was quite proud of his aristocratic tone, one he'd worked on for weeks. With it, and his swagger, things seemed to be going well. But perhaps he had gone too far in developing a story he couldn't confirm. He would have to watch what he said. Too many embellishments, too quickly, would be difficult to remember, and his cover story had already developed. Apparently, he was now working for his father. That detail would be all right, except, how would it mesh with his dealings with the OPR? He would have to get it right before he spoke with the mayor.

I was wondering about that, Stone commented dryly.

"I know," Rhone mumbled, suddenly feeling like his real self, and not one of the gentry he was playing. "So how can I make it work? I already said it, so now I have to live with it. You've got to help me." He glanced around the open room, making double sure no one noticed him talking to himself. Things were confused enough without them thinking he was crazy too.

Ah, yes, Stone said, happy with the prospect of a real task. *Try this for a story line. Your father works at The Stronghold, which would be totally explainable, and you were approached by Aundrea, which you were, so that she might use your father's connections to improve her own. Use a double front, and no one will ever suspect a different story.*

"You came up with all that in one second?" Rhone replied in amazement, then casually scanned the ceiling as he thought through the plot. "It actually sounds reasonable enough to work."

One word of caution, Stone continued. *Do not be too quick to throw all your cards on the table. Hold them until you need an out. There is no need to give it all away at the first hand.*

Stone's monotone instructions ran through Rhone's mind, but he quickly lost concentration as he watched the comings and goings of the harbor, wondering which boat he might soon be sailing on. After all, he didn't have to worry. If he got into trouble, Stone would be certain to remind him of it.

CHAPTER 9

Captain Black

Rhone's cup had been refilled, twice, before Bella stepped around the corner with a bobbed curtsy.

"Sir, your guest has arrived. May I introduce Captain Black, of The Backwater Mistress." She looked embarrassed at even saying the ship's name, but the captain stepped past her curtly and strode up to Rhone, hand outstretched.

"I heard you were looking for a tour around the harbor. Wouldn't normally do anything as paltry as that, but just so happens, I need a trial run before we load up. Killing two birds with one stone won't hurt none that I can see."

The big man's hand was meaty and strong, proving both that he had plenty to chew on, and that he was a worker. His scraggly grey beard stuck out in several directions at once, but that might have been from the wind blowing outside, more than any intended design. His high leather boots looked like he had waded through the shore's waves, with the piece of seaweed sticking to a buckle merely confirming it. But it was the multiple holsters, and weapons strapped to almost every conceivable space on his body, that lit up Rhone's eyes in question.

Noting the look, the captain glanced down, quirking his mouth in thought. "I suppose you're wondering about all the weaponry," he said matter-of-factly. "Well, see, my Mistress ain't a big ship. More like, she's a beacon for pirates, thinkin' they can take her whenever they want. So I need to prove 'em wrong. Now, she's a good ship, and fast, and my mates know how to keep her movin' along, not gettin' plundered like so many are around here. It's a serious thing, and I take it mighty personal if I lose my cargo."

The captain was a talkative man, and even though Rhone hadn't said a thing, he was learning more than he had hoped. Maybe this was the reason Aundrea had sent him here.

"A good afternoon to you, Captain... was it, Black?" Rhone feigned his attempt to remember. "Yes, Captain Black, of the Backwater Mistress."

Having been struck giddy at his first sight of weapons, Rhone had been lucky, as Stone slipped him the name.

"It is sir. At your service," the captain said with a short bow.

"Excellent. As I was telling the miss, I am new to the town, sent directly from The Stronghold, and I am in need of an overview of the area. It is vital to our business dealings to have a good lay of the land. I'm certain, as a businessman yourself, you understand."

That was well done, Rhone. Maybe we will evade being thrown out after all.

Stone's unimpressed words bubbled through Rhone with the feeling of coarse sand on bare skin. He had been trying out various new sensations to assist with verbal communication, but Rhone's quick grimace said it might have worked a bit too well.

Hey, I happen to be in a conversation here, Rhone snapped in reply, then became concerned as he noticed Captain Black glancing uneasily through the window. "Is there trouble?"

The captain returned his attention to Rhone with the twitch of an eye. Then putting on a cherubic smile, said, "Not at all. Got it covered, but you've got good senses. Just keeping track of some of the riffraff round about. It pays to know who you might be bumping up against in a squall." The smile made it clear he thought pretty highly of himself, but quickly turned serious again. "When were you wanting the tour? Tide turns in about two hours, so if you're interested, we should be goin' before then."

Surprised at his good fortune, Rhone asked, "What about the wind?" It had only gotten stronger since his arrival, and now he wasn't so certain about going out to sea.

"The wind? What about the wind?" the Captain asked, looking as though he really didn't understand the question.

Remembering his supposed position, Rhone tried to find a gentlemanly way to back out. "It looks a bit blustery at the moment. Is this a good time, or would it be better to wait for a more ...propitious occasion?"

He had learned the word from Bran just a couple of weeks prior, and was pleased that it had worked so well.

"Pro-who?" the captain asked with suspicion.

"Should we wait for better weather conditions," Rhone explained, allowing a tiny bit of impatience to show.

"Pro..per..sti..lishous means all that? Dad-gum-it. Guess I should have finished my schoolin'." A full-humored, crooked smile lit his rough features, before he shook his head savagely, sending his shaggy hair flying like it was already in the wind. "Naw, the weather's fine. Just gotta know when to hang on."

This may not be a good idea, Stone whispered cautiously.

Maybe, Rhone agreed, *but I doubt he wants to sink his own boat, so it should be okay.*

Thrusting out his hand in a gentleman's agreement, Rhone gave what he thought would be the deal maker. "Allow me to accompany you on your trial run, and I will speak to my father regarding our company using your services for shipping in the area."

It was a simple enough statement, but he could feel the shake of Stone's nonexistent head.

⁂

Rhone braced against the gunwale, gripping tightly to the rail with both hands as the frothy water surged past his boots, almost sweeping his feet from under him.

"Hang on!" Captain Black shouted gleefully, swinging the wheel to meet the next wave. "That one hit just a bit off-side, but we'll get the next one right. Waves are a wee bit raucous jus' now."

The captain looked pleased at his use of a big word, although Rhone wasn't at all sure it fit.

It is a plausible use, if not common, Stone interjected, almost breaking Rhone's concentration at holding on.

The bow rose again, tipping the deck skyward and sending the water already running on deck into a flowing torrent toward the stern. At least the Captain's warning gave Rhone time to brace for the next crash, as the boat's bow smashed down onto the far side of the towering wave, sending huge volumes of salty water spraying away from the hull.

The Captain seemed in seventh heaven, guiding the boat through the wind-driven waves. His crew worked just as hard manning the sails, though Rhone had no idea what they were actually doing. He simply watched in disbelief as the sailors nimbly scampered up the rigging, masts swaying violently back and forth, out over the deep grey of the water, then a moment later, back over the deck and out again on the far side. The little ship took the beating in stride, battling furiously to make headway against the wind.

Cackling like a madman, Captain Black make the boat follow his will. The sailors were shouting just as loudly, but with stoic resignation, as they attempted to change the sails at their Captain's whim.

So far, Rhone had kept his stomach under control, but it began to complain with the violent and unexpected shifts of the deck.

At least Stone was quiet, but Rhone could feel his mental gears running through calculations of some sort, which wasn't helping with his motion sickness.

This was not quite the tour he had expected, and Rhone was already regretting his recent agreement with Captain Black.

He had begun to wonder when the good captain had agreed with such rapidity, but was now fully questioning his own sanity.

As the contents of his stomach began to match the fervor of the ocean's waves, he hoped the outcome wouldn't be the meeting of the two, with him hanging over railing, meeting the next swell head first. The thought of cold seawater in his face became an abrupt reality, as a massive wave washed entirely over him.

If it hadn't been for the strength of his vice-like grip on the rail, and the hands of the sailor that grabbed him as his feet came off the decking, it could have been far worse.

"Get a good grip sir," came the helpful voice shouting in his ear. "It takes a while to get your sea legs." Then he was gone, headed to his next task at keeping the boat afloat.

Rhone glanced back and saw the Captain waving happily. His cheerful bellow of, "A great day to be sailing!" didn't make the cold dousing any warmer.

"Whatever," came Rhone's quiet if caustic reply.

But within the hour, the Captain had turned the vessel about. Their tremendous up and down heaving settled to a mere running with the wind, and the occasional surge as they raised over the crest of a wave they had outpaced. Finally, Rhone had time to see the shoreline they had been racing past, now that his attention wasn't entirely focused on staying aboard.

As far as he could see, broken cliffs and rocky beaches stretched down the length of the coast. Several sections of rock, no longer attached to the mainland, stood valiantly against the ocean's harsh waters, rising high above the surface. Even Rhone's limited knowledge told him those would be dangerous to a ship running anywhere close by.

Far sooner than expected, the tall stone lighthouse of Corgy appeared, flashing its warning. A foundation of wave-scarred spit gave a firm anchoring to the sturdy structure, but could only be reached at low tide. No captain would ever attempt a landing while the tide ran high with its treacherous currents. Rhone had noticed the tower on their way out of the harbor, and had been filled in on the unique light that could be seen far out to sea. The entire coastline was well known for its history of shipwrecks, and the region's commissioner had requested funds from The Council to have the tower built and manned. It was well worth the effort and money, lessening the deadly toll along the coast.

Rhone wondered if it was a possible connection to his placement at Corgy.

"A good trip, no?" Captain Black bellowed, even though the wind wasn't nearly as strong with them heading in this direction.

"It is. Thank you, Captain," Rhone replied truthfully, now that he was able to stand without holding on for dear life. "I have a much better understanding of the area, seeing things from here. The view from the land side simply doesn't make the same impression."

"Heck no. Not even close," the captain agreed. "It would take you days to see what you can from here, especially with all the trees and hills. Nope, this was a good idea of yours," Captain Black stated, very forthcoming with his praise of Rhone's foresightedness. "I would be proud to make my ship available to your business." He paused, in what could only be a calculating moment. "And what exactly would we be shipping?"

And now the problem. Rhone had no idea.

Ask him what goods he ships most often, Stone whispered silently. *Determine the normal shipping in the area, and work from there.*

Rhone quickly sent his thanks, *and keep them coming,* then he turned to the captain. "Tell me Captain, what goods do you ship most often?" He continued playing his part, but it was beginning to feel like a trap closing.

"Oh, goods and bads," the Captain said with a chuckle. "Did I mention the load of salt pork we shipped? Turned out to be fresh meat, not salted. Oh Lordy, did that load stink. Almost wouldn't let us tie up to the wharf, and that was after we dumped it all at sea. It took a week of scrubbin' before we had it clean enough to take on another load. Even then we had to smoke out the hold first."

The Captain liked his own stories, which luckily helped ease his rough exterior.

Rhone forced his own laugh, "What other things Captain? Surely you have a few basic commodities you transport routinely."

The captain made a squinty-eyed face before answering. "Nope, jus' whatever comes up. We like to stay... flexible, you might say."

A vivid orange flash crossed Rhone's visual receptors, as Stone tried to catch his attention. *I believe he is trying, very discreetly, to 'not' say, he is a pirate.*

Suddenly Rhone understood, and began his own version of discretion. "I believe I understand," he said with a knowing look. "A good captain needs to be available for whatever shipment comes along."

Captain Black nodded vigorously with a look of relief. "Exactly, my good sir. A specialty shipping company you might say, for those shipments needing rapid transport."

It also explained the weapons Captain Black wore.

"Well, Captain, I believe I have had enough viewing for the time being. Could I offer you a drink at The Common House tonight?"

Captain Black was all attention now. "Would be might neighborly of you. Guess we'd best be heading in then. Give you time to get cleaned up and all."

Rhone could see the avarice in the good captain's eyes, even without comment from Stone. But who could blame him, blessed with a contract, and a stiff drink, all in the same day.

CHAPTER 10

The Tide Goes Both Ways

Mayor Dugan kicked his wheeled office chair to an almost reclined position, and considered the possibilities. He was peeved, and wanted answers. There was a new kid in town, and he hadn't been warned. Was he really from The Stronghold, or was he a plant? Did it even make a difference? And finally, could he get rid of him now, or later?

He wasn't new to the game. He had been Mayor for a dozen years now, and knew all the tricks. Somebody was always trying to gain power. It didn't matter how far from The Stronghold you went, power grows or it dies, and everything strives to live.

So far, he had held his own, even against the powers-that-be in the government offices. But he had no doubt, his only reason for still being in office was because he was so isolated, not worth the time or effort. Perhaps things were about to change.

The clerk at the port office couldn't say enough about 'The Young Gentleman' needing to speak with the mayor, babbling on incessantly until he had almost had him thrown out. But finally, the comment of, "Don't you have work to do?" was enough, and blanching, the clerk quickly found adequate reasons to leave.

The Backwater Mistress, and their tour of the area, had given the mayor more to think through. Why would this newcomer want to look over the area? What could he see from the ocean view that he couldn't see from land? The fact that the kid's horse was at the stables, and he had spent some time at The Common House, meant he might be staying, and another sign of trouble.

Mr. Jorstad, the crook who owned the place, wasn't someone to be played around with. Too many strings around too many of the townsfolk to make the place all happy and smiley. Then there were the rumors, his ships didn't seem to get attacked the way everyone else's ships did, and there may have been more than just old wives and empty cups to the tales. There were simply too many hands in the pot, especially for a small town like Corgy.

Mr. Jorstad had explained it all with the comment, "It is simply that I keep renowned marine troops on my ships," which was true, but they had only been added last year, while everyone else had been getting hit for several years now.

The Mayor's eye searched the ceiling panels for answers. He may not be a fisherman, but even he could tell when something smelled fishy.

But how was the kid from the city involved? It was time for a talk.

Mayor Dugan kicked his chair into the upright position, and called for his secretary. "Mrs. Randle, can you come in here?"

"Good evening Mr. Mayor." Isabella dipped a deep curtsey as Mayor Dugan entered The Common House, casually dropping his heavy coat and fine hat into her waiting arms.

"Good evening, Bella. I'm here on business. Did you happen to see a young gentleman come through today? I've been looking for him." Without waiting for a reply, and as one who knew his way around, he strode into the tap room and found himself a seat.

Bella delivered his items to the cloak room before hurrying in to check on him. The Common House no longer had many employees, leaving her with several jobs to do.

"What would you be having tonight Mr. Mayor? I'll fetch it for you straight away."

"Just coffee for now. As I said, I'm on business."

"Yes sir, coffee will be right up," she said, heading to the kitchen.

In no time at all, she was back. "Here you go sir, and to your other question regarding the young gentleman." She waited for him to take the cup and settle comfortably on the overstuffed divan before continuing. "The gentleman sir?"

"Yes, go ahead. You saw him?"

"I did, sir," she said, instantly wary and adding another short dip. "A very fine young man. I spoke a few words with him, and he asked about you. Said he had business to attend to here in town, and would probably be staying awhile."

"Business," the mayor frumped. "I'll bet he has business. Probably wants my job too." He glanced up at Bella, realizing it was poorly said with the staff at hand. "Forgive me Bella. I've got a grumpy tummy today. Always makes me a bit irritable. Now, did he mention anything else? Forewarned is forearmed, as they say." Taking a hanky from his jacket pocket, he noisily blew his nose before looking back to her. "Well, anything?"

"Not much, sir," Bella replied, used to the treatment of those in power. "He said he was expecting someone, and when Captain Black came in, I introduced them."

"Of The Mistress? That Captain Black?" The mayor grew more tense with the information. He knew there was something wrong about The Backwater Mistress and her sketchy captain, even if he couldn't put his finger on it. "Now what would this new gentleman be wanting with Captain Black? Did you get any information? Did you manage to listen in at all?"

Bella looked appalled at his question. "Of course not, sir. I make it a point never to listen in. It wouldn't be proper, and Mr. Jorstad would fire me outright if he even thought I was."

Makes sense, Dugan thought. *Being a crook himself, Jorstad would be very cautious of the staff overhearing conversations.* But to Bella, he said, "That's a good girl, and I'm glad to hear it. But if you happen to acquire any further information, it would certainly gain my appreciation." He gave her a crafty smile that made her stomach turn.

"Yes sir. I expect him back soon. I understand he was going out for a tour of the harbor. The Mistress headed out to sea some hours ago, so they must have gone down the coast a ways."

Mayor Dugan smiled, at least on the inside. With a bit of information, and and a new informant, his stop had been well worthwhile.

Bella wasn't on duty when Rhone finally entered the lobby and asked for a room, but the chubby middle-aged clerk quickly showed the way to a room overlooking the harbor.

"This is our best sir. There's a grand view from the window, and if you would be wanting anything, just ring, and I'll have it brought up fast as a swallow." He motioned to a pull cord and bell arrangement, with a convenient speak tube beside it.

Rhone was tired from his morning's ride, and the sail, and was not only dirty, but still a bit wet from the rough ocean tour. All he wanted was the bed, and maybe a bath, which sounded even better as the thought stuck. "Is there any way I could get a bath? I'm about worn to a frazzle."

His question must have conveyed real need, because his attendant snapped to attention. "Absolutely sir. I'll have one drawn up in no time."

Rhone sighed, and before the man had even left the room, sank thankfully into the couch's soft upholstery. He ached from one end to the other, but as bad as it was, he had to admit, it was nothing compared to his trials in the badlands. He had practically died there. Twice, or was it three times? He was still thinking about it when a knock came at the door.

"Yes?" he answered, reconsidering the need for a bath. At the moment, bed sounded even better.

"Your water sir. Are you decent?"

"Yes, come on in. It's unlocked."

Two young teens carried steaming buckets of water to the big claw-footed tub, set singularly in the side room. Rhone heard the heavy splash as they were unceremoniously dumped, then a harsh clatter as a bucket banged against the enameled side.

"Careful there! Don't chip it," the older of the two commented in fear. "It's worth more than our year's pay together."

Both teens glanced abashed at Rhone, still sitting where he had collapsed.

"Don't mind me," Rhone said, remembering the big galvanized tub at home. "How long will it take to fill?"

"Another few trips sir. But it won't be too long," the older commented apologetically.

"Fine, but just come on in. Don't worry about knocking."

He was almost asleep when the door opened again, with the sound of the sloshing water rousing him slightly. He began to time the trips, and was already waking when the older of the two announced they were done.

"It's still hot sir. Made sure the last batch was good and warm."

Rhone had a few coins stashed in his pocket, and handed them to the boys. "Thank you both. That was a lot of work. I know, I've done it myself a few times."

"You did?" the younger one asked, amazed that a gentleman would have carried bath water.

"Absolutely, you'd be surprised what I've done."

"Come on, Luke. Give the man some peace," the older chastised. "Thank you, sir. Have a good soak."

When the door closed, Rhone climbed wearily from the couch, the warm water drawing him to the tub. It looked almost as good as the lake buried deep in the badland's maze.

Maybe better, Stone commented, as Rhone unfastened the buckle holding the collar in place.

Again, Stone was right. This was better.

B ella's, "Good Morning, sir," caught Rhone mid-step as he exited from the stairway.

"Are you always on duty?" he asked, happily surprised to see her. "And is that coffee I smell?"

He had gotten used to the unique drink during his time at the OPR, and with a grin, followed the smell wafting invitingly from the dining room.

"Would you care for a cup?" Bella asked with apparent innocence, her thoughts overshadowed with the task the Mayor had set on her. "And how was your tour yesterday? It seemed pretty windy out."

"It certainly was," Rhone said, taking the cup with a laugh. "I've never sailed before, and honestly, had no idea what it would be like, but riding a bronco bareback might be a good comparison. I simply couldn't keep my feet under me, no matter how hard I tried. I almost went over the side at one point. Barely managed to hang on with both hands, when a sailor walks up without a care, and grabs me. Sets me back on the deck and says, "Best get a good grip sir. It takes a while to get your sea legs.""

Rhone's terrible sailor accent made Bella laugh, before she realized he was telling the truth. Her expression changed to one of dread as she listened, thinking of his going overboard in the rough seas.

"Honest, he did," Rhone vowed, "and I'll tell you what, I couldn't grab the rail hard enough. I should check to see if I left finger prints."

Bella blinked in horrified awe. She knew many people couldn't swim, including most sailors. What good would it do when you were out in the ocean, miles from land. But here was her chance. Steeling herself, she launched into what she hoped was a reasonable question. "You're not from around here. That's pretty obvious, but you haven't sailed?"

"Is it that easy to see?" he asked with humor. "I was hoping no one could tell."

Bella made an odd face, wondering how he could even consider that a possibility. But what if she had said too much already? She hated trickery, but still didn't have information for the mayor. Finally, she simply shrugged and said, "You don't exactly look like a deck hand."

Which was very true. This morning, Rhone had dressed in black knee-breeches and high boots, with a sea green cut-away jacket covering his normal leather vest. With the burgundy silk shirt, and Stone centered in his leather collar, he did make a statement. No one in three counties could have afforded the outfit, let alone actually worn it. Not unless they were undeniably wealthy, and perhaps at their own wedding.

But Rhone felt he wore it well, and the pretty girl before him seemed to agree. She may only be an employee, but he could still enjoy the company.

Putting on a concerned face, Rhone tried to come up with a believable answer. "No, I've never been to sea. You won't tell anyone will you? I'm here to check out the area, and see if it will be suitable for an extension of the company. I won't be able to do that if people are all over me, trying to make headway into our doings."

"Wouldn't tell a soul. Cross my heart," Bella said, making the appropriate motions, and not understanding half of what he had just said. But now what was she supposed to do? The mayor had hinted at a possible job in his office if her information proved of value. The thought had excited her, but now felt underhanded.

Bringing the talk back to safer ground, she asked, "Did you see what you needed, or did you get sea sick? I know I do if the water's too rough."

"I was worried for a while," Rhone admitted, still in good humor, "but I managed to hold it together. I think Captain Black took pity on me, and we came about, making for a much smoother trip coming in." He paused, considering his next words. "Did you know The Mistress has cannons on board? I went below deck for a few minutes, and there were all kinds of weapons."

"I wouldn't doubt it," Bella answered honestly. "There have been reports of pirates, and some ships never come back. It's a dangerous game they play, saying it's just business. I hear them talking."

Then she realized how dangerous her own words were, especially having just told the mayor differently. She may not intentionally listen in, but she did hear things on occasion.

Having already spent too much time with this young gentleman, she asked, "Can I warm that cup for you? They don't pay me to stand around," knowing she would be called to task for dalliance if she didn't get back to work.

"Please, and thank you, Bella," Rhone said, holding his cup out for a refill. "You have brightened my morning."

Smiling shyly, she refilled the proffered cup and gave a dip, before turning quickly to the kitchen area.

It was none too soon. Rhone heard her name being called as she entered, and felt guilty for holding her from her work.

Enjoying yourself? Stone asked with his normal curtness. *Now you have even more business issues to remember. And when exactly are you planning to make your contact with the Mayor, instead of flirting with the staff?*

Just doing my job, Rhone countered silently, but not really concerned. *Besides, Bella makes a good contact, and meets all kinds of people. If I set things up right, all I have to do is drop information to her and see where it goes. It's certainly easier than me running all over the coastline, trying to find people to talk to.*

Trying to think words to Stone while sipping coffee was not as easy as it had once been. He had gotten out of the habit during training, but sitting in the middle of The Common House was not the place to be seen talking to himself.

Ummm-hmmm. The vibrated comment replaced any need for words. *Just be sure your efforts are aimed in the right direction. Remember, you are not here to go lady hunting.*

CHAPTER 11

What the What?

"Have you heard the news?" Bella asked quietly, speaking low as in confidence, then without waiting, continued in a worriedly excited voice. "One of the ships got hit. I heard they barely made it to port."

Rhone carefully set down his cup, his raised eyebrows making it patently clear he had not heard. His voice merely confirmed it. "Hit, by what? Was it badly damaged?"

He remembered all too well, the deep grey-green water and the powerful waves smashing against the tall stone lighthouse.

Bella bounced in place, the excitement making her lose her caution. "It was the Liberty. She's a quick two-master, and runs coastal trade from here to the northern border. She came limping in early this morning, and they say half her side is blown away. The good captain managed to slip into the fog and escape, but they took on water and spoiled most of her goods."

"Hit, or blown away? Did her powder catch?" Rhone knew a fire on ship left nowhere to go, and if the powder caught, would blow the vessel wide open. He hadn't been around long, but even he understood that much.

"Pirates, dummy!" came Bella's instant critique. Then her eyes went wide at the recognition of her own words. "Oh, I'm so sorry, sir," she muttered, looking shocked by her own indiscretion.

Rhone couldn't have cared less, and had heard far worse. "Stop worrying. We, you and I, are either going to be friends, or you are going to have to stop talking to me. I can't keep forgiving you for something I would have done myself. Now, which is it going to be?" With studied patience he waited for an answer.

Bella looked unsure. It was totally improper for her to speak with someone of his position, unless it was a direct request and a desire for her to respond. To call him dumb was enough to get her whipped, and fired. Still, he was waiting for an answer.

Finally, dipping her head, she accepted his challenge. "I would like to be friends. If that doesn't seem too improper? I'm just a serving girl, not someone you would even know in the real city."

Rhone had a difficult time holding to his story. He wanted to tell her who he really was, but that could cause big problems for his assignment. Instead, he nodded. "Thank you. I wouldn't ask if it wasn't correct, now would I?" It was another challenge, and he held his face immobile, managing not to crack a grin at her confused look.

"Well, I... suppose not. But it still seems pretty iffy." At least she was talking, and more like a friend.

"All right then," Rhone said with pleasure, "Tell me more about this ship. You say it was pirates?"

Pirates were far more interesting than anything else he might end up doing for the day.

Bella began bouncing on her toes again, sharing his enthusiasm, which made it very difficult for him to keep his mind on her words. But being the gentleman he played, he raised his eyes expectantly, awaiting her news.

"I'm sure it must be. I know they've been having trouble for years. When I heard the commotion, I ran out to see, and saw the torn sails." At Rhone's questioning look, she answered before he asked. "That would be from grapeshot. It shreds the sails to keep the ship from getting away."

Rhone was impressed with her knowledge, then realized, she did live in a sea port, probably hearing all the incoming news. She was indeed a good source of information, even if second hand. He made sure to flick the knowledge to Stone.

"What's grape shot?" he asked. "I may be an in-lander, but I doubt they would be firing real grapes at anyone."

Bella rolled her eyes and giggle cutely. "No, grape is something like using a shotgun. They load the barrel with pieces of metal they call grape, and fire that instead of a cannonball. It doesn't do much damage to a ship, but it will do terrible things to sails and sailors. Then, when they're done taking over the ship, it's still seaworthy and they can claim it as salvage."

Rhone smiled invitingly, hoping for more details.

"The rest isn't so nice," Bella said, her nose wrinkling in disgusted horror before she continued. "I didn't see it mind you, but I overheard how they had to sluice the decks, just to keep from slipping on the blood. It sounds horrible." She gave an involuntary shudder at the thought. "Why would people do something like that?"

Rhone shrugged as he answered. "People get greedy I guess. There's always someone who wants what someone else has, and is quite willing to take it. I've met a few myself."

His words brought a look of alarm to Bella's face. "You have? I know you have a lot of things, but someone actually took something of yours?"

Rhone wondered briefly if he should mention losing his collar, and Stone.

Best not, Stone warned, ever diligent to Rhone's doings. *Do not get the young lady involved where she does not need to be. And do not drop crumbs when you do not want a bite. It could end up being dangerous information.*

Rhone nodded his agreement, which fit into the discussion well enough.

"I did, but it could have been worse. I ended up retrieving the lost goods. Still, it only goes to show what people will do." He let it set for a moment, but still wanted more information. "Are pirates a big threat? I should know if we plan on doing business here."

Bella shook her head in a way that set her curls dancing. "I don't believe so, but you could speak with the mayor. He would know everything there is to know about it. You said you wanted to speak with him anyway, so here's a good reason." And, it relieved her from needing to pass on information the mayor had requested.

"An excellent idea," Rhone agreed. "I believe I will take a stroll after breakfast, and drop by the mayor's office for a chat." Having made up his mind, he placed his order. "Just make it the common breakfast please."

Once again, she had let time slip by, and quickly resumed her proper station. "A good choice, sir," she said, dipping her head in acknowledgment. "Just let me run that to the kitchen."

While his breakfast was no problem, she was appalled at the thought of, 'just dropping in' on the Mayor. But then again, she wasn't used to the ways of her betters. With a quick curtsey, she left to get his food.

As soon as the plates were delivered, Rhone began to eat, greedily digging in to the bacon and eggs. They were always good, but so was the sausage with black pudding, and that was before the grilled tomatoes even got to the table. His favorite though, was the amazing fry-bread with butter and marmalade. He could never get enough bread, and even after stuffing himself full, sat back with a sigh, savoring the last few bites. He'd never had anything this good. Mom had cooked, and he had eaten, but there were very few changes in their daily diet. But here, he was eating something different every day, and even if he didn't know what something was, all he had to do was act as if he was in deliberation, then say, "I can't quite decide. Which would you suggest?" It worked like a charm, and he had discovered some wonderful new meals.

For now, though, his belly was full and the morning bright. He stretched in exaggeration as Bella came to pick up the plates. "A beautiful day isn't it Miss Bella? Too bad you're working. It would be a great morning for a stroll."

When she bunched her brows and tightened her lips, Rhone had to ask, "Did I say something wrong?"

"Master Rhone," Bella scowled with defiance, "I am employed at this establishment, and I am not, as you seem to be, able to take my days in a stroll around town. Even if I managed to do so, I would be chastised to no end, thinking to act above my station. Do you not understand this?"

Surprised at her outburst, Rhone merely stared in confusion as she continued.

"I believe that we can be friends, but any further instigation upon my person will not be looked upon with favor. Do I make myself clear?"

With eyes wide, Rhone simply nodded his head, unable to understand what he had done to deserve this.

Bella held her strength for a moment longer, before her countenance abruptly changed. Quickly gathering her skirts into one hand, she hurried from the room, wiping her eyes with the other.

Rhone cautiously glanced around the dining room, checking to see if anyone had noticed their interaction.

Do not even ask, Stone broke into his thoughts. *I am not a human, and if 'you' do not understand your women, how would you expect me, a...what did you call me, a rock-thing? How can I possibly do so? Yet even I am not as hard headed as some.*

More befuddled than ever, Rhone refused to have his beautiful day brought down for something he didn't even understand. He would have to ask Aundrea about dealing with women. Then he rethought the idea. Bran might be a better option.

Carefully folding his napkin, as he had been painstakingly taught, Rhone lay it beside his plate, then stood and slid his chair up to the table. He looked for Bella, but she was nowhere to be seen, so he finally left The Common House, and headed down the boardwalk toward the quay. When he saw The Backwater Mistress tied at its berthing, he thought it was a good time to make a reacquaintance. He needed to learn more.

As the day before, dockworkers and seamen crowded the walkway, carrying and hauling all manner of goods to and from the ships they were servicing. It was a busy place for such a small harbor, and everyone had an urgency to their motion.

Rhone could feel the energy as he headed for the ship, ever watchful for an errant bundle, or leg, to set him over the edge. The day may be nice, but the water would be cold, and didn't look all that clean here at the dock. Sludge, oily scum, and debris lay in a slimy coating over the surface, sticking like tarry glue to the ships. Some ships had men hanging over their sides, scrubbing and refinishing the wood before heading out to sea where it would be tarnished all over again.

Rhone's casual stroll eventually took him to where The Mistress was tied. Stopping at the end of her ramp, he called to one of the hands on the deck, his well-worn clothing stained with sweat and oil. "You there. Is the Captain aboard?"

The deckhand, irritated at having his task interrupted, glanced down ready to vent. But seeing Rhone in his finery, swallowed heavily, his Adam's apple bobbing in alarm. "Why yes, sir, he is," then nervously dipped his head to touch hand to forelock. "I'll have him called up in a trice."

"Thank you. I would appreciate it," Rhone answered with the appropriate aplomb. The well-to-do had very little interaction with the common worker, and though it still felt odd, it was becoming easier to hold to his part.

It was only a few moments before Captain Black's head stuck above the railing, bellowing a welcome that might as well have been in a gale.

"Why good morning young sir. What brings you out to my Mistress this fine morning? Although personally, I can't think of a better place to be." His crooked smile was almost covered by the bushy beard still sticking in all directions. Then with a thoughtful expression crossing his face, he continued without a pause. "Except maybe, lying about with a fine lady or two, but you might not be knowing about such things yet, so, kindly disregard an old codger's imaginations. I do get carried away at times."

The Captain was his normal talkative self, holding both parts of the conversation. He knew where he stood and that was good enough for him, and therefore his crew.

Rhone smiled at the captain's babbling, but decided to break in or his day might never proceed further. "Captain, sir, might I come aboard? I have a few questions."

"What? Well of course you can come aboard. Why aren't you up here already? There's things happening, and we've got to make ready."

The gleam in the captain's wild look was something Rhone hadn't expected, but he quickly made his way up the squeaking, complaining ramp. "And again, good morning, Captain," Rhone said as he reached the deck.

"And a good day to yourself," Captain Black beamed, pleased to be addressed so by a gentleman. "How can I be of service? We could offer you some tea. I'm afraid it wouldn't be in one of those dainty little cups you're used to, but tea we have." Without waiting a response, he bellowed to a crewman. "Tea for the gentleman. And be quick about it."

"Aye, Cap," came the cheerful call, not in the least concerned by the gruff manner of the command.

Then in all politeness, Captain Black swept an arm forward, inviting Rhone aboard. "Now sir, if you will follow me to the quarterdeck, we'll see what brings you out so early."

Placing his heavy arm around Rhone's shoulders, Captain Black escorted him to where a crewman was hurriedly setting out chairs.

"We've got a good view from here, and I can keep an eye on the men. Can't have them lollygagging about when there's work to be done," he commented loudly, giving Rhone a conspiratorial wink.

"Why, no sir," Rhone agreed quickly, recognizing the importance of keeping command. "I must say, you keep a remarkably tight ship. I was lucky to find you, seeing some of the others around."

"We do indeed. It's the only way to stay afloat," he said, jesting as usual.

Another crewman hurried up and Rhone took the proffered cup, lifting it to the Captain in acknowledgment of the pun. "Now sir, I have a real question, if I may?"

"Of course. I didn't figure you came all the way out to The Mistress for some tea. Now what's on your mind?" But his eyes took on an undefinable gleam. "Mind you, we are pretty busy this morning, with all the goin's on."

"Then perhaps we are on similar tasks," Rhone nodded sympathetically. "I am questing as to the situation with The Liberty, which I heard came in damaged."

"Aye, she was indeed. Practically blown away she was. Course, since she managed to make it back, she'll be reworked in no time. The shipwrights here are pretty darn good at their jobs."

"Exactly, sir. But what caused the destruction? Did she blow from the inside, or was she hit?"

The captain winked in a knowing way, before slyly answering, "I see where you're going. I knew you were a bright lad. So I'll tell you right out, it was pirates, and no doubts about it. Talked to Captain Stenson myself, first thing."

"Pirates," Rhone almost whispered, but his mind was shouting, *What the What? Real pirates?*

There is no need for such racket, Stone said caustically, not nearly as thrilled with the concept.

Rhone didn't pay him the least attention. "Pirates? Are you certain?" he asked, totally intrigued by the subject.

"Indeed I am. So was Captain Stenson. Attacked the Liberty from the fog, almost ghost-like he said, quiet as a mouse. They were fired on broadside, with no chance to beat to quarters. Only the roll of the sea kept them from being beaten right there. But Captain Stenson was quick on his feet, an' made for the same fog that hid them dad-gum pirates. He knows his stuff. Cut back close while the other ship swung about, then sliding off real quiet-like, managed to slip away. He said they dropped sails when he thought they had gone far enough under cover, and stayed silent all night, praying for the fog to hold. When morning came, the fog lifted and they were alone. Came limping in to port, dragging their tail behind them, as it were." He bobbed his heavy eyebrows with a grin, enjoying his word play.

"Pirates," Rhone whispered again, deep in thought.

"Yep. Captain Stenson made comment on seeing a red sail atop the mizzen. Stood out bright as a cherry, even in the fog."

Rhone had never considered pirates beyond stories. The thought excited him, until he wondered, *what if it had been us out on the tour?* He would have been on board, and quite possibly, right where the ship's side had been taken out. A chill ran down Rhone's back, realizing he could be dead right now.

But pulling himself together, he asked, "Have you ever had problems with pirates?"

Which he realized, might have been a poor question, considering Captain Black might be one. Talk about stepping right in it. Even Bella had thought he should talk to the mayor, not the Captain.

But too late now, the captain was answering with a devilish grin.

"Well, yes and no. See, I get around a bit, and as I said, my Mistress here is good and quick. Had her built a ways back, after doing a bit of sailing off the far coast. There's some quick ships down there, and I decided to design one up myself, just the way I wanted. Bits of this and pieces of that, and I came up with my Mistress. Course, I had a ship builder do the real work, with proper layouts and such, but the design idea was mine. She's a good girl, and I don't mind sayin' so myself."

Rhone heartily agreed. "She is a beauty Captain, and she sails like a bird."

The captain nodded, accepting Rhone's words as a true accolade. "Is one thing about her," he rumbled, rubbing his nose in apology. "She doesn't do heavy weather too well. Sides are cut a bit too low for that, so I tend to keep her close to shore. But she's got a shallow draught, so we do just fine, going where others won't. An' if we get becalmed, we have oars we can swing out, and work our way home. It's a lot of work of course, but other ships just have to sit there an' wait out the doldrums."

That was all good, but didn't answer the question, and Rhone try another tack. "I saw you had guns on board. Have you needed to use them?"

With a shrug, and a calculating squint, Captain Black made little of the question. "Not in a real battle, no. Haven't needed to. Like I said, we're fast, and outrun most problems."

Rhone didn't respond, thinking of the large waves the captain said they shouldn't have been in.

But to Captain Black, Rhone's lack of response was the same as being called a coward, and he continued with a sudden touch of hot ire.

"Now listen up fella. Battles aren't something to play with. You never know which way it's gonna turn, and it doesn't take much. A gun misfires, or the wind drops. A line lets go at the wrong time, or maybe it's a sail. It's a dangerous business, and not to be trifled with, but if it ever came down to need, I know what to do. How do you think I got the money to build her? I didn't come by any rich uncle's inheritance."

The unexpected distaste for his status evaporated before Rhone was even sure it was there, but it was enough to make Captain Black begin to squirm, acting like he had been caught with a hand in the cookie jar. His chair groaned as he shifted his weight, until abruptly he turned to Rhone. "Sorry fella. Sometimes my mouth gets away from me."

Rhone felt slightly disjointed by the admission, until Stone rephrased the issue in more understandable terms.

I believe our good captain may have a problem with your supposed position, but not you as a person. Does that help?

Rhone took a moment to think about it. *Does everyone think that way?* he asked silently. When Stone didn't reply, he had his answer.

It was obviously time to redirect the conversation.

"I take no offense, Captain, and your ship truly is beautiful, but I believe we were speaking of pirates."

"That I was," the captain said, delighted to away from slippery footing and onto solid ground. "There aren't as many as there could be, what with all the trade shipping up and down the coast, but they've been increasing. Seems like they know where and when a boat's going out, and what their carrying. Likely they've got somebody close, but I don't know what to do about it, so I pick my cargo carefully, and do quick runs."

Rhone's face lit with a flash of insight. "That would be the part about staying flexible you mentioned."

"Good, you understand," the captain said happily, "If I keep my schedule loose, and ship fast and valuable, we stay ahead of the game. But if need comes, the cannon stashed below deck won't hurt either." He nodded his shaggy head sagely.

It was a good action plan for the Mistress, which was probably why they were being hit, but how would it work for everyone else? It made sense.

"Captain, doesn't the government know? And what about the military? Certainly, the navy would assist."

"The government?" Captain Black chortled. "Why would The Council worry about pirates? Shoot, half of them are probably in cahoots, and get paybacks, but all legal-like. You know, like the rest of us gettin' taxed the way we do. The money has to go somewhere, so why not their pockets? Why do you think they're all so stinking rich? Shucks, everybody knows that."

But suddenly the captain stopped, realizing who he was talking to. Luckily Rhone was picking up his tea, too busy with his own thoughts to notice.

Rhone had also used the moment for a quick meeting with Stone, who reluctantly agreed to an uncertain move. It was risky, but worth the try.

"Sir, I have a confession to make. I am not who I appear to be."

Rhone's abrupt words effectively caught the captain's attention. His eyes swung up to meet Rhone's, their hard intensity very unlike the cheerful man Rhone had come to know. Scowling through his beard at the deception, Captain Black's hand slid nearer his weapons.

Rhone held the captain's stare without a flinch, but fortified himself with a steadying breath before explaining. "My name is indeed Rhone, but I am an agent for The Office of Public Recrimination. I am beginning to think the OPR has heard of these offenses to the shipping trade, and I was sent to look into it."

He waited for a response, but there was none, other than a huff and the continued scowl. Actually, he thought it was going pretty well. He hadn't been thrown overboard, clubbed, or shot yet, so he continued his reasoning with the captain.

"Captain, I need to find if the situation is true, or simply misdirected stories to divert our attention from other, more pressing matters. Since I am here, perhaps we could work together and both be winners. What say you?"

The captain's scowl deepened as he squinted in concentration. "So you're not here for your daddy's shipping interests." It was more of a condemnation than a question.

Rhone held his poise as he searched for an answer. "Not from my father, no, but I was sent to check on shipping interests, yes. Yours too, if I'm not mistaken."

It at least gained a grimace from the stoic face. Then the hard features began to unravel into a more thoughtful look. "I suppose that could be true, if you look at it like that."

Taking the impetus, Rhone barged ahead. "Since I now know the Liberty was hit by pirates, I need to determine exactly how much of a problem they are, and what can be done."

Still unconvinced, the captain gave a one-eyed squint and broached another issue. "You say you're with the Public Recriminations Office? Dang, everybody's heard of them, but aren't you kinda young to be an agent?"

There it was. The one thing Rhone couldn't disagree with.

Gritting his teeth in determination, Rhone held his course. "I am, sir, undoubtably, but I can assure you, I am a fully graduated officer of the agency, and have been sent specifically to this location. It is up to me to make determinations and report my findings to the office."

"Now, no need to get all worked up. I believe you." The captain chuckled with the amusement, his grin growing as he talked. "Nobody could just come up with that kind of spoutin', unless of course they were a whale."

When he began to chortle at his own joke, Rhone knew things were back to normal.

"So what's the plan, now that you know there's pirates about?"

The question was cheerful enough that Rhone wasn't bothered. "I may know there are pirates, but there is a lot more information I need before I can make any kind of recommendation."

"Now there you go again," the Captain said, sticking a finger into his ear and squirreling it around. "You sound more and more like a bureaucrat every time you open your mouth. Sorry I asked." Which he really wasn't.

Rhone didn't know what to say to that. "What would you do in my place?" he asked, really wanting to know.

"Me?" The captain asked, eyebrows lifting. "Why that's easy. I'd go hunt 'em down. Prove who's boss, and make them start paying taxes too. That would teach them something."

Rhone began to laugh, but stopped suddenly, mid-thought.

Rhone, what are you thinking? came Stone's panicked voice. *Were we not in enough trouble with The Commissioner? How could you even consider going against pirates?*

But Rhone clamped down on Stone's voice and turned to the Captain. "You would hunt them down? But how would you know where to go, and what would you use?"

Captain Black's laughter drained away like wine from a broached keg. "You're serious? But I was just funnin' you. You can't go hunting pirates. You don't have a ship, or men, or even know how to sail." He snorted at the stupid humor of it. "You just can't be that dumb. You'd be dead in a week, and only because it took you that long to get out of the harbor. Now listen, Master Rhone, or... what should I call you now? Officer Rhone?"

"Rhone will do just fine. I need to remain in my part, at least for the time being. It wouldn't do to get tongues wagging before I even get started."

"Yeh, I can see problems there," the Captain agreed with a frown. "So let's get this straight. You're an agent, and you're here on assignment, and you want to fight pirates. Have I got it so far?"

"Pretty much," Rhone agreed. "But I need to figure out a lot more, including sailing, I think. It seems pertinent. Although maybe just enough experience to know what they can and can't do. Would you be willing to give lessons? That would be a start."

Captain Black scruffed at his beard as he thought it over. "And what's in it for me? I hate to put it that way, but I am a business man, and have a crew to take care of. You have no idea how many women and kids up in these hills are attached to my income," then looked askance at Rhone's innocent smile. "No, they ain't mine," he grumbled, "but they are something I worry about."

"And I thought you were just a pirate yourself," Rhone said mockingly.

"Me?" the captain sputtered indignantly, "Why I'm a hardworking, honest to goodness... Okay, maybe not so much of the goodness part, but dang it all, I work hard."

Rhone let the Captain stew as he started working on something close to a plan. "So, will you teach me?"

He let the words hang, while the Captain chewed it over some more.

"If I weren't such a good citizen and all," the captain said, still grumbling, "I'd just say no, and go haul a load or two. But dang it, I try to do right, and if that means getting my little Mistress shot out from under us, well... I guess it's meant to be." He grimaced and blew sputtering noises before finishing. "Okay, I'll teach you something about sailing, but we'll have to see what goes beyond that. And... don't forget the pay. I'll need something to tempt my boys out, now that the Liberty got herself all shot up. They weren't all that far out either."

"Sounds good," Rhone said, allowing himself a smile. "Shall we start tomorrow? I need to get a report sent off, and let the office know what's happening in Corgy. *I'll also need some additional funds*, he thought to himself. He had enough funds to live on, but was pretty sure renting a ship would be over his limit.

I believe, Miss Aundrea will find your report quite interesting, Stone added, sounding hopelessly resigned.

CHAPTER 12

Back in Style

For the next several days Rhone got up early, headed to The Backwater Mistress, and sailed up and down the coast, around small islands, into and out of shallow inlets, practicing all the things a coaster needed to know. His main objective was trying not to ground the ship, or smash into a cliff wall on an inflowing tide. When Rhone wasn't handling the sails and lines, he was calling commands, quickly realizing why Captain Black spoke with such volume most of the time.

When the wind blew strong, the sound of waves bursting against the sides of the ship added to a cacophony of squealing tackle, slapping sails, and the groans of the ship itself, laboring against the weight of the ocean, all capped by the shouts of the men as they worked, and the squawking calls of the gulls flying alongside. Altogether, it made for an unbelievable din. Rhone was constantly forced to raise his voice, shouting just to be heard. Still young, he just didn't have the depth of chest the Captain did, and had to work that much harder to make his commands heard.

At least the crew had accepted him with an almost humorous glee. But it was more than once a sailor had to stop and cup a hand to his ear, signaling he couldn't hear. Then in embarrassment, Rhone would call the command again.

There were also times when the ship would need a quick correction, or when immediate action was required for the ship's safety. Perhaps a log floating on the waves before them, or a quick shift of sails for an oncoming squall. Rhone loved the craft of sailing, but it was also very tiring. Most of the time he wasn't even doing the heavy hauling, simply calling commands and trying to stay on his feet. But he was learning, and beginning to feel more comfortable. Luckily, he was a fast learner and had Stone as a backup, just in case he forgot the name of a sail or line, with names like jibs, sheets, and halyards. It wasn't as simple as, 'turn here', or 'lift that sail thing', and with so many men setting sails and hauling on ropes of different kinds, it took some doing. Far more than he would ever have guessed.

"You're doing fine, Master Rhone," Captain Black shouted, as Rhone made a course correction, swinging past the tip of a rocky outcropping jutting sharply from the cliffs. "No need to worry about grounding in this section. Probably a good twenty fathoms here." Seeing Rhone's blank expression, he cheerful explained. "Fathom, it's about the height of a man. Plenty deep enough we don't have to worry about losing our keel on the bottom. Specially with this ol' girl. Remember I told you she's got a shallow draught? Some ship's keels stick way down, helping to stabilize the weight of the sails up top. Think of it like balancing a stick across your finger, with equal weight on both sides."

Rhone gratefully accepted the simple explanation, while the captain continued his training, undaunted.

"Now, some ships use ballast to balance, so as the wind pushes the sails over to the side, the ballast weight helps to balance that force. If it didn't, the whole thing just topples over, and we capsize, hopin' we can tread water."

Rhone listened closely, but he knew Stone was paying even more attention, working to figure out the necessary equivalencies.

I have been working on the calculations, Stone commented sagely. *I have managed to develop a good equation for the process,* and *believe we will do quite well, unless of course, you call an incorrect command.*

Thanks, Stone, but I'm pretty sure I've got it, Rhone thought dryly.

Very good then, but if ever you need assistance, remember, I am very good at calculating.

Their talk ended as the ship passed the rocky spire, drawing Rhone back to the task of calling commands. With a swing of the wheel, they set on a new tack, working their way into the light wind. What a marvelous way to live.

His revery, however, was interrupted by a loud call ringing from the man on watch.

"Sail off the larboard bow sir. Tops just showing."

Captain Black's bellowing reply showed he was instantly back in command. "Thank you, Jolly. Ten miles off the larboard bow! Keep an eye on 'em!"

Without needing a comment, Rhone stepped back, now playing the part of first officer. "Is that bad?" he asked.

There were lots of ships trading along the coastline, but they hadn't seen one since their first day still near the harbor.

"Probably not," the captain admitted, scowling as he considered their next course. "But best to be cautious. Most captains are cautious. It saves a lot of heart ache. Now, if we were running across the ocean to some other coastline, we might just meet up and share a bit of news, but this close to land there's no reason to risk it. Pirates don't tend to wander the big ocean. Too far between targets. You could sail out there for months and never see a soul, so they tend to stay closer to shore, where everyone has to come to harbor."

It made sense, but there was just so much to learn, it was starting to overwhelm him.

"So what are we going to do?" Rhone asked. He couldn't play at sailing forever, so every new situation was knowledge to be gained.

"We'll hold our course for now. We'll keep an eye on them for sure, but not to worry. It would take some doing to catch us. We aren't carrying much in the way of goods, so we're even faster than we would be if we were loaded. That's what pirates look for. A heavy-laden ship, lugging' along the shoreline. If it's heavy and slow enough, they could catch up and board. If they can't, they set up to drive them onto a shoal or the shore, where they can pick up the goods from the wreckage. It's a nasty business, but it's there, and no doubt about it."

Rhone quickly filed away the information. As long as a ship was light and quick, they probably wouldn't be confronted by pirates.

The lone ship obviously had the same thoughts, as the lookout reported a change in sail, just before they disappeared over the horizon.

R hone knew he should have met with the mayor soon after his arrival, but he'd wanted to understand Corgy's problem first. Now with a good guess to why he had been sent here, he needed the mayor's support before he could deal with the pirates. And with Captain Black knowing of his real purpose, it was definitely time.

His chosen outfit for the day attempted to evade the fact he was young. Instead, he hoped to give the look of proficiency, and knowing what he was about. He had even cornered Bella, pleading with her to look it over. He needed to know if it worked.

Reluctantly Bella agreed, and now stood outside his door, waiting until he said he was ready. Even knowing his rank and privilege, her eyes rose in wonder as the door opened. A zillion pockets covered the fitted long-coat neatly set over his trim vest. His leather britches were more like a second skin, tucking into the high cuffed boots, with their shiny brass buckles running up his calves.

She didn't say anything for a moment, just stood with wide eyes and an astonished expression on her pretty face. Rhone wasn't sure if that was good or bad, but was too happy just looking at her to worry overly much.

Until her gaze switched to his. "Where are you going? Will you be gone long?"

Instantly his worry evaporated. She was talking to him again, and he loved the sound of it.

"I'm going to see the mayor, just like you told me to," he reminded her. Although that had been days ago.

She blinked at the memory. But the additional memory of the mayor's orders brought color to her cheeks, recognizing the thin line she was dangling by.

135

"Yeah, that's good, but I thought you already had. But now's good too," she corrected herself, looking away, and not liking what she was doing.

"Well, what do you think? Will it work?"

"Will it work?" Bella exclaimed, her mind stumbling, and not tracking his words as guilt assailed her. "For going to see Mayor Dugan? Rhone, he's just the mayor, not a king." Her real frustration only strengthened her need to say it.

"Well... yeah," Rhone murmured in embarrassment. "I just didn't want him to think of me as a kid."

"A kid?" Bella stammered in disbelief. "You may be young, sir, but no one in the entire county would consider you a kid. Why would you even think it?"

Rhone blushed, and raised a shoulder in a half shrug. "Captain Black made some comment of me being too young for the job, so I didn't want the Mayor to think so too."

Bella's fists knuckled to her hips, and a very serious face showed Rhone exactly what she thought. "Master Rhone, you are one of the dumbest people I've ever met."

Rhone stood dumbstruck, now understanding what the word really meant. He couldn't think of a single thing to say, which was fine, since she took over, filling in for his blankness.

"You must be the most conceited man on the entire earth if you are worried about Mayor Dugan thinking you're a child. At the moment, you could be Prince Rhone, and nobody would be the wiser. You could probably call up the entire county to arms, and have every man-jack around fighting to get in line. How could you possibly worry about such a trifling thing, and then ask me to verify your conceit? Oooooh!" She let out a frustrated groan, almost stomping her foot as she tried to contain herself. "Men can be so stupid!"

Rhone was lost to the entire thing, still standing in disbelief, as he finally tried a comment. "Bella...I..."

"That would be, Miss Bella, to you!" she snapped.

"Of course... Miss Bella, but, would that be a yes, or a no?"

Her single puff of breath seemed to dissipate the anger, and she dropped into a chair, skirts billowing. "I give up," she sighed. "I don't know how to help you. You're beyond anything I've been taught to deal with." Planting her head back against the cushion, she stared blankly at the ceiling, hoping it would give her answers.

"I take it, that would be a no," Rhone said quietly, not wanting her riled again, but needing an answer. He honestly knew nothing about clothes, or what was appropriate.

Bella rocked her head from side to side in hopelessness, not willing to hear him. But he remained standing there, unmoving. Finally giving up, she sat up and straightened her skirts, then looked up at his tall form as he stared down at her. His confusion caught her unexpectedly and she couldn't help the laugh that escaped.

"You are totally hopeless," she breathed in disbelief. "How did you ever survive this long on your own?"

Rhone smiled uneasily, not sure how to take her comment. "Is that good, or bad?"

"It's fine," she said with a sigh, far more relaxed now. "I really do wonder how you got here all by yourself." Then jokingly added, "Sir."

Rhone couldn't help his growing grin, but his eyes were still hooded, pleading for an answer. "So it's all right to wear? I really need to know."

She glared, but with humor at his neediness. "Like I said, you look as good as a prince on tour of his country. So yeah, you look fine." He was such a boy, for all his being a man.

"Well, okay then," Rhone said, suddenly perking up. "I have an appointment with the mayor, and I had best not be late." His genteel demeanor had returned, and he gave it his best, mostly for her benefit.

Bella rolled her eyes with at least a hint of a smile, and asked, "Will that be all, sir? I'd best be back to work, or rumors will fly."

"Yes, of course," Rhone responded, only now realizing she was still on duty. "Just let me see you down stairs, and I'll be going."

As they descended to the lobby, Rhone quietly whispered, "Thank you, Bella. I've missed you."

CHAPTER 13

The Problem Is...

Rhone stepped forward, surreptitiously reading the small nameplate on the desktop. "Excuse me, Mrs. Randle?"

The dowdy middle-aged lady glanced up from her heavy ledger, a severe question on her well-powdered cheeks.

"If you would be so kind," Rhone began, taking the opportunity to hand her a bright yellow daisy, accompanied by his equally bright smile, "I would hope to find the Mayor in, and available for a few words."

Despite herself, Mrs Randle couldn't help a prim smile of her own. "Certainly, sir. Let me see if he is available."

Rhone waited, hoping he looked more at ease than he felt. But within minutes he had been led into an ornate office, made his introduction, and now faced an irate mayor pacing back and forth in front of his desk, hands clasp behind his back.

"I'm as serious as a nest of hornets, mister," the mayor sputtered. "I don't need the government, or anybody else for that matter, sticking their nose into my business. Not here in my town, or my harbor. I have things well in hand, and will not take it lightly if anyone comes messing around, making accusations and looking to lay blame on me."

Rhone sat facing the mayor's scathing diatribe, realizing he had made a big mistake. "But, Mr. Mayor, how can I be assured of our goods getting shipped safely? You agree there are pirates, yet you do nothing. Is that not a dereliction of duty?"

"Dereliction of duty?" the mayor bellowed, practically spitting the words. "I'll have you know, I have been mayor here for going on twelve years, and in that time, I have been able to hold my own against all comers. That goes for on land, as well as by sea."

Quickly tiring of this one-sided conversation, Rhone threw in a retort of his own. "And yet only last week, The Liberty, under Captain Stenson, was almost sunk, and lost most of her cargo. How does that make things right? Nor have you been open about the problem, refusing to even acknowledge the severity of it." Then feigning a lack of interest, he sat back and casually dropped a comment. "I suppose father was right. This is simply too far out to make a decent port of call. He said it wasn't safe, but I disagreed. Now you say there are no pirates, yet your ships come in, blown apart, and you do nothing."

Mayor Dugan glowered, thrusting his hands deep into his pockets to still them. "Now, I didn't say anything about not working on the problem. I just don't want it going around that we have problems with pirates. It's not good for business. You can understand that," he said hopefully.

"Of course I can. And that is all I hoped to hear, although my next question may be more difficult."

The Mayor looked worried, but recovered quickly. "All right, let's hear it."

"What plans can I look forward to for the correction of our pirate problem?"

The question dropped into the air like a thunderbolt, and Mayor Dugan began chewing his lip, brows scrunched as tightly as a knot.

"I'll give it to you straight, Mr. Rhone. I can't fight pirates without ships, and we don't have a coastal defense to help, so we're stuck. I have a port, and we keep it clear. I don't know what else we can do. If that doesn't suit your needs, then I'm afraid you'll just have to look elsewhere, but I doubt you'll find it any better anywhere else."

At least he was being honest. Stone had sensed the mayor's energy, and passed on the data. The mayor was worried, but told the truth.

"Thank you, Mr. Mayor, I appreciate your honesty. Perhaps it will all work out, and we will get past this small inconvenience."

Rhone had played his part, and learned what he'd come for. The mayor was powerless to do anything to affect the growing problem. The one thing Rhone hadn't done was to mention he was from the OPR. Why mess up even a small win?

<hr />

Hardly a week later, the Backwater Mistress rounded a cluster of small islands, and ran onto the remains of a ship floating just off the shore.

"I knew these islands were a dangerous place," Captain Black grumbled, disheartened by the scene and the future it threatened. "Too many little coves and inlets to hide in. Don't know what made their Captain run so close to 'em, but it undoubtably cost him his life. Crew too, although some may have shipped on with the rogue that did it. They do that sometimes, if they're given quarter. Better that than bein' dead, I suppose."

Rhone scanned the debris, seeing bits and pieces of crates, clothing and rigging. An oil lamp floated by, peacefully rocking upright in the gentle waves. the scene was both a bit exciting, and more than a bit scary. At least he didn't see any bodies among the debris that was once a ship.

It was no longer just gathering data for a report. It had become real.

A s Rhone entered The Common House, hoping for a quiet corner to nurse his thoughts, a harried clerk flagged him down like he was late for the coach.

"A note for you, Sir."

"A note?"

Maybe a message from Aundrea? He hadn't received word of any kind since he had arrived.

"Yes sir. It was dropped off early this morning. Not an hour after you left."

The clerk appeared relieved to have it delivered, and handed off the missive before Rhone had more than entered the building.

"Thank you," Rhone responded automatically, but when he saw the scrolled lettering on the envelope, he looked up, suddenly unsure.

"Ah, yes sir," the clerk answered, seeing his question. "It's from the Mayor's office. He requested your presence as soon as possible."

"The mayor?" Rhone asked, covering his surprise with an air of nonchalance, totally appropriate for someone of prestige receiving an unsolicited summons. He paused as in consideration. "I suppose I could find time. If you would you be so good, let him know I will make my appearance as soon as I might adequately dress for the occasion."

The harried clerk stood in horror at the thought of Rhone making the mayor wait over something as middling as clothing. Besides, he was already dressed better than anyone in the entire town.

Rhone turned for the stairway without waiting for acknowledgment. The meeting wasn't something he had expected, but it was timely.

In no hurry, Rhone eventually made his way to the mayor's office and made his presence known.

"I believe the Mayor is expecting me," Rhone declared, greeting Mrs. Randle with a patrician's dip of his head, and his young man's smile.

"The Mayor is waiting," she replied evenly. Then surreptitiously added, "But you may find him a wee bit touchy this afternoon. I am not certain he is feeling well."

"I appreciate your warning," Rhone answered, feigning a look of concern. "I will do my best to be patient."

With a quiet knock on the door, she led him into the mayor's private office.

Mayor Dugan paced the windowed wall of the wood paneled room, noting Rhone's presence with a curt nod and a condescending snort, before returning to his pacing. Abruptly he spun and started in with a monologue, not allowing Rhone much in the way of response. "I expected you to make a point of dropping in this morning, just to rub my nose in the news."

He glared at Rhone as though it was his fault, but continued before Rhone could say anything in his own defense.

"Of course it could have been pirates. It could also have been any one of ten thousand other things. They could have grounded and broken up, or their powder could have blown. Damn, they could have been rammed by a rogue whale for all we know. Just dozens of possibilities that we aren't going to go into."

Although Rhone thought he was doing a pretty good job of doing just that.

"But no, you're out playing rich and snobby, not even giving me the benefit of the doubt. Probably going around behind my back, talking me down to the Captains and crews. Perhaps even trying to place yourself in a position to take over. Oh, I've seen it all," he said, shaking his head until his wattles wobbled grotesquely. "You won't get far. I've got people, and they have my back. I'll tell you right now, I will not be dragged under the keel by some little rich kid. It isn't going to happen."

Not having been offered a chair, Rhone stood where he was, trying not to feel the insults.

The mayor finally paused for breath, but Rhone missed the opportunity for a rejoinder as the mayor suddenly started in again.

"Don't try to deny it, because I'm not listening," he fumed, waving a hand as though shooing a bothersome fly. "You even managed to redirect my own connection to your ends, keeping them from passing me information on matters of importance. So I'm telling you again. I won't have it!" He glared at Rhone in self-righteous anger. "Now what do you have to say for yourself, Master Rhone?" He purposefully used the term for young man, not the Mister he had used previously.

Rhone was no more prepared for this version of attack than he had been for the previous. Besides, he had his own position to consider, at least as far as the people of Corgy were concerned. He had learned about duels while in the city, and apparently, the higher the rank of those involved, the greater the preference for this type of, 'Repair to one's honor', as it was put. Unfortunately, he had barely learned a stroke of sword play, and didn't carry a gun. It seemed that throwing words was his only real option. *What should I do?* he silently asked Stone, his face drained of color from the shock of the mayor's words.

Find the problem, Stone said, sounding almost as concerned as Rhone felt. *This is most irrational.*

Rhone took a deep breath, allowing time to pass, as much as to clear his head. Then blowing out the lungful in a heavy sigh, he stared the mayor directly in the eye, something quite improper for someone his age.

"Are you quite done, sir?" Rhone queried. "I have no idea, what so ever, of what you are speaking of. I most certainly do not desire your position, or your title. Nor am I undermining your authority with anyone. If that is indeed occurring, it is because of your own misdealing, and not of my actions." He was feeling good about his delivery, deciding to take an offensive step to find the problem. "Obviously, things are not going well at the moment, but if you would take a seat, perhaps we can move past this rigamarole and find the real issue. In so doing, we may...and I do say, may, be able to correct the problem."

There was nothing more to say. He waited, while his feet wanted desperately to remove himself from this tyrant.

Mayor Dugan's face went red, fists clenching until Rhone heard his knuckles pop. But a moment later, his look unexpectedly eased, as perhaps his saner side took over. At least he hadn't thrown Rhone from the room.

Finally, the mayor stalked to his desk and sat heavily, clasping his long fingers together on the top. "What's your game, Rhone? I can't seem to get you figured. I've sent out for information on you, but I wasn't expecting to need it so soon." His gaze never faltered as he searched Rhone for a weakness. "I want to know what you're up to. I know you've been hangin' around that Captain Black, which surprises me. Someone of your obvious rank wanting to spend time with a low-ball creature like him, just doesn't seem right."

But Rhone wasn't going to stand there and let the Mayor talk down his new friend. "Excuse me, Mayor. My business is no business of yours, unless I am doing something illegal, or otherwise dangerous to your community. I do not see that as an issue here." Rhone truly looked regal as he stood straight-backed and tight-jawed.

But Mayor Dugan wasn't one to give up easily. Pulling his feather quill from its holder, he studied it minutely for a full minute before pointedly leveling it at Rhone, a sneer curling on his lip. "You still haven't told me what you want." Then he settled back in his chair, waiting for an answer.

Rhone worked at soothing his own feathers, thinking carefully of the words that would make, or break, his standing with the mayor, and any support for his being here. He wouldn't tell of his place with the OPR. The man obviously didn't deserve the truth, and his failures were his own.

Take it back to the pirates, Stone said slyly. *They are the real problem, not you, or him.*

Rhone couldn't agree more, *I like it,* he silently replied, unable to control the slight muscle pull of a smile.

"What is it?" the Mayor rasped irritably.

Rhone inclined his head regally, and took a seat without being offered one. "Mayor Dugan, we need to take this battle to the pirates, not each other. I can guarantee, I have done none of the things you are so adamantly accusing me of. None, but I do have a thought that would remove our disagreement forthwith."

The Mayor looked both suspicious and dubious, but perhaps intrigued too. "What is it, Rhone? Tell me what you've got up your sleeve, because I'm not interested in theatrics or game-playing."

Rhone's posture relaxed now that he was in control. "I want your permission to fight the pirates."

"You what!" The words burst from the mayor, and Stone, at the same time. The mayor's were almost a laugh. "You kid? You want to fight pirates? Oh wait, I get it. Like a penny novel, with pirates and brigands, and you'll be the hero. And get yourself killed!" He almost bellowed the last words, heat flaming back in a mere moment. "Next, your dad will come looking for me, wanting to know if I have any control at all over what goes on around here. He could probably get The Council to remove me too. That's the way with the big-and-mighty." His hands made a set of air-quotes to make his point. "You go about doing whatever you want, and everyone else gets the blame. Well it ain't gonna happen. Not in my town."

The mayor puffed like a bull ready to charge, but Rhone sat unfazed as he answered.

"Yes, I for one, would like to do what I can, and I will be sure to remove any blame from your head. But I do intend to find a way, with, or without your approval."

The Mayor's eyes closed to slits. "How do you plan on doing all that without a ship? Or are you planning to use Captain Black's little shoe skate? The Backwater Mistress isn't big enough to tackle a squall, let alone a pirate brigand and his horde. You'd be lost before you even get into firing range. Oh, she's fast all right. I'll give her that, but a single ball would splinter her to kindling."

Seeing the concern growing in Rhone's eyes, the mayor dealt his final punch.

"Don't believe it? Just go ask the good captain. He'll tell you the truth of it. And if you do try something unbelievably stupid, I'll have you arrested and brought up on charges so fast, your head will swim. Now get out of here. I've got a town to run."

The interview was over. Dugan picked up a stack of papers, patently ignoring Rhone as he began to read.

Rhone rose and gave a curt bow. "Thank you for your time, Mr. Mayor. Until we meet again."

"Not likely," came the growl, eyes never leaving the papers.

Angry with himself, Rhone paced the entire length of Corgy's docks before his mind cleared enough to look up. Pulling himself together, his flustered gaze centered on a large warehouse standing at the very end of town, its old faded sign precariously hung above the barn-like doorway. The sign was so weathered he couldn't make out the name, but even from here the place smelled absolutely awful. Rhone rubbed at his nose from the stench, but at least it would take his mind off the mayor. Hesitantly he stepped into the shadowy entrance.

Within moments, he tugged the almost dainty handkerchief from his pocket, holding it to his nose as he waved his other hand through the putrid air, hoping for a clearer breath.

"This place stinks," he exclaimed to no one in particular.

Unexpectedly, a snarling reply answered from the dark interior. "What were you expecting? Perfume? That part comes later."

Rhone peered cautiously into the building to see who had spoken. His search found not only a balding man standing just inside the shaded warehouse, but the body of a huge whale drawn up onto the slime-drenched wood of the sloping deck. Workers clambered up and down the poor creature's sides, laying open the thick meat with heavy cleavers, as they filleted entire slabs of blubber from the bones. Giant meat hooks then snagged each section, lifting them out and over to a huge cauldron, where it was rendered down into oil. While the scene was ghastly, it was also fascinating. The massive carcass was being systematically dismembered, from the outside in, with every piece being used in one way or another.

Rhone's interest was drawn to the flow of entrails spilling out onto the decking. He was so curious that he simply walked in, until he was standing alongside the enormous creature.

The balding man followed, offering an introduction of sorts. "I'm the owner here." Then almost without interest, asked, "Whatcha lookin' for?" He was here to sell, and if somebody wanted to buy, the reason really didn't matter. With Rhone's look of an aristocrat, the man had simply followed the power, as any knowing person would.

But the question brought Rhone to the realization of how closely he stood to the leviathan, and stepped back a pace. "I apologize, good sir. I am not normally quite so intrusive, but I must say, I was not expecting such an extraordinary find, and no two ways about it. Simply incredible."

"Yup, quite a sight ain't she? Now, you just buyin' a look, or lookin' to buy? We got work to do around here."

"Sorry for any inconvenience," Rhone apologized, tipping his head in salutation. With one last inquisitive glance, he carefully made his way up the slippery planking.

The man looked a little confused by the formalities, but took it in stride. "No problem. But if you're ever lookin' for whale oil, you know where to come." His hooded eyes showed sadness at missing a sale, but it paid to be polite to the gentry.

With the long walk and the intriguing stop at the whale cutters, Rhone's mood had eased, and he set his steps back toward town. When he came to The Backwater Mistress tied in her usual berth, he saw Captain Black standing at the bow, supervising the men at work on the windlass that held the anchor chain.

"Captain, might I come aboard?" Rhone called.

The captain peered suspiciously over the rail, but seeing Rhone, waved a greeting. "Mister Rhone, my friend, come on aboard. Absolutely come aboard, and would you be caring for some refreshment? I myself am as dry as a bone with all the shouting it takes to get things done. Lazy crew I tell you. Almost ready to get rid of 'em all, and do it myself." His woeful nod merely acknowledged his defeat.

Rhone barely covered his sputtered laugh when a crewman rolled his eyes.

"Tell me captain," Rhone said, throwing a jest of his own, "do you plan on climbing the rigging, and hoist the sails yourself, or am I missing something here?"

With an offended look, Captain Black blurted a reply. "I'll let you know, I spent my youth climbing rigging, and probably pulled a good twenty miles of lines and halyards. Why my hands got so worn, you could nigh-on see through 'em."

It was the captain's puppy-dog pout that got past Rhone's final reserve, and with honest laughter he replied, "But not recently I'm guessing."

The crew was barely controlling their own mirth, until Captain Black righteously demanded, "And what are you laughing about?" glowering at his crew. "Every word is the gospel truth. I swear it."

Instantly, the grinning crew turned studiously back to their work, and Rhone remembered his reason for being here. "I have no doubt Captain, but if you have a moment more, I would have a word with you."

His words must have held something of seriousness, as Captain Black raised an eyebrow. "Certainly, sir. We'll take coffee on the bridge." Turning to his first mate he ordered, "See see we're not disturbed."

"Aye, Captain. Good as done," and made off at speed to accomplish the deed.

"Now, what's this about?" the captain said with concern. "I've got a bad feeling."

CHAPTER 14

Trouble in Paradise

"I am quite serious, Miss Bella. I need a guide. Someone who knows the area. Consider how it would look if I head out by myself and get lost, and you have to admit that I asked for your assistance?"

Rhone gave her a wide-eyed look of innocence, which was actually pretty honest, although he was just hoping for an afternoon with a friend.

"Mr. Rhone, You know it would be inappropriate. We hardly know each other, and we would be alone. With you part of the upper-crust and all, why, I'd most likely be flayed, and rightly so."

"Not at all," Rhone denied expansively. "I simply wouldn't permit such a thing. Besides, we're only going for a picnic, and I've already requested a basket." At her unconvinced look he continued, "As I'm required to see more of the country, I thought it would be a swell time if you could come along and show me the sights. You do know your way around, don't you?" he asked, almost as a challenge.

"Of course I know my way around," she fumed. "I've lived here my entire life."

"As I thought. So who better to know what and where?" Having made up his mind, Rhone gave her no further out. "I will pick you up at eleven, if you're available. But I already know you're off duty, given the shift schedule on the wall."

His look of satisfaction was only matched by Bella's barely controlled ire, that slowly dissipated into dutiful acceptance. While she wasn't smiling, she was at least answering with a modicum of control.

"All right, Mr. Rhone. I will guide you for the day's outing. But there will be no...extension of my services. None, and nothing. Do I make myself understood?"

He seemed to mull over the idea, as she glared at him a few seconds longer.

"I'm not certain what you are expecting of me, my lady, but I am going for a picnic, and you will be guiding me." He liked the feel of winning.

Though hot under the collar at being handled so smoothly, Bella knew it really would be fun. She hadn't been on a picnic since her thirteenth birthday, and that was years ago. Finally dropping her pretense of fighting, she nodded agreement. "All right, but pick me up at the back entrance, at ten. Maybe it won't make the headlines that way."

Rhone gave a respectable nod, "Until ten," as his mind shouted, *Yessss!*

Exasperated by his nonchalance, Bella asked, "If you could tell me exactly what you're looking for, it might help in finding it."

Rhone had rented the little buckboard rig from the stables for a very reasonable price, and Blue seemed happy pulling the light load. They sat comfortably side by side on the springboard seat, driving up the rutted road out of town and into the hills. Unfortunately, Bella had asked a very reasonable question.

"I certainly think there should be water," Rhone answered, nodding wisely as his mind raced. Since he wasn't really looking for anything, he couldn't give her an accurate answer, but unless he came up with something more coherent, she was going to figure it out far too soon. "Not ocean though. I believe a lake or a stream would do. Fresh water will of course be a requirement."

He certainly couldn't tell her he was just happy to be out for a ride with her, and quietly thanked Stone again for the picnic idea. Social customs were a pain, and didn't make much sense as far as he was concerned. But they were what they were, and he was here on a job, not, as Stone kept reminding him, for the dating scene.

She gave him an appraising look, wondering again at his motives. "Water, okay. Just water, or are there other things about this location we're looking for?"

"Yes, of course," he said, as though trying to eliminate obvious elements. "Not totally flat, and at least some of it needs trees. Other than that, I am fairly open in my discretion."

Personally, he thought he was sounding quite confident on the issue, but Bella didn't look all that impressed.

"Water, with some trees, and not totally flat. You certainly drive a hard bargain, Mr. Rhone. I don't think we will be able to fulfill that request, with anything other than every single section of land in the county. Are you serious, or just simple?" She was actually trying to decide, but as soon as the words came out, she blanched, realizing how they sounded.

While surprised, Rhone didn't take offense. He was getting use to her scratchy personality. Putting on an amused smile, he said, "Well, probably both actually. I am looking for something that fulfills those requirements, and I really don't know what else it will entail. I am, of course, still looking."

Resigned, Bella sighed. "All right. Water, trees and land, but you're not making this easy." Then, with an almost surprised look, she brightened. "Actually, a place just came to mind, and one of my favorite spots, although I haven't been there for years. How much time do we have? It's a few miles out."

"Sounds good, and I have no time requirement," Rhone responded cheerfully. Then glancing at her, asked, "As long as you don't."

"I'm fine, as long as we're back before dark."

He even received a smile. Unfortunately, her thoughts were of seeing the lovely place again, not of him.

It really was lovely. The rutted road ran past a small lake, fronted by a grassy meadow. Mounds of blackberry bushes grew along one side, with treed hills forming behind it, cradling the lake into a corner. The entire thing looked out over hills that rolled gently down to sharply-defined cliffs dropping to the ocean's edge.

Rhone sat in awe. "This is absolutely gorgeous. How did you know of it?"

"We would come here on weekends," Bella answered, appreciating his obvious joy in the place. Somehow, it almost made him a real person. "I was just a kid then, so I'm sorry it's grown over so much."

"Doesn't look overgrow to me," Rhone said easily. "I'm used to desert rock and dry grass. This looks great."

Stone's rumbling vibration gave a soft warning, before his silent words ran through Rhone's mind. *Careful what you say. No need to get her in trouble, telling more than she needs to know.*

They had been through this before, and Stone was right. Rhone held his tongue, not saying more, simply pleased she was talking to him again. Working the reigns, he pulled the buckboard off the rutted track and stopped in the shade. Bella hadn't said anything further, which, Rhone thought, might be better than another caustic rejoinder. She tended to ramp up her heat whenever she disagreed with him, which was often, but at the moment she was peacefully quiet.

As Bella sat quietly looking at the beautiful reflection of the cloud-filled sky on the still water, Rhone climbed down and reached into the back for the basket. When she was finally ready, he was there, hand out to assist.

Bella's brows gathered, at him thinking her incapable of doing herself, but his actions were so genteel she really couldn't find fault. Taking his hand, she stepped down as Rhone dipped his head.

"Milady, why don't you pick a spot while I unhitch Blue. I don't think he'll mind a chance to graze."

She could hardly complain. "Thank you, Rhone, I think I can manage that much." She had meant it as a rebuff, but by the time it came out, she was smiling.

As Rhone took care of the horse, Bella reveled in the sun's warmth, releasing even more of her anxiety. It really was as beautiful as she remembered. After a moment or two absorbing the sun, she took a deep satisfied breath, and began spreading the blanket. Once smoothed to her liking, she went back for the wicker basket, gasping silently as she bent to pick up. The basket must have weighed thirty pounds, maybe more. If she had asked The Common House kitchen for a picnic basket, she would have received leftovers, and would have been perfectly content. She was a girl after all, and hired help, but Rhone's basket was something totally different. She vaguely wondered if they really expected him to eat it all, and tried not to be jealous.

Hauling the loaded basket to the blanket, she flipped back the wicker lid and began digging under the linen covering. The top layer held plates and goblets, silverware, embroidered napkins, and a huge carving knife. Her quirky smile came without thought, as she realized she now had a weapon if needed. Below that was an entire section dedicated to meats. A haunch of beef, a shoulder of lamb, and an entire game hen stuffed with diced breads, celery, and apple, baked with enough butter that it was practically dripping. Then came a half loaf of fresh bread, a crock of butter and a chunk of hard cheese. But it was the smell of an apple pie with its crisscrossed crust that had her mouth watering. In the very bottom of the basket, packed in their own bedding of sawdust, lay an entire layer of bottles. Ginger beer, lemonade, cider and red wine waited at his desire. No wonder the basket weighed so much, and he had only asked for a picnic. She could have lived for two entire weeks off of this much food. He was of the gentry of course, and they had their own ways, but that still didn't make it fair.

When Rhone walked up brushing dust from his jacket sleeve, Bella had to school herself not to frown over the inequity of it all. But it wasn't his fault, probably. At least they would eat well.

"This looks like a real feast," Rhone said, appraising the items she laid on the blanket.

His obvious surprise at least made Bella feel a little better.

"I hope you're hungry," she said, making a space for him on the blanket. "but you should have had it catered. Then we wouldn't have to pack it all up after." The snarky reply slipped out as her normal spunk returned.

He grinned, enjoying her banter. "You said you came all the way out here to fish? Was it with your family, or did you come out on dates?"

"Sir?" Bella responded, shocked he would even ask such a thing.

So much for their smoothing things out.

But Rhone quickly covered for his error. "You said you came here to fish. Was it with your family?"

She appeared nervous, wondering how to skirt any deeper discussions of her past, and slowly tried again. "Yes, when I was young, my family would come here when we could. This is where my dad taught me to fish. Mom wasn't all that happy about me learning, but it made Da happy. Me too I guess, since it makes me smile to think about it."

Listening to her made Rhone happy. He could almost picture her running along the bank, pole in hand, laughing and scaring all the fish in the pond.

"I bet your dad was happy to teach you. I never had a dad to teach me."

It was obviously the wrong thing to say, as Bella's brows knit in confusion. "You mean, your dad never taught you."

Rhone, what are you doing? Stone rattled in his mind. *Get your story together, or there is going to be trouble.*

Realizing his goof, Rhone's mind searched for ideas, but sinking into the ground didn't seem plausible. He finally came out with a vague excuse. "Yeah, he never had time, and I doubt he even knew how himself."

He knew he was a terrible liar. Already Bella was drawing back, intuitively knowing something was wrong.

"Mr. Rhone," she began, fiddling with the lunch. "I believe we will need to eat and start our way back. I do not intend to be caught out after dusk."

Things could have been worse, but the joy of the moment had gone. Nodding, Rhone guiltily tore a leg from the chicken, inspecting it as though he didn't know what it was. Then he came to a decision.

"Bella...," he started, but stopped, as Stone's panicked voice cut into his beleaguered mind.

Rhone, what are you doing?

"I am going to tell her the truth," he stated aloud, then watched as Bella's expression turned from question, to real concern, and a feeling of hopelessness began to flow from his collar.

Growing uneasy from the two-sided reproof, Rhone lay the chicken leg on a plate before wiping his hands with the embroidered napkin. "Miss Bella, I have a few things I need to clear off my conscience."

As Bella's growing confusion edged towards fear, she gathered her skirts, readying for a more rapid departure. She was alone, miles from anyone. No matter what Rhone did, his position would bear him out, while her words would do little but bring condemnation for attempting to attach herself above her station. Slowly she began to put things away, obviously no longer waiting until they had eaten.

"Wait," Rhone pleaded. "I need to talk to you." With hopeful eyes he waited for the worst.

At least his quiet waiting eased the worry lines on her face. This wasn't the look of a vicious man, or one hoping for illicit activities. It was more the look of a hurt little boy.

Bella stopped her cleanup and knelt, smoothing out her skirt before lifting her chin with defiance. "I will give you five minutes, then we will pack and leave. Best make good use of your time, sir." Resolutely she awaited his words.

Rhone gave a thankful breath and a half-hearted smile, wondering how he was going to fix things.

Best start from the beginning, Stone stated in resignation. *Since you are heading into deep water, it would seem better to dive, than to fall.*

Which really wasn't much help.

Thanks, Stone, Rhone sent to his friend. *How did I manage without you?* His woeful smile was for Stone, but it worked for both.

Not sure what was going on, Bella stubbornly restated her position. "You only have five minutes, so if you are going to say something, you had best get it done."

Rhone nodded, beginning to chew his lip as his mind went into overtime. But when she suddenly began gathering her skirts again, he bleated out for her understanding.

"Bella, I am an agent with the Office of Public Recrimination, and I'm here on an assignment. Please listen."

She stopped, although poised as though ready to run, and finally turned to face him, fists to hips. Belligerently she asked, "Why should I believe this story? Your last was at least more believable."

With all the sincerity he could muster, he answered, "Bella, I'm playing a part. It's my assignment. My very first one after graduating. I don't know a lot about how it works, but I'm not lying." He was so overwrought at hurting her, he began to say it all over again. "It's my job. I know it sounds stupid, but it's true."

"So, you're an agent," she said, mulling it over and not quite sold yet. But she didn't leave. "Pretty young for an agent aren't you? You're no older than I am."

"Yeah, I know," he said in resignation. "That's another story, but I could tell you if you want?"

His hope went up a notch as her forehead wrinkled in thought.

"If you're an agent, then why are you here? There isn't much in Corgy to draw the government's attention."

Rhone's heart soared, realizing she was at least willing to listen.

"At first I thought Aundrea, my boss, sent me here for an easy assignment. But when I got here, I found out about the pirate problem. I'm not sure if that's the real purpose for me being here, but as long as I'm in Corgy, it's my job to find out what I can, and fix it. If it's good for the people, it's good for the government. That's our motto," Rhone said proudly.

For the first time, Bella looked like she was beginning to believe. "It sounds pretty farfetched," she reasoned aloud, "but nobody would come up with something that dumb on purpose." She let out a long slow breath as she made her decision. "I guess I need to hear the rest, and we should probably eat some of this food too. It would be a horrible waste to let it go bad. Would you like some ginger beer or cider?"

While it wasn't exactly a smile, her face had softened with her thoughtful look. Maybe the day wouldn't be a total disaster.

B ella sat, legs outstretched on the blanket, listening to Rhone's account as he reconstructed his confrontation.

"You actually told Mayor Dugan you were going to fight pirates, whether he helped or not? I don't think I could ever do something like that. I can hardly face my own boss, let alone the Mayor." Then guiltily realized, she did indeed have that very problem. "How were you planning to do it without a ship? And honestly, it would probably take several to round up and destroy all the pirates."

While he couldn't disagree, he also didn't want to admit it.

"Somebody has to do it, and I don't see any other volunteers standing in line. But yes, the boat is a problem." He frowned, thinking through his options. "I have some discretionary funds, but it wouldn't come close to buying a ship. Even then, I don't really know how to command one. I'm taking lessons with Captain Black, but it only showed me how little I know." With a huff of mild frustration, he realized just how far he was from a valid idea.

Bella squinted into the bright sun, before asking, "Would you like to walk a bit? My backside's getting numb sitting here." Then she blushed at sounding so common, and tried to cover her slip. "There's another little ponding just over the lip of the hill. I thought you might like to see it while we're here."

"Sure, I'm game," Rhone replied, grateful to be rescued from his own thoughts.

Climbing to his feet, he offered Bella a hand up, and with Blue chomping placidly in the deep grass, they walked side by side around the edge of the lake and over the low hill. Just beyond was indeed another ponding of water, but much smaller, and covered with green scum. While it may not have been a calm, clear lake like the one where they had picnicked, it was an active place, full of life. Tall grasses grew up through the thick muck as flocks of birds flitted about, hanging onto the willowy grasses or snatching up insects as they dove in barely-seen patterns over the scummy green water.

"I'm not sure I want to go for a swim," Rhone commented dryly, "but it is pretty in its own way."

Bella nodded her agreement. "I'm afraid it smells too, so we didn't come over here much."

"It smells?"

She nodded, wrinkling her nose cutely. "It does. Just watch. Sometimes the green coating lifts like a big bubble, and pops. You can hear them at night when it's quiet, but it's probably too noisy right now."

Rhone thought the spot was perfectly quiet, especially after having spent his recent time in the big city, but listening carefully, heard the birds singing and the chirp of insects, making a constant musical backdrop to the scene.

"Bubbles?" he began with interest. "I never saw a lake that makes bubbles, but I've never seen a lake covered with so much green either. Is there water down there or just swamp muck?"

"Oh, there's water," Bella said knowingly. "The slimy stuff grows on top, but the water's clear beneath it. There are fish too."

He watched as she stepped carefully through the tall grasses, skirt lifted to boot tops. The day hadn't turned out so bad after all.

CHAPTER 15

Mountainous Waves aren't Actually Mountains

Corgy's pirate problems grew at an alarming rate, until no captain wanted to head out by themselves. Most hired on extra men, or formed up as convoys, working to simply outnumber the thieves. Still, almost weekly, a ship limped in from an attack, or wreckage was found floating on the waves.

Mayor Dugan could do nothing. He didn't have a navy, or even an armed ship to use for an escort. All he managed was to simmer in anger.

Rhone made a point to stay away from him, but it was a small town, and the fact that they both spent a good deal of time at The Common House didn't help either.

Bella did her best to stay on a professional level with Rhone, but their day together had changed a lot of things. It just seemed correct to exchange comments as they passed, or when she served him at his table, but he couldn't understand why she was grumpy so often, or her flashes of frustration.

After all, he had his own frustrations to deal with, and while he was living quite comfortably, he wasn't getting anything done as far as his assignment. Even his letters to Aundrea was merely passing on data about the problem, but nothing about fixing it.

"I don't know what to do, and I'm getting bored waiting," Rhone complained, playing with his fork as Bella laid out his breakfast dishes. "What do you suggest?" He didn't mind sharing his problems.

Bella made a wry face as she rebalanced the heaping plate of fried pota- toes she was juggling. Her other hand slid the cup full of coffee with its saucer onto the table, all done without spilling a drop or crumb. It was no more than she did every day, for every customer, but with him just sitting there nonchalantly waiting, her building ire, never far beneath the surface, began to boil.

Sensing her growing mood, Rhone attempted to help by reaching for the cup. "Here, let me take that," he said, flashing her a smile. "I'd just as soon not wear it."

But Bella's piercing blue eyes sharpened to slits as she grated out a sharp reply. "Why thank you, Mr. Rhone. I appreciate your help more than you could possibly imagine. Unless you can imagine the entire plateful of potatoes in your lap." The tight line of her lips dared him to make another inane comment.

Somewhat startled, Rhone tried to figure out what he had said wrong, but it was just the Bella he had come to know. Always a bit on the sharp side of almost anything he said. Still, he enjoyed their few times together, as she worked almost constantly, and he didn't at all.

But as with other things, Bella seemed to have forgotten the issue already. "Why don't you go see Captain Black today? I'm sure he wouldn't mind having you, and at least you'd be down where you can hear any news from ships coming in."

"That's a great idea. Thank you, Miss Bella," Rhone said regally, still playing his part.

Careful with her response, as being rude to so distinguished a customer was certainly grounds for dismissal, Bella covered her glare with faked politeness. "I'm glad I could be of assistance, sir. And will there be anything else?"

But Rhone saw right through it, for once enjoying his position of power. "Too bad you don't have the day off," he commented casually. "It looks like it is going to be beautiful once the fog burns off."

With lips already in a tight line of aggravation, she tried to think of a descent way to respond, finally answering with a less than sincere smile. "I'm sorry too, but at least some of us have to work."

She could have left then, but even though aggravating, their combative camaraderie was more fun than gathering the dirty dishes from other tables. With calculated insolence, she turned away, saying, "I'm terribly busy right now, so I might not make it back to refill your cup. Enjoy."

Her quick snipe left Rhone an odd feeling, but this was how it always ended. He would get in trouble for something he said, and she would stomp off, full of righteous indignation. His slow shrug wasn't much of an answer, only acknowledging that girls were odd creatures.

Luckily, the food, and the thought of heading to the docks, perked up his mood.

The tap room of The Common House was dark and elegantly furnished, especially for a small harbor town like Corgy, offering a more private, intimate setting than the main dining area and common rooms. Bella would never have chosen it as a meeting place with the mayor. In fact, she would rather not meet with him at all. Feeling trapped, even though he was seated and she was standing, Bella tried to hide her discomfort. He had called, and she was required to respond.

"Yes, Mr Mayor. Is there something I can get for you?" Her half-hearted smile hoped that was all he wanted.

"No. Nothing. I believe we have some business to attend to, and as I will not be in the office for a few days, I thought this a convenient time."

It might have been convenient for him, but obviously non-relevant that Bella was on duty.

With a shallow curtsy she answered, "Certainly, sir, but I'm not sure what I can offer?" almost blushing as she realized her response may not have been well thought. At least being at work made her safe from some propositions, and she released a sigh in thankfulness.

Not having noticed her chagrin, Mayor Dugan took time to clip and light a cigar, drawing in the noxious fumes before artfully exhaling a plume that changed shape as it drifted across the room, slowly to dissipate and mix with the odors of leather, oiled wood and liquor.

It was their second meeting, and Bella felt her stomach churn.

Captain Black seemed eager to show off his new toy, beaming affably as he asked, "Care to try the new swivel gun?"

Rhone greedily eyed the shiny brass mini-canon, newly mounted since his last appearance. The gun's heavy barrel hung in a unique metal harness, balanced to allow it to swing up and down, as well as back and forth. The polished brass made it deceptively beautiful for a tool of destruction.

"You'd let me shoot it?" Rhone asked in surprise. "I'd need instruction."

"No problem. All the boys need training, and since you never know who's going to be around it when need comes, it's best they all know. You might as well learn right along with 'em."

"I would be honored, Captain. It was indeed good timing that I came down this morning."

He didn't mention Bella's telling him to come. Some things were personal.

The captain nodded his acceptance of all things timely. "Got a keg of powder and some shot delivered this morning. We'll head out to deep water and give it a try. Even had the boys grab a few old crates for target practice, just to see how good a shot you are."

It sounded fine to Rhone. He doubted he would hit anything, but it was better to miss with a group, where everyone was having fun.

The Mistress drove at an angle into the sharp breeze, the oncoming waves sending spray far up the sides and drifting back in a fine mist. Rhone was getting used to the feel now, the mist cooling his windburned face as he stood watching the horizon. The push and pull of wind and sea thrilled him as they sailed away from the coastline, but the memory of the captain explaining how their low sides could take on water in heavy seas kept him nervous. Even so, the low sides were worth the risk, allowing oars to be run out if the wind died, or if they needed maneuvering in the tight confines of the harbor. Other ships only had oars on their small captain's gigs, used to ferry men to shore when they were anchored.

"Captain Black, sir," Rhone asked, taking the moment to gain information. "If we were to be attacked by pirates, what would you do? I know we're fast, but would you set for action, or just run?" He felt the Captain's calculating eye scour him to the core.

"Gettin' pretty worked up, aren't you?" the captain growled, scowling deeply at the possibility of being called a coward.

Rhone shrugged noncommittally, beginning to pace the quarterdeck in restless agitation. "Sir, I don't know the first thing about fighting. Even less than sailing. So what I mean is, what would I do if I was being attacked by pirates? I figured, you already have some pretty good ideas on the issue, so why should I piece something together that has already been done?"

The captain took his time, looking Rhone up and down as if searching for something. Maybe it was manhood, or the ability to lead. It was hard to tell, but the close scrutiny made Rhone's cheeks warm.

"Come, have a seat," Captain Black said, patting one the empty chairs just set out by a crewman. "We need some talkin'." With pursed lips, he leaned forward and stared at Rhone, as though reading his soul. Apparently having made up his mind, and using slightly less volume than he would in a gale, the captain gave his verdict. "So you want to fight pirates."

Relieved, Rhone nodded with sincerity.

"Well, I suppose, thinking something ahead of time is better than thinking about it too late," Captain Black stated, his grin making his wiry beard stick out like thorns on a cactus. "So I'll tell you straight. The best plan I know is: don't get caught, and you won't lose." He chuckled, liking his own words.

Rhone could see the truth of it, even if it wasn't very satisfying. "But, what if you were forced to fight? What tactics would you use? There must be something that works."

The captain bobbed his head thoughtfully. "There are ways," he agreed. "But mainly, you gotta see the entire picture of what's happening, and not get frozen into one particular element of the attack. If you could see the fight, as from a bird's eye flying over, you could plot it out as it develops. Often times, a person sees one move, but misses what the first prophesied. You gotta understand, each action sets up the next. If you could see everything ahead of time, you could probably figure a way to be somewhere else, and not in the place where it all goes south. If you get my meaning." He watched Rhone's eyes, looking for the spark of understanding.

Rhone thought through the process, segment by segment, feeling Stone doing the same thing in the background.

It makes absolute sense, Stone murmured thoughtfully. *It is something I should have observed myself. If you know the outcome, you merely need to change the cause. Very elementary, but I can see it taking an entire career to perfect.*

"Ah ha, you understand," Captain Black commented, watching as a tight smile finally overcame Rhone's drawn brows. "It is the one thing that makes a good captain great. Some can do it, and others never get the concept. If you can just stay ahead of the game, you have a good chance to win."

"Now, if I could just see it with a real bird's-eye view, it would be a lot easier," Rhone added with a mischievous grin.

"Aye, that it would," the captain nodded in agreement. "Wouldn't it be great to fly over an action, before you engaged? You could hardy lose." He cackled merrily, raising his cup in a salute. "To our newest captain. Maybe we could call you, Flyboy, or Captain Cloud..."

Or, Bird Brain, Stone threw in.

Rhone barely managed to contain his eye roll as Captain Black moved on with the discussion.

"Yep, It's definitely a good way to see the problem, but you still need to deliver when the time comes."

"I get it. Just seeing, isn't going to win a fight."

"Right enough. Now, there's a few other concepts to master. For starters, don't get caught in a broadside, and hold the weather gage."

Rhone's obvious stall was enough for the Captain to explain the term. "Stay on the upwind side of the action, and you steal their wind. Leaves them unable to maneuver."

"But that's cheating," Rhone said, aghast at the concept.

"Shoot, it's not cheating if you're the one being attacked. It's good common sense, and a way to stay ahead of the game. Dang it boy." Captain Black was heating up to his topic now, and gave Rhone a wary eye. "Are you just wantin' to get in a fight, or are you fighting to win?"

Rhone had never considered the difference. To him, a fight was a fight.

Seeing his thoughtfulness, the captain leaned on an elbow and asked, "Have you ever been bullied? Ever get beat up? It's scary. Nothing like fighting in a boxing ring."

His words had taken on a hard edge, and Rhone wondered if there was something behind them.

"There's no rules. Just survival," the captain continued. "You fight to win, because losing may truly be your life, or your family's."

Rhone took time to swallow before responding. "I can see the difference. If I was being attacked, my following rules they weren't, would only help them win."

"There you go," the captain beamed proudly, slapping his meaty thigh. "Hit it right on the noggin."

This was serious stuff, but Rhone couldn't help his grin. He was beginning to see just how dangerous the game could be.

"Captain, could you diagram a few possible winning scenarios on paper? I'm pretty new to all this sailing stuff, but at least I know enough to know how much I don't know.

The captain's chortle agreed with every syllable of his twist of words.

CHAPTER 16

On to Other Things

The back steps to The Common House were well-placed for catching the evening sun. Even better, they were out of view of the street. Rhone sat next to Bella, giving a rundown of his morning aboard The Backwater Mistress.

"Captain Black was good enough to draw out a few attack scenarios," Rhone said, with a bit of superiority in his voice. "I actually think I'm beginning to understand his concepts."

Interested, Bella looked over the sketches, intuitively noting each vessel's advantages. "This isn't so hard. I thought it would be some crazy play-book, with symbols and notations only an admiral could understand."

"You understand it?" Rhone asked in surprise. "I think I got the basics, but even that took me awhile."

Bella looked up quizzically, trying to decide if he was joking. Her look of, 'You couldn't figure this out?' spoke loudly enough she didn't need to say the words.

"Yeah, well, I did have some problems with some of it," he admitted, mentally blaming it on his lack of education. "I could see my own maneuvers just fine. But I get lost thinking what someone else might be doing."

Bella nodded. "It must be the gentleman in you," she said graciously. "If you wouldn't do it, you wouldn't expect someone else to. That could definitely get in the way in a fight. I saw a real fight once, and they didn't fight fair at all. They kicked, and bit, and threw dirt. It would have been funny, except they both got hurt. The whole thing was dumb, but the rest of the guys were all excited, saying what a great fight it was."

Rhone nodded thoughtfully. "You're good at this stuff," wondering how he had gotten so lucky as to run into her in a little town like Corgy. "Too bad you're a girl."

He meant it in support, but quickly learned his error.

Bella's eyes flashed like fire as she scrambled to her feet, fists on hips, glaring daggers at him. "And what's the matter with me being a girl?" It was less a question than a verdict. "I know things, and I am good at them too. Maybe not as a waitress," she conceded, "but I do know how to fish. I hunted too. My dad used to say I could shoot the eye out of a potato. Can you do that?"

Rhone flinched at her heat. "I never shot a potato," he said meekly, trying to lower the sudden tension, "but I did manage to hit a crate today with a swivel gun."

Eyes still flashing, Bella let him know exactly what she thought. "I'm serious Rhone. I'm good at this stuff, but nobody would even consider me. It's totally dumb. If I'm good at something, I should be allowed to do it. Who said, just because I'm a girl, I can't do things. Times are changing, just you watch."

Rhone wasn't sure either way, but he wasn't going to say so. He wasn't the one in charge of what girls did, or didn't do. He just knew they looked nice, but was also pretty sure she wouldn't want to hear that right now. For perhaps the first time in his life, he was glad he hadn't grown up around girls.

"I didn't do it," he said, raising his hands in mock defense. "Well, I did hit the crate, but I didn't say anything about not wanting girls to do things. I grew up with my mom, and we did everything together. There was no one else."

Bella's glare lost most of its heat, finally changing to a soft frown. "Sorry, I guess I got a little carried away," she said, dropping back to the step in a dramatic slump. "But it's just so unfair. I would rather be out on the ship with you. I hate being stuck here, catering to everyone's wants. And it's just wants. Nobody actually needs anything."

It was odd, but Rhone understood. He had been stuck in a life just as void as anything she could see in front of her, but had gotten out. By accident, yes, but he had gotten away. Now Bella was stuck here without a future for herself, other than waiting tables, and only if she didn't get fired first.

Seeing her defeat, Rhone tried to lighten the mood. "So you're a crack shot? Got to be better than me. I managed to hit the crate today, but only because the gun was loaded with grape. I must have missed a half-dozen times with the waves tossing it around."

Bella smiled ruefully, recognizing his attempt to ease her hot temper. "At least you got to shoot at it," she said in resignation. "I'll never get the chance."

Rhone slid in beside her as he worked at a thought, then brightened.

"Since you're so gung-ho good at understanding these sheets, why don't you try explaining them to me? I could use a few more pointers."

She sighed and leaned on an elbow, gesturing with the crumpled pages still in her fist. "Okay, but you should probably smooth those out a bit or I might get seasick just looking at all their waves." With the tension broken, she actually smiled.

Grinning, Rhone smoothed out the crumpled sheets and settled himself more comfortably on the wooden step.

"It all comes down to controlling the wind," Bella said, taking on her school teacher's tone. "Those who control the wind, win."

Rhone nodded, already enjoying her lecture. Changing positions slightly, he not only got a better look at the sheets, but ended up closer to her.

Keep your mind on her words, not her looks, Stone warned. *And you had best pay attention. There will be a test after.* Not only was Stone an implacable chaperone, he wanted to hear what she had to say.

"Great," Rhone grumbled to himself, but he did focus a bit more.

Unfortunately, Bella had stopped mid-sentence. "You said something?"

Caught, again, Rhone tried to pull himself out of hot water. "Ahh, Great perfume you're wearing. I like it." Which he thought was a pretty good come back.

But she looked at him curiously. "Dish water and table scraps? I'm not wearing perfume. I don't waste it coming to work."

"It must be you," he said, shrugging eloquently. Then quickly changed subjects. "Don't stop. I was just beginning to understand."

Bella's face still held questions, but she let them drop as she finished her lecture. "So, by controlling the wind, and your position, you force your opponent into predictable moves."

"Got it!" Rhone said, slapping his knee just as Captain Black had. "It's like the captain was telling me. If you know what the other guy's going to do, you're one step ahead of him."

"He said that?" Bella asked in surprise. "He said it better than me. But he's probably been in lots of fights, while I just fight boredom."

Rhone laughed at her dismal tone, then solidly bumped shoulders with her, purposefully tipping her off balance.

Incredulous, Bella righted herself before demanding, "What was that for?" Then primly settled herself with an added lilt to her voice. "Just because I'm better at this, is no reason to be a bully." She tried not to smile, and almost succeeded.

Rhone was rather pleased with his move, and simply shrugged. "Captain Black also said, if you plan on winning, don't plan on being a gentleman." With a wicked grin, he added, "I suppose that means, I won."

His moment of satisfaction was quickly broken as Bella flung herself at him, attempting to regain her position on the step. She would have done pretty well in a flyweight division match, but against Rhone, she simply ended up wrestling.

Until the door opened behind them.

"Miss Bella!"

Bringing their joy to a screeching halt.

R hone watched as the sea battle raged far below. His lofty position made it difficult to see through the billowing cannon smoke and whips of clouds, but when he saw the first ship with its single red sail, turn sharply, cutting across the wind, he knew the battle had shifted.

Although the ships still ran full-sailed, it seemed almost in slow motion, as they crashed bone jarringly into the waves, and bucked with canon fire. Before long, the second ship found itself in dire straits as the first swung in, blocking the wind with its wall of sails and stealing the second's wind. As the sails began to luff, going slack and powerless, the first ship's captain saw his opportunity. A single massive broadside into the sails of the floundering ship, and it was done. With sails torn away, there was no way to evade the coming fight. Grapples flew, fastening the two ships together, as swarms of shouting men clambered over the rails or swung from the spars, weapons drawn.

"Rhone, are you paying any attention at all?" Bella waved a hand in front of Rhone's face, shaking her head as his blank stare refocused. "I've been talking for two minutes, and you aren't even here."

Rhone cheeks flared crimson as he blinked, rapidly regaining his where-abouts. "Sorry, I guess I dropped out for a moment," he mumbled, pulling his mind from the vivid picture of his daydream.

"Really?" Bella asked, already knowing his lame excuse for what it was, but she didn't push him. After all, he had come to her rescue. The least she could do was go easy on him. But she did raise an eyebrow, her tilted head inviting an explanation.

"Okay, I was daydreaming," he admitted.

Which got him the same response, but with a smile.

"All right," he whined, "When I asked Captain Black to explain his winning attack scenarios, he said something about seeing it from the view of a bird. 'Remember,' he said, 'If you could just see what was happening, the way a bird would see it, you would be forewarned, and could prepare accordingly.'" His mind was still caught up in his daydream. Somehow, the mental image of flying like a gull, watching the world drift past below, had gotten completely mixed with the scene of pirates. "Wouldn't it be great to fly out and find the pirates. "There's nothing they could do about it either."

Bella rolled her eyes. "You do realize they could shoot you down, dummy. Maybe not with a canon, but a long rifle would work just fine."

"Party pooper," Rhone replied, frowning sarcastically.

Actually they were getting along much better since he had hired her. When Mr. Jorstad, owner of The Common House, had walked out and caught Bella wrestling with him on the back steps, Rhone had stepped in and taken the verbal assault, saying he had instigated the entire affair and she was not to be blamed. She had still been released, as it was a major impropriety, but Rhone had decided to hire her as his assistant, with a pay check to match. Bella called it a rescue, claiming the verbal abuse she would have received had she stayed. Having more time together now, he appreciated her new kindness.

"And I am not a party pooper," Bella answered, glaring in an obvious intent to finish the issue.

It was just as obvious, he didn't take the hint.

"I'm merely saying," She huffed, as she tried again, "if you were just hanging in the air like a bird, a good marksman would pick you off with no problem. I once saw a guy throw a pie plate, pick up a gun and shoot it down while it was still in the air. You're a lot bigger than a pie plate, so you'd be an easy target."

But Rhone was into his mind again, her words barely reaching him as he tried to understand a concept he could almost feel.

When another odd thought crossed his mind, he sent Stone a query. *Are you doing something in there? I keep seeing things.*

Stone's immediate response should have given him a heads up.

Sorry. But you keep going on about your conversation with the good captain, and as I have nothing else to do at the moment, I am working on calculations for lift versus mass. I thought perhaps I could answer your concerns.

Confused, Rhone silently asked, *My concerns? What concerns?*

Stone's mental reply was not only succinct, it was staggering. *Flight, you ninny.*

Rhone's brow wrinkled in consternation, as he answered, *I am not a ninny. And I'm not a bird. I was just trying to get an idea what it would be like to see from up there, not actually fly.*

Unfortunately, Bella's expression made it quite obvious she was watching.

Covering for his lack of discretion, Rhone absently rubbed at his neck. "I ah...I had a kink," he stated, instantly guilt-laden by his deception.

She was his friend, and he hadn't told her what was arguably the most important part of his life. But it was a difficult situation to balance. He couldn't go around telling everyone about Stone. He had already broken his front, telling her he was an agent. Now, he couldn't quite decide which was worse. Stone was his friend and collar-mate, but the O.P.R. was his job. They both mattered.

Feeling the weight of indecision, he finally decided to split the difference.

"I guess I was thinking about flying," he conceded. "Could you imagine drifting through the sky, seeing everything below like they were toys?"

Bella's gaze shifted skyward as she considered it, then shrugged. "It would be interesting, but totally impossible. We're simply not birds, and not even all birds can fly."

Rhone was ready to agree, when Stone popped into his thoughts. *Of course you could not fly like a bird, but floating is a possibility.*

"Floating?" Rhone burst out in surprise, then sheepishly looked at Bella, expecting a caustic retort.

Unbelievably, she didn't appear to question his sanity, so he answered her question before she could ask.

"Floating, you know, instead of flying. I know we can't fly. That would be silly, but I bet we could find a way to float."

"Floating? Like in water?" Bella asked, trying to catch his meaning. "But air isn't like water, so how would that work?"

In total truth, he didn't have a clue.

Until Stone whispered into his mind. *More like smoke in the air, than a boat in the water.*

Which Rhone repeated for Bella.

"I think I understand," she said in awe. "If smoke can float, then maybe we can capture it, and float with it. Is that what you mean?"

"You think it might work?" he asked, actually impressed. His heart began to race as it caught the heat of possibility. "I was just thinking out-loud, not actually considering it as possible."

Like a school teacher correcting an errant student, Bella assumed her favorite position, fists to hips, as she gave her opinion. "It seems to me, things have to be a thought before they can be studied."

Rhone was embarrassed by her loyalty. Especially since it had been Stone's concept, not his.

Not true my friend, Stone corrected. *I merely put into practical application the thoughts you were already dealing with. I told you we make a good team.*

Going with the flow, Rhone began to work with the idea, gathering odd bits of information drifting around in his head. "Smoke does rise," he said thoughtfully, "but it drifts away. So, we would need some way to capture it. Then, if I could strap the container to my back, maybe it would lift me off the ground."

It was a big 'if', but the more he considered the idea, the more excited he became.

"I don't know. It sounds pretty dangerous," Bella commented, her concern growing at the same rate as his enthusiasm.

"Maybe, but probably not any more than fighting pirates," Rhone said with a grin. "It might actually be safer."

"Safer than fighting pirates?" she asked skeptically.

Rhone raised a noncommittal shoulder. "I haven't done either yet, so it's hard to say."

Stone added additional data into his already loaded thoughts. *In actuality, the contained element would not need to be smoke. Any lighter than air gas would work. Smoke is only lighter because of the heat. Remember, heat rises.*

"That's right," Rhone murmured, totally forgetting Bella's presence.

"What's right?" she asked, watching him closely.

Rhone was finding it difficult keeping up with two discussions at once. Thinking quickly, he said something that might take her mind to another track. "That I probably wouldn't get hit. A shot would be from a long distance, not up close like a sword fight."

"Maybe, but it still sounds dangerous. Besides, distance just gives them more time to aim."

Rhone sighed. "Anyway, I was thinking about why smoke would work, and realized it was because of the heat. Heat makes it lighter somehow, but it's possible there are other things that would work."

Bella squinted as she processed the information. "But if they were lighter, wouldn't they just rise up and go away?"

Again, Rhone was surprised at her mental quickness.

Explain gases, Stone instructed. *Remember your elements. They come in solids, liquids and gases, and heat can be used to excite the molecules, creating expansion and lift.*

Really? Rhone sent in a quick reply. *I was never good at that stuff.* But while he might not be good at it, he still had to convince Bella the idea was his. *Sorry, Stone. I don't mean to take credit for your thoughts. I just don't know how else to explain it.*

With the mental equivalence of a snort, Stone replied. *Not a problem, my friend. The We do not have issues with self, as humans seem to. You and I are a team. Since I am not able to speak to Bella, I will do the thinking. You do the talking. Does that make it easier?*

Happy to have an answer, Rhone responded silently, *If you're sure it's okay.*

It might have been okay with Stone, but Bella had noted Rhone's habit of 'phasing out', turning to what she considered his internal self. She was beginning to consider him an honest to goodness genius as he appeared to calculate problems in his mind.

Which wasn't far from the truth, except for the calculating part.

"I've got it," he said with a snap of his fingers. "Matter comes in three forms, solid, liquid and gas. When wood burns it produces smoke, although it's not really the wood that's burning. The wood is converted to gasses by the heat, and the gasses are what ignites."

"I never knew that," Bella said in amazement. "Is it true?"

"It is," Rhone said, nodding dramatically. "And because the gasses are warmer than the air around it, they rise." Silently he asked Stone, *Am I right? I think that's what you said.*

The feel of Stone's chuckle vibrated at Rhone's throat as thoughts echoed in his mind. *It is close enough for now. But do continue. Even I am interested in where you are going with this.*

Mildly annoyed, Rhone gave a begrudging, *Thanks,* before turning his attention back to Bella.

"I think I understand," she replied, not sounding sure at all.

Rhone's own mind struggled to connect the pieces, working to place them in sequential order.

Suddenly he knew. "I have a plan," he stated dramatically. "I'm going to fly."

Bella's confidence in him showed as she began bouncing on her toes in enthusiasm. "When do we start?" she asked excitedly. She had many more questions, but she was a believer.

"Sure, I get it," Rhone said, beginning to laugh at her energy. "You want this to work, so you can try shooting me down."

"Ha. Wouldn't even be a fair fight," she threw back with a grin. "I just want to fly."

Her sincerity made Rhone feel small. She was being honest, and he was far from it, trying to straddle the issues.

"I'm pretty sure it is possible, and I still have to work it out, but if I can come up with a design, and we can find the resources, it just might work."

"It will work," Bella said in full belief. "I have faith in you."

Words that made Rhone feel even worse about his deception.

CHAPTER 17

Do, or Die Doing

Rhone's mind was crowded with thoughts, leaving his feet to wander their typical path toward the docks. But instead of heading to the ship, he found himself walking the quay's length, barely noticing where he was. Finally raising his eyes from their view of his boot tips, he saw the Whale-cutters Warehouse standing forlornly at the end of the docks. A moment later, inspiration hit, and he changed pace, walking briskly toward the building's stinking miasma.

The balding owner was standing in the exact location of his previous visit, and raised an eyebrow at Rhone's approach.

"Good day, sir. Would you have a moment?" Rhone asked.

The owner looked as though he was questioning his hearing. "You talkin' to me? An' are you back to buy somethin', or just here for another look?"

Rhone answered with a short nod. "Sir, I am in need of a containment vessel for a gaseous substance, and thought perhaps some portion of entrails might suffice."

The man scratched at his chin as he considered his options, but Rhone's lofty demeanor forestalled any further questions. "Well now, you'd be talkin' guts," he stated blandly. "They hold stuff all the time."

"Exactly my thoughts," Rhone agreed.

Now that they were talking sales, the man's haggard expression transformed into a wreath of smiles. "You might even be thinkin' lungs," he began, nodding at his own expertise, "but they're not hollow like you might expect. No, you'd best go for something else, like maybe a bladder. We got guts of all kinds though, and they'd all be available, for a price. How big are you wanting?" His bright eyes gave Rhone the once over, and saw money.

"As large as I can get," Rhone answered. "I will need a great deal of containment." Then not in the mood for pointless conversation, asked, "And how long would it take?"

"Not an hour, sir. You're lucky. We're at the point where we can get right to it." He was almost fawning at the thought of making a sale on guts. "

"Excellent. May I have a look?"

"A look? Well certainly, sir. Not a problem. Right this way."

A few minutes later, Rhone had not only gotten a peek at the still-connected organ, Stone had done a quick visual measurement.

"I believe this will suffice," Rhone said perfunctorily. Returning to the office, he took up the quill and scribbled a note. "Have it delivered to this location, and I'll take a second as soon as it's available."

The owner could do no more than bob his head in ecstasy.

Business done, Rhone gratefully left the stinking warehouse, barely exiting before Stone's excited voice broke the silence.

According to my calculations, the bladder will enlarge to approximately eight times its original size when fully inflated.

His knowledgeable summary was everything Rhone hoped, and with a spring in his step, headed back to tell Bella the good news, forgetting all about The Mistress.

———

"How did it go?" Bella asked excitedly, bouncing in anticipation. "Any problems?" As usual, she was full of questions, and couldn't wait for him to get inside.

"Actually, I didn't see the captain," Rhone apologized. "I got sidetracked, but I think I found our answer. Whale."

"Whale?" Bella asked with a frown.

"Yes, but I honestly don't know how they can work in that place. The smell was absolutely horrid." His contorted face supported his words.

"I believe you. I can smell it from here," she grimaced, fanning the air in front of her face. "But, what place?"

Realizing the disconnect, Rhone told her of The Whale-cutter's Warehouse and his find, leaving her in startled amazement.

"Bladders? So you bought them?"

His grin was enough that he didn't need to answer.

With a yip of excitement, she asked, "So, when do they come?"

"The first should be delivered by this evening," he said, posed as though preening. "I believe I was quite aristocratic, throwing pretense around like it was real money. I wish everyday would go as well."

Bella rolled her eyes, but had one more question. "Can we start tomorrow?" She seemed as happy as if he had invited her to an ice cream social, instead of a day working with whale guts.

R hone covered a yawn as his attention drifted, pretending to listen as Stone lectured on about the requirements for lift. He was into his daydreaming again, trying to regain the feel of flying.

The main problem of course, is weight, Stone droned. *The greater the weight, the more lift it will require. At a minimum, it will need to carry itself, and the payload, which at this point is you.*

Whatever, Rhone thought, but managed to drag himself up a little straighter.

It really was important information, but they had both been working late into the nights, designing various methods of containment and the required structural support to carry it. The entire concept was fraught with problems, as size, volume, weight and construction materials all had to be considered. Yet each obstacle only made them more determined. Rhone had finally resolved that he would make this thing fly, or float, if it was the last thing he did.

Which it just might be.

As the days wore on, other problems began to emerge, such as the bladder tissue wanting to dry and crack. If the precious gasses leaked, the entire creation would potentially drop back to earth. While it was all theoretical so far, the design was progressing at a rapid pace.

Rhone worked so diligently he almost forgot the reason they had started, until he overheard comments from a neighboring table in the Common

House discussing more ships being attacked. It was a dreary trip back to the worksite as he considered the future. So far, floating above the earth was still just a daydream.

To top it off, he and Mayor Dugan were still at odds, which hadn't done anything to help the town, or his job. He knew he wouldn't be staying here forever. Once his assignment was completed, he would be moved somewhere new, which only made his frustration grow.

He glanced toward Bella where she worked, confident in his ability to control things, but not understanding his awkward position. She was still unaware of Stone and his vast input into the project. Yet without Stone he would never have come up with the system. Stone was the genius, not himself. Having people believe he was rich and intelligent might have been fun, but the falsehoods constantly wore on his conscience.

He was almost relieved when he heard Bella's concerned call.

"Rhone, how does this attach to the lower support? I'm pretty sure this tissue won't wear very well, and any attachment I make will tear through." Then she laughed, despite the fact that it sounded like a real problem. "At least I won't need to shoot you down. You'll simply fall out of the sky. But with my luck, you'd probably land on me."

"Ha, ha," Rhone replied dryly, not finding it nearly as funny as she did.

His idea of floating through the air did not include a quick trip to earth the old-fashioned way. Although landing on her might be interesting.

Only slightly annoyed, he answered, "I was hoping a good job of oiling would help."

"It might," she admitted, "but probably not for long. The tissue is just too thin." With her brows furrowed in light creases, she asked, "What if we wrapped it, or cover it with something that would wear better?"

Rhone had already thought of that, but had only come up with one option. "I thought of using leather to wrap the whole thing, but that much leather would weigh a ton."

Not quite a ton, came Stone's unasked for response, *but certainly more than we would desire. So we should look for a better option.*

"Not leather," Rhone repeated for Bella's benefit, "but there must be something lighter we could use. Weight is the problem."

He was beginning to feel defeat looming. The entire project probably wouldn't work, and they would have wasted tons of time and effort, let alone money.

Bella tried to help by ticking off items as she listed them. "Okay, light weight and durable. Anything else?"

"It's a good start," Rhone acknowledged with more cheerfulness than he felt. "If we can manage those two we'll be getting close."

I am very proud of you, Stone said, dropping into his thoughts. *You have learned a great deal since we first met. It was not all that long ago, I was the one attempting to pull items from your mental confusion. Now you are doing the searching, almost on your own. With Bella's help of course. I just thought I would let you know.*

Rhone didn't know what to say. It was the biggest complement Stone had ever given. He had always felt so inferior next to the crystalline entity's mass of stored data, and never considered himself the one to lead. Humbled, he silently replied, *Thank you Stone. If I'm any good at all, it's because I have the best teacher in the world. Or even from out of this world.*

If Stone thought he was doing well, then maybe this project could work.

Bella raised a hesitant hand, flagging for his attention. "What would you think if I said, seaweed?"

R hone drew back the sliding doors, giving Bella her first clear view inside the rented warehouse. The building was mostly empty, except for the giant bellows sitting propped in a corner, its thick leather sides hanging like heavy drapery between the iron support struts. The center of the room held the partially fill whale bladder, its ballooning envelope waiting patiently, ready to be oiled and wrapped in seaweed. Even partially inflated, the monstrous bubble took up the majority of the nearly empty work space.

Finding enough seaweed had taken much longer than expected, but constant search of the tidal flats eventually produced piles of the long, slimy leaves. Then it was Bella's task to weave the slippery strands around the bladder. Not even Stone knew exactly how well it would work, but as a prototype, it would give a tremendous amount of data for redesigning the model to a true working unit.

Bella now considered her release from The Common House as an auspicious occasion, freeing all her time for the warehouse. Rhone agreed, knowing there was no way he could have done it all himself. She may have been somewhat small in stature, but she made huge efforts for their cause.

Their cause. The words struck him almost like a physical blow. If it wasn't for Bella and her work, he probably wouldn't be doing this at all. She needed to be a true part, not just a worker on the sidelines.

I'll talk to her, he thought. *If this contraption works,* putting it off to a better time.

Feeling better, Rhone doubled his efforts at oiling the stretchable strands. His work was accompanied by Stone in his instructional mode monotonously rolling words through his weary mind.

We have two options for lift. Either heat, or lighter than air gases, of which there are several, Stone commented.

"Do we really have an option?" Rhone asked skeptically. "I don't happen to have a gas-filling tank sitting around, so isn't heat our only real choice?"

I understand your question, but gases are everywhere. Some are natural in the environment, and some produced through conversion. Finding them is not as difficult as the refining, or singling out of a particular gas.

"How does that make a difference if we can't do it?"

I am merely stating, Stone replied in a grump, *there are options. Both will lift, since they are lighter than the air.*

Stone could be just as hard headed as Rhone. He was a rock thing, after all.

But Rhone was already drifting on the subject, and Stone finally gave in with a mental shrug. *Let us just say, if we can find an available gas, it will be more stable and give longer flight than using heat.*

"Okay, I get it. But we still don't have any," Rhone replied wearily.

As you wish, Stone commented in exasperation, *but while you continue with your envelope preparation, I will work on the lift compensation problem.*

Which was where they were before the lecture.

When the harness-maker looked up from the set of plans with eyes full of restrained questions, Rhone could only shrug, and say, "It's actually designed to fit me," which didn't seem to help. "I realize it is quite unique," he tried to explain, "but it is part of a project I'm developing." He stopped as the worker raised a hand.

"Not sure I want to know, but I'll take the job. Do most anything for a buck."

"Very good then," Rhone agreed, relieved, and not needing more than the work completed. "If you would have it delivered, I will pay in advance."

Two days later the harness arrived.

Bella was so excited her eyes seemed to glow, actually sparkling in the lamp light. "Rhone, you've got to try it on."

But he wasn't nearly so sure. The way her teeth gleamed simply made him nervous. Regardless, within minutes he was fastened securely to the underside of the envelope. It was only a test fitting, but Bella seemed to have far too much fun securing the heavy straps, binding him in place until he could barely move.

Still, the harness seemed to work, and once in the air, he wouldn't be doing anything other than watch the earth fall away and pray he would come down in a controlled manner. Bella would follow in the wagon, attempting to keep up, then retrieve him and the unit. The entire project was crazy, but he was so far into the planning, he couldn't draw away far enough to even be afraid. He was going.

Stone had finally decided on the lifting agent. They would be using hot air, instead of the not-yet-discovered gas version. They chose steam for heating the air. A method far easier to control, and almost as easy to come by as smoke. Like smoke, steam had a built-in control factor. As the air cooled, it would lose lift, lowering Rhone back to earth. Another gas might take days, or even weeks, before it lost lift, which may be good for a finished product, but not a good way to start out with a new concept.

The sketch of a plan, and a little more money, prompted the local smith to build the heavy iron boiler. The odd contraption looked something like a giant teapot, simply converting water to steam. A long-armed valve released the steaming hot air, injecting it through a tube into the balloon envelope.

It was something more than a suggestion, when Bella asked Rhone to speak with Captain Black about the project. Having a rescue vessel would be handy if the wind carried him out to sea.

The Captain only needed a single look before he rubbed his weathered nose with an equally weathered knuckle, and squinted in consideration. "Might work," he said skeptically, "but if it was me up there floatin' along with the birds, I'd want to make sure I wasn't coming' off unexpected like. Try wrapping it in a net, and hook it to your harness. Nothin' wimpy 'bout havin' a little protection. It only makes sense."

Following the captain's suggestion, fishnet cording now wrapped the ballooning bladder, showing the interlaced layer of woven seaweed that covered it. It was a rude affair, not really a craft, but it was a start.

Rhone stood uncertainly below the billowing bladder, feeling much like an ant carrying a bubble. Bella did her part, double checking the harness buckles securing him to the netting. The breeze was light, but there was a briskness to the day. His jacket would do double duty, keeping him warm and keeping the leather straps from chaffing badly.

Altogether, the rig was hardly what one would call handsome, or maybe beautiful, since a ship is always a she. It wouldn't do to ignore tradition, for as Captain Black said, 'tradition is a jealous mistress'.

Suddenly Bella stopped, as realization dawned on her. "She needs a name!" she exclaimed in horror. "She can't fly without a name."

"But it's only a test flight, or float, or whatever," Rhone said with a dismissive look. He was far more worried about the unit failing, with him in the air, than whether it had a name.

Bella didn't seem to hear his complaint. "Let's name her Bo," she declared, bouncing happily.

"Bo?" Rhone questioned, with a look that said he wasn't all that sold.

"Yes you ninny. Bo, as in, bo-loon. Get it?"

As Bella's nose wrinkled in joy, Rhone instantly changed mind. She was so unbelievably cute, he couldn't keep from smiling.

"I guess it works," he admitted with a shrug. "So, Bo it is then."

"Yessss!" she said, fists squeezed tightly in excitement.

"Hey, enough already. I'm getting so nervous, I'll have to pee again if we don't get started soon."

Bella giggled at his inappropriate words, but she was getting use to his unique ways.

The fire in the boiler had been burning for some time, and the little vent happily puffed steam into the cool morning air. Like a teapot, a light whistling sound said it was ready. Having gone through the motions several times in rehearsal, Bella gave the signal. Her job was to divert the steam into the bladder envelope, and hope.

At the last moment, Rhone clipped the anchor rope to his harness. The other end was already tied securely to the wagon. It was mostly for emotional support, since he didn't expect to need it, but if something went wrong, the wagon's weight would be enough to hold him down.

Blue stood patiently harnessed to the wagon, ready for pick-up duty, or a quick getaway if Bella needed it.

Taking a firm grip on Stone's collar, Rhone silently asked, *Are you ready? I think I'm afraid, but I'm even afraid to admit it.*

There was a pause before Stone replied, his words a mix of emotions. *I am fine my friend, and I am proud of you. Both of you. And... if this goes wrong, allow me to say, it has been the pleasure of my long life to be able to make this trip with you. Rhone... I am here,* words that were special between the two.

Feeling their impact, and understanding, Rhone dropped his hand and shouted, "Let's... do... this!"

Gritting her teeth, Bella used her entire weight to pull the long, iron-armed distribution lever, its squeal of complaint un-noticed as the valve slowly opened.

Steam rocketed through the leather hose, once used to reduce a ship's bowline chafing, but now running directly from the boiler's valve into the base of the balloon envelope, giving life to its placid form.

Life and lift, but it was all theoretical, at least for a moment longer.

Already Rhone had difficulty staying on his feet, his balance being played with by the changing weight of the inflating envelope fastened to his back.

Bella stood beside the noisy boiler unit, waiting to close the troublesome valve. They were tense moments, but filled with excitement.

So far, the envelope was holding, gradually expanding into an odd oval shape. It was definitely not a beautiful spherical bubble, more a lopsided, elongated, black-green squash looking thing, with Rhone strapped awkwardly to the bottom of the netting.

Bo's continuous growth made it difficult for Rhone to keep his feet under him, the shifting weight threatening to topple him onto his face. Then a light breeze caught at the fabric, lifting him free of the ground. A startled yelp broke from his lips before he was dropped solidly back to mother earth, grinning like a crazy man. The next moment, he was swept totally off his feet and dragged away.

"Hang on!" Bella screamed, both in fear and excitement.

But Rhone had nothing to hang on to. Swinging awkwardly from his harness straps, he bounced and skidded across the road, trying desperately to fend off the worst of the bruises. Suddenly, the ground dropped away, with Bo rising into the air. Rhone was just starting to congratulate himself, when a terrible ripping sound riveted his attention. He watched In horror as the leather hose pull free, whipping through the air like the mouth of a giant, steam-spewing dragon.

Captain Black would have been proud of his bellow, as he shouted, "Shut it off!"

But Bella was already doing her job, wrenching frantically at the long lever, shutting off the flow of whooshing steam. In the sudden stillness, the hose stopped its violent whipping, falling almost gracefully into an untidy heap.

"Rhone, are you alright?" Bella shouted, watching in amazement as Rhone rapidly rose to the end of the tether. Her comical expression showed part fear and part disbelief at the spectacle of Rhone dangling like a spider, hanging almost upside down from his balloon's webbing.

It had been an abrupt departure, but the gentle swinging motion quickly eased Rhone's somewhat panicked heart. He was just beginning to relax, when the sudden stinging slap of the rope tether striking his thigh made him grunt in pain. Again in near panic, he lunged for the rope, an action that only sent him rotating wildly, barely managing to snag it as he swung past. At least with rope in hand, he had an emotional life-line to safety.

Hanging head down, almost fifty feet above ground, Rhone's eyes followed the taught yet gentle arc of the rope tether stretching back to the wagon. While the view was incredible, it was not a particularly secure feeling. More like diving off a bridge into solid earth.

Below, Blue stood unimpressed, contentedly chewing grass like it was just another day at the farm.

"Bella, we did it!" Rhone shouted. "We're floating!" Then not needing to worry about being overheard, spoke directly to Stone. "You did it, Stone. Thank you. Can you imagine what mom would say if she saw me now?" But as happy as he was, the somber thought almost drowned him with emotion.

As usual, Stone caught him. *Indeed my friend. But I did nothing, other than a few calculations. You did the work. You and Bella.*

Bella! How was she taking this? In sudden concern, he shouted, "Bella? Is everything okay down there?"

"No problems here," she called back, shading her eyes to see better.

"Hey, watch this," he called, beginning to climb head first, hand over hand down the hanging rope. Then with a devious grin, released his grip, floating gently back to the full length of the tether, the slight jolt causing the balloon to bounce softly before coming to a resting position, drifting gently in the breeze.

"Rhone, please be careful," Bella shouted, her voice again caught between bubbling happiness and fear.

But when a new idea came to him, he called, "Bella, get in the wagon. Try driving up the road. I want to see what it's like to float along."

"Are you sure?"

She certainly wasn't, but immediately began clearing the area. It wasn't a minute before she clucked to Blue, and with a flick of the reins, began a slow arc out to the road.

Rhone felt the gentle tug as the line tightened, then the slight drop in elevation as he began a slow descent, swinging in behind the buckboard. No training in the world could have prepared him for this experience. It was beyond... anything, but maybe something like Stone floating in space.

Stone caught the thought and responded. *There is a similarity, but still very unique,* he commented. *In space however, there was no sense of motion. We simply were.*

"You're awesome, Stone. Just think what we can do from here."

Indeed, a momentous occasion, Stone commented grandly, *But I do not believe fighting pirates would be a good option at the moment. We are far too low, and as Bella mentioned, far too easily shot down.*

Rhone almost said, 'party pooper', but knew from previous experience, Stone simply wouldn't understand the odd term. Totally caught up in the moment, he shrieked, "Yaaahoooeee!" just like a kid.

Hearing Rhone's shriek, Bella blanched, instantly pulling back on the reins, certain she would see him falling head first from the sky. Instead, she saw a crazy grin on his face, with him frolicking like the child he was too old to be. But her tight-lipped glare was wasted as Rhone continued to cavort through the sky, not paying her the least bit of attention.

With a shake of her head, Bella felt the painful fear ease away. "You're too much for me," she murmured quietly to herself. "I'm just a small-town girl, and you are... truly... something else. But thanks for this opportunity. I'll never forget it."

And she had thought him such a boor when he first showed up at The Common House. In fact, he had almost gotten her fired, several times, but he did grow on a person. A mix somewhere between totally annoying, and an absolute wonder, with perhaps a little genius thrown in. He would make some lucky girl quite a catch someday.

But at the moment she could only laugh as she wiped away her tears, watching as Rhone tried to fly, waving his arms like a bird.

When his forward motion finally stopped, Bo drifted directly overhead, bouncing slowly up and down with Rhone's exertions. Her prediction of his falling out of the sky and landing on her might still be a possibility, but she shrugged unconsciously. It as at least one way to get a hug. A little rougher than a girl could want, but beggars can't be choosers. With a rueful smile matching the worry lines creasing her brow, she shook her head, one word coming like a judgment to her lips.

"Boys!"

CHAPTER 18

Bigger is better

Rhone's head-down position had been great for viewing, but the extended flight had his head throbbing in time with his rapid heartbeat. Luckily his flight was coming to a close. The hot air in Bo's envelope was following the laws of physics, slowly losing lift as it began to cool, and dropping inexorably earthward.

When Rhone finally touched down on hands and knees, he gratefully collapsed on the green grass of the roadside, landing undignified, but at least not flat on his face. Bo gently settled over his form, burying him under the seaweed-covered bladder.

Bella wasn't sure whether to laugh or cry as she scrambled madly to his rescue, hauling the draping fabric to the side. Dropping to her knees beside his hunched form, she engulfed him in her arms, almost smothering him again in her relief and joy.

"What was it like? Was it awesome? When can you do it again? What does it look like from up there?" Her sentences ran together, making one long string of words. Finally, with emotion outweighing her restraint, Bella buried her head in his side, weeping tears of joy.

With no idea what was going on, Rhone's first thought, and far too familiar, was wondering if he had done something wrong.

"Bella, what's the matter?"

Having Bo still strapped to his back only compounded the problem, as the draping balloon fabric made righting himself extremely difficult, especially with her holding on so tightly. Not knowing what else to do, Rhone carefully squirmed an arm free, and managed a tentative hand on her shoulder. He knew nothing about girls, other than they were very nice to be around, most of the time.

It was yet another thing mom had never mentioned. His only other connection with females had been Aundrea, now his boss, and MaryEllen, the absolutely fabulous co-worker in the OPR. They were both older, and so far beyond him that there had been no serious question of their roles. But this was different, and he had no idea how to help.

Finally regaining a measure of control, Bella scowled dramatically before shaking a finger in his face. "You idiot. What were you thinking? You could have gotten yourself killed, and you were shouting like an entire herd of red-butted baboons." But again the emotion caught her, turning her into a blubbering mess.

Rhone was in the process of asking, "What's a red-butted—yaaaahh!" when a static jolt cut his question short.

Annoyed, and totally confused, he mouthed a silent, *What?* to Stone, as he rubbed at his neck.

I am sorry, Stone counseled his young friend, *but the intervention was necessary. While it may not seem rational, I have now associated with the human female enough to understand at least some of her condition. Allow me to say, it is well within the parameters of their emotional instability. I warn you however, this is not something you should mention to Bella.*

It may not have answered everything, but Rhone was glad for Stone's words of wisdom. He knew his back-country upbringing didn't teach much in the way of social customs, which left him constantly worried about doing something improper. Even Stone had far more knowledge of such things as he observed people all day while Rhone worked.

"Bella, I'm fine," he attempted. A bit woozy-headed from hanging upside down for so long, but I'm better already." Reluctantly, he released her shoulder, spreading his arms wide to prove his words.

But Bella's head stayed buried in his side, her mumbled words almost impossible to hear. "I'm sorry. I just got afraid... but not until it was over."

"Are you kidding? You did great," Rhone said, happy to discover the problem. "The way you handled the boiler and wagon was perfect, and I certainly couldn't have done this alone. In fact, I think you were awesome."

Still buried in Bo's billowing fabric, Rhone put his arm around her, protecting her from the movement of the rough material. He closed his eyes, absorbing the peaceful warmth that suddenly raced through him.

Adjusting her position, Bella wrapped even closer, snuggling into the crook of his arm. For several minutes they simply sat, neither wanting to change a thing.

Until a shrill shrwwissshhhheeeeeeeeeee shattered the morning's quiet, the screaming shriek of the boiler's pressure valve breaking the spell.

Startled from his revery, Rhone came fully awake, eyes wide at the sight of a non-stop plume of steam blasting into the air. "It's the boiler," he shouted needlessly, unintentionally dumping Bella onto the ground. "We have to release the pressure!" his words simply repeating what Stone was shouting in his head.

As Bella quickly scooted from the folds of fabric and scrambled to her feet, Rhone attempted to, but was bound in place by the harness still buckled to Bo.

Not waiting, Bella ran to the boiler, while Rhone worked frantically to disconnect from the balloon. She knew what needed done. They had gone over it several times in rehearsal.

The boiler's heat was almost overpowering as she reached for the release valve's heavy arm. All she had to do was haul it to the open position. But the thick steel bar seared her hands, simply too hot to hold. With a scream of pain, she released the arm, and in tearful frustration began searching for another way to fix the problem.

Bella's pain-filled scream tore at Rhone's heart, and with finesse forgotten, franticly fought at the harness, fingers refusing to do what he wanted.

Crying openly as she waved her burned hands in the air, Bella searched for something she could use, but seeing nothing suitable, finally grabbed her own skirt, lifting the hem above her knees and wrapping it around the lever's scalding arm.

Rhone was almost mad with frustration as he finally disentangled the last buckle. Nearly tripping on the billowing material, he raced across the short distance to where Bella still hauled stubbornly at the long lever.

Tears ran freely down Bella's face as she worked at the stuck valve. Even her skirt couldn't entirely protect her burnt hands from the unrelenting metal. Swelled with heat, it was truly stuck.

Rhone was in no mood to temporize. Racing up, he grabbed the material from her tender hands and swept her bodily to the side, away from the boiler. Wrapping the remainder of the skirt around the handle, he lunged, using his entire weight to wrench at the stubborn lever. He felt relief at the sound of a muffled groan he thought might be the valve moving, before realizing the sound was coming from him.

Again and again, he slammed bodily against the arm, until slowly, inch by inch, it creaked, and grated, noisily sliding into the open position. The sudden release sent billowing steam rocketing down the leather tube, whipping it back and forth like a dragon's head gone berserk.

Diving to the side, Rhone covered his head with his arms, protecting it as best he could. As the hose swept passed in a near miss, Rhone scrambled behind the relative shelter of the boiler, frantically looking for Bella through the blistering cloud. He finally caught sight of her, sitting partially covered in the ruined remains of her skirt.

Defeated, Bella sat with teary rivulets running down her face, hands held awkwardly in the air trying not to touch anything. Her skirt, what was left of it, exposed most of her legs, the rest lay in a smoking ruin wrapped around the lever's handle.

But she wasn't out of danger, as the whipping tube arched across the ground, swinging back in her direction. Without a thought, Rhone launched himself forward, leaping the flailing leather tube in his effort to protect her.

The tube may have missed him, but the steam didn't. If it hadn't been for the leather pants tucked into his high cuffed boots, he would had been cooked like the crab legs he had so recently learned to love. Even so, the searing heat was almost more than he could endure.

Landing hard, Rhone bellowed with his own pain and anger before scrambling further out of reach of the almost-living demon.

Bella screamed in fear at seeing him go down, her blistered hands making her powerless to protect herself or him.

With two lunging steps, Rhone was there, scooping her up as though she weighed nothing. Then dodging un-romantically across the remaining distance, made it to the safety of the wagon.

As though disheartened by its failure, their dragon-like demon gave up, hose sagging as the pressure lowered, its shrill shriek sinking to a mere warble.

"It's okay," Rhone cooed shakily. "I've got you. Let me put you in the back of the wagon. You'll be okay there."

Blue turned to look at them, his own fear causing the whites of his eyes to show. He didn't much like the big noisy thing behind him, but stood true to his duty, awaiting direction.

As gently as he could, Rhone deposited Bella onto the wagon's bed, trying to keep his eyes from her legs. But they were easily the most beautiful thing he had ever seen. No wonder she kept them covered all the time. A man could go crazy, trying to get any work done with them around. Even thinking the thoughts clouded his mind, and he blushed.

Her hands, Rhone. Her hands require care.

It was enough. Rhone brought his eyes to hers, feeling the full intensity of her pain.

"Let me see," he said softly, reaching for the hands she held up in pleading supplication. Carefully taking her wrists, he turned them over, and blanched. The skin was already bright red with large white blisters forming over a large portion of the palms and fingers.

The pain must have been unbearable, but she had done her job the best she could. He would never ask for more than that.

Bella's crying slowed as she watched, fully believing in his ability to fix it. Her faith almost broke his heart.

Having been burnt before, he knew at least something about its care, and tried to remember what his mom had done. First, he needed water. Soaking her hands in cold water would reduce the heat burning in the skin.

Hoping he appeared calmer than he felt, Rhone swept the area with his eyes, finally, spotting Blue's scummy and half-full canvas bucket. It would work for now. The skin wasn't broken, so dirty water wouldn't matter too much.

Now that he was moving, his confidence grew. "I'll be right back," he said.

Rushing to the bucket, he unconsciously made a sour face at the bits of vegetation and horse slobber floating on the surface, but it was all he had. With a shake of his head, he carried the bucket to the back of the wagon, trying not to spill it all before he got there.

Bella's legs sat on dramatic display, stockings folded neatly over her boot tops, but Rhone barely allowed himself a glance as he got to work. Setting the bucket near, he took both her hands and gently dipped them into the cool water.

"Ooooooh," she moaned, tears again filling her eyes. As though embarrassed by her outburst, she clamped her lips tight, refusing anything further.

Rhone saw the white ring around her mouth as she grimaced, and knew what it must be taking for her not to scream.

"The cool water will help," he instructed. "Just keep them in there. Don't move until I get back. Got it?"

She looked ready to ask a question, but his stern look got a tear-streaked nod. Releasing her hands, he ran to the front of the wagon where the picnic basket sat under the bench seat. Drawing it out, he flung back the wicker top and dug through the food stuffs, looking for the little glass jug he had noticed earlier.

Bella's hands were still held in the scummy water, but she had moved, now sitting cross-legged, with a small tear-filled smile. "I'm sorry I'm a problem," she whispered quietly.

"What problem?" Rhone asked, honestly confused. "You were the one fixing the problem. I was too slow. If I had been doing what I should have been doing, and unhooked from Bo, you wouldn't have gotten burned trying to fix it."

A look of horror registered in her eyes as she connected the dots. She had been the one to distract him, and was the real cause of the trouble.

But before she could think further along those lines, Rhone gripped her shoulders. "No! If I hadn't been playing around up there like an idiot, I would have been down here in time to see it was shut off, before it became a problem. It was me, not you, you gorgeous thing."

He stopped awkwardly at hearing his own words, and looked cautiously to see how she had taken them.

A stunned expression crossed Bella's tear streaked face, eyes deep and wide. "But I kept you from doing your job," she whispered, fearing his response. "If I hadn't been draped all over you like seaweed on a rock, you would have been up and had it taken care of."

"There's nothing wrong with those drapings," Rhone mumbled with an embarrassed grin. His sideways glance took in her long legs crossed unconcernedly beside him.

Suddenly conscious of her condition, Bella started to shift to a more lady like position, but Rhone put a calming hand on her shoulder. "It's no problem at the moment. Right now, I need to take care of your hands. I even have something that should help."

At least he hoped it would. It had done wonders for him.

"First we need the heat gone. It won't all go away of course, but most will. Let me know when it's better, and I have a salve we can use."

Her shallow nod said she understood, but Rhone continued to watch her eyes, worried she would go shocky from the pain. A single tear made a run to the end of her nose, and instinctively he reached out, catching it on his finger tip. Holding it up for her to see, he softly commented, "I think I'll keep this one for you, just in case you need it back someday."

They both smiled shyly, until she winced and dropped her gaze. The pulse in her hands had begun to throb.

"It hurts," she whispered, trying not to sob. "I think the heat is leaving, but it's really throbbing."

"Okay, good," Rhone said lightly, although his heart was still thumping wildly from the moment before. "Well, not good exactly," he stammered, "but I think it's time for the salve. Are you ready? It's going to hurt as I put it on, but it will feel better in a few minutes, and it'll help it heal without scarring."

Bella stared as though not comprehending his words. She knew a girl with scarred hands was about as good as a swaybacked mare. Both would be stuck out in a pasture and left until the wolves got her. Her heart sank.

Blind to her worry, Rhone reached for the little pot, unlatching the metal ring holding the top in place. Gently holding her hand in his, he prepared to work. "I only have my finger to spread this with, but I'll try to be gentle."

Nodding in a wordless reply, Bella closed her eyes and waited for the pain. She almost shrieked when the sticky salve touched her swelling palm, but biting back the sound, pressed her lips together so hard they puckered white as her face drew into a mask of pain.

"I'm so sorry," Rhone whispered, but didn't stop applying the salve. With gentle motions he smeared the sticky substance across her tender palms and fingers.

Bella didn't move, eyes squeezed shut as though not seeing would make it feel better. Or perhaps it was the fear of seeing the burns.

When he finished with one, he started on the other, carefully covering each burned finger. It was almost mesmerizing, stroking her palm as lightly as if she was a butterfly. The warmth of her hands quickly melted the stickiness into an oil that soaked into the damaged skin.

Finally finished, he whispered as gently as he had to a fawn he had once found in the wilds of his valley, "Hey, I'm done. Now I need to wrap it. We have to keep it clean, and keep things from sticking to the salve. Are you doing okay?"

Bella slowly unclenched her eyes and focused on his handiwork. "What is that stuff," she asked with a grimace, "and where did you get it?"

He smiled, knowing it was something unexpected. "It's honey from the picnic basket. It was supposed to be for the rolls with butter, but I think this is a better use right now. How does it feel?"

"Honey?" She asked, almost angry in her disbelief.

"Yes, honey. It's pretty magical stuff, and can help things heal. My mom used it on me more than once, including when I got burned. Look, no scars," he said, holding up his own hand for her to inspect.

"Really?" she said in wonder. "Will it really keep them from scarring? If I was scarred, I would be almost useless." She stopped, fighting off a sob of dread. "There was an old lady on the outskirts of Corgy. I heard she was scarred from a fire. Everybody hated her because she wasn't pretty anymore, but I think they were frightened of her."

Bella stared at her hands until Rhone finally had to prompt. "Did she do okay?"

Numbly shaking her head, Bella mumbled, "Her house burned one winter night, and no one went to put it out. They were afraid. Some even said she was a witch." With angry tears threatening, she gritted her teeth, then continued savagely, "People are so stupid! She was just an old lady. It wasn't her fault she was scarred. It just happened!"

"I'm sorry," Rhone said, shaken by the story, "but don't worry. We've got this. The honey will make it better. Not right away of course, but pretty soon, and I'm pretty sure it won't scar. I know it's blistered, and must really hurt, but the honey will help that too. Honest." Carefully reaching past her out-held hands, he wrapped his arms around her and gently began to rock. "It's going to be all right. Just hold on. The pain will get better."

They sat, rocking, until her tear streaked face began to smooth. As the muscles of her jaw relaxed, her creased forehead again became flawless perfection.

Bo lay like a giant squash caught by an unexpected winter frost and gone bad. Its sides sagged, draping over the ground with only occasional flutters as the breeze caught on the woven seaweed fabric. It had flown, or floated, or whatever version you wanted to use. They had done it, and it could be done again.

Bella's injury, however, was like rain on his parade. Maybe it was time to put it all away, and do something more productive for the community. Perhaps something a bit more reasonable.

Rhone pulled his eyes from the fallen balloon and closed them, resting his head against Bella's. With another breath, he too drifted off, the weight of the day having used his normally boundless energy, leaving him totally exhausted.

CHAPTER 19

Tangled Webs

Even with bandaged hands, Bella looked almost ready to fight.

"You are not going to quit on my account! I won't have it," she almost shouted, stomping her foot in emphasis. "You flew, or floated, or whatever, but you did it and you're going to do it again."

Rhone's raised hands signaled his defeat and ended her tirade.

"It wasn't just you," he started, then saw her lips tighten, and quickly corrected his comment. "Well, it was, but maybe I should do something a little more constructive, that won't get you hurt." He had already tried to discuss his reasoning, but she stubbornly refused to listen. Her determined scowl proved that she still wouldn't. Finally, with a disconsolate shrug, he gave up. "Okay, I suppose we can try again." He tried to smile, but his worried face probably made it more of a grimace.

"Alright then," she said, instantly switching to a cheerful grin. "There will be no trying to bail out. It's a great idea, and you floated. You actually floated! How many people can say they've done that?" She looked like she wanted to clap with her excitement, but her bandaged hands quickly changed her mind.

＊＊＊

That had been weeks ago.

Now, with the tether in one hand and the other shielding his face, Rhone shouted over the steady huff of the boiler. "Are you ready?"

The little vent hissed merrily as a slim plume of white steam vented into the cool morning air.

Bella looked tense as she stood beside Bo, and had a right to be. She was the one buckled securely into the balloon's harness, but in a slightly different location from where Rhone had hung. A little recalculation from Stone had corrected the placement, taking her slight form into account so she wouldn't end up head-down as Rhone had. Now they were ready again.

This flight was scheduled as a simple up and down, giving Bella the chance to float like a cloud. It definitely wasn't flying like a bird, with no control of where she went, but an unbelievable experience none the less. She was bubbling with excitement.

Rhone spoke loudly over the noise of the boiler, ready to release the steam valve and finish filling the balloon envelope. "I hope you'll be warm enough. My coat will protect you from the harness rubbing, but I'm not sure it fits well enough to keep out the chill."

He worried about her, and had since she burned her hands. They were almost healed now, and only slightly tender to the touch. A far cry from her first few days slathered in sweet honey. He had spent most of his time caring for her, bringing her whatever she needed.

More than once she had complained about 'not being an invalid', rolling her eyes whenever she reached for something and he jumped up saying, "I'll get that." It was cute, and almost fun at first, but she wanted to do things for herself. She wasn't used to people waiting on her. Maybe it wasn't so great waiting for someone to do everything for you. It did give her a new view on what the high-and-mighty must go through, and a new perspective on why waiters were called waiters, with everyone waiting for things to get done.

"You worry too much," Bella scolded. She wasn't concerned about a little chill in the air. She was ready to fly.

Then with a move that surprised Rhone almost to disbelief, she lifted her skirt, grabbed the back hem and pulled it between her legs, tucking it into the front of her belt. The long swaths of bare leg showing from mid-thigh to boot top were more than Rhone knew how to deal with. He stared in total shock, wide-eyed and a dumb look on his face, until the noise of Bella's throat-clearing dragged his awed glance up to meet hers. His own instantly burned in a blush.

Bella's crystal-toned laugh rang in the brisk morning air, her bright blue eyes sparkling in mischief, knowing she was teasing him. "What's the matter?" she asked innocently. "You might as well have seen a ghost with that look on your face. Now, if you're done, we have a balloon to fly."

Tucking her gloved hands under the harness straps, she stood waiting for him to open the valve.

"I ahhh... Yeah, I guess I am, now," he said, getting his breathing back in working order. "But... aren't you going to get cold?"

Seeing his still-befuddled reaction, Bella gave a truly evil grin before rolling her hip, knee bent and heel lifted in a pose. She had his full attention. Her control had nothing to do with her being the pilot and he the ground crew. She felt like a woman.

But enough was enough. "Let's go!" she chided, snapping him out of his revery. Sweeping an arm across the heavens, she shouted, "I want to fly!"

Rhone blinked at the apparition before finally getting the hint. With a call of, "Valve opening," he pulled the long-armed lever, allowing steam to shunt into the leather hose.

For several nervous minutes they waited as the envelope filled, the bladder needing to finish expanding inside its seaweed wrap. The hot gasses slowly stretched the fabric, until suddenly, it began to inch its way upward, lifting a wide-eyed and grinning Bella off her feet.

"I'm floating. I'm actually floating off the ground," she shrieked with delight. "Thank you, Rhone! Oh thank you!" Then giggled, "I'm flooooat-inggggggg!" expanding the word as though it too was being stretched. "This is the best gift I've ever had."

Bella rose into the bright morning sky as Rhone let out the rope tether. He had gladly offered her the flight, but also planned on keeping a tight hand on the reins. She wouldn't be floating away on his watch.

The view of her bare legs dangling from her hitched-up skirts held his rapt attention. As hard as he tried, he simply didn't have the strength to look away. Her booted feet, moving in a slow mid-air dance of joy, certainly weren't helping the issue, and with her arms gliding through the air in soft waving motions, it was indeed like she was floating in the soft currents gently buffeting the balloon. Bella was in heaven, and to Rhone, she might actually have been an angel.

Having found her haven from the world, Bella never wanted to come down, but Rhone's anxious call cut into her revery.

"Bella, are you doing okay? Are you feeling sick?"

Almost dreamily, Bella opened her eyes, and with a sigh, called, "No, you ninny. I'm dancing with the wind," then again closed her eyes, feeling the wave-like motion of Bo drifting on the breeze.

Far too soon, however, her legs began to feel the cold. She was glad they were free from the confines of the heavy skirt, but the breeze blowing over them was definitely chilling. In disappointment, she called an end to her flight.

"I think it's time. Haul me down please."

"Got it," Rhone called back, beginning the task of hauling in the tether hand over hand.

For the five minutes it took for the balloon to descend, Bella kept her eyes closed, feeling the flow of the air around her and the unique sensation of weightlessness. It was something she would never forget.

"It was absolutely unbelievable!" she bubbled, as Rhone unhitched the harness buckles for her to step free.

When Bo lurched suddenly, catching the breeze and beginning to swing this way and that as though wanting to go back to the sky, Bella could only agree. But first, she wanted to get warm. Un-tucking her skirt hem, she dropped it back to its proper position, feeling instantly warmer, though costing her the freedom of bared legs.

"Next time, I'll wear heavy stockings to help keep warm," she commented thoughtfully. "I never realized how cold it can be up there. But it was wonderful. When can we do it again?"

Rhone just grinned, admiring this daredevil girl, who was not only willing, but excited to fly. He understood. He felt the same way.

When a flickering thought flashed through his mind, Stone was quick to pick up on it.

Of course we could build a larger unit. It would require larger containment vessels, but there is really no limit to the size, only the source and volume of the gasses required for its lift.

It was good news, but sounded too simple, and Rhone had to question it. *But if it was really big, wouldn't the air cool before we got it filled?* He could see that as a real problem.

Possibly, Stone agreed. *But as I have said, there are other gasses. Our steam process was simply the most available at the time.*

"Other gasses?" Rhone questioned aloud. He had already shut down the boiler, not wanting to go through that particular dance again.

Tying Bo to the wagon he turned to find Bella standing close, watching him with a calculating look.

"What?" he asked guiltily, feeling like he had been caught at something, but with no clue what.

"Did you know you talk to yourself?" she asked, with a raised eyebrow.

"I do?... Well maybe," he admitted, knowing instantly what she meant. Silently, he asked Stone, *What should I do?*

There was only a short pause before he felt Stone clear his non-existent throat. But when he did speak, it was as though Rhone was listening to an old grandfather speaking words of wisdom. The depth of the time-weighted words almost frightened Rhone, putting everything else on hold.

If this woman creature is special to you, then you can no longer withhold information. To do so will damage her trust. I leave this up to you, for you are the human, and I am merely an attachment to your life. The choice is yours, but you had best make your choice quickly. She is waiting.

Rhone's mind froze as he stood rooted, watching her, watching him.

Her look changed from surveillance to concern, as she asked, "Are you all right?" The exact words he had asked her a couple of weeks prior.

Guiltily, Rhone bobbed his head, not sure what to say, then shrugged, and sighed. "We need to talk. I meant to after my first landing, but then you got hurt and things changed. I suppose this is a good time."

He honestly thought he was doing a good job, but the shocked confusion on her face told him, it wasn't going as well as he thought.

Bella's color drained as her mind began to fill in the blanks, then spiral in disbelief.

She looked as though she was going to be sick, and Rhone jumped forward to catch her. "Bella, did you get hurt on the flight? Let me help." He couldn't think of any other reason she would be falling.

"No," she mumbled, her face ghost-like pale. Then grimacing at the pain on her still sore palms, pushed his hands away, forcing him away.

"No?" Rhone questioned, not at all so sure. "But... but you need help. Here let me hold you until you're stable."

"I said no!" The anger in her voice was enough to stop him cold.

He was shocked by the hardness in her eyes, where only moments before there had been so much joy.

"I don't understand," he whispered hoarsely. "What's wrong?"

"I'm done here," Bella said with total commitment. "I'm done with you and your, 'pretense', as you once said. And I'm tired of playing your games, waiting for you to do whatever it is you're going to do, and hanging around like I'm your toy. Well, I am not a toy!" she almost shouted. "Do you understand? I am not a toy! And I'm done."

As close as he was, her words actually rang in his ears. Rhone stepped back abruptly, catching a heal on the tangle of the balloon's tether, and hitting the ground hard. Totally dumbfounded, his mind couldn't understand a thing she had just said.

Bella didn't wait for a reply as she haughtily continued. "If you would be so good as to assist me in getting the wagon hitched up, I will be out of your way, and you can just go play with yourself. I really don't care." Then with minimal use of her hands, awkwardly stepped around Rhone's frozen form. Unfortunately, her bandaged hands made her unbalanced, and as her own foot caught, as Rhone's had, toppled with arms flailing.

Again Rhone jumped to assist, catching her before she hit the ground. "Bella, wait!" he pleaded, "You must have something wrong. Just wait."

A flash of memory reminded him how she had been when she was still a waitress, thinking him a well-to-do braggart looking for a good time. She had been hot then, but that was only a steaming kettle compared to this rampant boiler.

Bella's eyes flashed like fire as she hissed words of condemnation. "Touch me again, and I will bring you up on charges with the Mayor. He already doesn't like you, so this will give him all the reason he needs. Now let go of me!"

In furry, she ripped her arm from his grip.

Rhone knew her resolve. She would not only do as she threatened, she might actually attack him. But the violence of tearing her arm free unbalanced her again, and with her heel still caught, she tripped once more. Falling awkwardly, she barely managed to catch herself on still tender hands.

Her cry of pain and frustration burned livid scars into Rhone's already bruised conscience. Not knowing what to do, he flopped ungracefully down beside her, his action sending her into a panic.

"Get off!" she screamed, "Get off! Get off! Get off!" thrashing wildly with no thought to anything but defending herself from his obvious unwanted advances.

Recognizing her fear, Rhone instantly scooted back, giving her space, his eyes pleading for understanding and forgiveness. He tried one last time. "Bella, whatever you're thinking, it's not like that. Honest."

With panicked motions and bandaged hands, Bella worked to extricate herself from the tangle. Suddenly her anger and fear changed to tears of frustration, and she began wailing at herself, not him. "How could I have been so stupid? I fell for some dumb rich kid who couldn't care less for a small-town girl like me. No, he's too rich and powerful to see anyone but himself, and proves it every single day with his stupid collar and jewels! Even the Mayor knows you're no good, and I'm forced to report everything. I'm done! I'm done with it all!"

Her anger was talking now, building in force with its new direction to vent.

"Every day you wear that thing, and I have to stand here and look at it, proving I'm a nobody and you're the real thing." As her beautiful face fell into hopeless anguish, she shouted, "I hate you! And I hate it!" Her last words were almost a scream, filled with weeks of her frustration. Then she broke into the deep, honest sobs of a broken heart.

And what have you got to say for yourself? Stone rumbled in Rhone's weary head. *How do you plan on fixing this mess?*

"Me?" Rhone said aloud, too stunned to even think straight.

His surprised word cut through Bella's sobs in equal disbelief.

"You are such an ass," Bella whispered in disgust, her voice as dead as if she were speaking from the grave. "You wonder how I could possibly accuse you, because you're so special. You, who grew up in plenty, not in the run-down, back-country streets of a little worn out harbor town like this one. No, you grew up having whatever you might possibly want, from clothes, to toys, even your stupid jewelry for goodness sakes. What self-worthy man wears something like that? Particularly around town every day. But to you, it's nothing, just another bauble. Another pretty thing to play with, just like you tried to do with me. I hate your guts, which undoubtably smell worse than the poor creature's you use in your balloon. Who does those kinds of things? Who? No one! And for a good reason. People aren't supposed to fly. Birds fly! NOT PEOPLE!" She screamed the words in frustration and guilt.

But Rhone was so buried in his own guilt, he barely heard her scathing words.

A sliver of guilt crossed Bella's face, knowledge she couldn't blame him for, even if it meant allowing him a tiny piece of equity. She had flown. Regardless of the wrongs, she would never have done that without him.

When Rhone saw her glance swing to Bo, he didn't waste the moment.

"Bella, I'm not rich. I've been trying to tell you, I'm not anything. I grew up in a town far smaller than Corgy. In fact, I didn't even live in town. I lived in an old rundown house with my mom, until she died, when I was thirteen. Then it was just me. I'm nobody, except, I do work for Aundrea, my boss. She runs the OPR in the Capital Stronghold. Remember, I said this is my first job, ever. Being rich is just my front for this job. That's all. It's not real." He paused in his hopeful ramblings, then went for broke. "And I really, really, like you. I don't know what just happened, but I was going to tell you everything, and then everything sort of fell apart." His throat caught, and he could hardly hold it together.

Exhausted by her rant, Bella looked unsure, but began to work through his announcement. There had been so much strength in her fight, changing directions mid-stream was almost impossible.

Finally, the pain in her hands overcame the pain in her heart. Breaking eye contact, she glanced at the now dirty bandages, and her skirts wrapped tightly around her thighs, binding her in place. A length had even pulled up her leg, showing the bare skin of her thigh, but neither of them had enough energy to care at the moment.

As quietly as if talking to a kitten, Rhone asked, "Can I help you up? And I need to check your hands again. They look like they may need to be re-wrapped."

Bella looked from bandaged hands to him, her sad painful frown making her shoulders droop.

He gave a small, hopeful grin. "I didn't expect you to be crawling around on the ground. You were going for a float in the sky, and you were absolutely gorgeous. I could hardly breathe, watching you dance with the wind. It was breathtaking, and something I will never ever forget." His words lost power as he came to the end.

She may not have been convinced, but she was listening.

CHAPTER 20

Perchance to Dream

S ome parts of the story, Bella already knew. Now Rhone had to explain in its entirety, allowing it to unfold in series, like the pictures of a story book.

Stone, of course, made his presence known, flaring his light to the accompaniment of Bella's astonished, "Ooo's."

She was a picture of wonder, sitting with knees pulled to her chin, arms wrapped around them, and skirts tucked in snuggly, listening in rapt attention as Rhone told of rescuing Stone from Commissioner Dodge, and the lake in the badlands that had saved his life. He was going to mention Jewel and her partnering with Aundrea, but Stone broke in.

Excuse my interruption, but I do not believe that is your story to tell.

With a quick nod of understanding, Rhone apologized to Bella. "Ahh, Stone just reminded me, there are some things I can't tell you. Some is government business, and I don't have clearance to pass it on. Is that okay?"

With eyes still swimming with question, Bella tightened her lips into something not quite a smile, but accepted the rightness of it. Then came her big question. "So where do I fit in?"

It was a fair question, but one Rhone didn't know how to answer.

"I'm not sure, but you floated today. You've been part of this since the day I arrived. We wouldn't be anywhere near getting off the ground if it hadn't been for you. The part I don't know is, where this is going. I think it's my job to find a way to beat the pirates, but all we have is Bo. How it goes together from here is anybody's guess." With a shrug, he let it drop.

Bella released her knees and stretched, then leaned back on her elbows. Her hands had been re-bandaged, and she glanced down at them before lifting her eyes to Rhone. "I floated today," she said with deep sincerity. "It was the greatest thing I've ever done. I don't want to leave. I want to stay and be part of this. I don't know if it's my fear of you, of who you really are, or how much I want to do whatever you're doing, but I don't care what the rest of the world says. I want to float."

Rhone was about to nod in agreement, when a sudden outburst from Bella sat him back in surprise.

"No wait," she blurted, bandaged hands raised to stall his question. Sudden tears gathered in her eyes as she pushed on. "I need to say something, but I'm afraid."

Her attempted smile came out as a painful grimace, making Rhone unsure he wanted to hear, but he didn't stop her.

Bella's words seemed to scrape across each other as she whispered, "I've been spying on you, for the mayor."

Rhone was caught totally by surprise. "For the mayor?" he asked blankly. "But, I don't understand? Why? What would you even tell him? That we went on a picnic? I... I don't understand?"

Bella's chin began to waver, as the shame of what she had been forced to do finally came out in the open. "He came to me the first day you showed up, wanting to know who you were and what you were up to. I didn't want to, but he was The Mayor. How could I say no? I never told him much, only what he could have seen with his own eyes, but it was still wrong and I'm sorry. Then I got burned, and things changed. Now I've floated." She raised her hands in desperation, as if it answered all. "I can't take it anymore. I needed to tell you, even if you hate me for it."

As her tears started their run down her cheeks, he didn't have the heart to mention she had screamed those very words at him only minutes before. It no longer mattered.

"You want to stay?"

Her forehead creased as she tried to make her point. "If I can float again. Not every time. Just once in a while."

"Are you kidding? I loved watching you float."

He tried to clamp down on the image of her bare legs dancing with the wind, but she must have caught at least a whiff of his thoughts.

"I will be wearing stockings next time," she said with mocking eyes. "It's far too chilly for bare legs." Her snarky reply was much more the Bella he knew.

"Yeah, of course," he muttered, mentally slapping himself.

She grinned, probably recognizing those thoughts too.

Now that she wasn't threatening to whack him upside the head, Rhone took the opportunity to slide several feet closer.

"We do make a good team, and I couldn't have done this without you, but there's more that needs done. So here's what I'm thinking…"

Rhone dove in with enthusiasm, starting with his thoughts for improving Bo. It might not have been his best option, but it seemed the safer ground.

Within moments, Bella was nodding along absently. She had been hoping for something a little more personal, but beggars can't be choosers, as her mother used to say. Even so, Rhone's next words were enough to break into her thoughts.

"Maybe if we made it larger, it could be big enough for us both to float."

"Both of us?" she asked, doubting she had heard correctly. "We could do that? But who would work the boiler?"

"I'm not sure," Rhone admitted with a wrinkled brow. "We might need some other arrangement. And instead of strapping ourselves on, maybe we could make a bag we could hang below to sit in."

"How about a basket?" she asked hopefully. "We would be squished in a bag, and wouldn't be able to move very well."

"Ahh, yeah. That's true," Rhone mumbled, embarrassed that he hadn't seen the problem. On the other hand, it might not have been so bad, considering the other occupant.

It is feasible, Stone commented. *I will work on the lift calculations, but off-hand, consider it as requiring several of the bladder containment vessels for sufficient lift.*

Dutifully, Rhone passed on the information. "Stone just said we can do it, but we'll need more bladders."

The relief of being part of the team allowed Bella to breathe deeply again. At least her near future looked secure. Where it would go from there, as Rhone had said, was anybody's guess.

The owner of the Whale-cutters Warehouse nodded knowingly at Rhone's order. "Don't usually get much call for bladders, but if you're lookin' for more, we've got 'em."

"Excellent," Rhone answered, once again in his aristocratic demeanor. "Have them delivered to the same location, and one more question if you would. Do you know the location of a basketer in the vicinity?"

"Basketer? Oh, a basket maker, hmmmm," the shop owner mumbled noncommittally before giving his verdict. "Nope. Sorry. Not my zone of expertise," then smiled. Two-bit words were a rarity for this end of the dock.

"Well thank you, and I appreciate your effort."

Rhone was nothing if not polite, and really, the four huge whale bladders were quite a find on their own. Not so good for the whales, he supposed, but at least they wouldn't be wasted. He still had no idea where to find a basketer.

When Stone's calculations on needed lift again brought up the possibility of other gasses, Rhone didn't pay much attention, until Stone mentioned the possibility of the balloon going down over the ocean, if the air cooled too soon. The memory of dark waves and cold wind brought the terrifying realization that while he might be willing to wait for The Mistress to pick him up, there was no way he was going to let Bella do so. He would never forgive himself.

"You mentioned other gases," Rhone said, evading the fact that he hadn't been interested a moment ago. "How do we find them? I can't have the balloon going down with Bella onboard."

A very good point, Stone agreed readily. *There are only a few options, and some would not be available in the needed quantity, but I do have an idea. Would you mind another picnic?*

"A picnic?" Rhone asked in surprise.

"A picnic?" Bella repeated, having just walked over. "What a great idea. Where do you want to go?"

Already defeated, Rhone sent a comment to Stone. *Now see what you've done? How am I supposed to get any work done if we're traipsing all over the countryside?*

Stone's chuckle actually vibrated his collar. *Be patient my friend. Remember the little green lake with the bubbles? We need to do some testing.*

Testing? Rhone stopped working as his mind focused. *You think those are gasses? Wait... of course they are. How else would the muck lift up?*

His interested expression prompted a raised eyebrow and a comment from Bella.

"Hold on there, fella. Just because it's a picnic, doesn't mean you're getting anything but food."

Bella had tried to keep some distance between them since their last escapade. It was obvious, at least to her, he was not interested in her as a woman. So keeping her desires under wraps, and keeping to her work, made their close proximity manageable, if not what it might have been.

"Food?" Rhone asked, his attention rerouted. "I suppose it wouldn't be much of a picnic without food."

He had missed the other connection entirely, which was probably just as well. With a sigh, Bella gave a half-hearted smile. "I'll see to the food, but what made you bring up a picnic?" It obviously wasn't to spend time with her.

"Stone just asked about the pond, where we went the first time. The little green one. He thinks there might be gasses we could use in place of steam."

Bella's blue eyes lit up, almost forgetting her disappointment.

"I'll get the wagon hitched and meet you at The Common House," Rhone said, leaving the food detail to her.

"How about, I get the wagon hitched, and you go get the food?" Bella countered, still uncomfortable dropping in at The Common House. She didn't need the reminder of her past, and how out of place she was now. Corgy was a small town, where everyone knew she was employed by Rhone the rich kid. She felt the eyes of her fellow town's folk following her whenever she went out.

When Rhone's questing look showed he didn't understand, Bella sighed and headed into town.

At least Blue was hitched by the time she made it back to the stables.

With the wisps of clouds racing across the bright sky, Rhone was pleased he had thought to bring a lap-robe, a welcome addition that kept their legs warm in the crisp breeze. The wind always seemed to pick up along the coastline, but it served as a good excuse to sit close, leg to leg, with the heavy blanket tucked in around them. They rocked back and forth with the bouncing of the buckboard along the rutted road, laughing easily to comments about various people of the little town. It was about as good as it could be without their getting closer, and that wasn't on the table for the day.

With their conversation moving along no faster than Blue's plodding, Rhone began explaining more about their newest endeavor.

"Stone isn't sure the bladders will be strong enough for the extra load, and recommends staying low during the trials. But I'm not too worried. I don't plan on you going up until they've proven they can handle it."

"Sound's reasonable." Bella agreed, but made a sour face, appalled at the thought of the balloon giving out mid-flight. "But are you planning to go up? I might have suggested shooting you down, but I wouldn't want you landing on your head, or mine."

Rhone gave an easy chuckle. "No, I'm not dumb enough to bet against Stone. But I was thinking, since we already have a bladder for another steam balloon, we should probably try them grouped together. Then we'll have them ready if we do come up with a gas."

Bella's learning about Stone had caused her to drop Rhone's genius status somewhat. He wasn't dumb by any means, just not up to Stone's level. Besides, trying out a multiple-bladder version might get her a ride sooner, before they converted to a new gas.

"Sounds good to me."

Rhone was relieved. Bella had become tense when he was around, and it was hard to guess how she would react to most things. Maybe she was jealous of Stone? It was possible, but not something he could ask about.

Far too soon, the miles had rolled past, and they arrived at the two lakes tucked into forested hills. Although they had come to see the smaller lake, Bella chose a location very close to where they had picnicked on their earlier trip, where the smell was better. She spread the blanket while Rhone dug out the lunch basket. Since she had been the one picking up the food stuffs, the lunch was considerably lighter than the first had been, but the picnic was merely an excuse for the day's outing. They had real work to do.

Bella unwrapped the cold chicken breast and rolls, while Rhone uncorked a bottle of cider, pouring two glasses. Handing one to her, he gave an elegant dip of his head and raised his glass. "To a great day, and great company," clinking their glasses together with a crystal chime.

Bella was the first to lower her eyes from Rhone's bright smile. Her insides warmed at his words, but she knew he was simply practicing his well-to-do manners. Regardless, she could at least do the same.

"It is indeed beautiful, good sir, and thank you for inviting me."

It was fun to play the part.

They had no more than started the meal when Rhone sat up and rolled his eyes. "Stone wants to know when we'll be ready to get on with his investigation."

Bella tried not to show her disappointment, but she understood. "Stone, if you would give us five minutes please. There's no need to waste the food."

Rhone's apologetic shrug said he was right with her on that point.

A few minutes later, Bella began gathering the remains.

"Alright, Let's get to it," she exclaimed in resignation, brushing off her hands as though from real labor. "So much for a nice relaxing lunch, but we came here for the lake, not for the company."

Arms filled with a large clay jug, a stopper, and a funnel tucked tightly against his side, Rhone carefully stepped through the clumps of coarse grasses edging the ponded swamp. The dark water was almost invisible, covered as it was with sludge-like green scum. The slimy muck wrapped around his legs, making him grimace as he slid through like it was thick porridge. Thankfully, he'd removed his beautiful boots, refusing to immerse them in the muddy water, hoping he wouldn't slide in deeper than the pant legs rolled above his knees. With jug in one hand and funnel in the other, he stepped around the clumped grasses, working deeper into the pond.

Stone had given strict instruction on collecting the gas, and Rhone worked like he knew what he was doing, hoping to show his worth in front of Bella.

Once clear of the grasses and into more open water, he stuck the funnel's small end into the jug's mouth and stood waiting. Stone's implicit directions weren't too complex, but had been given twice, verifying that Rhone understood. Still, the work itself was more difficult than he would have guessed, and his palms began to sweat as he focused.

Bella had brought the blanket and spread it out, drawing her skirts to mid-thigh as she lay down to enjoy the sun's warmth on her bare legs.

Rhone's wide-eyed stared earned him a quip.

"You sir. Stop making such a fuss. You've already seen my legs. Now get your work done while I sun, and make sure you don't drown."

Rhone nodded a reluctant agreement, tearing his eyes away, before heading deeper into the pond. He had tried the drowning thing in his previous life, and definitely didn't care for it.

When he saw a bubble starting to form, he slid over to it, and flipped the unit upside-down directly above it. With the jug carefully positioned to balance against his shoulder, he reached into one of his many pockets for the sharp stick placed there for just this purpose. With an aggressive flourish, he stabbed the thick green bubble, skewering it like a sword thrust into a despicable pirate, then grinned in success as he watched, knowing the smelly gasses were beginning to fill the jug. He counted to a hundred while the sample gathered, then turned to let Bella know of his progress, and maybe sneak a peek. Unfortunately, his quick turn caused his bare foot to slide on the slimy bottom, squishing thick mud up between his toes. His awkward hold on the jug made it impossible to stop his slide, and with no traction, he slipped deeper into the muck, feeling himself falling. Rhone grabbed franticly at the jug, and in an acrobatic contortion, managed to save it from tipping off his shoulder.

"Good catch," Bella called cheerfully from her place in the sun.

Rhone glowered in her direction, growling, "I've got it," then slipped again, dropping seat first into the chest-deep water. He was a sorry picture, sitting head above the sludge, jug held securely in the air. He may have fallen, but he wasn't going to lose the sample.

His slip brought a shriek from Bella, but it swiftly changed to a shrill laugh. "Are you all right?" she asked guiltily, words stuffed between her laughter.

Rhone gave an exaggerated sigh. "I'm fine. A tad wet, but nothing that won't dry."

"Did you lose the cork," she called back, remembering the task wasn't done yet.

"I've got it, but it's in my pocket. I can't get to it without lowering the jug." His squirming around, trying to get his feet back under him, had only worked him deeper into the mud.

"I'm coming," Bella giggled, scrambling to her feet and stripping out of her skirt.

By the time Rhone got himself turned to face her, Bella was wading out into the muck, in her underthings.

"I told you I wouldn't let you drown," she said with a grin. "Now where's the cork?"

Pulling himself together, Rhone muttered something about it being in his pants pocket, but when she dipped her hand into the murky water and began digging around, his eyes grew to the size of hen's eggs. "What are you doing?" he gasped.

Bella grinned like a catfish at his obvious discomfort. "I'm searching for the cork. What do you think I'm doing?

"Ahh, well... it's in my front right pocket...not there!" he gasped again, sending her into yet another chorus of laughs. He was trying desperately not to tip the jug, as he sputtered, "It's not all that funny," going a bright crimson at her obvious enjoyment.

A moment later she announced, "Got it!" jubilantly drawing the dripping cork out of the water. With a face denying anything out of the ordinary, she stuffed it into the jug's mouth, and asked, "Can I help you up?"

With a deep sigh, Rhone allowed her to assist him back to a standing position, feeling the slimy, muddy water, run down his body. Bella herself was wet to the waist, but she, at least, was having fun.

"Come on," she bubbled. "Let's get out of this soup."

In slow slogging steps, they made it back to dry land.

With solid soil beneath his feet, Rhone confidence grew. He turned to glare at Bella, ready to make some cutting remark, but stopped short, as his eyes riveted to her, wringing mucky water from the dripping underthings that barely covered her wet thighs.

Feeling his gaze, Bella smiled shyly with a shrug. "You've already seen my legs, so, just don't stare too hard, and I won't get too embarrassed."

"Ahh... sure," Rhone agreed, not able to come up with anything more appropriate. But he couldn't help noticing the thin material wrapping wetly against a very shapely rump. After a very, very, deep breath, Rhone managed to focus on a nearby tree instead. Sometimes, it was difficult being a gentleman.

With apparent nonchalance, Bella walked to the blanket and bent to pick up her dry skirt. Rhone was more than aware of her presence, but kept his glances to a minimum as she pulled it on. Then turning her back, she slipped her wet things from under it, piling them on the ground.

Nothing in Rhone's life had taught him how to deal with this, and he felt the hot blood rush to his face.

Glancing over her shoulder, Bella saw his condition. "Sorry, but it really would be uncomfortable if I wore them all the way back."

Finished, she turned to a still dripping Rhone, and sighed deeply. "You're impossible," she mumbled. "You act like you've never seen a girl before," then paused, realizing he probably hadn't. With a solemn shake of her head, she took over. "All right. Your turn. Strip out of those, and we'll wring them out. They won't be dry, but it will be better than dripping muddy water all the way back to town. Just try to keep your shirt pulled down until then."

Nodding a dumb agreement, Rhone started to unbuckle.

Bella didn't have as much objection to watching as he had, and even helped when the wet pants stuck to his legs. By the time they were off, he was able to grin again, and with each of them grabbing an end, they began to twist, wringing out the muddy water. When they were as dry as the wringing would get, Bella flipped out the wet material, laying them on the grass alongside her own frilly things, then plopped down on the blanket, motioning for Rhone to sit next to her as though it was an everyday occurrence.

"At least we got the sample we came for. Now what?" she asked, looking at him expectantly.

Very mindful of the drape of his shirt, Rhone lowered his lanky form to the blanket, understanding better how Bella must have felt at his curious gaze. But she had a fair question.

"Stone is going to do some tests. We'll know more after that," he explained, trying to remain casual. It was an evasion, but right now it was the least thing on his mind. "I think we have an hour or two before we need to head back, if that's okay? Maybe we can just lay here in the sun for a while? It might actually get warm if the breeze dies down a bit."

Bella propped herself up on an elbow, nose crinkled in consternation, as she asked, "Let me get this straight. You're asking if it's okay to lay in the sunshine, on a blanket, without your pants on, next to a girl that just took off half her clothes? Are you a priest or something?"

Instantly, Rhone felt as stupid as she was suggesting. While he didn't know what to say, he knew enough to face it like a man. With ears turning a deep red, he gave it his best.

"To answer at least one thing, no, I've never seen a girl, like that." He didn't mention seeing his mom in her underthings, but he was pretty sure that wasn't the same.

Bella raised her eyebrows, unsurprised by his answer. "It's okay," she said, smiling lightly. "You're a gentleman. That's a good thing."

"I'm sorry," Rhone continue uncertainly. "I just don't know much about women. In fact, I've never been around girls. I don't want to make a mistake, or make you afraid, and I've already done that."

Bella tipped her head to the side, considering him. "I think all you need is experience. Having a little information might make it easier."

"Maybe," he said carefully, "but what exactly does that mean?"

Leaning forward, she kissed him lightly, experimenting.

Rhone flinched involuntarily as her lips touched his, but the warmth behind them drew him back for more.

As he soon found, even the sun had something to learn about heat.

CHAPTER 21

Bigger is Better

R hone smoothed his expression, trying, without much luck, to keep from grinning constantly. It had been an amazing day, and he still wasn't sure what to make of it. Whistling tunelessly, he checked the calendorium Aundrea had given him before he'd left on assignment. It was a match to hers, and could tell the exact time, the moon phase, season, tide, and sun-sign, but he hardly ever used it. He was a country kid. When the sun rose, it was time to get up. When it set, it was time to go to bed. Winter was cold, and summer was hot. What else did he need to know? But it was a beautiful piece, and he was proud of the mechanical device strapped to his wrist.

When the calendorium's timer chimed, Rhone plucked the cork from the jug. Flipping it over, he dumped Stone onto the table with clunk, watching as he spun like a drunken top.

"Is everything okay?" he asked, scooping Stone into his palm.

I must say, that was interesting, Stone said with a humorous chuckle, *but I am perfectly fine, and thank you for asking.*

"Good. So... Will it work?" Rhone asked, not realizing how anxious he had been.

The infusion of warmth answered even before Stone's voice filled Rhone's mind. *Better than suspected. Excellent in fact. The algae can undoubtably be cultivated, and their outgases are indeed lighter than air.*

"Bella, it's a go!" Rhone shouted, unable to contain his enthusiasm.

Used to his outbursts, Bella smiled as she turned from her task of oiling bladder tissue. "How big will it need to be?"

Which was something Rhone didn't know.

Tell her I will work up the numbers, Stone said silently. *It shouldn't take long, but I want to calculate in a safety factor, and possible regeneration tables. So perhaps tomorrow.*

Obediently, Rhone passed on the information. "Stone said maybe tomorrow."

"What's taking so long, and what's he been doing in there?" Bella asked with interest.

"Oh, he's just doing research on the swamp algae, the little plant things on the water. See, when they breathe, they give off a gas, just like we do, except their's isn't really breath, but it works the same way." Rhone was beginning to confuse himself, and tried to re-explain an issue Stone had explained, but he barely understood. As far as he was concerned, his understanding didn't really matter. If Stone said it would work, it would.

Bella however, took in the information, nodding in agreement as the concept firmed in her mind. "And if we can harvest the gas, we can use it to fill the balloon envelope." Her eyes got bigger as she began to understand the process. "We'll have all the lift we want! We won't have to come down when the air cools." Her face took on a cherubic expression as she whispered, "We might never have to come down."

"Maybe," Rhone agreed carefully, not having thought that far along. "But remember, I still need a way to fight the pirates. That's why I'm here."

She may have known, but as Bella returned to work oiling tissue, there were stars in her eyes.

Concerned, Rhone had to ask, *Stone, is it true? Could she just stay up there forever?* For some odd reason, he felt a bit jealous.

Technically, yes, Stone answered carefully. *Of course there is the food and water issue, but aside from that, the balloon contraption itself could stay aloft for a very long time. I am also considering the possibility of algae regeneration, which would allow a continuous gas replacement. It would certainly require a much larger containment envelope, and there would be an output barrier with size constraints, but I see no major element to curtail its use.*

"Okay, thanks," Rhone mumbled, deep in a mind-clouding fog. The longer he watched Bella humming sweetly as she oiled the whale bladders, the more he rethought the issue. Maybe it wouldn't be so bad.

But as nice as it was, it merely evaded the real question. How could he use a bunch of ballooning whale bladders against pirates? It was time to talk to Captain Black again.

"Good morning to The Mistress," Rhone called cheerfully from the bottom of the ramp. "Is the Captain aboard?"

A shaggy head rose questioningly above the rail, its familiar grin a standard on the captain's face. "Well hello there young sir. Thought you up and floated off on that giant bubble you've been spoutin' about. Figured you must have loftier sights than visiting an old sea captain. But since you're here, you might as well come aboard."

Rhone trotted up the rickety ramp, and made his way to the quarterdeck where Captain Black cuffed him on the shoulder in a hello. "So you decided to come court the ne'er-do-well captain did you? It must be difficult, finding time in your social calendar for us un-gentried types."

The Captain knew Rhone wasn't the little rich kid he appeared to be, but Rhone felt as guilty as charged.

"I'm sorry, Captain. I have been busy, but I should have made time."

"Aww, you're fine. Glad you showed up in fact. You just out for a stroll, or is there something on your mind?"

The Captain's grin took most of the steam from his words, but he was also correct.

"A very simple thing," Rhone commented, taking the offered cup. "Would you know the whereabouts of a basketer?"

"Really? You show up to ask about shopping?" He actually looked affronted by the question. "Do I look like a common fish-wife, hawking her wares on the street corner?" Not only did he roll his eyes, but his entire head rolled in a display of exasperation. But pulling a pipe from his vest pocket, he stuck it between his teeth and settled himself comfortably. "Just so happens, you came to the right person," he said, using the pipe's stem to punctuate his words. "Now, not that it's a normal choice, expecting a ship's captain to know such things in a port. The nearest tavern, sure. Fancy ladies, you betcha. Even the jail, where he might have to draw some of his men, but basketers? Well, this is your lucky day. Of all those people who depend on the services of this little ship, turns out there's a couple basket weavers among them. They don't have a shop in town, but I do tote their wares from time to time, when there's a bit of cargo space left from other, more prosperous ventures. Basketry tends to sell better in further ports than at home. It's all about trade you know."

"That would be perfect," Rhone responded eagerly. "But I need something special."

An eyebrow raised on the captain's scraggy face, as Rhone continued.

"See, I'm in need of an overlarge basket, strong, but light. Perhaps an arm-span in width and waist deep. Not exactly normal."

Captain Black gave a great guffaw and whacked his knee. "Dang me if you aren't something. You've got more plans than a shipwright."

His cackling continued until Rhone became embarrassed. Even the crewmen turned to look.

"So, the basketers?" Rhone asked cautiously. "Where would I find them?"

Wiping his eyes, the captain returned to a somewhat more serious demeanor. "Oh, they'd be pretty hard to find back up in the hills, but I can get a message sent."

"Perfect," Rhone sighed. "Have them go to the warehouse I rented on the far side of town. I'm there most days now."

"Setting up shop, are you? Well good. Somebody's got to get some work done. Now, speaking of it, if you'll excuse me, I've got to holler at my crew. They're workin' about as slow as a sunburned crab."

Rhone nodded absently, wondering how slow a sunburned crab was. He would have to ask Bella.

But as the captain started to rise, Rhone stopped him with a serious request. "Captain, one more question if I could? If you just happened to

244

own a big balloon envelope, and you wanted to help take care of a pirate problem, how best would you use it?"

It was a pretty straightforward question as far as he was concerned, but Captain Black merely scratched at his scraggly beard for a full minute, taking so long, Rhone began to wonder if the captain had fleas.

The scowl was the first sign of a problem.

His words were the next.

"If you're seriously considering the issue, then you must be crazy," the captain stated harshly, but unexpectedly, his scowl became a shrug, as though the statement didn't really matter. "Shucks, you couldn't do much by yourself anyway. True, you might well be able to find a ship, and with flags, pass on the information, but dang-it fella, your balloon-thing couldn't change course to make any type of attack. Remember, control the wind and you control the battle, but you've got no way to control the wind. You just float along where it blows. Even if we drag you along, tethered to the Mistress, the moment we cut you loose, you'd just drift away. I admire your spunk, honest, but I just don't have an answer you'd want to hear."

Rhone's heart fell as if he had dropped from Bo's harness. If Captain Black, with all his fighting history, couldn't see a way, then all their efforts were wasted.

Barely able to speak, Rhone mumbled, "Thank you, Captain. I appreciate your honesty."

"I'm sorry too. If it would work, I'd be all over the idea like flies on a dead fish. It'd make trading a ton safer. It's bad enough fighting the weather and the sea, but having pirates going for your goods too, just about takes the fun out of it."

Numbly, Rhone nodded his acceptance. "Thank you again, Captain. I had best be getting back. I left Miss Bella at the warehouse, working on our newest project. This one is much larger, which will give more lift, but I'm not sure what good it will do now."

In a mind-numbing fog, Rhone rose and made his way down the rickety ramp, his blank stare missing the solemnness in the captain's eyes.

"I'm really sorry, fella," the captain called to Rhone's departing figure, "but it's still a pretty nifty achievement. Now you take care and I'll send the basketers tomorrow."

Rhone acknowledged the comment with a quick nod, then hands in pockets, absently paced the worn and sunburned boardwalk. He had been so sure of his plan, but after putting all that time, effort, and money into the project, he had nothing worthwhile. It was hopeless. How could he tell Bella?

When Stone's unique throat clearing interrupted his drifting thoughts, Rhone responded with a short, "What?" the querulous answer more abrupt than he intended.

What? Stone commented in uncharacteristically good humor. *But I must say, it is at least the right question. I have been considering your recent conversation with our good captain, and as I understand, his only dysfunctional element was our lack of control over the wind. Would you say that is a fair assumption?*

"Maybe," Rhone answered moodily, "but why worry about it? We can't control the wind. It's wind! That's just common sense. Nobody can tell the wind what to do." His frustration showed in the frown creasing his forehead.

Oh, contraire my friend. The good captain controls the wind every time he sails. So why can we not do the same from a balloon?

Rhone's response would have been quite vocal, but he was on the docks, and instead focused inward. *What are you talking about? Bo is a balloon envelope, not a ship.*

If rocks could smile, Stone would have been beaming. *Perhaps, if I were to be more specific. If I were to call it an airship, would that catch your attention?*

"A what?" Rhone choked out in amazement. "A boat in the air? Could we actually do that?"

Perhaps not an actual wooden boat, but something similar, yes.

With a new and vital energy surging through his body, Rhone quickened his pace. He needed to talk with Bella.

B ella's first words were less than complimentary, making Rhone wince.

"An airship? We haven't even completed BoToo, and you're already off on some new harebrained scheme?"

Her fist-on-hips posture, which she had developed to an art, doused cold water on his growing enthusiasm.

"BoToo?" he asked cautiously. "Ahh, that's different."

"Well, we already have Bo, so of course this is Bo Too."

And that was enough said. Without the energy to fight back, and with Captain Black's verdict hounding his thoughts, Rhone continued his work on BoToo. He wouldn't allow his project to flounder. Not if there was still a chance.

For the next several nights, Rhone sat up sketching designs on brown wrapping paper, the cheapest kind in town. He was so deep into his work, even Bella was all but invisible. Luckily, she had her own work to do, oiling both the new bladder tissue and the batch of seaweed they had washed clean of sea salt and sand.

Rhone's new ideas truly had been exciting, but Bella insisted on 'slow and steady', completing the envelope they were working on before plunging headfirst into a different pool. It was tedious work, but had to be done.

When a light knock sounded at the warehouse door, Bella gratefully untangled herself from her work. Rhone was far too deep into his designing to even hear the knock.

Sliding open the heavy door, Bella saw an older, grey-haired couple, eyes to the ground and obviously unsure of themselves.

"Can I help you?" she asked politely, her time as a waitress making her tone well-practiced and welcoming.

The sparsely-haired man stepped forward, wringing his frayed flat cap in both hands, likely explaining why it was so worn. "Excuse me, miss. I was told to meet a Mr. Rhone at this address."

"You have the right place. Can I say who's calling?" she asked, smiling warmly and trying to alleviate his concern.

"It's actually my lady wife he wants to see. I'm just her chaperone for this trip. We don't get out much, and I'm afraid she's a bit shy."

To prove his point, the older gentleman nodded toward his lady wife, as busty as he was wiry. Recognizing their scrutiny, she quickly returned her eyes to the ground, blushing a brilliant red glow from her already ruddy cheeks.

"This is Cara, and I am Grenn," the man stated, quickly diverting attention from his wife. "Captain Black sent a message sayin' you might have a need for our services."

Bella was cautious as she asked, "Your services?"

"You didn't request basketers?" Grenn questioned, his aged face turning to disappointment.

Like a sunbeam shining through the clouds, Bella brightened, and stepped back to usher them into the room. "Please, do come in. I'm sorry I didn't make the connection. Rhone is at work on a project, but will be with you in just a moment."

Leaving the two beside the door, Bella scurried to find Rhone. She found him, madly scribbling inky lines onto brown paper. The piles of scroll-like paper scattered on the floor, betrayed how long he'd been working.

"Rhone, there are people here to see you," she announced, placing a gentle hand on his shoulder.

Rhone dragged weary eyes from the newly inked lines, his voice scratchy as he asked, "People? What people?" furtively glancing over his shoulder to the doorway.

Not to be put off, Bella smiled brightly to the two, and gestured for them to come over. "This is Grenn and Cara, the basketers you asked Captain Black about."

Grenn stepped up, bowing stiffly as he attempted to do justice to Rhone's supposed position of power. Cara simply blushed an even brighter hue, dipping a shallow curtsy, her face almost buried in her busty chest.

Rhone blinked twice before a flash of recognition crossed his features. The next seconds were like a biblical miracle, as Rhone rose from his seat into a regal stretch, instantly becoming the young noble he was professed to be.

"Pray excuse my delay," he began, addressing the older couple with a respectable bow of his own. "I am more than pleased to meet the both of you. Thank you for making the trip. As to why the request, I find myself in a most interesting situation, where your skills might be of use."

Bella marveled at his instant change. In one moment, the tired, unsure youth had become every bit the nobleman she had first met.

Slightly embarrassed, Grenn glanced around the spacious warehouse, noting the billows, fiber, jugs and other odd items scattered about. With raised eyebrows, he cautiously asked, "Would this be a laboratory? I've heard tell of some strange doin's hereabout, but I can't imagine what use you might have for us. We're both a tad past our good years I'm afraid." Then realizing his words might get them sent off without employment, quickly added, "We can still produce good work though. Cara is a true marvel at the weaving, and no doubts about it." The hopeful look on the old man's face made Rhone smile for the first time all day.

"Not questioned in the least," he said graciously. "Captain Black would not have sent you if you didn't do good work. I have full belief in his judgement."

As worry dropped from the man, a look of pride took its place. "Very good sir. You can be sure we'll do our best. Won't we Cara?" He turned lovingly to his wife who still retained her brilliant coloring. "That would be a yes," Grenn explained with a crinkling smile. "If it wasn't, you can bet I would be hearing about it already." His light chuckle ended as he remembered who he was speaking to. "Sorry Sir," he mumbled in embarrassment.

"Please, call me Rhone, or we won't get very far on this project." Then, not waiting for a reply, he led them across the warehouse, stopping before a large pile of seaweed. "This is a floating balloon envelope," Rhone announced, "or will be, once completed."

The couple glanced at each other as if questioning his sanity, until Bella stepped in to assist.

"It's true," she insisted. "It floats up in the air."

The comment didn't improve the worry lines etching Grenn's leathery brow. It wasn't until Cara's quick tug on his coat-tail drew him down to her quiet whisper, and his nodded acceptance, that he straightened with an apologetic smile. "Cara would like to know what you use as a lifting agent?"

The question caught both Rhone, and Bella, by total surprise.

"She knows about lighter-than-air gasses?" Rhone asked.

Grenn's grin transformed his face as he explained, "She was a school-marm once, a long time ago."

Amazed, Rhone wondered how she could possibly teach school when she was this shy, but respectfully gave Cara a slight bow. "You are absolutely correct, Mum. We used steam for the first flights, and will again for this larger unit as we test, but eventually we hope to use a gas for lift."

Cara's smile glowed behind Grenn's shoulder, her enthusiastic nod causing more than just her chubby cheeks to bounce.

"And exactly why we need you," Bella stated, getting right to business. "We're hoping you can create a giant basket, large enough to ride in, but as light as possible. Our balloon is big, but won't lift very much weight."

Cara pulled Grenn down for another whispered conversation, then released him, her cheerful smile giving a good portent of the answer.

"Can do sir," Grenn announced. "We can work up a design in no time. She's thinking, something like a giant egg basket, thick at the top edge, and strong enough to carry your weight. If it's woven from coarse willow-like branches, it would be plenty strong, and you could have it as big as you like." Then he cautiously added, "As to timeframe though, better give us a week," glancing to Cara for his own confirmation. "It'll take us a couple of days to gather the reeding, and a couple more to weave. Once we get going, it comes along quite apace. Cara here is a certified whizz at it, and I help as I can."

Rhone's heart was leaping as he answered, "Excellent. The timing will be perfect."

"Well, we'd best be off then. Plenty to do," Grenn said good-naturedly.

He was already herding Cara to the door, when she unexpectedly turned back. "It's a wonderful project," she whispered, her voice barely loud enough to be heard. "Simply wonderful." Then ducking her head in embarrassment, once again disappeared behind Grenn's solid shoulder.

As the door closed, Bella began to laugh joyfully, clapping her hands as she moved in a sinuous dance, her sing-song voice chanting, "We have a basket."

"So it seems," Rhone agreed, watching appreciatively as Bella danced.

It had indeed been an interesting meeting. While he may not have all the answers, he would have a basket, for two. Whether he had a balloon envelope to lift it was another matter.

When Bella finally noticed him gawking, she scolded, "What are you standing there for? You have work to do."

CHAPTER 22

A Strange thing You Have There

B o Too may have been a bit bulky, as their creation rose in the still morning air, but Bella considered her majestic. It was definitely a unique sight with the big basket swinging below the odd contraption.

Rhone had tethered the balloon to the wagon as usual, but at Stone's suggestion, had loaded the wagon with rocks, compensating for the lift of the multiple bladders. Bella's white knuckles, gripping tightly to the double-thick edging, didn't take away from the fact she was having the time of her life. This was even better than flying Bo, since she was standing on her own feet rather than being buckled to the balloon. She waved to Rhone, where he waited beside the windlass he would use to haul her back in. He had refused to send her up without testing the unit first, and luckily, all had gone well. Now it was her turn.

When a quick gust blew in from the ocean, Bo Too danced on its long tether, the added strain causing the balloon to drop lower, then rise rapidly as the breeze let up. Bella's shriek of laughter brought a grin to Rhone's face. She was made for floating.

Rhone kept track of the time on his calendorium, and after the twenty minute chime, called to Bella. "How's it going up there?"

Reluctantly, Bella answered, "I think it's time to pull us in. I'm starting to get cold."

Giving a thumbs up, Rhone began cranking the windlass, drawing Bella and the floating balloon contraption back to earth.

As soon as the basket touched down, Bella hopped out, flashing a bit of stockinged leg in the process. "It was awesome. Totally awesome," she bubbled appreciatively. "The wickerwork creaked and squeaked, but I was never worried about it coming apart. Cara did a great job, and she's so pretty."

Rhone's questioning look, caused Bella to roll her eyes.

"BoToo! Who did you think I was talking about?"

Rhone shrugged innocently, which really didn't matter since she had already passed the issue.

"Don't you just love the designs they wove into the sides? It's almost like having a blanket wrapped around you." Bella said appreciatively, running her hand along the edging.

Again Rhone winced, mumbling to himself, "A really stiff blanket," not able to get a word past her enthusiasm.

Bella was fully into her experience, hands floating dreamily through the air. "Imagine flying over the countryside, watching everything below? It would be like drifting through a dream."

Rhone loved seeing her happy, but his assessment was aimed more at structural safety than her daydreams, and commented as he looked speculatively at the netting. "I think these connectors need to be changed. They'll work okay for now, but with anything bigger, I'm afraid they'll pull apart."

As his comment drew Bella from her dreamy experience, she remarked, "Can't you ask Stone? He knows pretty much everything."

But Rhone's mental connection with Stone, got a stiff reply. *Why ask me? I know nothing about connecters, brackets or casements. Those are hands-on, human things. I deal with numbers and projections. If you wish my assistance, request data on things I know.*

Rhone was a surprised by Stone's answer. But how would he know? Stone wasn't human.

Sorry, he projected to his friend. *Sometimes I forget how hard this must be for you.*

Stone's rumble felt like a far off thunderstorm, but eased, quickly coming to his more normal sigh. *It is not your fault. I am simply feeling useless. I sit here and wait, while you two do all the work.*

That much Rhone understood. Being rock-like, Stone may be good at waiting, but doing nothing while everyone else was working, could wear on a soul.

"I get it," Rhone said quietly, "But remember, you're the one who came up with this whole thing. I just put it on paper."

There was a moment's silence before Stone answered, *Not true. It was all your concept. I simply converted your somewhat haphazard thoughts, into more concisely arranged data. You simply do not believe in yourself.*

Glancing at BoToo tethered to the wagon, Rhone realized he had done some pretty neat things, but he hadn't done it alone.

Stone? I hate to correct you, but Aundrea sent us out together, as a team. It's not me, and it's not you. It's us, and together we'll get this assignment done.

They did make a good team. All of them.

The unexpected blast ripped through the oiled tissue, throwing Rhone backwards like a discarded doll. He lay there, flat on his back, his mind clouded, not understand why he had an unobstructed view of the sky, and not BoToo's looming form. Even his mental reach for Stone found only scrambled words, too disjointed for recognition.

It took several moments to understand what had happened, but finally the words, 'bladder rupture', made their way through the one-sided conversation he was having with himself.

Finally dragging himself into a sitting position, Rhone stared in dismay as the massive balloon whipped back and forth, before finally dropping sickly to the ground.

Bo Too's bladders had been inflated several times, attempting to get the connectors right and not rub on the sensitive tissue, but obviously, it had been once too many.

Bella gazed tearfully at her beloved BoToo, laying in a limp pile of seaweed and tissue, draped awkwardly over the beautifully-woven basket. A shiver of cold fear passed over her as she realized what would have happened if they had been aloft. Burying her sob in an armful of the blanket she was sitting on, she suddenly remembered Rhone, and fought to her feet, heart racing in panic. When her eyes found him hobbling unsteadily toward the wreckage, she ran to his side and wrapped an arm around his waist, steadying herself as much as him. "Rhone?" she questioned, needing no more than the word.

Rhone stood with vacant eyes, and a shaky hand, caressing the smooth seaweed wrap. He knew this was a system failure. The bladder tissue simply wasn't strong enough for dependable flight. The sadness in his eyes said as much as his soft words. "I'm sorry. I guess this means we need a better envelope."

Bella simply nodded in agreement, not needing to beat a dead horse.

With a deep breath, Rhone slid free and began the task of dismantling BoToo.

It took a full hour to load the basket and ruined balloon into the wagon. He would come back later for the steam boiler. They obviously wouldn't be needing it for quite some time. Still, he wasn't ready to give up. They would simply have to come up with another material. What ever that might be.

C aptain Black's reply was concise, "Tissues too thin," he said, nodding knowingly. "Think of it like sail canvas. A bed sheet would work, but it wouldn't hold up to a storm, and would wear out in no time. It's like that with your bladder tissue. It works, but isn't tough enough for the long haul."

It was almost exactly what Rhone had told Bella, but it sounded far wiser coming from the Captain.

"But how do I find tougher tissue?" Rhone asked petulantly. He didn't want to give up, but didn't know where else to look?

"Dang it, boy. What's the matter with your whale? You only tried the bladder. There's other parts you know." His raised eyebrow prompted Rhone to answer.

"Other parts? You mean like the stomach, or lungs? He made a sour face, thinking of working with more guts.

"Something like that. But I was thinking more like the throat. The rorqual grooves. Ever seen a whale eat krill?" He waited for the light to go on, but when Rhone's expression remained dim, the captain shrugged. "Guess that answers that. Any how, take those whales you've been going on about. Not all of 'um mind you, just the ones without teeth. Their throat stretches to a zillion times its regular size, holds tons of water, and filters out the good stuff, dumpin' the rest. If it's expansion you want, I'd try that."

It was hard to imagine, but since he had never seen a whale eat, he figured they all had teeth and ate meat like a shark.

The captain waited for the information to settle in before starting again. "Tell you what. Why don't you go back to that whale cutter's place and see what I'm talking about? I'd figure you could stitch a couple of those throats together and have a contraption tons bigger than that little bladder of yours. The hide's tough, too. Gotta be, to hold that much water."

I think you should agree, Stone whispered in Rhone's mind. *After all, you did come asking for Captain Black's experience.*

Rhone nodded, answering both Stone and the captain. "What did you call it? An inkwell?"

"Rur-kwel," the captain answered slowly, pronouncing it so Rhone could pick up the unique word.

"Right, a throat. I suppose it's no worse than a bladder," Rhone said thoughtfully. "Thanks, Captain. I'll give it a try. You are definitely a man of knowledge."

"Don't know about that," the captain said with a chuckle, "but you learn a few things when you've been at sea your whole life. Besides, we got that harpoon up front for more than just pokin' at sharks."

Rhone made his goodbyes, then walked up the dock with a thoughtful expression.

R hone learned a lot about whales from this visit to the cutters. The captain had been right. Some whales had teeth, but not all. And while toothed whales had a throat, they didn't have the grooved rorqual that would balloon out into a huge pouch, capturing tons of water along with the tiny creatures they ate. All in all, the throat was just another hunk of fatty hide.

"I'll take two please," Rhone announced. "As large as you can get."

If he was going to try, he might as well go for the prize.

"An' would you be wantin' that delivered?" The owner squinted with one eye as he calculated the load. "Might take two trips for that much meat."

"Meat? I wasn't looking for the meat, or fat. It's the skin I want. Can you just skin it out?"

A look of consternation came over the man. "The skin? But the fat's the only part that's any good. Shucks, if it wasn't for the work involved, I'd give it to you free, just to be rid of it." Then his face blanched at hearing his own words. His own father's words of wisdom had stated, *Never give away that which can be sold!* The old man would be rolling over in his grave.

Rhone tried not to smile at the man's obvious discomfort. "I will pay, but I do expect a decent price," he said amiably. "If we can come to terms, I would like the hide of two rorqual throats delivered to the same address as before."

As the owner was beginning to congratulate himself on an unexpected sale, Rhone broke into his happy thoughts.

"Excuse me, but I have a change of plans. If you would have them delivered to the tanners, I'd appreciate it."

With a relieved breath, the man nodded respectfully. "Good plan at that," and slumped weakly into a chair.

Rhone remembering the work it took to skin, scrape and work hides, glad he wouldn't have to that with these monstrous slab. With a quick nod, he left the warehouse and its horridly invasive smell. His clothes would need laundered before he wore them again.

⚜

The tanner was next.

"Ain't never done a whale skin," the tanner said, rubbing his sunburned nose in thought. "Whatcha need it for?"

He was looking for gossip. Small towns like Corgy didn't get a lot of news, and Rhone was a magnet for such things.

"I'm going to make a bubble," Rhone told him evasively, keeping things to minimum.

It was also a good way to hide the truth, since it sounded ridiculous. Rhone's mom had taught him to watch for lies, also explaining that the best of them were almost true, just not quite.

"Bubbles, yeah, that's a good one," the tanner said, recognizing a misdirect when he heard one. "Well, give me a couple weeks. It'll take the whole crew that long to work it over. First there's the fleshing. Then the salting. Then pickling..."

"Yes, I understand," Rhone intervened, dismissing the oration with a waved hand. "I've done my share of hide work. Now, to the job. What I desire is a finished hide, both flexible and pliable. Do it well and there will be a bonus."

"Better give me a month," the tanner reconsidered with a grimace. "Don't wanna skimp anywhere."

Rhone happily agreed. He now had an entire month to perfect his plans,

CHAPTER 23

Watch That Last Step

S ketches of unique bubbles were scattered across the brown paper, filling the space between anchors, windlass winches, and very odd-looking ships with billowing sails.

Rhone had been working non-stop for the last two days, until Bella
began to worry he would starve before he was done. She placed food close
at hand, but would find it pushed back, making room for another sketch.

He needed real data to finalize the plans, particularly the simple things,
like how large an envelope they would need to actually lift the ship. It
would determine the entire structure. Pictures were all well and good, but
without data the plans weren't complete.

"Stone, I can't finish this until I know how much space it's going to take.
Have you got the problems with the algae pans solved?"

I believe so, Stone began, *although it did require a recalculation of the pan
itself.*

Rhone paused, weighing the words against the feeling he sensed from his
collar. "So, what aren't you telling me?" he asked cautiously.

You are so suspicious, Stone complained. *I was simply referring our use of copper sheeting for the algae bed. It was both easy to work and readily available, but it seems to create a problem of its own. I have since discovered that copper is unable to support algae growth on its surface.*

"But that defeats the whole purpose," Rhone sputtered in shock.

Just settle down, Stone answered with an air of superiority. *It should be a simple enough fix, only requiring a coating of tar prior to the algae being transplanted.*

"That's it?" Rhone answered, slightly embarrassed of his outburst. "Well, okay then. But do you have size projections yet? I really need them to finish the hull design."

I do have a generalized projection, Stone said patiently, though not exactly what Rhone wanted to hear. *It depends on the lift versus area calculations of course, but by using the spherical boundary of the balloon envelope as the extent of the containment bed, there should be sufficient lift to rise, and hold at level. It is not, however, an efficient way to go up or down at will. In consideration of that need, I am considering an adaptation to our existing system, using both algae bed and steam, for better lift control.*

It took more than a moment for Rhone to process the information, but Stone only gave him the moment, before continuing almost hurriedly.

It might also be possible to use a steam generator for propulsion, and not leave us to the whims of the wind.

The very idea was shocking. Then Captain Black's words came to mind. *He who controls the wind, controls the battle.*

With his heart racing, Rhone asked, "What do we need?"

While math wasn't Rhone's best subject, he had spent tons of time working on it during training. He had no idea what math had to do with being an agent, but Aundrea had said he needed it, so he had given it his all. Luckily, he had Stone to double check everything he did. Honestly, the volume to lift calculations weren't too difficult. It was weight distribution and mass placement, that kept him working for untold hours. His vivid memory of hanging head-down on his first flight reminded him how error calculation of that kind wouldn't be acceptable when an entire airship hung in the balance.

Rhone continued redesigning, but the plans always had a remarkable similarity to The Backwater Mistress. Every time he thought he had a great layout, Stone would say, *I believe your design is front-heavy,* or, *This system design will be incompatible with the necessary structural and flexibility requirements.* While he knew Stone was right, he still fought the issue. He liked the slim waist of Captain Black's little Zebeck-style ship, with its far-reaching bowsprit and high quarter deck. It was his vision of perfect. He wanted to build something similar, even if it had to float under a funny-looking balloon of lifting gasses.

After days of work, he was finally satisfied.

"Here it is," Rhone said in relief, pulling a sheet of curling brown paper from the bottom of the stack. "Fins."

"Fins?" Bella asked, sure she hadn't heard correctly.

Ahh, an excellent idea, Stone chimed in. *Although technically they would be sails.*

"Stone likes it," Rhone said, ignoring the last comment.

"He would. You two like your toys," Bella teased, bending to scan the obvious different sketch. Fins seemed to sprout from almost every angle of the craft, some drawn in their closed position, while others were extended, with arrows showing the air-ship's responding movements.

"You did this?" she asked with honest praise, her eyes still on the drawings. "This could work. I don't know much about ships, but I can understand these." She began bouncing on her toes in excitement. "You could actually drive her like a boat on the water! When can we start?"

Rhone grinned, but put up both hands. "Slow down. It's just a design. I'm afraid there might be some flaws in the concept, so I want to take it to Captain Black tomorrow and see what he thinks. It's best to hear if there's problems, before putting all the work into building her, just to have her fall apart under us."

***

When Rhone saw the sails of The Backwater Mistress swing into the harbor, he packed up the plans, gave Bella a quick peck on the cheek for good luck, and took his mostly-completed plans for Captain Black's perusal.

"Dang me and hang me!" was Captain Black's raucous comment. He had been drawn like metal filings to a magnet by the designs Rhone had laid out on the table in his captain's quarters. His own maps were rolled neatly, tucked away in tiny compartments between the heavy beams of the low ceiling. Their placement kept them close to hand, but above any splashed water from the ship's daily floor-scrubbing.

With long years of practice, the captain swept out one of Rhone's brown sheets, setting an inkwell on one corner of the curly paper while holding down the opposite with his well-callused hand. The whale-oil lamp swayed gently in its hanger, giving a cheery glow to the room and bolstering the wane light from the one window.

Captain Black traced the lines with a thick, scarred finger, nodding as he noted location, distance and balance configurations. "Good choice using the lateen-rigged sails. They may only be triangles, not the footage of the square-rigged sort, but they'll be a ton faster to handle, and a bunch more manageable with a small crew. With only so much weight capacity, you can't have too many people aboard."

It was amazing how well he understood the plans, especially since the airship didn't float on water.

"You think it will work?" Rhone asked, almost dizzy with happiness.

"Looks more than fine, Mr. Rhone. Don't think I could have done better myself." Which was big praise from a man who truly liked who he was. "But she's a big girl, so you'll need to know when to sit out a storm. Just like my Mistress, she won't take heavy weather, and a good captain knows when it's best to find safe harbor."

Rhone was ready to start taking notes, when the captain surprised him with a slap on the back. "So this is what you've been planning for our pirate problem."

"Yes sir," Rhone managed, trying not to cough from the blow. "I had to come up with something. But really, it was your words that brought it together."

"Mine?" the captain blustered. "I'm pretty good, and I know a tad about sailin', but I don't know nothin' about floatin' through the sky like a bird."

Grinning, Rhone answered. "Remember when I was asking about fighting tactics, and you said, it would be simple if I could see the action from the eye of a bird flying over. And, if I could just see what they were doing, I would be prepared, and one step ahead."

"Well, I'll be." Captain Black mumbled, almost speechless, and a very uncommon situation. But a moment later was back to normality. "I just figured I was keepin' you out of trouble. You know, simple stuff like, don't be where the action's gonn'a get hot, an', it's okay to run away, so you can fight another day. An' that kinda stuff. Then you go and put a whole new spin on the game. You've made it three dimensions now, not just two."

"But the wind still controls the action," Rhone added with a smile.

Captain Black nodded wisely. "You're right about that. The dang wind's always got us by the short hairs. But I'll recommend one more thing, if I may. Get some ballast aboard. It'll be extra weight, a precious thing for sure, but you'll be able to dump it if ever you need an emergency get-away. Less weight means faster rise. Think of it like a ship. If you're setting too low in the water, you might get swamped, so lighten the load."

It was perfectly obvious once he thought about it. Even The Backwater Mistress had to watch out for heavy seas. If the waves got too big, she might have to jettison some of her goods to stay afloat. It was common enough that sailors called it jetsam.

"Sounds good," Rhone acknowledged, thinking over his design, but what would have to go in order to add ballast. He was still trying to decide when Stone's words came drifting through his mind.

When in doubt, ask someone with experience.

Rhone quietly thanked Stone before turning to Captain Black. "Captain, if I have to remove something to allow for the ballast, where should I look?"

"Good question" he said, chewing on a strand of his scruffy beard. "Don't want to cut the rations. So I'd say, dump the crew quarters. No bunks and no walls. Just hammocks an' canvas drapes. Works for the navy, and they know their stuff."

Rhone frowned as he leaned over the plans. With the walls gone there wasn't much room-division left. Just the quarter deck with the captain's quarters. The main deck as a working space, and the lower hold for storage. The small room in the bow for food stores could stay, and of course the copper containment tray for the algae matter, hanging above the main deck. That was essential, or they were back where they started. With the base of the balloon envelope encasing the tray, acting like a funnel to keep the precious gasses where they belonged, there was nothing left. No matter how he looked at it, it was still big, and heavy.

Why couldn't anything be easy? The project seemed to go from one problem to another.

Finally Rhone muttered, "I think the timbers are just too heavy." But a sudden inspiration hit him, instantly supported by Stone's enthusiasm. "Captain? What if we make the hull from basketwork, like we did for BoToo, but lots bigger?"

Captain Black took a long moment to work out the possibilities, screwing his face into a gruesome caricature of thought. "Dang it, boy. Might just work. But remember, you'll be sailing' over a lot of water, so best be able to settle on it if you need. Try splittin' the difference. Maybe a shallow hull of cut and caulked lumber. Then use the basketwork for the rest. It might need a bit of bracing here and there, and supports for the masts, but do it right and she might hold together."

When Stone said, *Give me a moment, and I will have a compendium of the necessary support calculations.* Rhone felt mental gears begin to turn.

Sure enough, within moments, Rhone could see the design changes unfold in his mind's eye.

"I like it," Rhone replied in awed.

And once again, he could hardly wait to show Bella.

R hone had invited Grenn and Cara back to the warehouse, with the four of them sitting around the table, plans stretched out for inspection.

"I realize this is a much larger project," Rhone was saying, "so first I need to ask, is it too much?"

He had already been to the ship wrights, asking the cost of a shallow hull of lighter-than-normal construction.

Grenn's frown said loudly enough, he thought the idea was crazy. But Cara continued to search the plans, finger lightly tracing the fine lines as they progressed from one area to the next. The furrowed creases of her forehead looked more like tree bark than fine skin, but her shyness had disappeared the moment she stooped over the paper. Her other hand tapped quietly against the table top, almost like she was counting. When she finally looked up, refocusing on Rhone, her brows raised with a look of wonder.

"This is the most intriguing project I have ever seen. The mere scope is boggling, but the idea is truly terrifying."

Rhone's hopes fell.

But Cara raised a hand for his attention. "I didn't say it couldn't be done. But you must understand. Building the big basket was a simple design, merely enlarging what we already do. This however truly is terrifying . What if my designs didn't work right? What if the material wasn't strong enough? What if weather caused stresses I didn't consider, and it fell apart?"

She looked like she wanted to cry just thinking about the number of possibilities for failure.

Rhone's glance sought Bella's soft eyes, looking sadly afraid. They had hoped so hard.

Then he faced Cara. "But is it possible?"

Cara set her jaw, then sagged at the mere thought of the daunting task.

Grenn sat like a stoic tree stump, giving Cara a tilt of his head, an okay for whatever she was going to say.

"Yes. It would be difficult," Cara acknowledged with a wipe at her eyes, "and there would need to be several very unique connections for supports and cross bracing. And I'm not even talking about the timber framework, just the wattle." She shook her head as though disagreeing with herself. "But yes, it can be done."

Momentarily stunned, Rhone tried not to grin. "If you have any suggestions, I could incorporate them into the plans. It might keep other problems to a minimum."

With an almost sad nod, Cara accepted the inevitable. "We will do our best, as always, but I'm afraid I can't guarantee the work. I simply can't. It's so far beyond my experience, I will be developing methods as we go. Are you sure you want to hang the airship, and your lives, on that?"

A shiver of fear ran down Rhone's spine as he felt the truth of her words. Bella would be aboard, not just him. His normally self-assured face carried a new look of worry. He rose and stepped up to Bella, stooping to look into her eyes.

"I need your thoughts," he said quietly. "It could mean both our lives, but yours in particular. This is my job, and I think I should try, but you don't need to do this. Beyond that, I want your honest thoughts on the entire project."

Bella's smooth forehead lined with her worry. He had asked, but she was afraid to answer. Moments passed as she tried, but it was simply more than she could do.

Rhone had his answer.

He turned to Cara, but was stopped before he could speak, as Bella grabbed his shirt, pulling him back to face her.

"I need to fly," she whispered, mouthing the syllables that were almost without sound. Her words gathered volume as will fought against fear. "We can do this. It will work. You know it will."

She wasn't a waitress anymore. She had to fly. This would be her new world.

CHAPTER 24

No Port Without a Storm

S tone's evaluation of the gasses had verified that they were indeed lighter than air, and proved the algae bed would work. Even so, the new system wouldn't be installed until the new envelope was tested. One blowout was enough.

With the steam boiler on standby, their massive beast was ready to rise into the heavens, or at least the 100 feet of line they had on the reel. All they needed to do was complete the filling, and find if the system held together. Once the new envelope was full they would let out the line and leave it until the balloon came down. It would hold, or it wouldn't.

"Ready when you are," Rhone called, signaling Bella to pull the long-armed lever .

The old boiler unit complained in its normal raucous hiss, belching hot steam through the leather hose. The mottled blue-grey of the whale hide was almost like camouflage against the cloudy sky, the mountainous rorqual balloon envelope continuing to stretch, straining the leathery material as it expanded. Finally it rose, lifting above the framework, and showing off BoToo's tiny basket hanging below. The basket looked very fragile, like an egg under a mother hen. It wasn't the much heavier, new hull, but it was enough weight for the test. The airship hull wasn't completed yet, and wouldn't be risked until the balloon was proven.

"Let her go!" Bella called excitedly, signaling Rhone to release the winch's latch.

Under Stone's guidance, several large anchors had been buried deep in the ground, connected to the windlass by heavy chains. It should be enough to keep the balloon in place, even if the wind increased. But like a steer at branding time, the balloon contraption wanted free. Even the light onshore breeze was enough to make the tether strain.

Rhone prayed that nothing would go wrong. If the envelope gave out, like the last time, their dreams would be over. He didn't have enough energy to try again. Nor the money. Playing the rich kid had been fun, but the funds were at their end. It was now, or never.

As the windlass drum spun, the giant balloon began its majestic ascent, unreeling the line as it rose faster and faster, fighting to break free. When Rhone finally put leverage on the brake wheel, the loud squeal of complaining wood made him wish he had brought cotton for his ears. It may have been called a brake, but that didn't mean he wanted it to break. Luckily, it did its job, slowly bringing the balloon to a stop.

The giant envelope floated gently over their heads, like an oversized squash in the sky. The description may not have been complementary, but it was accurate.

Relieved, Rhone set the latch, and walked to the wagon where Bella watched. Blue was an old hand at this by now, and continued his unconcerned grazing. Sliding up beside Bella, Rhone stared up as the balloon hung in the sky, jostled now and then by a gust, but remaining firmly tethered. Hours later, they packed their things, ready for the drive back to town. They had more to do than sit around watching their balloon fly like a kite.

"It looks good," Rhone commented, swinging a nearly-empty picnic basket into the wagon. "It will probably come down tonight, as the air cools. We'll check on it first thing tomorrow, but I think we can call it a go."

"It will be," Bella said proudly. "I trust Stone. He wouldn't give us information that didn't work."

Give Bella my thanks, Stone commented in a pout. *At least she believes in my abilities, even if you do not.*

Rhone sighed as he squinted up at the balloon, trying to figure out how to respond. *Of course I do. I wouldn't go up in it if I didn't believe in you. We simply needed to test it first. You might not break if we fall, but I would. Then where would you be?*

It was an old argument, and honestly, more friendly banter than anything. But Rhone did pass the message on to Bella.

"Stone says, thank you. He doesn't think I appreciate him enough."

Bella rolled her eyes at the comment. "Don't worry about it. He knows you do. You two just enjoy picking on each other, like siblings."

"Siblings? What's a sibling?" Rhone asked, unsure what she was trying to say.

"Brothers. You two act like brothers."

"No way!" the two exclaimed together. Rhone's out loud, and Stone's echoing through Rhone's head.

"Yes way," Bella replied with arched eyebrows. "You pick on each other all the time. You should be ashamed of yourselves."

She was actually enjoying their scolding. Rhone and Stone were just about her only friends since she had left the security of Corgy's community. The town's folk simply didn't understand her position, and she felt their judgment. It was hard even going into town for food, so mostly she stayed in the warehouse out of sight. She had plenty to do, and with Rhone going out often enough that she got the news, she wasn't even bored. It was enough.

But Stone's grumpy attitude demanded an answer, *Your brother? But I am more like your great, great, great, great grandfather than your brother. Does she not understand that?*

I'm sure she does, Rhone thought back, almost as peeved as Stone. How could she possibly think he was anything like his rocky friend? Stone was a grump.

Regardless, the project had gone perfectly. The balloon held.

With the hull and wickerwork under construction, they had just one more system to work on.

⸻

Rhone was bored as he listened to Stone lecture. It was important stuff, just not exciting as his daydream.

The algae off-gases will indeed produce lift for the airship, but unless you simply wish to float along with the wind, you will need a system for propulsion.

"Propulsion? That's the part that makes it go, right?" Rhone asked, attempting to catch up from his mental drift. "But won't the fins will do that?"

To an extent, that is true, but there are two problems. One, your fins are technically sails, and two, you would find it very difficult to go upwind. I observed how the Backwater Mistress uses water resistance against the hull and keel to keep from slipping sideways under the wind's pressure. Basically, the ship is squirted forward, caught between the wind in the sails, and the hull resistance on the water. Think of it as shooting a seed between the thumb and forefinger. Our problem is, there is too little resistance in the air to push against. Without that resistance, your direction will be limited to downwind, and some cross wind, but virtually no upwind.

Rhone's mind jumped seamlessly to the next conclusion. "So we need a propulsion method that helps us go upwind."

That would be the answer, Stone agreed. *We already use steam for lift, but do you remember the various odd machinery in the big city? They used steam to power the mechanisms, enabling their propulsion. We may be able to do similar, merely changing the energy transmission to thrust, pushing through the air instead of traveling along the ground.*

Rhone felt like slapping himself upside the head. Why hadn't he thought of it? He had already drawn sail plans, maybe they could become wings, and fly like a bird.

But Stone was way ahead of him.

I am sorry. It is a great idea, Stone commented wisely, *but to be honest, it would be exceedingly difficult. The airship has an exceptionally large volume, which in turn creates a great deal of drag. Theoretically, if the force is greater than the drag, it will move. But beyond that need, bird wings do not simply move back and forth like a fan. They flex and arch in quite a complex motion. No, I was considering more of an air wheel, with sails between the spokes. If the sails are set to scoop the air as it turns, the outcome should produce forward thrust. Remember, all action creates an equal and opposite reaction. All things must balance.*

A picture popped up in Rhone's mind, and he quickly moved to gather paper and quill.

He was already starting on the new plans when Stone interjected another comment.

One moment more if you would.

"What now?" Rhone asked, sagging back in the chair. Why couldn't anything be simple?

The system will require an on-board steam boiler, which of course will need fuel to heat the water.

"Of course," Rhone groaned, thinking of the piles of firewood he would need to split. Then he wondered how they would carry it. They already had problems with weight. Resigned, he had to ask. "I give. So how do will it work?"

You are correct that a wood fired boiler would not be very efficient. No, I had another thought in mind.

Rhone sighed in exhaustion. Working with Stone was great, but it had its share of ups and downs. "Lay it on me."

Lay it on you? Are you speaking of a blanket?

It was a typical Stone comment, and Rhone couldn't help but roll his eyes.

"Never mind. Just tell me what you were thinking."

Yes, well, it is quite exciting actually. When I was doing my evaluation of the lighter than air gases, I also determined they are flammable, which means they will burn.

That was news to Rhone. He knew they rose into the air like smoke, and smoke was already from burnt stuff, so how could it burn when it was already burnt?

Stone knew him well enough to guess his thoughts, and began explaining without being asked.

Take my word for it. The gases will burn. The difficulty will be keeping the fire gases from mixing with the lift gases. We would not wish them all to burn, or the airship would be destroyed.

Rhone couldn't agree more. Falling from the sky would definitely ruin his day. Falling while on fire would only make it worse.

"It sounds great, honest, but maybe we should stick with something a bit simpler. Like something that won't kill us the first time we use it. Besides, if it's impossible, why bring it up?"

I said it was difficult, not impossible. We simply have to discover a way.

Rhone closed his eyes, thinking back through all their trials, and how many times had he heard that particular line. But they had come a long way since the first bladder strapped to his back.

With another heavy sigh, he gave in, deciding it was at least worth another look. "Okay, sails for direction. Algae gas for lift. Wind wheel for propulsion, and burning gases for the boiler. Is that all, or is there more?"

You may be a genius after all, Stone said proudly.

Luckily, being in Rhone's head meant no one else heard the comment.

I am certain the design is beautiful, Stone commented dryly, *but it still requires minimal weight, and have balance. All ships carry the same requirements, though slightly varied.*

Rhone had heard it all umpteen times.

"I know, but I like the look. Besides, no matter how I design it, it won't carry the cannon we need. They're just too heavy." It was an old complaint, but had no answers.

That is true, Stone agreed. *You might be able to carry a cannon ball, but certainly not the cannon itself.*

Rhone slumped in weary resolution, dropping his mind-numbed head to the table. But a second later, he popped back up and asked, "Did you just say, a cannon ball?"

Suddenly worried for his young protege, Stone cautiously answered, *Yes, why do you ask?*

A small smile grew on Rhone's tired face. "Why would I need a cannon, when I could simply drop a cannon ball on their heads? It would probably punch right through the deck too!"

Excitedly, he called for Bella.

"What is it?" came her instant response. "What's wrong now?"

"We have an answer," Rhone announced proudly.

"To which question? We have dozens." She sounded more skeptical than normal.

"Not those questions," he said, waving an arm in exasperation. "The big one. How to deal with the pirates."

But she wasn't impressed. He had taken her away from her job, which, if he was only goofing around, would be a fighting offense. But she finally had to ask, "And just how would that be? Drown them in your BS?" She did smile then.

"No. We drop cannon balls on them."

When her expression didn't change, he tried again.

"Remember, we can't carry cannon. They're just too heavy."

He waited again, but got nothing more than a raised eyebrow.

"So, the simple answer is... we carry cannon balls. Not cannon."

It finally clicked.

"Of course. It's so simple! Why didn't we think of it sooner?"

Rhone's eloquent shrug excused all.

CHAPTER 25

The Lady Luna

The massive balloon was no longer a delicate bubble shape as Bo had been. Even BoToo had been similar in form, only bigger. But this envelope was different. Instead of upright, it was an elongated sausage shape with a blunt rump. The algae pan, mounted into the bottom of the balloon, was sealed directly to the pan, acting like a funnel and keeping the precious gasses from being blown away. The addition of the sail-fins along the sides and bottom, and the large tail fin in the rear, made the airship look far more like a fish than a bird, but Rhone wasn't complaining. It flew. Finally, with the addition of the very ship-like hull hanging below, it had become a real airship. It had everything but a name.

"I like Bella's Dream," Rhone said matter of factly.

But Bella's immediate response of, "Absolutely not," put an end to that thought. "Besides, this was your idea, not mine," she announced ungraciously.

Unconvinced, Rhone shrugged. "But it needs a name. I'm tired of calling it, The Balloon."

Looking disgusted, Bella finally said, "I don't care, just nothing about me in the name. I want to captain it, not be named after it."

Rhone was caught totally by surprise. A little put out by her comment, he sputtered, "You want to be the captain? I sorta thought I would do that." He didn't want to hurt her feelings, but it was, after all, his project.

Bella gave a soft shrug. "I know, but if she's going to be a fighting ship, who understands tactics better? You or me?"

She had him there. She had helped teach him.

Rhone felt himself slipping toward melancholy, his mind flitting through one thought after another, not knowing how to answer. Women didn't captain ships. They were the support structure that allowed men to work. It wasn't his fault, that's just how it was.

Then he remembered MaryEllen working right beside the men, and Aundrea as their boss. So maybe things were changing. Who was he to say?

When the picture of Bella dancing with the wind came to mind, he knew he had lost. He couldn't keep her from that. She needed it too badly. How could he stand in the way of that kind of need?

Glancing her direction, he caught a glimpse of her well-hidden pain. Concerned, he softly asked, "What's the matter? You don't look so good." The words may not have been poetic, but he really was worried about her.

"I... I have to fly," she answered in a whisper, barely acknowledging him as she settled unsteadily on a stack of pallets.

"Of course," he answered, somehow feeling relieved. "We'll go up as soon as we have the test done. I need to make sure she won't drop out from under us first, but that won't take very long."

"Thanks, that would be great," but her half-hearted smile didn't reach her eyes, sounding more like resignation than pleasure.

A painful realization came to Rhone. "You really mean it, don't you? You have to fly."

His words brought a deep shuddering breath from Bella, and a shallow nod, affirming her need.

Worry lines crossed his face as he tried to find an answer. "I never really thought about it, but you've been here for the whole thing. You never complained, never quit, and never gave up. I was the one bouncing around like Bo on the tether." He chewed a lip before voicing his next thought. "You know, it's probably a good idea if we both know how to fly this thing. What would happen if I got shot during an attack? You even said it could happen. We would need someone to get us back."

Mind racing, he started chewing the other side of his lip, working at it as though it was a prize jaw breaker. Bella was his responsibility. He was, after all, the reason she had been fired from The Common House. While she seemed more than happy to be gone, she would still be there if it hadn't been for him.

Then a new thought struck him. What would she do when he was reassigned? It was something he hadn't even thought about, but now the question stared him in the face. There was a lot more to consider than just her wanting to fly.

Trying to work the problem like Stone had taught him, he checked off the issues one at a time, and suddenly had his answer. And why not? He would be reassigned someday. Someone had to keep watch over their balloon. Why not her? No one knew it better, or would love it more.

It is a good plan, Stone commented warmly. *I too should have thought of this particular problem, but now it is up to you to fix. Do what you can. I will be here to support as I am able.*

Rhone did have a plan. But what would she think of it?

Bella's normally sparkly eyes were dull and filled with pain, but still held a flicker of hope as she waited for his announcement.

Rhone crossed his arms and leaned against a post in an attempt to appear casual. "I've got a plan," he stated, sliding his eyes to see her reaction. "What would you say if we start you out as a Lieutenant. That's number two on a naval ship. Since she's going to be a fighter, it only makes sense."

Bella almost stopped breathing, her face changing to a shocked white as her disbelief fought with his words. But her hidden dream was too big. It was too much, and she knew he had to be playing with her again. It simply couldn't be true, and suddenly it hurt. Tears that couldn't be stopped slid silently down her face.

Confused, Rhone saw her question, and answered with gentleness. "I know it's not Captain, but would Lieutenant be okay for now?"

Suddenly Bella flung herself off the pallet, wrapping herself around him like a starfish on a clam.

With his arms and legs tangled, Rhone almost went down, but caught himself with her head buried in his neck and hot tears scalding his skin.

"I'll take that as a yes," he said, wrapping his own arms around her slim waist, holding her close.

It was a wonderful feel, and he held her that way several minutes, until her snuffling began to tickle his ear.

With a grin, he ducked his head against the tickle, and asked, "Well Lieutenant. Is this any way for an officer to act?"

Bella started to disentangle herself with a laugh, but Rhone held her tighter, not giving an inch.

She snuggled back into his neck rubbing her nose on Stone's collar, whispering, "Stone, you did a pretty good job raising this guy. He turned out all right after all."

With a final hug, Rhone released Bella, turning to the monstrous airship, looking even bigger against the full moon hanging in the morning sky.

With a satisfied smile, Rhone commented, "I think it's time we learned how to fly this thing. What do you think, Lieutenant?"

Grinning, Bella gave a sharp salute. "Aye, aye, Captain. And, Captain... she still doesn't have a name."

Rhone gave a half snort of acceptance. "Well, I guess it's stuck with, 'The Balloon', but it could be worse. Could be called Buttercup or Blimpy, or something awful."

Bella simply frowned, knowing their ship deserved a real name. Searching for an answer, she squinted up at the giant blue-grey balloon, hoping for some clue. When she saw the full daytime moon eclipsed by its bulk, she had it.

"Luna," she exclaimed excitedly. "The Lady Luna. We did Bo, and Bo Too, now we'll work from the other end. Luna, like ba-Loon-a. Get it?"

Rhone shook his head in disbelief, then chuckled, "Not much of a name for a fighting ship, but if you like it, it's good enough for me." He tried the name again, checking its feel. "The Lady Luna. It is kind of catchy, and she's big enough to be one. I can hear it now. Someday, someone will tell our story, saying, Once on a blue moon a..."

But Bella cut him off with a laugh. "Rhone, did you know you're weird?"

I t was time.

Rhone sent a short query to Stone, hoping they hadn't forgotten anything. "I've checked all systems, but I'd prefer your view on it. Did I miss anything?"

All seems in working order. The envelope is full. The boilers are active and there is sufficient water for a short flight. Other details will require visual checks, but as long as you can descend safely, there should be nothing requiring immediate attention.

"I think that means yes," Rhone said wryly, considering the seriousness of a failure.

Bella stood close, fidgeting as she expectantly awaited his command.

Finally satisfied, Rhone allowed a smile on his tense face. "Stone says all systems are go. We'll check everything again once we're airborne, but there's no reason we can't make a trial flight."

Bella was all bubbles and bounces, until she stopped abruptly, caught in an 'Oh no' moment. With an apologetic look, she said, "I forgot my coat," and headed to the buckboard at a run. She was well acquainted with how cold it could get up there.

"Good idea," Rhone called to her retreating back. "Grab some food too, and some of the bottled cider, if there is any left. We might as well make it a party."

Okay, so he hadn't thought of everything.

T he Luna was a gorgeous lady, bow jutting forward in long flowing lines, securing the tip of the sails that lay securely reefed above.

Other sails dropped from below the hull like the keel on a ship, and along the sides like a gaudy fish displaying its fins.

Even with the fins, it was obvious, the airship's design had been heavily influenced by The Backwater Mistress. The similarity of line gave her a sleek profile, hopefully cutting through the air like the ship did through the water. But instead of the heavy rigging lines holding masts in place, they bound the giant balloon envelope to the hull, while somewhat lighter rigging worked the sails themselves.

The stern's raised quarterdeck wasn't just for looks. It was the way up to the service entrance to the balloon itself, and the algae pan it enclosed. By design, the algae pan's sealed envelope also kept the fumes tightly secured. No one wanted to stay in there any longer than they could hold their breath. Contained as it was, the rancid air inside was far worse than the water of the little lake.

The steam boiler, housed deep in the hold, had been entirely redesigned since the early days of Bo and BoToo. Smaller and much lighter, the output was still enough to spin the fan sails for propulsion.

Rhone had asked Captain Black to officiate the first real flight, hopefully connecting their new airship to naval traditions, and Captain Black's large frame seemed almost decorated with his various weapons, looking far more piratical than naval officer. Still, it was as official as they were going to get. Mayor Dugan was not as yet on speaking terms with Rhone, and the two kept their distance whenever possible.

With Captain Black doing the official duty, the ship naming ceremony and launch was a not to be forgotten experience.

"She'll be a fierce fighter," he assured them heartily, "Now let's get this girl flyin'." Then bellowing in his storm honed voice, he heralded the new airship's birth. "All right you scum-sucking pirate hoard. Know your end is near. We're here to christen the good ship...ah... good 'airship', Lady Luna. May she sneak up and sink your cursed souls!"

Rhone slid a covert look to Bella, gauging her reaction to the somewhat less than formal words, but her eyes were bright. At the nod from Captain Black, she swung the bottle against the wooden section of the hull, shattering the dark glass and sending deep red wine splashing onto the ship's keel.

To Rhone's eyes, it looked altogether too much like dripping blood, but luckily, The Lady Luna would be far out of reach from most attackers. Still, the wine accepted its part, running across the boards and dripping to the ground in glistening red beads, before being greedily absorbed by mother earth.

The shattering bottle signaled a chorus of "Huzzahs!" from the tiny gathering, as Cara dabbed at her eyes, and Grenn re-gained his footing after the back slap from Captain Black's massive hand.

Now it was Captain Rhone's turn. Stepping forward in the new uniform Bella had designed for him, he placed his palm against the wood and wicker airship, giving his blessing. "Do us proud," he whispered quietly, before grabbing Bella in a hug. Then standing tall, he gave his first command. "Lieutenant, would you be so good as to lower the ladder? It's time this ship got off the ground."

With her eyes sparkling like diamonds, Bella saluted. "As you wish, sir." Then with another quick salute to Captain Black for good measure, tugged the release, watching as The Lady Luna's wood-and-rope ladder unfurled down the airship's side, waiting for her crew.

Reverting to his more elegant training, Rhone gave a short bow, and addressed Bella. "After you milady."

Bella couldn't have cared less. With a wildly wicked grin, she scampered up the ladder and over the rail. She was home.

When a massive hand came to rest on Rhone's shoulder, he turned to receive Captain Black's last minute counsel. "Remember your sails, Captain. They pull as well as push, and anytime you cut crosswind, you'll need their pulling to get you there. Pushing only takes you downwind." His spiky beard quivered as his lips twitched, until Rhone could have sworn there was moisture in the old captain's eyes, but it must have been the bright morning sunlight that caused the blinking.

Rhone nodded, accepting his mentor's words. He had learned a lot under Captain Black's tutelage. He had commanded The Backwater Mistress numerous times, learning to work with the boat and crew, not to mention the weather. There was just so much to learn, and Captain Black could only make suggestions on how to deal with sailing in the air, but as long as they didn't fall out of the sky, there should be time. Learning was a process.

"Thank you, Captain. I couldn't have done it without you. As soon as I get the maneuvering worked out, we'll be back and do some pirate hunting."

"Now you're talking," Captain Black answered happily. "Never figured to actually go hunting the critters. Spent most of my time tryin' to evade 'em." With a nod and a wink, he gave Rhone his sendoff. "Now you be careful. I don't want to be scrapin' up your spattered remains, so you keep her up there where she belongs."

He was talking about The Lady Luna, of course, but it fit for Bella just as well.

"Yes sir. I'll do my best."

With a crisp salute, Rhone turned to the ladder and ascended to his command.

As his head reached the rail, the clear call of, "Captain on board!" rang through the crisp air, her sincerity not covering its joy.

Rhone grinned and snapped her a salute in acknowledgment. "Very good, Lieutenant. Prepare to lift anchor."

As Bella ran to the windlass, Rhone stepped to the rail and gave Captain Black a single wave. "See you when we get back," he called down, "and...ah..., would you mind unhitching the anchor line? I believe we'll need a fix for that."

With a delighted guffaw, Captain Black tugged the hitch loose and The Lady Luna slowly began her rise.

Climbing the ladder to the quarterdeck, Rhone stepped to the wheel calling out a command. "Set the mains and drop the keel, Lieutenant."

In far less time than he could have guessed, the sails fanned out in elegance, catching not only the wind, but the golden rays of the morning sun.

Unpracticed as they were, and with only the two of them to do the work, Rhone and Bella had little time to enjoy the sights. Bella had run miles crisscrossing the deck, managing sails and hauling lines. Rhone had his own work to do, learning to handle the massive rig that wanted to follow every cross wind and gust they met.

The airship's large triangular sails were the main form of propulsion, deployed by simply dropping away from the sides and keel, making them workable even for Bella's one woman show. Retrieving the sails was just as simple, hauling in the lines that connected to the stays, and reducing sail. Her time was spent running back and forth adjusting sails, hauling lines and staring over the rail at the passing countryside.

It was hard work, but she was happy. At least that was Rhone's assessment, seeing the crazy grin she wore all day, dancing about the deck in pure joy at their success. The Lady Luna didn't simply drift with the wind. They flew.

Once they had the simple flying mostly under control, it was time to test the boiler propulsion system.

"Furl the sails," Rhone called. "Time for the next test."

He smiled, seeing Bella's look of exasperation. She was tired, but sweeping a lock of hair from her eyes she straightened, a weary smile showing on her smudged face as she headed to her next task.

As wonderful as the airship was, it was the propulsion system that made it great. The new boiler design had come from Stone, translating the data to Rhone, and Rhone drawing up the specs for the smith. Now when the valve was opened, steam ran through a casing, pushing against impellers and spinning the shaft for the fan sails. The small angled sails scooped air as they spun, pushing the big balloon across the sky. It was almost unbelievable how simple it was, but it worked. Even so, Luna's profile made her more of a parachute than a knife.

As The Lady Luna criss-crossed the county, she drew curious eyes, gathering as much attention from their sudden shadow as from their distant sight.

Between tasks, Bella waved energetically to everyone, hoping to gain their approval, but they could see the unease of the people at having the large apparition hanging over their heads.

"Maybe it's a good thing we'll spend most of our time over the ocean," she commented with a worried look.

"Or maybe they'll get used to seeing us," Rhone commiserated hopefully. "I really hadn't expected this kind of a reaction."

Bella agreed, but understood why they would worry. "It's complete dominance," she explained. "We can fly over anything we want, day or night, and it probably gives people the creeps."

Rhone nodded in acknowledgment. "I hadn't thought of it that way. Maybe we should just fly at night, but I'd rather they learn to accept us."

With their trial a success, The Luna headed for home.

As they finished securing the airship, Rhone commented, "Let's celebrate tonight."

Bell stopped mid-step. "Wait. You mean it? Like, actually going out somewhere... or just partying at the warehouse?"

Rhone answered with caution. "I was thinking about a dinner at The Common House. But only if you're comfortable with it. I know you have some feelings about the place, but it is the best in town."

"Bella made a thoughtful face, then brightened. "I'll bet I can get over it. I'm not just a serving girl anymore. I'm Lieutenant of The Lady Luna. If that's not good enough for them, then it's their problem, not mine."

"It's a date then," Rhone said happily, and honestly relieved. But the look on Bella's face, made him realize what he had said. Even more cautiously, he said, "If you don't mind being seen with your captain."

"Is it appropriate?" she asked, not sure how it would be taken. "I never thought about that particular problem before. Maybe we should just call it a celebration, and keep things neater."

She, at least, was thinking of the future. What would happen when they had a crew? There had to be discipline. Captain Black said so.

Disappointed, Rhone forced a smile. "Good plan, Lieutenant. You'll be ready for command before you know it."

It wouldn't be the evening he had hoped for, but they would be going out.

When finally ready, Rhone's short coat and breeches, were far superior to anything in Corgy, but next to Bella, he could have been in his birthday suit for all it would have mattered. Bella had dressed in something a bit more roguish. Something more suited to her new self image. Besides, as number two of an airship, a fighting ship at that, she would do as she wished.

Rhone was already concerned about taking her to The Common House, knowing her feelings about the place, but one look at her, and he was far more concerned for the other customers and the ruckus she might cause, although he wouldn't be the one to complain. If her outfit meant his stepping in to defend her, it wouldn't be the first time. Besides, she was totally, and absolutely, stunning.

Little by little over the last few days, Bella had reworked her garb, making it easier to work around the airship. Her main problem was constantly tripping on her hem as she climbed ladders and catwalks. At first she had simply tucked the front into her belt, as she had with Bo, lifting the skirt off the ground and out of the way. But when it had pulled out one too many times, she tore the front off above the knee, freeing her boots and legs while leaving it long in the rear. It was a concession to the style of the era, yet allowed her to climb without stepping on her skirt front. There could be nothing worse than catching a hem at the wrong time, and pitching overboard for the long fall to the sea. It may be a bit scandalous now, but was certainly a safer option. Her burgundy and black striped hose had helped, making it a bit more modest, but Rhone had still bruised more than one knuckle, being constantly distracted from his work.

He had honestly felt slightly relieved when he had been sent to pick up a high-necked blouse for her to wear with her burgundy short coat, but it was the black velvet, boned cincher, and the dark green clip-fronted skirt that made the outfit what it was.

He tried not to stare, and almost succeeded. But woe be to the rest of town.

"Dining for two," Rhone stated to the waiter. He was more than aware of the stares of the other patrons in the establishment, most of whom he knew, but the feel of Bella's hand on his arm made him face all comers with the surety of his supposed wealthy position. Even so, he was also aware of the smiled glances Bella's new outfit received. The fact that she was easily the most beautiful woman there, only made him the more proud of her. Instead of fearful, she stood strong and true at his side, daring any to make comment or show.

"Absolutely, sir," replied the waiter. "We have a table set aside for you and the lady."

Rhone saw the flickered look of consternation, as the man suddenly recognized Bella. But he was well trained, and covered his surprise admirably.

"If you will follow me."

When the goblets of wine were brought more rapidly than he had ever experienced, Rhone wondered if it was to get them done and out of the establishment as quickly as possible.

"Are you doing alright?" he asked quietly, wondering how Bella was taking all the notice. "We can leave if it's too much."

Heartened by his care, Bella bolstered her spirit, setting the smile back on her face. "No, I need this. Besides, there should be enough rumors floating around to keep this town busy for weeks. It's almost too bad I waited so long."

"I can't blame them," Rhone said with a chuckle. "Every woman here is as jealous as a cat at the fish market, and their men don't dare to get caught looking, although they are."

The comment made Bella blush, feeling their looks even more.

Breaking into her obvious moment, Rhone raised his goblet in a toast. "To the Lady Luna, and her courageous Lady Lieutenant."

Relieved, Bella picked up her own goblet, returning the toast. "To The Lady Luna, and her Captain."

CHAPTER 26

What goes Up, Must Come Down

Corgy's rumor mill was working overtime, with the huge floating craft stalking the countryside as the main topic of discussion.

Mayor Dugan was putting in miles stomping about the office, grouching at everyone that came through the door. "I'll see him laid so low he won't be able look up!" the mayor sputtered angrily.

Mrs. Randle knew it wasn't personal. He was simply venting. "Yes sir," she mumbled, continuing her paperwork and allowing his incessant fuming to fade into the background.

It was a useful skill, since the mayor wasn't done.

"I've had my sources out trying to find information on this character, and they come back empty handed. How can that be? If he's so all-fired high and mighty, there has to be at least something connecting him to whoever is trying to take over my office." The mayor's hand punctuated each statement like he was a conductor at the opera. "Nothing in the big city is quiet, and I mean nothing. The entire government is covered with spies and watchers. That's why I left that place, to be free of the nonsense."

To make his day worse, another ship had gone missing.

Every captain knew shipping was dangerous. Storms, currents, rocks, sea monsters and pirates, all made it a dangerous profession. But the constant loss of ships was taking a toll on the town, and revenues were dropping. Not only that, the banks had just raised rates for insuring ships and cargo. Since everyone wanted to blame someone, the mayor was the popular choice. All in all, it had been a bad week.

With hands clasped behind him, the mayor stared out his office window at the ships in the harbor. It was a grey day, of which there were many in Corgy. Most, as far as he was concerned. Through it all, his pent-up ire found two easy targets, that damn rich kid, and the new gossip.

When the monstrous apparition had appeared in the sky, he, of course, was supposed to deal with it. The Common House was full of rumors, and everybody had a different idea regarding its intentions. Invasion was the favorite, but didn't make sense to him. Why would anyone invade Corgy? It was a far step to anywhere, and didn't offer much in the way of anything. With nothing blown up, and no troops seen, invasion was a low probability.

Besides, he knew the probable answer, but staunchly kept it to himself. If it was that Rhone character, or the pirates, his Mayoral chair might truly be in danger. The thought hounded him until he could hardly sleep, and the less sleep, the more he felt the noose tighten. Then another thought crossed his mind. What if Rhone was in collusion with the pirates? It was an odd concession to his own history, but how else would Rhone know so much about what was going on? And what better way to side-step an issue than to pretend to be against it.

It was a diabolically simple plan, one he would have been proud of himself, and if he wasn't careful, it would work. Not only would he be out of a job, he would look like a buffoon to boot, having denied the existence of the problem that overran him. He would not let that happen. He would fight back. It was simple math. What goes up must come down.

"Mrs. Randle, I need a sharpshooter."

C aptain Black shook his head sagely, as he mumbled, "Dang, this just might work."

He was all smiles as he watched The Lady Luna flying in and out of the slowly drifting grey clouds. It was perfect camouflage. At a distance, the big balloon looked almost like a storm cloud herself, the dangling hull nothing more than a displaced ship mirage drifting above the horizon.

"What's that, Cap?" his first mate asked. Being number two in the command structure, meant he needed to hear even the unexpected words he had missed.

Captain Black gave a serious scowl as he shouted, "Get those cannons on deck. It's time we started some firing practice."

"Yes sir! Give me a couple hours and we'll have them stoked and ready."

Again the captain scowled, before bellowing, "Do you think this is a tourist ship? Make it one hour. We're going hunting!"

"Aye, Captain," his seldom used salute accepting the challenge. "One it is."

Within moments, crewmen were running to haul block and tackle from the holds, readying to hoist the guns up from the lower deck. It was heavy work while at sea, but the captain wasn't about to leave the guns on shore when they might be needed, even if it took time to place the massive canon.

Such was the price of keeping them hidden from every Tom, Dick, and Harry's view. But it was a seaman's life, stuck between boredom and panic, a price not one of them would change. While the captain knew the risk of keeping the guns below deck, in reality, a sea chase could take hours before being overtaken.

But now the time had come.

<hr/>

"Guns at the ready, Cap."

Captain Black checked his new calendorium, the toy Rhone had given him in exchange for training. "Fifty minutes," he commented, sounding almost cheery. "Good enough. I'd hate to have to keel-haul one of you as a sloucher."

Just the mention of keel-hauling could bring wayward crews in line. With a man's hands and feet tied to long ropes, he would be dropped off the bow, and dragged under the length of the ship to the stern. If he managed to hold his breath long enough, and was still alive after being dragged over the keel's mass of barnacles, he would be allowed back to work.

It was not a desirable way to get a bath, but shipboard life was seldom gentle.

Luckily, unlike others of his trade, Captain Black's threat was more a way to keep up moral than as a punishment, and had never used the grizzly method.

"Target sir?" shouted his first mate.

Ten black cannons, five to a side, sat mid-ship on the main deck, their smooth muzzles peeking over the railing. Crewmen waited beside each, thick steel pry-bars in hand, ready to maneuver the canon into a firing angle.

When all was ready, Captain Black gave a nod and a command. "Fire as we go!"

Within moments, gouts of orange flame burst through billowing grey plumes of smoke, as one after the other the cannon fired. The thickening acrid cloud almost concealed the ship, as like ants on a downed bug, the cannon were drawn back, swabbed out and reloaded, ready for the next go-round.

Again, the captain glanced at his calendorium, and winced. "I trained you better than this," he bellowed. "My poor departed grandmama could have done it faster. We need twice that many shots. No pirate's going to give you time to eat lunch while he's trying to take it away from you. Now do it again! But this time, try setting down your tea cups first!"

The crew knew better than to believe their Captain was actually angry, but his voice still spurred them on like a riled horse.

Smoke again engulfed The Mistress as her lithe form slipped smoothly through the growing waves. Pirates also didn't wait for sunshine and calm seas.

While technically eleven guns, with the little swivel-gun mounted on the quarterdeck, ten cannon was a paltry number for any ship of war. But they were at least something, and would be a surprise on a ship as small as The Backwater Mistress.

And so went the afternoon. By the time the captain was satisfied, the crew was worn out, black-faced and red-eyed from powder smoke, but they were happy. They had in fact doubled their firing rate. Now if the Mistress ran up against pirates, they just might make it home.

"Number Two. Make for port!"

"Aye Captain," came the tired reply. "Returning to port."

In the far distance, barely seen amid the heavy clouds, The Lady Luna had also turned toward shore.

Satisfied with their day, Rhone guided The Lady Luna along the cliffs and beaches of the rough coastline. With their flying height, they didn't have to worry about the inhospitable terrain that would have taken days, if not weeks, to cover by land, and even on a cloudy day, the scenery was unexpectedly beautiful.

Their flight out had been almost whisper-quiet with the airship only using the large sails for propulsion, but the return flight required the boiler-powered drive-sails to force the giant airship forward through the wind, just like The Backwater Mistress did against the waves. Unfortunately, the steam boiler was as loud as it was handy. The constant pulse of hot steam venting into the impeller housing, and its high-pitched wheezy-whine, would take some getting used to.

The airship had passed its test, and it was time for the next phase.

T he Luna may be ready, but Rhone still felt awkward as he stood posed at the wheel, attempting to act the part of a captain as he had seen Captain Black do. He was as new to captaining as he was to the push-pull of their new wheel arrangement.

Stone's new rigging design had come from the block and tackle workings aboard The Mistress, but uniquely arranged to take in the needs of The Lady Luna. It had taken days for Rhone to rework the rigging, connecting her elevator fins directly to the wheel stanchion, but now, he could change the fin angles by merely pushing or pulling on the wheel. It was just one of the ways The Luna was different from The Mistress, and that much more to learn.

When Stone brought up another possible addition to Luna, Rhone passed the idea on to Bella, but was less than excited.

"Stone says he has plans for a new bombing aperture. Whatever that is. But as far as I'm concerned, we can simply drop the cannonballs over the side, and down they'll go."

Unfortunately, Stone was listening in.

I am quite aware of your thoughts, he responded, piqued at Rhone's obvious disregard, *and I am sure that you might, on occasion, hit what you were aiming at. But if you are steering the ship, and Bella is working the sails, who does the targeting, and how does the cannonade get deployed?*

Of course Rhone hadn't thought of that, but did passed it on to Bella. "I really never thought about it," he told her unhappily.

Stone merely continued his grumble. *And if we are indeed that close to our target, then we are back to the problem of you getting shot out of the sky. I'm sure they have marksmen on board.*

"Thanks, Stone," Rhone said with a roll of his eyes. "Now, if you're done making wise cracks, why don't you go ahead and explain your plan."

Bella smiled at the exchange, having fun watching Rhone talk to himself, and trying to figure out what they were saying.

Thankfully, when it came to talking about his plans, Stone was easy to redirect.

Yes, of course, Stone agreed, switching seamlessly to the explanation. The new targeting aperture and drop tube design. I recognize your lack of comprehension, but it is nothing more than a tube sight and a release mechanism. The system could even be designed to handle several cannonballs at one time, leaving you free to do other duties, like departing the scene of the crime.

"What crime?" Rhone responded grumpily. "I was sent here to stop pirates, and that's what I intend to do."

MmmHmmm, Stone rumbled dryly. *But it is also possible, you were to remove Mayor Dugan from office, as he so vehemently accused you of.*

Rhone didn't like the way this talk was going. "But we didn't," he responded with growing tension. "The Major's just a little confused."

But he still does not like you. Stone replied sarcastically.

Rhone couldn't disagree. He and the Major had spent most of their time banging heads. "Maybe it's time I talk to him again," he relented. "We have The Lady Luna now, so we at least have something to offer."

Stone was as implacable as he was honest. *That is true, but he might see it as more of a takeover.*

Rhone idly wondered why life was so difficult, but as mother used to say, "You can lead a horse to water, but you can't make him drink. And you can show a man a problem, but you can't make him think." Her words seemed oddly prophetic, and he reluctantly gave in. "Maybe I'll wait a bit longer before I go see him. After all, if we fix the problem, he might see us in a little better light."

And we will see how that goes.

"Stone, you're a pessimist." Rhone replied drearily.

A pessimist? No, I am a realist.

"Whatever," Rhone answered, still in a grump.

Bella had been listening to Rhone's raving, and was beginning to worry. Their discussions didn't normally go on with such intensity. "Hey guys," she broke in. "Forget your tiff and explain about the bombing thing."

"Yeah, sorry. I guess I got carried away," Rhone mumbled, managing to look embarrassed. "Okay Stone, what do we need?"

Stone's answer was similarly subdued. *The requirements are few. One pipe, the diameter of a coin, and a second, large enough to fit a cannonball.*

"That's it? Two pipes?

Yes, It does not take much. The first is used as a sight, and the other for the bombardment projectile. But let us just shorten that to bomb, as it is less time consuming.

Rhone considered it for a moment, before answering with a nod. "Sure. I know about bombs, but I thought they exploded."

They can, Stone commented easily, *but it is not required. There are many refinements we could include, such as the addition of a release mechanism, but simple is sufficient.*

Again Rhone acted as translator, adding his own take on it. "Stone says it isn't difficult, and simple is better."

"I think it's exciting," Bella bubbled.

As always, her excitement made Rhone smile, and he accepted his defeat with a shrug. "Okay, we'll work on it tomorrow, but first we should reload the water and food stocks."

S parks flew as the blacksmith beat the glowing metal, stretching and flattening the heavy rod into its new form. His thick leather apron was soiled with sweat and grim, his bulging work-forged muscles proudly showing on arms twice the size of Rhone's. Unexpectedly, the man's face was quite jolly, turning to an easy smile as Rhone walked into his shop. Any customer that paid up-front was a good customer.

"Good day, sir. So happy to see you again. Did your boilers work? I never built anything quite like 'em before, so if there's a problem, it may take some time to rework."

"Not at all," Rhone said, raising a hand of good will. "They worked perfectly. Thank you. But I have a much simpler request, if you have the time, of course?"

"A simple job? Need shoes for your horse?"

Rhone tried to cover his guilty grimace, realizing Blue probably did need shoes, but at the moment he had more pressing matters. "I need two pipes. One can be quite narrow, maybe the size of a coin. The other needs to be large enough a cannonball could fit inside."

"A what? I'll assume you mean that large, not to actually fit a cannon-ball."

"One would think so, but in this case, it is. Beyond that, it requires a mechanism to hold the ball in place, and a release, allowing it to fall free. Would you be able to accomplish such a thing, or should I look elsewhere?"

When the smith looked affronted at the question of his ability, Rhone finished his ploy. "I only ask as I would not wish to waste your time if you were not capable of the task."

"Not capable?" sputtered the smith. "Why, it'd be as easy as boilin' potatoes. If it's metal, I can do it. I've even got a few ideas on the release contraption you're wanting, not that I know what it's for. But it don't matter. I'm good for the work."

"Excellent. Then consider it a contract," Rhone answered cheerfully. "And if you could add a holding feature for additional cannonballs, I would be glad to offer a bonus."

The smith wagged his head enthusiastically. "Can do sir. I'll get right on it."

Rhone was still amazed at the effectiveness of his supposed position. Things that would have taken hours of finagling for someone else, took only moments, and he was on his way.

CHAPTER 27

Bombs Away

Rhone stood on the quarterdeck of The Backwater Mistress, staring wide-eyed at the elegant single-edged saber Captain Black had just presented him. The sun flashed blindingly off the polished steel, making it as difficult to follow the wavy lines of the intricate metalwork as it was to swallow past the lump in his throat.

"It's beautiful," he managed to whisper, "but it's too much. Besides, with me being up in The Lady Luna, I can't think why I might need a sword. It's not like I'll be down with you and the pirates." He was also worried, that while a sword hanging at his side would look grand, it might also make walking difficult. A true threat on an airship.

Captain Black just beamed, his beard poking out like a cactus gone wild. Slapping Rhone's shoulder, he cackled, "Dad-gummit boy, you're Captain of a pirate-huntin' airship. You gotta look the part. Anybody scannin' you through a scope has to know you're ready to fight. Besides, if they're watchin' an' worrying about you, they won't be nearly so worried about my little Mistress scootin' in for the kill."

Rhone was oddly overcome by the captain's sentiment. Squaring his shoulders, he gave a slight bow. "Thank you, Captain. I'll cherish it."

The captain accepted Rhone's gesture with a nod and a wink. "Looks good on you too, and that don't hurt none." Then stepping to the map, he took on a more serious tone. "Now, I've been doin' some research, an' I've got a pretty good idea of where to look for those low-down scum of the seas. With so much broken shoreline, shallows and sea towers, there's plenty of areas most captains don't want to go. So I figure, if I was tryin' to stay hidden, that's where I'd be. Out of sight, and out of mind."

Rhone's interest perked at the comment. It was exactly the information he needed to finally strike at the pirates.

The next hour was spent with heads together, going over maps and planning for possible scenarios.

T he Lady Luna flew high over the Mistress, allowing Rhone to search the little bays and estuaries, even the areas behind the sea towers, without danger to the little ship far below.

Unfortunately, the clouds that often hid their balloon also hindered his own sight, taking as much as they gave. Rhone again scanned the wave-scared water, but this time searching for The Mistress. It seemed as though every time he turned to the shoreline, he would lose track of the little ship as she dipped between rolling waves. It was amazing how well she could hide in the broad expanse of water. From any distance, white caps and sea spume looked just like sails, set against the blues and greens of the corrugated surface.

Luckily, their meeting had come up with several good points, such as Captain Black's recommendation of using flags for signaling.

"Which ever of us see something of interest, fly your signals and the other will come running." He had been very assertive in the need to keep in touch. "How do I know what you're planning, if you don't let me know?"

With their plans made, their excitement grew. The speed of The Backwater Mistress and her newly-placed cannon, combined with the overhead attack of The Lady Luna, was sure to bring utter devastation to their foes.

At least that was the plan.

T he rocky sea spires were just beginning to show through the shoreline haze, their weathered stonework sticking sharply from the surface of the white-capped ocean below. With each wave, great plumes of spume rocketed skyward, drifting lazily with the breeze, until finally dropping back like rain into the churning blue-grey ocean. Seabirds screamed raucous cries as they circled the rocks, searching for the niche they called home, and the brood awaiting their return.

As The Lady Luna drifted sedately toward the towering rocks, Rhone kept a careful eye on Bella, grinning as she hung far over the rail, pointing excitedly at each new feature she saw. He was so enjoying the moment, he almost forgot why they were there, until they lifted over the crest, and a dark shape of a ship lay anchored in the protected water between the spires and the shoreline cliffs.

Recognizing the shape for what it was, Rhone swept up his long spyglass, sighting in on the deck, then up to furled red topsail.

Almost immediately, Stone announced, *I believe we have found our target,* sounding a bit apologetic, as if he too had been caught daydreaming.

"Hold on!" Rhone called sharply, spinning the wheel and kicking up the boiler.

Slowly, far too slowly for Rhone's liking, The Lady Luna fought her way into a turn, circling her bulbous form back the way they had just come. Rhone's racing heart didn't settle until they were once again hidden behind the rocky spire.

Bella leaned against the rail in shock, looking caught between the wonder of her observations, and panic at having been so rudely pulled into real action.

"I'm pretty sure they didn't see us," she stated shakily, as though waking from a dream.

"I hope you're right. They're not used to looking up for a threat, and hopefully, the surf drowned out our noise. Either way, get the signal flags ready while I set course toward The Mistress."

With their initial panic passed, Rhone cut back on the boiler power. "Set side sails," he called to Bella. "We'll let the wind do its job, and save the steam power for the attack."

With the push of the offshore winds, it only took ten minutes before Bella pointed excitedly into the distance. "Sails off the port bow."

Sure enough, Rhone quickly spotted the familiar sails of The Mistress showing against the horizon.

It took another twenty minutes, working their way cross wind, before Rhone ordered, "Signal Captain Black, 'target found', and watch for his response."

His words may have held somewhat more bravado than they had when he had cut and run, but Bella didn't make comment as she searched through the piled signal flags. When she found what she wanted, she connected the flags to the weighted line and dropped the end over the rail, watching expectantly as the line pulled taught, signal flags snapping in the breeze.

The Mistress had obviously been waiting. Within moments, a similar stream of flags rose on The Mistress, running from bowsprit to masthead.

"Got it," Bella shouted, pleased at having memorized the code. "They say, 'lead the way', and 'attack', 'plan two'."

"Plan two," Rhone repeated, smiling at her excitement.

Plan two included The Lady Luna dropping into view, and passing close to the targeted ship. While their crew was distracted by the odd-looking airship, The Backwater Mistress would sweep down from the far side, fire a round across their bow, and force a surrender before they could react. It would be shame to destroy the unsuspecting ship.

As Bella attached flags signaling their agreement, Rhone angled The Lady Luna back toward shore. The Backwater Mistress would be heading for the far more dangerous area between spires and cliffs, where the narrow strip of water wouldn't leave much room to maneuver. Even small as she was, timing would be critical.

Rhone gave the sea spires plenty of clearance, knowing a wayward gust could swing them at the wrong moment. Hitting the rocks might only be considered a beginner's error, but it could also be a fatal one.

"Ready for the approach," he called over the wind, quickly followed by, "Coming about!"

With a spin of the wheel, the airship rolled to her new heading. Only then did Rhone engage the boiler power, driving the fan-sails and edging the behemoth balloon forward. Wind was fine for general sailing, but he wanted full control during the attack.

His next command was, "Reef the side sails."

With the fan sails giving thrust, the side sails were only creating drag, acting as a parachute and slowing their progress.

Bella gave a cheerful salute, and ran to adjust the rigging, glad she had taken care of her skirt problem. This was no time to trip on a hem.

As soon as The Lady Luna cleared the majestic spire, Rhone shoved the wheel stanchion forward, adjusting the angle of the tail's elevator fins to drop the nose. The sounds of the heavy surf covered their approach, as The Lady Luna closed on their unwary foe.

The sudden drop and sloping deck caused Bella to grab for a nearby rail. She held on tightly as The Lady Luna swiftly slid toward the ocean far below. With the Luna acting more like a swooping swallow than a soaring buzzard, she would have to think about a safety harness of some kind. Skirts weren't the only hazard on airships.

Suddenly, the raucous and repeated sound of a ship's bell rang from the anchored ship, its strident clamor easily heard above the crashing waves and boiler's wheeze.

Rhone edged The Lady Luna downwind, sailing in stately review as they passed the gawking crew.

Meanwhile, on the far side, unobserved in the hubbub of the Luna's arrival, The Backwater Mistress, full-sailed and racing with the wind, swooped down on the anchored vessel.

Rhone's chest swelled with pride at their maneuver, until Bella shrieked, "Rhone, they're going to shoot! Get us out of here!"

A cold shiver ran the length of his spine as he glimpsed a long-barreled rifle being hauled up the masthead. Again, he spun the wheel, using the oncoming wind to help the airship pivot like a dancer. With the boilers already going at full steam, the Luna swung away and out to sea. Hauling back on the wheel's new stanchion, Rhone used their new fan-sail technology to rise rapidly on the breeze.

It was magnificent, feeling with the wind lift the hull up and over the spires. The disturbed birds screamed their defiance as loudly as the ship's crew far below. But Rhone wasn't finished. Once it was obvious they were in a running retreat, he once again spun the wheel, and none too soon, as the resounding crack of a rifle shot echoed off the rocky cliffs.

Rhone actually felt the air whip past his head the moment before Bella screamed, "We're hit!" pointing at a dark hole appearing in the balloon envelope above him.

With a quick wide-eyed glance at the hole, Rhone turned to see the tiny form of their attacker standing in the crow's nest of the ship below. He had been a good shot, just as Bella had predicted, but they were still afloat. At least for now, that part of her prediction hadn't come true. He would be sure to let her know.

When the sound of a much heavier blast shook the air, Rhone spun to see The Backwater Mistress emerging from a thick cloud of grey smoke, her full sails taut with the brisk breeze. One of her starboard guns was still trailing smoke from its mouth, and was already being pulled back to reload.

Aboard the pirate's ship, splinters exploded from rails and planking as the deckhouse shattered, the shock of the blast lifting men from their feet, while others ran to their own cannon.

"Coming about," Rhone shouted, preparing Bella for their next maneuver. Again, Luna turned, although not quite as smoothly as before. They had barely settled into their new heading when Rhone gave another command, "Ready the bombardment!" shouting in what could only be considered his 'storm voice'.

Releasing her grip on the rail, Bella ran to the newly placed aperture and waited as The Lady Luna began her approach. Eye to the tube, she scanned for her target, her breathing coming heavy from fear and excitement. "Please don't let me miss," she whispered.

"Ready...," Rhone called as he raised an arm. With a last look over the side, he shouted, "Release one!" and stood waiting. With a feeling of horror, he realized there had been no response. Bella simply knelt there, looking through the sighting tube. *What's she doing, sightseeing?* he questioned Stone. When no answer came, he began to panic. He was ready to give the command again, when he saw Bella smoothly punch the release.

The first of her ten cannonball projectiles rolled neatly into the bombardment tube, and without a sound, dropped toward the pirate ship far below. Without the noise of gunfire, or a canon's blast to sway the airship, Rhone almost questioned whether it had worked. But a quick glimpse caught sight of the quickly disappearing ball as it began its rapid descent.

The pirate crew had all but forgotten The Luna, with The Mistress rushing down on them, cannon blazing, but they were obviously well-practiced. Already the sails were rising, as men came to action, some scurrying up the masts, while others loaded the cannon. They were quick at their work, knowing an anchored ship was as good as a sitting duck.

With their distance above the action, Rhone had time to watch, seeing it as from a bird's eye, just as Captain Black had told him so long ago.

The Mistress's first cannon was still being reloaded as Captain Black continued his assault, using the remaining four on that side. Those of the crew not working the sails, or manning the guns, gripped their weapons of choice as they prepared to board.

The pirates began to fire back with scattered rifle shots, then a lone cannon spoke in a huge billow of smoke and flame. But they'd chosen haste over precision, and Rhone saw the shot go wild, skipping off a wave far to the side of The Mistress. Unfortunately, the pirate's sharpshooter had proven better. One of The Mistress' crew gripped futilely at the rail, before sliding to the deck, hand to his chest.

Captain Black stood proudly on the quarterdeck, urging his crew on. As soon as their volley fired, The Mistress turned sharply, cutting back against the wind to slow themselves and bring the port-side cannon to bear.

Blinking away the scene, Rhone called to Bella. "Prepare for continuous bombardment." Then as The Mistress had, turned The Lady Luna into the wind.

With the ship held in place directly above the pirates, Bella tightened her lips, and again, placed her eye to the sight. Within moments, the cannonballs were rolling forward, one after the other, dropping into the void.

The Luna's solid-bottom hull would keep them fairly safe from the sharpshooter. And while a shot might possibly pierce the hull, its power would be spent.

But before The Backwater Mistress could close on their prey, the deck of the pirate ship burst apart, sending splinters flying. Another projectile punched through a rising sail, shattering the heavy spar. Screams mixed with shouts from the angry crew as the slightly-deflected cannonball careened downward, holing the deck and nearly striking a running crewman. With cannonballs raining from the sky, The Mistress fired her port broadside, engulfing the two ships in billowing smoke. A minute later, the two ships ground together with the sound of snapping woodwork.

"Grapples," bellowed Captain Black as he drew his own saber.

With The Mistress engage at close quarters action, Rhone called a halt to their bombardment, watching in fascination as the resulting confusion allowed their men to board. In a mass, the men rushed across the narrow gap, charging to meet the harried pirates. The disordered ranks fought bravely, but had been caught unprepared, and in mere minutes, a surrender was called.

In wide-eyed wonder, Rhone gazed over the rail to the damaged ship slowly settling in the rough water. The destruction was hard to believe. Bodies floated in the salty waves, next to splintered railing, and spars still attached to sections of sails.

Rhone felt himself go cold as he realized what they had done. Men who had been alive mere minutes before were now dead, just more trash of battle. He felt himself sickening, then heard Bella climbing the stairs to the quarterdeck. Her swagger and triumphant grin abruptly changed as she looked his direction.

"The hole! We have to patch the hole!" she shouted, pointing fearfully up at the balloon.

She was right. In the midst of battle he had forgotten they'd been hit. Worse, hole patching was not something they had practiced. How could he have been so dumb?

"What do we do?" Bella shrieked in growing panic.

Rhone's mind spun, forgetting entirely about the beleaguered ship below.

While it was only a small hole, logic said two, since the bullet would have pierced the entire balloon easily. With the gasses escaping through both, it wouldn't be long before they felt the loss of lift.

"Get a blanket," Rhone shouted as his adrenaline kicked into action. "We may not get it patched, but we can at least slow the leak."

What he didn't say was, if they didn't, they might not make it back to Corgy.

With a shaky but understanding nod, Bella ran for the ladder. In no time she was back, blanket in hand.

"Bella, you have the helm," Rhone called, clasping her hand firmly over the wheel. Then grabbing the blanket, he tucked it under his arm and headed for the entry to the balloon's interior.

It wasn't far from the quarterdeck to the enclosed algae pan, really only a few steps, but with his knees already feeling weak, Rhone had to take a steadying breath before he drew back the draping whale-hide cover, and slipped through into the dark interior. As the flap closed, the sunlight was sealed off, leaving it truly dark. It took a moment for his eyes to adjust. He took a thankful breath, but instantly regretted the action, as he gagged. The smell from the algae pan was worse than a hen house in summer, but he had a job to do.

Careful of his footing, Rhone waded into the algae bed, making his way through the thick muck. His mind churned with thoughts of the recent action, and his plans for the repair.

The bullet had come from below, so it should have struck the envelope near the bottom. *Do you see it?* he thought to Stone, not wanting to open his mouth to speak.

Ahead and to your left, Stone directed.

At least it should be simple to work on. But a moment later a sudden gust caused the airship to lurch, and with nothing to hold on to, Rhone went down to a knee, thankful it hadn't been face-first. Staggering ungracefully to his feet, he continued his sliding steps toward the tiny spot of bright light ahead.

The interior air was thick with the smelly gasses, allowing Rhone only shallow breaths as he slogged his way to the small hole. The soft whoosh of venting air was enough to make him cringe, knowing how quickly they would lose lift as their precious gasses escaped. Feet wide to stabilize, he peered upward, spotting the second hole shining brightly near the top. But one task at a time.

Shaking out the blanket, he attempted to tear the material, but it was just too tough. Frustrated, he was stumped on how to proceed, until Stone's voice broke into the quiet.

Rhone, use the sword. Just be careful to not puncture the envelope.

Got it, Rhone replied in a thought.

Carefully pulling the sword free, he sawed away at the blanket. It was far more difficult than he had expected, as the material simply whipped back and forth in the dark, following the action of the sword. But finally it cut through, almost dumping him again in the sudden release. With the blanket in two, he had one piece for each hole. But how would he get it to stick?

Again, Stone came to his assistance. *The interior air pressure should be some help in holding the blanket in place, but try wetting the material first, as it might give some added adhesion against slippage.*

"Good idea," Rhone said, then coughed, having forgotten to keep his mouth shut.

After dunking the half blanket into the soupy algae bed, Rhone flopped the soggy material over the hole and was actually surprised when it seemed to work. The sound of escaping gasses had stopped.

One down and one to go.

Surprisingly satisfied, Rhone slipped and slithered his way back to the center of the airship, staring up at the hole far above his head. He could hear the boiler steaming away in the lower hold, and felt the rise and fall of the airship as it drifted over the ocean far below, but looking into the envelope's disorienting darkness only proved his inability to reach the upper hole. Staring upward into the gloomy interior, he suddenly felt woozy from the shifting motion of the airship.

He was still shin deep in the muck, searching for inspiration, when another sudden shift dumped him backward, dropping him seat-first into the ooze. With a shoulder-wracking shudder, he sank into the mucky algae up to his waist. Then a cheerful thought popped into his wandering mind, that once again he had managed not to go in face first. The disconnected thought made him chuckle, then cough, as he inhaled more of the gross air. Then he began coughing in earnest, sucking in huge lungfuls as his body struggled for clean air. But the new air was no better than the last.

Coughing continuously now, he nearly retched as he dropped to hands and knees, then began crawling toward the exit.

His mind spun as he wallowed forward, dragging himself to where he was sure the entry was. He barely recognized it when he bumped headfirst into the leathery side, until he slowly realized, this wasn't the way out. With hands sweeping over the smooth whale-hide wall, he searched, but only saw the wall disappearing into the darkness.

He was lost.

CHAPTER 28

Winning is not all it's Cracked Up to be

With their recent naval engagement all but forgotten, Bella fought the winds that threatened to pin them to the mainland cliffs. Buffeted by the gusts, the bulky craft bucked wildly in undignified lurches, skillfully handled by her use of both the wheel and boiler drive.

Rhone hadn't returned from his task, and she was begin to worry. How long did it take to patch two holes? On a normal day, she could simply tether the wheel and go check on him, but Luna wasn't acting her normal placid self. She shuddered violently as a new gust shifted her position, flying more like a chicken than a sparrow. She was heavy and slow to react, making Bella grip the wheel with white knuckles. No matter what she did, The Lady Luna sagged, slowly dropping lower toward the ocean's surface.

T otally unaware of the situation outside, Rhone dragged himself forward through the slimy muck, no longer sure of where he was going, only that it was vitally important that he got there.

If he could only remember.

Then a hazy memory surfaced. Stone. Of course. He had been searching for his friend. Stone had been stolen.

Rhone tried to focus, certain he could hear his friend's call in the darkness. He knew Stone had to be rescued. Stone certainly couldn't do it by himself. He was a rock-thing.

Rhone? Can you hear me? The words rolled through Rhone's thoughts as hollowly as a rock through a pipe.

Stone? he answered uncertainly. *Where are you? Don't worry, I'm coming.* They were after all, best friends. Collar-mates, and Stone wasn't even a people. Somehow Rhone found that funny, and began laughing, then choking, drowning in the desert. Or was it the algae pan? It was hard to keep track.

Rhone, pay attention. Can you hear me?

The concern in Stone's voice caught Rhone's attention.

"Stone, I'm sorry," Rhone mumbled between coughs. "I didn't mean to let you get taken, but I died. Remember? I died in the desert. Then I died in the water. But I had to come rescue you."

Rhone coughed again, fighting the numbness of his mind, then a sharp jolt coursed through his body, and he stiffened, teeth clacking together with a snap. Stunned by the unfairness of it, Rhone started to complain, but another coughing fit racked his tortured body.

When he was finally able to breathe again, he all but cried, "Why'd you do that? I'm coming to rescue you."

Rhone! Pay attention! Follow my light. Can you do that?

"Follow the light," Rhone numbly recited, as a glowing pinpoint began to reflect off the algae bed in front of him.

Yes, follow the light, Stone encouraged.

"Sure. Follow the light. Easy peasy, if you would just slow down."

No, we can't slow down. Bella needs us.

Rhone considered that for a moment. "Bella? Bella needs us?" his oxygen-starved mind working to make sense of it all. "Stone, we have to hurry. Bella needs us!" But saying the words only made him cough again, spitting out the taste of algae water that had somehow gotten into his mouth. "Tastes really bad."

Yes, I am sure it does. Now keep your mouth closed, and do not talk. Follow the light. We are almost there.

Drawing scum-covered hands from the slimy surface, Rhone pushed wearily forward, slithering through the muck as he followed the bright light. The journey seemed miles long, his eyes going hazy by the time he was semi-alerted by Stone's now flashing light. Bumping into the hide of the doorway, he raised a hand for another push, and slid headfirst over the lip of the algae bed, through the overlapped covering of the entrance, and into the brilliantly bright golden sunshine.

Instinctively, Rhone raised a hand to cover his eyes, and sucked in huge lungfuls of fresh, clean, ocean air. Then his body rebelled, and he retched, emptying his churning stomach onto the clean deck.

Bella had been watching expectantly for his exit, but hadn't expected this. Hastily tying off the wheel, she ran to his side. The Lady Luna would have to wait.

Gripping his arms with now slimy hands, she dragged him away from the opening, then quickly reversed course to reseal the entrance. No need to lose more of the precious gasses.

Sadly, she gave him the bad news. "I know this isn't the best timing, but we're going down. There just isn't enough lift gas to stay afloat, and I don't know what else to do."

Even his slowly functioning mind could hear her worry.

Desperately he tried to focus on the problem. "We need more lift," he said unnecessarily.

There was only a moment's pause before Bella asked, "What about the boiler? Could it create enough lift to get us to shore?"

Rhone was still fighting his mental fog, but remembered that steam had been the only lift method for Bo and BoToo. Maybe it would work here.

Still on hands and knees, he asked the now quiet Stone, *Will it work?*

Sorry, Stone answered guiltily, *I was doing calculations. But yes. Diverting the steam boiler from drive sails to the envelope, should help, though perhaps only for a few minutes.*

With his mind finally clearing, Rhone passed Stone's directions on to Bella.

"Of course," she replied, a renewed hope bringing the glow back to her smudged face. "I'm not exactly sure how, but I'll try. You drag yourself to the wheel and keep us off the cliffs, and I'll get it done."

Nodding wearily, Rhone gathered enough strength to climb to his feet, while Bella hiked up her skirts and ran to the lower deck. There was no time to waste.

It didn't take more than a glance for Rhone to see the situation wasn't good. The Lady Luna was not only drifting toward the cliff, but dropping toward the waves. Even untying the wheel took him longer than normal, but he managed a course change, hoping to gain some time. The hull had been built to settle on the surface if needed, but they would never survive the churning water of the sea towers.

Rhone was glad he had a good grip on the wheel as the frenzied wind tried to throw them against the cliff. But with the upthrust winds, if Bella could somehow manage the steam rerouting, it just might give them enough lift to rise over the top. If not, it would be a smashing end to their dreams, hitting the cliff face and dropping to the boiling surf below.

Rhone searched for options, but all he could see was holding course, and the likelihood of getting Bella killed. Like the bullet hole, they had never planned on changing the boiler lead, having never considered the need. He was frustrated at his lack of foresight, and had no idea how she could manage it. His only comfort was that she wouldn't see the end. A small consolation indeed.

As Rhone wiped muck from his face with an almost-as-slimy sleeve, he caught a flash of motion below. The Backwater Mistress was rushing toward them under full sail, leaping across the wave tops, throwing clouds of spume into the air as it battle the waves of the narrow waterway fronting the cliff.

It was beautiful, watching The Mistress fly so elegantly, defying the waves, but Rhone smiled sadly at the futility of their effort. The balloon was so low now, he was able to tell the men apart by their clothes. Captain Black himself stood at the bow, looking like the giant figurehead of a god, arm raised pointing up at them. For a moment, Rhone thought they might even collide with the masts, but The Mistress cut slightly, the angle bringing them in even closer.

He watched in confusion until he saw the captain step back, and a seaman take his place, harpoon in hand. With a heart-breaking realization, he understood. They were going to pop his balloon. Bringing it down meant they wouldn't hit the cliff, and could be rescued, but he felt sick at the loss.

The Luna dropped even lower, until Rhone was close enough to see the scruffy windblown beard on the captain's anxious face. Then like an ancient Greek warrior, the seaman flung the harpoon.

Rhone couldn't see where it struck, but even he could hear Captain Black's bellow ring over the sounds of the surf. Oddly, nothing happened, until The Backwater Mistress suddenly changed course.

A massive shudder ran through the wallowing airship, bringing Rhone to his knees. Then a stomach-dropping dip toward the waves swung that The Lady Luna around, pivoting her away from the cliff, but directly toward the tall rocky spire.

Rhone clutched at the wheel with white knuckles, mostly for balance since it made no difference to their course. Their destruction was almost upon them. By cliff or spire, their hours were numbered. They were done.

Suddenly Rhone panicked, remembering Bella working in the hold. "We're going down," he shouted in panic. "Get out of there!" This wasn't the way it was suppose to happen!

Almost immediately Bella's head popped up from the ladder. Her worried look didn't giving a clue whether she had heard, or gotten the boiler converted, but at least she was back on deck. They would go down together.

"You're making for a pretty rough ride," she said almost calmly. "Are we crashing?"

When Rhone's answer was to point toward the rocky spire directly ahead, her face turned white.

Even Luna must have recognized her end was near as she gave another deck-creaking shudder, staggering both Bella and Rhone. They had only seconds left.

Rhone watched enviously as The Backwater Mistress's new tack barely managed to evade the spire's frothing waves. At least The Mistress would be safe. It was better than both of them going down.

Then he noticed the taut line tied to the stern of The Mistress, and recognition slapped him in the face. Captain Black hadn't tried to pop Luna's envelope. The harpoon must have lodged in the hull. The Mistress was dragging them away from the cliffs!

Instantly energized, Rhone turned back to the wheel. "Hang on!" he shouted.

He could see the question on her face, but Bella nodded and gripped the rail.

With their new forward motion giving life to the slowly dying airship, Rhone turned the spoked wheel, pulling The Lady Luna into a gut-wrenching turn.

Bella watched in resignation as the broken-sided rock slid closer. So close, she wondered if she should try jumping to safety. But the choice was easy. She would go down with her ship. This was her life, and if need be, it would be her death too. At least she had flown. She would ask for nothing more.

The Lady Luna leaned like a swing at the bottom of its run, carving a very un-balloon like arc past the towering spire with mere feet to spare.

But while the sudden swing kept the Luna from crashing into the spire, it also had an effect on their saviors. Within a boat's length, The Backwater Mistress stopped all forward progress, practically standing on her nose in the rough water. As the weight of the airship jerked The Mistress's stern to the side, her sails luffed, then crack back into their full bellied shape as they once again came under the influence of the wind. The ship's crew grabbed for anything near, attempting to stay on their feet. Men went down, loosened from their perches in the sails. Those on deck found that even experienced sea legs weren't ready for this kind of motion. The cries of birds and crash of waves couldn't hide the cries of the men and creak of the mast as the ship took the strain. Then the sound like a gunshot rebounded from the spire as a mast gave way, tearing a ragged gash in one of the sails, and littering the deck with falling debris. Through it all, Captain Black's storm voice boomed, somehow calming in its orders.

With The Backwater Mistress suddenly losing headway, the massive shape of The Lady Luna quickly caught up.

Rhone stared in horror at the oncoming collision, but unexpectedly they began to rise, slowly climbing up and over their damaged rescuer, their hull almost grazing the masts as they drifted past.

Rhone swung to stare dumbly at Bella still holding to the railing. "Did you get the boiler redirected?" he asked in amazement.

He didn't even notice the dirty smudge crossing her grin, as she saluted. "Yes, sir. Redirected as ordered, sir."

When Stone candidly remarked, *A very capable woman, is she not?* Rhone could only agree.

"She sure is," he whispered in absolute awe.

CHAPTER 29

Beginning of the End

The Lady Luna limped back to port, staying well within sight of The Backwater Mistress. With two masts still working, The Mistress had no difficulty cutting handily through the waves, and staying ahead of the barely-managing airship. Losing a spar was one of the normal failures while out to sea. Masts too. They even had a spare, but they would wait to swap it out until they were safely in harbor.

The pirates hadn't fared so well. With the hull holed, the ship had quickly taken on water, destroying their goods and losing men to the vagaries of the churning ocean. Most sailors couldn't swim, and few survived wrecks. When out at sea, swimming only lengthened the time it took to drown. They had been close to shore in this fight, but the waves smashing against the rocky cliff left very little uncertainty as to their fate. Few had been taken on board The Mistress.

The Luna had made it back to Corgy, but all in all, it wasn't what Rhone had imagined. He had hoped to take over the pirate ship, and sail it back as a hero, with very little damage to goods or men. Now his spirit hurt thinking of those souls lost because of his actions.

Bella tried to console him. "It isn't your fault they became pirates," she said quietly. "They made their choice. If they hadn't been attacking other ships, we wouldn't have needed to deal with them. In fact, I suspect the town may even throw a party in your honor."

She held his hand as they talked, but his face stayed gloomy.

"Thanks, I know you're trying to help, but men died because of me."

It was a hard road he had chosen.

With a sigh, Rhone drew his hand from hers. "I need to write an incident report, and get it sent off. I'll see you in the morning, okay?"

Without waiting for her reply, he left to find his desk.

<hr>

Mayor Dugan happily worked his way through the process of arrest papers, citing Rhone and his newfangled contraption for destruction of property, cows not producing milk, and chickens not laying. He was just getting to the good part, where Rhone's floating menace had scared the good people of Corgy, causing civil unrest, when Mrs Randle stepped into his office doorway, with a light rap on the jamb.

"Sir, you have visitors."

"Just tell them I'm busy," he griped, a gargoyle-like smile plastered to his mug.

"Yo, Mayor Dugan," came an over-pleased call from the outer office. "We need your esteemed presence."

"What now," The mayor mumbled, rubbing both hands over his bothered face.

But he was too late. The doorway was suddenly filled with the bodies of several of Corgy's business owners, each vying to be the first in.

Mrs Randle looked aggrieved at their intrusion, but wisely chose to back out of the way, wringing her hands as she retreated to her own territory.

"We are calling an emergency meeting of the city council," said a tall man now holding center stage.

The mayor greeted the entrants with feigned concern, putting on his political face. "Now what's all this about? I've got work here that needs done."

"Well, Mr Mayor. We, your friendly voters and constituents, want to know what you plan to do about this wonderful young man that's saved our town?"

"We must do something," puffed a rotund man, barely able to fit through the doorway. "He deserves a medal at least."

"A party," responded a third, speaking over the previous conversation. "The town should sponsor a party in his honor."

Mayor Dugan cringed at the notion of Rhone parading around like a victorious soldier, home from the war with medals plastered to his chest, but being the politician he was, simply smiled with raised eyebrows. "That's an amazing idea. I should have thought of it myself." Luckily, the sound of his curdling stomach was covered by the cheerful backslaps of his guests.

The first speaker again made his presence felt, as he said, "It seems the harbor captains are also behind this young man. They can't say enough about his service to shipping and their trade. Why, they're even ready to recommend him to The Council proper."

"You don't say," Mayor Dugan whispered, feeling the strength go out of his legs. "Let me discuss it with my secretary, and see what we can do, although I can't guarantee a date for the festivities. I'm terribly busy right now, so I... "

"Perfect," replied the rotund man from across the room. "Look, there they are now," waving out the window to the flying contraption hovering over the harbor.

The mayor grimaced as his stomach growled forlornly. "What the town wants, the town gets," he said through gritted teeth. "Mrs. Randle, would you mind seeing these gentlemen out?" Then with a last half-hearted wave, managed an almost believable smile. "It's always a pleasure to have you drop by."

Plopping into his chair like a bag of turnips, the mayor groaned and began banging his head repeatedly on the desk top.

As gut-wrenching as the thought was, he had to admit, the airship had made a difference. In only two weeks, two pirate ships had been destroyed, and the town was jubilant. His town, at least for now. Luckily, it had all happened while he was in office. The public's short memory might at least remember that much, and as tooth-grinding as it might be personally, he was a politician, and knew he needed to make a public statement, applauding the airship and its crew.

Then there was that Captain Black creature, another thorn in his side. He was the one spreading the news through the harbor, expounding the exploits of the airship. What was its name again? The Lady Luna? Stupid name for a ship, but The Backwater Mistress wasn't any better. Didn't they know a good name when they heard one? Something like, The Challenger, or The Liberty. Those were names any good captain would love.

Utterly disgusted, he called to the outer office. "Mrs. Randle, set up a gala event for the town."

"Certainly sir, and what's the occasion?"

Grinding his teeth again, Mayor Dugan managed, "An award of excellence," in words barely discernible through his partially covered curse.

"A splendid idea sir. I'll get right on it."

"Whatever," he said under his breath. "Just get it done."

The Mayor's stomach gurgled sickly as he felt its acid churning. He and his ulcers had a working relationship. They made themselves felt whenever he worked.

R hone's brisk stride slowed at seeing Bella's excited eyes.

"Rhone, you have a letter."

"A letter? From the OPR?" he asked hopefully.

He had continued to send updates to the office, but had yet to receive a single response.

"No, from the Mayor," Bella said, hardly able to contain her excitement.

"Rats and barnacles. It must be a summons," Rhone muttered.

The Mayor must have found a way to have him arrested, probably using The Lady Luna as a pretense. Slowly, he crossed the room for the proffered letter.

In elaborate script, the envelope said;

From the office of
Mayor Dugan, Corgy.

Taking the letter from her outstretched hand, Rhone cautiously slid a look from it, to her. Bella's eyes were sparkling at the thought of a missive from the town's mayor come to their door. Obviously, she didn't share his concerns.

With a sigh, he took a pen knife from the table, and slid it under the top flap of the thick envelope, slicing it neatly along the fold. Hesitantly, he pulled out the fine parchment and began to read.

Bella couldn't wait for him to finish. He was only part way through when she began bouncing in place, hands clasped together, almost bursting with anticipation.

"Hold on and I'll read it to you," Rhone said, deciding it was safer than having her bust a button,

Bella nodded happily and sat, waiting impatiently for his delivery.

It appeared to be an invitation, and Rhone briefly wondered if was to his own hanging. With his brow showing his question, he began to reread the fancy script.

A cordial welcome to you.

I, and the town of Corgy, ask your presence at the meeting of the town and council, tomorrow evening, Thursday. We would wish the honor of presenting you, an Award of Excellence for your heroic effort on our behalf.

The presentation will be followed by a minor dessert buffet, where your fellow townsmen and women may meet with you and deliver their own congratulations.

I thank you ahead of time for your acceptance of this honor.

Mayor Dugan, Corgy.

"An award, from the Mayor?" Rhone sputtered in disbelief. He would have been less surprised if the couch had transformed into a frog. "I must say, it's not quite what I expected."

Bella sprang to her feet, clapping excitedly as she bounced. "I knew it," she cried happily. "You're such a grumphead sometimes. You never expect things to go right."

"I'm a grumphead?" he asked stupidly. "I just thought I was doing what needed done." He took an unsteady seat, face mirroring his confused expectations.

Bella saw his dismay and came to his rescue. "Don't worry about it. He did treat you pretty bum. But let's get to serious matters. What shall I wear?"

Bella was nothing if not practical. With only her two options, the normal in-town and boring outfit, or the fabulously-uptown, clip-skirted ensemble that was honestly very practical on shipboard, there wasn't much choice.

Rhone wondered briefly on how much devastation one woman could bring to a town. But it was a celebration, and she had as much right to the award as he did. Probably more.

"Go for it," was all he said.

With Bella doing her utmost to wow the town's folk, Rhone could hardly do less. He had seen the big city, and had developed several new accoutrements for himself. Between the two of them, he was almost sorry for the town's people, certain they would never be the same.

Still uncomfortable around the town, Bella asked Rhone along on her shopping spree, searching for the best material the mercantile had. The selection wasn't great, but she knew that before they went.

Finally, after working non-stop for hours upon hours, she was ready.

Rhone's eyes almost bulged out of his head as she stepped from the room. Bella's hair was tied back loosely, allowing strands to fall innocently over her ear, but Rhone's gaze was glued to the high-collared blouse, un-buttoned down the front to a dark leather bustier that cinched snuggly around the slim curves of her waistline. It fit her like the proverbial glove, the boning and buckles only accentuating her shape.

He stood in stunned silence, not at all certain he would be able to protect her, from predatory eyes if nothing else. Even he was breathless, just looking at her.

Golden-hued laces tied her almost knee-high boots, and if he hadn't been taken by the bodice, he certainly was by the fine legs showing just above those boots. The lacy netting of her stockings was something he had never seen before, and was so captivating he had to drag his eyes back up to hers. Her dark green, clip-fronted skirt he had seen the evening he had taken her to dinner, and was almost commonplace next to the rest of the outfit.

But all of this together? He couldn't come up with anything to say, simply standing open-mouthed, like a fish out of water.

"You like?" Bella asked, a little shy now that she had made her daring entry.

"Do I like?" Rhone stammered. "Am I alive? I thought you were awe-some when I took you to The Common House, and you were. But this...

you...," he stuttered to a stop, his eyes taking in every inch of her, willing his mind to memorize the picture.

"Okay, I guess I did good," Bella chirped pleasantly, stepping the rest of the way into the room. "You look pretty good yourself by the way. And you finally found things for all those pockets and buckles. I like." She grinned at him playfully, fully aware he couldn't respond in any sane manner.

Hoarsely, Rhone whispered, "You're absolutely gorgeous. But are you sure you want to go out in public like this? What if they talk about you?"

"They already talk about me," Bella explained with a shrug. "I heard a few comments when we went shopping. Actually, I'm the talk of the town, next to you. I'll admit, there are probably a few things I could have done differently, but this is me. The new me," she said, giving a flourishing wave of her hand, "and I fly on The Lady Luna. If they don't like it, then we'll just... fly somewhere else, and let the pirates return."

Rhone knew she meant every word. She would work to save this town, but it wasn't hers any more.

"I think I understand," he said supportively. Then schooling his expression, gave a slight bow and asked, "In that case, would you accept my arm? I believe we have a ceremony to attend."

Bella searched his face, looking for something. Maybe laughter, or perhaps peevishness at her actions, but there was nothing other than his joy at being by her side. Drawing her lips together in a tight line, she returned his nod. "I would love to. Thank you, Captain."

Mayor Dugan could have chewed gravel, had he been able to unlock his teeth from their grinding grimace. He had planned on capturing the hearts of his townsfolk with his fluid oration, as he granted the Award of Excellence to The Lady Luna's victorious crew.

The speech had been a masterpiece. One of his best. He would have been magnanimous in his praise of the heroes, and their defeat of the vulgar pirates that had besieged his town.

Even now, running the speech through his mind, he could feel the glory of its cadence. A true masterpiece. Or, it would have been. Until that conniving rich kid had shown up looking like a damned prince. Worse, he had the gall to have his so called 'lieutenant' on his arm, dressed in her flaunting, almost indecent contraption of a dress.

Between the two of them, nobody even heard him, their own mayor, as he attempted to gather the crowd's attention for his speech. The entire room cheered and applauded the two in utter pandemonium.

Disgusting is what it was. Pirates or not, he still wasn't convinced they weren't part of it from the beginning. It was all too convenient for his liking. Besides, the gods knew, nobody should be that rich, young, and good looking. It just wasn't right.

The ceremony had gone on, but not the way he had planned it. His voice shook as he tried to smile, and his ulcer had gone into overtime, curdling his stomach and giving him the ague until he could hardly stand, let alone give an effective address. The speech was an absolute failure, making him look a fool.

After graciously accepting the award, Rhone had stood, hand raised to the crowd, and given a short response, acknowledging practically everyone for their help in providing pieces and parts for their airship.

It had been too much. The mayor had quit listening, looking for a way off the stage, his stomach insisting it was time to be elsewhere. Only now, somewhat recovered, could he rage at the unjustness of the world. Corgy was, after all, his town.

Or had been.

___※※※___

While The Lady Luna was inaccessible, ranging far and wide over the county and sea, The Backwater Mistress, captained by the infamous Captain Black, usually made port at Corgy every week. Her captain may trade mostly in commodities needing rapid transport, but she still had regular routes, and called Corgy her home.

That was all Mayor Dugan needed. Still furious over the ceremony fiasco, he needed a win, no matter what it took. He had done it before, and he could do it again. A win was a win.

___※※※___

The cold evening wasn't the most comfortable, but it did match the cold snarl of self righteous determination on the mayor's face. "Captain Plo..." he began, only to be cut off with a quick motion.

"No names!" came the pointed threat. "You know the method. If you can't abide, find someone else."

The gruff command wasn't respectful, but the mayor gave a simple tip of his head in acknowledgment.

"My apologies. I'm afraid I forgot in my excitement. Now, I want The Backwater Mistress on the bottom of the ocean, and I don't care how you manage it. They're a menace to all, parading around like everybody owes them something. I would torch the little skiff myself, but it would simply clog the harbor with its rubbish. No, I want it done out of sight. If she never comes back, I doubt there will be any questions. The seas are a dangerous place from what I hear."

The jest was matched by the dark humor glinting in his listener's eyes, sending an involuntary shiver through the mayor, and making him draw his coat tighter in the chill of the evening.

"I'll see it done," the man growled. "I've got my own reasons to see to Captain Black."

"The sooner the better. I appreciate your service in this, our hour of need. Payment will come in the usual manner. Half now and half on completion." He pulled a small bag from his coat pocket and handed it to the dark man.

"As I said, I'll see it done," came the aggravated response. Then hefting the bag as though checking its weight, deftly slid it into a now-bulging pocket. With a sly grin and a wordless nod, he left the mayor standing in the dark.

The drift of sea spume, wafting through the night sky, gave a chill embrace to the already murky environment.

"Dang pirates," Mayor Dugan muttered under his breath. The cold plume of steam lifting from his exhalation couldn't cover his shiver, going from shoulders to toes.

Shaking himself free of the feel, the mayor strode to his horse standing with drooping head, looking as if he too would much prefer to be home.

"Why do they always choose such inhospitable times to meet?" he grumbled." It simply isn't civilized."

Gathering the reigns, he tried a couple poor efforts to mount, before settling himself onto the cold leather of the saddle. But his tight smile knew his problems would soon be over.

Not two days later, a heavily armed ship lay quietly tucked behind a towering spire, impatiently waiting her prey.

As The Backwater Mistress slid elegantly past the towering water-sculpted stone, canon shots blasted through the sounds of the surf, bringing a ringing echo off the near shore's cliff face.

The sound of tearing sail cloth followed, barely heard above the responding bellow from Captain Black. "Man the guns! Hard about! his storm-honed bellow almost as deafening as the shot had been.

Men ran to their positions as though their lives depended on it, which in truth, they did. Gunners prepared their shots as other crewmen manned the halyards and lines, hauling the sails to better catch the wind as the ship turned. With a spin of the wheel, The Mistress worked to come about. Triple-masted and gaff-rigged, rather than square-rigged as most ships in the area, she was able to drive ahead with the rearward sails, while the forward set turned, using the wind to whip the bow around. The crew worked in a well-practiced ballet; men, sails, wind and water doing with the little ship what other captains would have found impossible.

Captain Black may have been taken unaware, but now had the element of surprise. With unexpected agility, The Backwater Mistress spun back to sea, cutting briskly around the towering spire and disappearing behind solid rock. The attacking ship, setting secure and certain of a kill, now struggled, fighting wind and waves to begin moving. Their square-rigged sails could not hold as close to the wind, and required a large swing to come around the stony towers. When they finally managed their arc, The Mistress was gone, blending into the misty clouds scudding across the rough seas.

Even with sails holed in several places, The Backwater Mistress easily outran their larger attacker, never even hearing the curses flung at them.

Mayor Dugan was too weary to pace his office, choosing simply to glower at Mrs. Randle whenever she entered. He expected bad news, and got just that. The dang little ship had managed some kind of miraculous maneuver, and gotten away with barely a scratch. Now they had changed routes, seeming to disappear whenever they left port.

He could see the writing on the wall, but at least he wouldn't have to pay the second half of the fee.

CHAPTER 30

Recalled

I have just received a message from Jewel.

Stone's quiet announcement was the last thing Rhone would have expected.

Coming to an abrupt halt, he re-ran the echoing words, his thoughts instantly going to Aundrea, wondering if she was alright.

"A message? What kind? How'd you get it?" Rhone asked, his urgency surprised even himself.

Settle yourself, Stone answered ungraciously. *If you will give me half a moment, I will pass on the information I have.*

"Sure. Of course, you're right," Rhone apologized. "Now, what did she say?"

It wasn't much better, but he was trying.

As I said, I have received a transmission from Jewel. It was similar to our normal contact, but I will admit, somewhat different. I am not certain how it was accomplished. While the signature was the same, the methodology was definitely not. My theory is, she has developed a method of wave transmission.

We had discussed the possibility, but have not had the time to work on the concept. If it is true, we will be able to make contact at almost any distance. Absolutely wonderful, but as I stated, it is merely conjecture at the moment.

"Wave transmission? That would be awesome," Rhone said approvingly, but barely understanding what it meant. The mere thought was staggering. Instantaneous contact from a distance could change everything. "That really sounds great, but what was the message? Are they all right?"

Method could wait. The message couldn't.

Yes... as to the message... Stone's uncharacteristic pause brought Rhone an instant sense of panic. Then the words, *We are being recalled,* landed like a hammer's blow striking an anvil.

"Recalled? But why?"

His thoughts floundered in the bleak unknown, but snapped back to focus as the worst rose to the top.

"But, what about The Lady Luna, and... and Bella?" His pulse spiked until he had to sit down with sudden dizziness. "Was there anything more to the message?"

I am afraid the message was quite short. After the initial connection, verifying our reception, the message simply said, and I quote, "You are being recalled. Please present yourself to headquarters. Jewel."

Rhone felt his heart drop. He was done. He must have failed his assignment, or caused enough problems that he was being removed.

"That was all?"

Yes, In its entirety. I am sorry.

Rhone's head swam with the implications. Maybe the mayor had finally gotten him replaced. Then another thought crossed his mind. Maybe he had spent too much on the airship, or something was wrong at the office? The list of possibilities was suddenly endless.

But the message had gotten through, and Aundrea knew it. He would be expected to return, and from the sound of it, as quickly as he could make it happen.

His assignment at Corgy was over. He simply couldn't see a way around the requirement that would change his life, again.

But Stone felt him falling into despair, and found a different approach. *Perhaps you are needed elsewhere, and possibly where time would make a difference.*

Rhone brightened at the thought. Maybe things weren't quite so bad, and Stone's not knowing how to duplicate Jewel's connection was another good reason to return. How had she done it?

He could feel Stone's excitement to know.

With Bella's hand on his arm, they took their casual stroll down the worn boardwalk toward the docks. He hadn't told her yet, having decided to wait until he could talk to both her and Captain Black at the same time. Why go through the pain twice?

Stopping at the bottom of the short ramp, Rhone called, "Captain Black, might we come aboard?"

All signs of their recent skirmish had been cleaned up, and everything was shining with spit and polish. And if not actually polished, it was at least neat and tidy.

When the head of a sailor popped up over the rail, a flash of recognition crossed his face. He had spent many an evening retelling the story of how he had saved the little rich kid from becoming fish food during their early excursions. It was a favorite story on The Mistress.

Rhone had heard the tale, grinning along with the rest of the crew. But hadn't been funny at the time. He truly had almost gone overboard in heavy seas.

"Evenin', Sir," the seaman called happily. "You wantin' the captain?"

"If he's available, yes. If you would let him know, Rhone and the lady Bella are here to see him, I would appreciate it."

"Certainly, sir. Not but a moment," and the head disappeared as quickly as it had appeared.

Bella had seen The Backwater Mistress many times, but had never been aboard. Many sailors believed it bad luck for a woman to board a ship, and she didn't wish to cause a problem. Tonight though, Rhone hadn't asked, simply escorting her directly to the boat. That was fine with her. She had seen it in action, and was quite interested in seeing The Mistress up close.

It really was 'not but a moment' when Captain Black's rough bark came floating up from the lower deck. "Captain Rhone! You've certainly stirred up a hornet's nest."

Head and shoulders quickly followed the voice, as Captain Black climbed to the main deck, and crossed to stride down the ramp, making it buck and bounce with every step. His grey beard was just as scruffy as on Rhone's first visit.

Rhone winced as Captain Black's callused hand slapped him on the back, almost knocking the wind out of him. "Good to see you too, Captain," Rhone managed with only a single cough.

The captain beamed. "Ahh, and Lady Bella too. It's so good to see you again," he said, giving her a wink and a smile. "I heard you changed the lady's styles in town. Good for you! Wish I had been there myself."

Captain Black carried on the conversation, mostly by himself, as Bella blushed at the mention of her garb, but her grin quickly returned.

"I want to thank you again, Captain," she said sweetly. "Your service certainly saved us from getting our tails wet. Without it we might well have drowned."

"Or been smashed against the cliffs, dropped into the crashing waves, then drowned," Rhone muttered quietly. It hadn't been their best day.

Then again, it had. Life was confusing that way.

Captain Black was in his usual high humor, and answered in his jovial way, "Well, don't just stand there gawkin' at my comely features. Come on aboard already."

Bella led as Rhone followed her up the ramp, but found it difficult to maintain his sense of the present with his mind slipping to his impending departure. His preoccupation had apparently missed a few comments, as Bella turned to look back at him questioningly.

Luckily, the captain seemed not to have noticed, continuing his monologue as he led them to the open area of the quarterdeck. A table and chairs were being set out by the crew, and the captain motioned them to take a seat.

"Too fine to be cooped up inside," Captain Black boomed merrily. "Care for some wine?" He was enjoying the chance to show off his hospitality to a beautiful woman.

When Rhone didn't respond immediately, Bella glanced his way, then seated herself without his aid. "That would be wonderful, Captain." she answered, giving Rhone another odd look.

Rhone felt himself blush, knowing he was doing this badly, but he simply wasn't ready. He would never be ready. Uncertain as how to proceed, he sat groping for words. His mind had gone blank with despair as his upscale training failed him, leaving nothing more than a simple teenager facing his nightmare. With the weight of the world setting heavy on his shoulders, he plunged headlong into his dilemma.

"Captain, sir... well, and Bella," he said shakily, thinking the guillotine couldn't be worse. "I have the unfortunate need to make a very painful announcement."

Rhone cringed as Bella's eyes took on a totally stricken look he remembered from past experience.

Just get it done! Stone scolded in frustration. *The longer it takes, the more pain there will be.*

At Captain Black's raised eyebrow, Rhone raced on with his announcement.

"I... I've been recalled."

There, it was said, as little as it was.

A look of fear swept over Bella, her grip on his forearm strangling it with more force than he would have guessed she had. "Recalled?" she asked. "How do you know? I didn't see a letter."

With a chortle, Captain Black came to Rhone's rescue. "Hold on girl. Give him a chance or he might just pass out before we hear it." The words were easy enough, but held their own questions.

Rhone thanked him with a pitiful glance as he plowed on. "I received notice earlier today. It simply said I was being recalled, and to report to headquarters. I honestly don't know any more than that."

"It must be really important," Bella whispered, now seeming more worried than angry.

When a crewman scurried up with the wine, Bella took hers, and downed most most of its contents.

"Easy there girl," Captain Black said, adding a bit of his normal grin. But Rhone noted the captain's faraway look as he processed the news.

Captain Black knew of his assignment. At least bits and pieces of the truth. It was like watching a chess player consider a move, checking all the pieces to find where the danger lay, and the most effective play. In only a moment, the captain's face was no longer grinning. It had taken on the serious look of battle.

"So you'll be leaving soon," the captain stated matter-of-factly. "Don't see any way around it. But you, son, have tons to clean up prior to your departure. First and foremost is the two-fold issue of the Lady Bella, and The Lady Luna. It isn't gentleman-like to run off and leave his ladies holding the gauntlet."

He was speaking in metaphors, but was absolutely correct. The Lady Luna was a fighting airship, and Bella... well, she was a fighter.

Bella's face had gone white as she too saw the implications. She had written off her town and its connections, and was now totally alone.

"I don't really know how it all works," Rhone tried to explain. "I've never been on assignment before. But I know I have to do something."

Captain Black nodded understandingly, but simply waited, not giving away his thoughts.

Like a ship in a growing storm, Rhone plowed on, almost unable to breathe as he carefully said, "So I have a thought," looking imploringly at Bella. "I would like to turn over Captaincy of The Lady Luna to you. You know her better than anyone else possibly could, and you're even better at tactics than I am." With a half smile he looked to Captain Black for confirmation.

The captain only stared back poker faced, making Rhone swallow before he continued. "Captain, if you could keep an eye on her, the two of you could continue to patrol the coast. I plan on talking to Mayor Dugan tomorrow to make a deal. I know he wants me gone, so I'll tell him I'm leaving, but The Lady Luna will stay and protect his harbor and shipping routes. I'll also try to get a fair protection fee in the bargain, to help Bella maintain the airship and herself. It might even become profitable if the shipping recovers sufficiently. What do you think, Captain?"

The idea held a lot of ifs, but it also had merit.

As Bella was still in shock, Captain Black took the lead, responding in his normal forceful demeanor.

"It could work," he agreed, with some reluctance. "But here are some stipulations I... we, will require." He looked to Bella for her acceptance of his intrusion.

Rhone hadn't expected negotiations, and broke out in a cold sweat. What could they possibly want that he could give? He had nothing but The Luna. Everything else was make-believe.

Scowling into his beard, the captain turned to Bella, sitting like a wilted flower, showing no recognition of his words. "If you plan on accepting this proposal, then I have a recommendation or two. One, change your name to Belle. Not only does Captain Belle have a much bigger bite, it will distance you from the Isabella the people of Corgy knew. And two, you'll need a crew. You can't go flying that contraption all by yourself. Just not possible. Now, that's not as big a problem as you might think," he admitted, his gruff face becoming a frustrated frown. "I know a whole hillside of good people, and a pile of them need a job. I've even trained some myself. So a crew, a new name, and a contract with the Mayor. Honestly, its not a bad start. Then of course, I'll be down amongst the waves, keeping an eye out for you too, if you'd be so good at to keep an eye on my Mistress from the skies. We have our own enemies it seems." His bushy eyebrows raised as he asked, "What say you? Can you handle it?"

Bella's painful look softened as she came to terms with reality. Drawing herself up straighter, she raised the near empty wine glass, staring vacantly into its depths as her determination firmed. "With your help, good Captain, I'll do my best."

Rhone's heart almost tore as he slowly began to breathe again. This was an answer he hadn't seen, but it would work.

Captain Black raised his own glass. "To Captain Belle," he declared, his words validating her new position in a toast.

"Captain Belle," Rhone repeated numbly, realizing he was no longer captain of an airship. He was a simple agent working for the OPR, and he was headed back to the big city.

Life had turned again, and he had no more idea where he was headed than when he had left the badlands.

But we do know, Stone interjected quietly. *There will be new puzzles to solve, and projects to complete. Let alone this wave transmission method of Jewel's. It will be forward and onward my dear collar-mate.*

His friend's unwavering support lessened the pit forming in Rhone's chest. *"I get it. Tally-ho and off we go?"* he said with a low chuckle.

Exactly! Stone purred, warming where he lay in his collar setting. *Now, say your good-byes like a good lad. We have a job to do.*

The end

About the Author

An award winning, first place author of the Chanticleer International Book Awards, Strider began his writing career after twenty-five years as a fire fighter/EMT. The emotions and experiences of those calls carry themselves through every story, bringing true 'been-there' reality to the scenes.

With additional years as a business owner, general contractor, designer, wildland firefighter, big game guide, ski instructor, back packer and sword fighter, his wide range of knowledge is intricately woven throughout his stories.

To date, Strider has written YA (young adult), NA (New adult), and general fiction in the realm of: sci-fi western, light steampunk, dystopian (post apocalyptic), gaslight (early mechanism era) and just fun reading.

Contact at: DuramenPublishing.com
or: DuramenPublishing@gmail.co

Final Thanks, and Your Review

Customer reviews

While Luna has professional reviews done, it's always desirable to get customer reviews from you, our reading audience. If you would be so kind, your personal customer review would be greatly appreciated. Go to your on-line source, weather you purchased the book there or not, and look for the section on reviews. For Amazon, scroll down the book's ad page to this section.

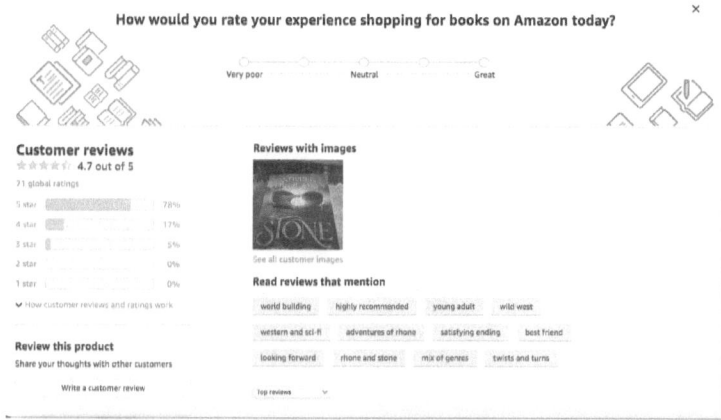

Amazon reviews clip

In the bottom left corner is a button marked, 'Write a customer review', which will take you to a page to do just that.

⚜

Thank you for reading <u>Luna</u>, book 2 of, The Adventures of Rhone & Stone.

S<u>tone</u>, book 1 starts the story, with <u>Recalled</u>, book 3, coming next, as Rhone & Stone expand their horizons and their knowledge, dipping into the gaslight-era of invention, and the ever-furtive attention of The Brotherhood.

www.ingramcontent.com/pod-product-compliance
Lightning Source LLC
Chambersburg PA
CBHW022146010726
47493CB00002B/363